I0885593

PRAISE FOR

THE CRUEL PRINCE

A *New York Times* bestseller
An IndieBound bestseller

"Black is a master at world-building, conveying integral details without that information ever seeming tedious or encyclopedic, whether you're well versed in faerie or a newcomer to the genre. . . . **The experience of reading a novel like this is something like being surrounded by magic**."
—*The New York Times Book Review*

"**Lush, dangerous, a dark jewel of a book.** Black's world is intoxicating, imbued with a relentless sense of peril that kept me riveted through every chapter of Jude's journey. And Jude! She is a heroine to love—brave but pragmatic, utterly human. **This delicious story will seduce you** and leave you desperate for just one more page." —Leigh Bardugo, #1 *New York Times* bestselling author of *Six of Crows* and *Crooked Kingdom*

"I require book two immediately. **Holly is the Faerie Queen**."
—Victoria Aveyard, #1 bestselling author of the Red Queen series

★ "**Spellbinding**. . . . Breathtaking set pieces, fully developed supporting characters, and a beguiling, tough-as-nails heroine enhance an intricate, intelligent plot that crescendos to a jaw-dropping third-act twist." —*Publishers Weekly*, starred review

★ "Another **fantastic, deeply engaging, and all-consuming** work from Black that belongs on all YA shelves."
—*SLJ*, starred review

★ "Jude, who struggles with a world she both loves and hates and would rather be powerful and safe than good, is a compelling narrator. Whatever a reader is looking for—heart-in-throat action, deadly romance, double-crossing, moral complexity—**this is one heck of a ride**." —*Booklist*, starred review

"This is a heady blend of Faerie lore, high fantasy, and high school drama, dripping with description that brings the dangerous but tempting world of Faerie to life. **Black is building a complex mythology; now is a great time to tune in.**"
—*Kirkus Reviews*

★ "Black, quite rightly, is the acknowledged queen of faerie lit, and **her latest shows her to be at the top of her game**, unveiling twists and secrets and bringing her characters vividly to life." —*VOYA*, starred review

"With complicated characters, a suspenseful plot, and a successful return to the Faerie setting of many of her popular books, **Black's latest is sure to enchant fans**." —*The Horn Book*

"**Another enthralling story** in Black's fantasy catalog." —Paste

THE CRUEL PRINCE

BY HOLLY BLACK

The Folk of the Air

The Cruel Prince

The Wicked King

The Queen of Nothing

How the King of Elfhame Learned to Hate Stories

The Stolen Heir Duology

The Stolen Heir

The Prisoner's Throne

Other

The Darkest Part of the Forest

The Coldest Girl in Coldtown

THE CRUEL PRINCE

HOLLY BLACK

LITTLE, BROWN AND COMPANY
NEW YORK BOSTON

Little, Brown and Company
Hachette Book Group
1290 Avenue of the Americas, New York, NY 10104
Visit us at LBYR.com

Originally published in hardcover and ebook by Little, Brown and Company in January 2018
First Trade Paperback Edition: December 2018

Little, Brown and Company is a division of Hachette Book Group, Inc.
The Little, Brown name and logo are trademarks of Hachette Book Group, Inc.

The publisher is not responsible for websites (or their content) that are not owned by the publisher.

The Library of Congress has cataloged the hardcover edition as follows:
Names: Black, Holly, author.
Title: The cruel prince / Holly Black.
Description: First edition. | New York : Little, Brown and Company, 2018. | Series: The Folk of the Air ; 1 | Summary: Jude, seventeen and mortal, gets tangled in palace intrigues while trying to win a place in the treacherous High Court of Faerie, where she and her sisters have lived for a decade.
Identifiers: LCCN 2016049232 | ISBN 9780316310277 (hardcover) |
ISBN 9780316310284 (ebook) | ISBN 9780316310307 (library edition ebook)
Subjects: | CYAC: Fairies—Fiction. | Sisters—Fiction. | Orphans—Fiction. | Princes—Fiction. |
Courts and courtiers—Fiction. | Fantasy.
Classification: LCC PZ7.B52878 Cru 2018 | DDC [Fic]—dc23
LC record available at https://lccn.loc.gov/2016049232

ISBNs: 978-0-316-31031-4 (pbk.), 978-0-316-31028-4 (ebook)

Printed in Indiana, USA

LSC-C

Printing 29, 2025

For Cassandra Clare, who was finally lured into Faerieland

Crooked Forest
Palace of Elfhame
Milkwood
INSMIRE
Lake of Masks
Madoc's Stronghold

Map of the Shifting Isles of
ELFHAME
Locke's Estate
Tower of Forgetting
INSMOOR
INSWEAL
Hollow Hall

Book One

Children born of fairy stock
Never need for shirt or frock,
Never want for food or fire,
Always get their heart's desire:
Jingle pockets full of gold,
Marry when they're seven years old.
Every fairy child may keep
Two strong ponies and ten sheep;
All have houses, each his own,
Built of brick or granite stone;
They live on cherries, they run wild—
I'd love to be a fairy's child.

—Robert Graves,
"I'd Love to Be a Fairy's Child"

PROLOGUE

On a drowsy Sunday afternoon, a man in a long dark coat hesitated in front of a house on a tree-lined street. He hadn't parked a car, nor had he come by taxi. No neighbor had seen him strolling along the sidewalk. He simply appeared, as if stepping between one shadow and the next.

The man walked to the door and lifted his fist to knock.

Inside the house, Jude sat on the living room rug and ate fish sticks, soggy from the microwave and dragged through a sludge of ketchup. Her twin sister, Taryn, napped on the couch, curled around a blanket, thumb in her fruit-punch-stained mouth. And on the other end of the sofa, their older sister, Vivienne, stared at the television screen, her eerie, split-pupiled gaze fixed on the cartoon mouse as it ran from the cartoon cat. She laughed when it seemed as if the mouse was about to get eaten.

Vivi was different from other big sisters, but since seven-year-old Jude and Taryn were identical, with the same shaggy brown hair and heart-shaped faces, they were different, too. Vivi's eyes and the lightly furred points of her ears were, to Jude, not so much more strange than being the mirror version of another person.

And if sometimes she noticed the way the neighborhood kids avoided Vivi or the way their parents talked about her in low, worried voices, Jude didn't think it was anything important. Grown-ups were always worried, always whispering.

Taryn yawned and stretched, pressing her cheek against Vivi's knee.

Outside, the sun was shining, scorching the asphalt of driveways. Lawn mower engines whirred, and children splashed in backyard pools. Dad was in the outbuilding, where he had a forge. Mom was in the kitchen cooking hamburgers. Everything was boring. Everything was fine.

When the knock came, Jude hopped up to answer it. She hoped it might be one of the girls from across the street, wanting to play video games or inviting her for an after-dinner swim.

The tall man stood on their mat, glaring down at her. He wore a brown leather duster despite the heat. His shoes were shod with silver, and they rang hollowly as he stepped over the threshold. Jude looked up into his shadowed face and shivered.

"Mom," she yelled. "Mooooooooom. Someone's here."

Her mother came from the kitchen, wiping wet hands on her jeans. When she saw the man, she went pale. "Go to your room," she told Jude in a scary voice. *"Now!"*

"Whose child is that?" the man asked, pointing at her. His voice was oddly accented. "Yours? His?"

"No one's." Mom didn't even look in Jude's direction. "She's no one's child."

That wasn't right. Jude and Taryn looked just like their dad. Everyone said so. She took a few steps toward the stairs but didn't want to be alone in her room. *Vivi*, Jude thought. *Vivi will know who the tall man is. Vivi will know what to do.*

But Jude couldn't seem to make herself move any farther.

"I've seen many impossible things," the man said. "I have seen the acorn before the oak. I have seen the spark before the flame. But never have I seen such as this: A dead woman living. A child born from nothing."

Mom seemed at a loss for words. Her body was vibrating with tension. Jude wanted to take her hand and squeeze it, but she didn't dare.

"I doubted Balekin when he told me I'd find you here," said the man, his voice softening. "The bones of an earthly woman and her unborn child in the burned remains of my estate were convincing. Do you know what it is to return from battle to find your wife dead, your only heir with her? To find your life reduced to ash?"

Mom shook her head, not as if she was answering him, but as though she was trying to shake off the words.

He took a step toward her, and she took a step back. There was something wrong with the tall man's leg. He moved stiffly, as though it hurt him. The light was different in the entry hall, and Jude could see the odd green tint of his skin and the way his lower teeth seemed too large for his mouth.

She was able to see that his eyes were like Vivi's.

"I was never going to be happy with you," Mom told him. "Your world isn't for people like me."

The tall man regarded her for a long moment. "You made vows," he said finally.

She lifted her chin. "And then I renounced them."

His gaze went to Jude, and his expression hardened. "What is a promise from a mortal wife worth? I suppose I have my answer."

Mom turned. At her mother's look, Jude dashed into the living room.

Taryn was still sleeping. The television was still on. Vivienne looked up with half-lidded cat eyes. "Who's at the door?" she asked. "I heard arguing."

"A scary man," Jude told her, out of breath even though she'd barely run at all. Her heart was pounding. "We're supposed to go upstairs."

She didn't care that Mom had told only *her* to go upstairs. She wasn't going by herself. With a sigh, Vivi unfolded from the couch and shook Taryn awake. Drowsily, Jude's twin followed them into the hallway.

As they started toward the carpet-covered steps, Jude saw her father come in from the back garden. He held an axe in his hand—forged to be a near replica of one he'd studied in a museum in Iceland. It wasn't weird to see Dad with an axe. He and his friends were into old weapons and would spend lots of time talking about "material culture" and sketching ideas for fantastical blades. What was odd was the way he held the weapon, as if he was going to—

Her father swung the axe toward the tall man.

He had never raised a hand to discipline Jude or her sisters, even when they got into big trouble. He wouldn't hurt anyone. He just wouldn't.

And yet. And yet.

The axe went past the tall man, biting into the wood trim of the door.

Taryn made an odd, high keening noise and slapped her palms over her mouth.

The tall man drew a curved blade from beneath his leather coat. A *sword*, like from a storybook. Dad was trying to pull the axe free from the doorframe when the man plunged the sword into Dad's stomach, pushing it upward. There was a sound, like sticks snapping, and an animal cry. Dad fell to the vestibule carpet, the one Mom always yelled about when they tracked mud on it.

The rug that was turning red.

Mom screamed. Jude screamed. Taryn and Vivi screamed. Everyone seemed to be screaming, except the tall man.

"Come here," he said, looking directly at Vivi.

"Y-you monster," their mother shouted, moving toward the kitchen. "He's dead!"

"Do not run from me," the man told her. "Not after what you've done. If you run again, I swear I—"

But she did run. She was almost around the corner when his blade struck her in the back. She crumpled to the linoleum, falling arms knocking magnets off the fridge.

The smell of fresh blood was heavy in the air, like wet, hot metal. Like those scrubbing pads Mom used to clean the frying pan when stuff was really stuck on.

Jude ran at the man, slamming her fists against his chest, kicking at his legs. She wasn't even scared. She wasn't sure she felt anything at all.

The man paid Jude no mind. For a long moment, he just stood there, as though he couldn't quite believe what he'd done. As though he wished he could take back the last five minutes. Then he sank to one knee and caught hold of Jude's shoulders. He pinned her arms to her sides so she couldn't hit him anymore, but he wasn't even looking at her.

His gaze was on Vivienne.

"You were stolen from me," he told her. "I have come to take you to your true home, in Elfhame beneath the hill. There, you will be rich beyond measure. There, you will be with your own kind."

"No," Vivi told him in her somber little voice. "I'm never going anywhere with you."

"I'm your father," he told her, his voice harsh, rising like the crack of a lash. "You are my heir and my blood, and you will obey me in this as in all things."

She didn't move, but her jaw set.

"You're not her father," Jude shouted at the man. Even though he and Vivi had the same eyes, she wouldn't let herself believe it.

His grip tightened on her shoulders, and she made a little squeezed, squeaking sound, but she stared up defiantly. She'd won plenty of staring contests.

He looked away first, turning to watch Taryn, on her knees, shaking Mom while she sobbed, as though she was trying to wake her up. Mom didn't move. Mom and Dad were dead. They were never going to move again.

"I hate you," Vivi proclaimed to the tall man with a viciousness that Jude was glad of. "I will always hate you. I vow it."

The man's stony expression didn't change. "Nonetheless, you will come with me. Ready these little humans. Pack light. We ride before dark."

Vivienne's chin came up. "Leave them alone. If you have to, take me, but not them."

He stared at Vivi, and then he snorted. "You'd protect your sisters from me, would you? Tell me, then, where would you have them go?"

Vivi didn't answer. They had no grandparents, no living family at all. At least, none they knew.

He looked at Jude again, released her shoulders, and rose to his feet. "They are the progeny of my wife and, thus, my responsibility. I may be cruel, a monster, and a murderer, but I do not shirk my responsibilities. Nor should you shirk yours as the eldest."

Years later, when Jude told herself the story of what happened, she couldn't recall the part where they packed. Shock seemed to have erased that hour entirely. Somehow Vivi must have found bags, must have put in their favorite picture books and their most beloved toys, along with photographs and pajamas and coats and shirts.

Or maybe Jude had packed for herself. She was never sure.

She couldn't imagine how they'd done it, with their parents' bodies cooling downstairs. She couldn't imagine how it had felt, and as the years went by, she couldn't make herself feel it again. The horror of the murders dulled with time. Her memories of the day blurred.

A black horse was nibbling the grass of the lawn when they went outside. Its eyes were big and soft. Jude wanted to throw her arms around its neck and press her wet face into its silky mane. Before she could, the tall man swung her and then Taryn across the saddle, handling them like baggage rather than children. He put Vivi up behind him.

"Hold on," he said.

Jude and her sisters wept the whole way to Faerieland.

CHAPTER 1

In Faerie, there are no fish sticks, no ketchup, no television.

CHAPTER 2

I sit on a cushion as an imp braids my hair back from my face. The imp's fingers are long, her nails sharp. I wince. Her black eyes meet mine in the claw-footed mirror on my dressing table.

"The tournament is still four nights away," the creature says. Her name is Tatterfell, and she's a servant in Madoc's household, stuck here until she works off her debt to him. She's cared for me since I was a child. It was Tatterfell who smeared stinging faerie ointment over my eyes to give me True Sight so that I could see through most glamours, who brushed the mud from my boots, and who strung dried rowan berries for me to wear around my neck so I might resist enchantments. She wiped my wet nose and reminded me to wear my stockings inside out, so I'd never be led astray in the forest. "And no matter how eager you are for it, you cannot make the moon set nor rise any faster. Try to bring glory to the general's household tonight by appearing as comely as we can make you."

I sigh.

She's never had much patience with my peevishness. "It's an honor to dance with the High King's Court under the hill."

The servants are overfond of telling me how fortunate I am, a bastard daughter of a faithless wife, a human without a drop of faerie blood, to be treated like a trueborn child of Faerie. They tell Taryn much the same thing.

I know it's an honor to be raised alongside the Gentry's own children. A terrifying honor, of which I will never be worthy.

It would be hard to forget it, with all the reminders I am given.

"Yes," I say instead, because she is trying to be kind. "It's great."

Faeries can't lie, so they tend to concentrate on words and ignore tone, especially if they haven't lived among humans. Tatterfell gives me an approving nod, her eyes like two wet beads of jet, neither pupil nor iris visible. "Perhaps someone will ask for your hand and you'll be made a permanent member of the High Court."

"I want to win my place," I tell her.

The imp pauses, hairpin between her fingers, probably considering pricking me with it. "Don't be foolish."

There's no point in arguing, no point to reminding her of my mother's disastrous marriage. There are two ways for mortals to become permanent subjects of the Court: marrying into it or honing some great skill—in metallurgy or lute playing or whatever. Not interested in the first, I have to hope I can be talented enough for the second.

She finishes braiding my hair into an elaborate style that makes me look as though I have horns. She dresses me in sapphire velvet. None of it disguises what I am: human.

"I put in three knots for luck," the little faerie says, not unkindly.

I sigh as she scuttles toward the door, getting up from my dressing table to sprawl facedown on my tapestry-covered bed. I am used to having servants attend to me. Imps and hobs, goblins and grigs. Gossamer wings and green nails, horns and fangs. I have been in Faerie for ten years. None of it seems all that strange anymore. Here, I am the strange one, with my blunt fingers, round ears, and mayfly life.

Ten years is a long time for a human.

After Madoc stole us from the human world, he brought us to his estates on Insmire, the Isle of Might, where the High King of Elfhame keeps his stronghold. There, Madoc raised us—me and Vivienne and Taryn—out of an obligation of honor. Even though Taryn and I are the evidence of Mom's betrayal, by the customs of Faerie, we're his wife's kids, so we're his problem.

As the High King's general, Madoc was away often, fighting for the crown. We were well cared for nonetheless. We slept on mattresses stuffed with the soft seed-heads of dandelions. Madoc personally instructed us in the art of fighting with the cutlass and dagger, the falchion and our fists. He played Nine Men's Morris, Fidchell, and Fox and Geese with us before a fire. He let us sit on his knee and eat off his plate.

Many nights I drifted off to sleep to his rumbling voice reading from a book of battle strategy. And despite myself, despite what he'd done and what he was, I came to love him. I do love him.

It's just not a comfortable kind of love.

"Nice braids," Taryn says, rushing into my room. She's dressed in crimson velvet. Her hair is loose—long chestnut curls that fly behind her like a capelet, a few strands braided with gleaming silver thread. She hops onto the bed beside me, disarranging my small pile of threadbare stuffed animals—a koala, a snake, a black cat—all beloved of my seven-year-old self. I cannot bear to throw out any of my relics.

I sit up to take a self-conscious look in the mirror. "I like them."

"I'm having a premonition," Taryn says, surprising me. "We're going to have fun tonight."

"Fun?" I'd been imagining myself frowning at the crowd from our usual bolt-hole and worrying over whether I'd do well enough in the tournament to impress one of the royal family into granting me knighthood. Just thinking about it makes me fidgety, yet I think about it constantly. My thumb brushes over the missing tip of my ring finger, my nervous tic.

"Yes," she says, poking me in the side.

"Hey! Ow!" I scoot out of range. "What exactly does this plan entail?" Mostly, when we go to Court, we hide ourselves away. We've watched some very interesting things, but from a distance.

She throws up her hands. "What do you mean, what does fun entail? It's fun!"

I laugh a little nervously. "You have no idea, either, do you? Fine. Let's go see if you have a gift for prophecy."

We are getting older and things are changing. We are changing. And as eager as I am for it, I am also afraid.

Taryn pushes herself off my bed and holds out her arm, as though she's my escort for a dance. I allow myself to be guided from the room, my hand going automatically to assure myself that my knife is still strapped to my hip.

The interior of Madoc's house is whitewashed plaster and massive, rough-cut wooden beams. The glass panes in the windows are stained gray as trapped smoke, making the light strange. As Taryn and I go down the spiral stairs, I spot Vivi hiding in a little balcony, frowning over a comics zine stolen from the human world.

Vivi grins at me. She's in jeans and a billowy shirt—obviously not intending to go to the revel. Being Madoc's legitimate daughter, she feels no pressure to please him. She does what she likes. Including reading magazines that might have iron staples rather than glue binding their pages, not caring if her fingers get singed.

"Heading somewhere?" she asks softly from the shadows, startling Taryn.

Vivi knows perfectly well where we're heading.

When we first came here, Taryn and Vivi and I would huddle in Vivi's big bed and talk about what we remembered from home. We'd talk about the meals Mom burned and the popcorn Dad made. Our next-door neighbors' names, the way the house smelled, what school was like, the holidays, the taste of icing on birthday cakes. We'd talk about the shows we'd watched, rehashing the plots, recalling the dialogue until all our memories were polished smooth and false.

There's no more huddling in bed now, rehashing anything. All our new memories are of here, and Vivi has only a passing interest in those.

She'd vowed to hate Madoc, and she stuck to her vow. When Vivi wasn't reminiscing about home, she was a terror. She broke things. She screamed and raged and pinched us when we were content. Eventually, she stopped all of it, but I believe there is a part of her that hates us for adapting. For making the best of things. For making this our home.

"You should come," I tell her. "Taryn's in a weird mood."

Vivi gives her a speculative look and then shakes her head. "I've got other plans." Which might mean she's going to sneak over to the mortal world for the evening or it might mean she's going to spend it on the balcony, reading.

Either way, if it annoys Madoc, it pleases Vivi.

He's waiting for us in the hall with his second wife, Oriana. Her skin is the bluish color of skim milk, and her hair is as white as fresh-fallen snow. She is beautiful but unnerving to look at, like a ghost. Tonight she is wearing green and gold, a mossy dress with an elaborate shining collar that makes the pink of her mouth, her ears, and her eyes stand out. Madoc is dressed in green, too, the color of deep forests. The sword at his hip is no ornament.

Outside, past the open double doors, a hob waits, holding the silver bridles of five dappled faerie steeds, their manes braided in complicated and probably magical knots. I think of the knots in my hair and wonder how similar they are.

"You both look well," Madoc says to Taryn and me, the warmth in his tone making the words a rare compliment. His gaze goes to the stairs. "Is your sister on her way?"

"I don't know where Vivi is," I lie. Lying is so easy here. I can do it all day long and never be caught. "She must have forgotten."

Disappointment passes over Madoc's face, but not surprise. He heads outside to say something to the hob holding the reins. Nearby, I see one of his spies, a wrinkled creature with a nose like a parsnip and a back hunched higher than her head. She slips a note into his hand and darts off with surprising nimbleness.

Oriana looks us over carefully, as though she expects to find something amiss.

"Be careful tonight," Oriana says. "Promise me you will neither eat nor drink nor dance."

"We've been to Court before," I remind her, a Faerie nonanswer if ever there was one.

"You may think salt is sufficient protection, but you children are forgetful. Better to go without. As for dancing, once begun, you mortals will dance yourselves to death if we don't prevent it."

I look at my feet and say nothing.

We children are not forgetful.

Madoc married her seven years ago, and shortly after, she gave him a child, a sickly boy named Oak, with tiny, adorable horns on his head. It has always been clear that Oriana puts up with me and Taryn only for Madoc's sake. She seems to think of us as her husband's favored hounds: poorly trained and likely to turn on our master at any moment.

Oak thinks of us as sisters, which I can tell makes Oriana nervous, even though I would never do anything to hurt him.

"You are under Madoc's protection, and he has the favor of the High King," Oriana says. "I will not see Madoc made to look foolish because of your mistakes."

With that little speech complete, she walks out toward the horses. One snorts and strikes the ground with a hoof.

Taryn and I share a look and then follow her. Madoc is already seated on the largest of the faerie steeds, an impressive creature with a scar beneath one eye. Its nostrils flare with impatience. It tosses its mane restlessly.

I swing up onto a pale green horse with sharp teeth and a swampy odor. Taryn chooses a rouncy and kicks her heels against its flanks. She takes off like a shot, and I follow, plunging into the night.

CHAPTER 3

Faeries are twilight creatures, and I have become one, too. We rise when the shadows grow long and head to our beds before the sun rises. It is well after midnight when we arrive at the great hill at the Palace of Elfhame. To go inside, we must ride between two trees, an oak and a thorn, and then straight into what appears to be the stone wall of an abandoned folly. I've done it hundreds of times, but I flinch anyway. My whole body braces, I grip the reins hard, and my eyes mash shut.

When I open them, I am inside the hill.

We ride on through a cavern, between pillars of roots, over packed earth.

There are dozens of the Folk here, crowding around the entrance to the vast throne room, where Court is being held—long-nosed pixies with tattered wings; elegant, green-skinned ladies in long gowns with goblins holding up their trains; tricksy boggans; laughing foxkin; a boy in an owl mask and a golden headdress; an elderly woman with crows crowding her shoulders; a gaggle of girls with wild roses in their hair; a bark-skinned boy with feathers around his neck; a group of knights all in scarab-green armor. Many I've seen before; a few I have spoken with. Too many for my eyes to drink them all in, yet I cannot look away.

I never get tired of this—of the spectacle, of the pageantry. Maybe Oriana isn't entirely wrong to worry that we might one day get caught up in it, be carried away by it, and forget to take care. I can see why humans succumb to the beautiful nightmare of the Court, why they willingly drown in it.

I know I shouldn't love it as I do, stolen as I am from the mortal world, my parents murdered. But I love it all the same.

Madoc swings down from his horse. Oriana and Taryn are already off theirs, handing them over to grooms. It's me they're waiting for. Madoc reaches out his fingers like he is going to help me, but I hop off the saddle on my own. My leather slippers hit the ground like a slap.

I hope that I look like a knight to him.

Oriana steps forward, probably to remind Taryn and me of all the things she doesn't want us to do. I don't give her the chance. Instead, I hook my arm through Taryn's and hurry along inside. The room is redolent with burning rosemary and crushed herbs. Behind us, I can hear Madoc's heavy step, but I know where I am going. The first thing we have to do when we get to Court is greet the king.

The High King Eldred sits on his throne in gray robes of state, a heavy golden oak-leaf crown holding down his thin, spun-gold hair. When we bow, he touches our heads lightly with his knobby, be-ringed hands, and then we rise.

His grandmother was Queen Mab, of the House of the Greenbriar. She lived as one of the solitary fey before she began to conquer Faerie with her horned consort and his stag-riders. Because of him, each of Eldred's six heirs are said to have some animal characteristic, a thing that is not unusual in Faerie but is unusual among the trooping Gentry of the Courts.

The eldest prince, Balekin, and his younger brother, Dain, stand nearby, drinking wine from wooden cups banded in silver. Dain wears breeches that stop at his knees, showing his hooves and deer legs. Balekin wears the greatcoat he favors, with a collar of bear fur. His fingers have a thorn at each knuckle, and thorns ridge his arm, running up under the cuffs of his shirt, visible when he and Dain urge Madoc over.

Oriana curtsies to them. Although Dain and Balekin are standing together, they are often at odds with each other and with their sister Elowyn—so often that the Court is considered to be divided into three warring circles of influence.

Prince Balekin, the firstborn, and his set are known as the Circle of Grackles, for those who enjoy merriment and who scorn anything getting in the way of it. They drink themselves sick and numb themselves with poisonous and delightful powders. His is the wildest circle, although he has always been perfectly composed and sober when speaking with me. I suppose I could throw myself into debauchery and hope to impress them. I'd rather not, though.

Princess Elowyn, the second-born, and her companions have the Circle of Larks. They value art above all else. Several mortals have found favor in her circle, but since I have no real skill with a lute or declaiming, I have no chance of being one of them.

Prince Dain, third-born, leads what's known as the Circle of Falcons. Knights, warriors, and strategists are in their favor. Madoc, obviously, belongs to this circle. They talk about honor, but what they really care about is power. I am good enough with a blade, knowledgeable in strategy. All I need is a chance to prove myself.

"Go enjoy yourselves," Madoc tells us. With a look back at the princes, Taryn and I head out into the throng.

The palace of the King of Elfhame has many secret alcoves and hidden corridors, perfect for trysts or assassins or staying out of the way and being really dull at parties. When Taryn and I were little, we would hide under the long banquet tables. But since she determined we were elegant ladies, too big to get our dresses dirty crawling around on the floor, we had to find a better spot. Just past the second landing of stone steps is an area where a large mass of shimmering rock juts out, creating a ledge. Normally, that's where we settle ourselves to listen to the music and watch all the fun we aren't supposed to be having.

Tonight, however, Taryn has a different idea. She passes the steps and grabs food off a silver tray—a green apple and a wedge of blue-veined cheese. Not bothering with salt, she takes a bite of each, holding the apple out for me to bite. Oriana thinks we can't tell the difference between regular fruit and faerie fruit, which blooms a deep gold. Its flesh is red and dense, and the cloying smell of it fills the forests at harvest time.

The apple is crisp and cold in my mouth. We pass it back and forth, sharing down to the core, which I eat in two bites.

Near where I am standing, a tiny faerie girl with a clock of white hair, like that of a dandelion, and a little knife cuts the strap of an ogre's belt. It's slick work. A moment later, his sword and pouch are gone, she's losing herself in the crowd, and I can almost believe it didn't happen. Until the girl looks back at me.

She winks.

A moment after that, the ogre realizes he was robbed.

"I smell a thief!" he shouts, casting around him, knocking over a tankard of dark brown beer, his warty nose sniffing the air.

Nearby, there's a commotion—one of the candles flares up in blue crackling flames, sparking loudly and distracting even the ogre. By the time it returns to normal, the white-haired thief is well gone.

With a half smile, I turn back to Taryn, who watches the dancers with longing, oblivious to much else.

"We could take turns," she proposes. "If you can't stop, I'll pull you out. Then you'll do the same for me."

My heartbeat speeds at the thought. I look at the throng of revelers, trying to build up the daring of someone who would rob an ogre right under his nose.

Princess Elowyn whirls at the center of a circle of Larks. Her skin is a glittering gold, her hair the deep green of ivy. Beside her, a human boy plays the fiddle. Two more mortals accompany him less skillfully, but more joyfully, on ukuleles. Elowyn's younger sister Caelia spins nearby, with corn silk hair like her father's and a crown of flowers in it.

A new ballad begins, and the words drift up to me. "*Of all the sons King William had, Prince Jamie was the worst,*" they sing. "*And what made the sorrow even greater, Prince Jamie was the first.*"

I've never much liked that song because it reminds me of someone else. Someone who, along with Princess Rhyia, doesn't appear to be attending tonight. But—oh no. I do see him.

Prince Cardan, sixth-born to the High King Eldred, yet still the absolute worst, strides across the floor toward us.

Valerian, Nicasia, and Locke—his three meanest, fanciest, and most loyal friends—follow him. The crowd parts and hushes, bowing as they pass. Cardan is wearing his usual scowl, accessorized with kohl under his eyes and a circlet of gold in his midnight hair. He has on a long black coat with a high, jagged collar, the whole thing stitched with a pattern of constellations. Valerian is in deep red, cabochon rubies sparkling on his cuffs, each like a drop of frozen blood. Nicasia's hair is the blue-green of the ocean, crowned with a diadem of pearls. A glittering cobweb net covers her braids. Locke brings up the rear, looking bored, his hair the precise color of fox fur.

"They're ridiculous," I say to Taryn, who follows my gaze. I cannot deny that they're also beautiful. Faerie lords and ladies, just like in the songs. If we didn't have to take lessons alongside them, if I didn't know firsthand what a scourge they were to those who displeased them, I'd probably be as in love with them as everyone else is.

"Vivi says that Cardan has a tail," Taryn whispers. "She saw it when she was swimming in the lake with him and Princess Rhyia this past full moon night."

I can't imagine Cardan swimming in a lake, jumping in the water, splashing people, laughing at something other than their suffering. "A *tail*?" I echo, an incredulous smile starting on my face and then fading when I remember that Vivi didn't bother to tell me the story, even though it must have happened days ago. Three is an odd configuration of sisters. There's always one on the outside.

"With a tuft on the end! It coils up under his clothes and unfurls like a whip." She giggles, and I can barely understand her next words. "Vivi said she wishes she had one."

"I'm glad she doesn't," I say firmly, which is stupid. I have nothing against tails.

Then Cardan and his companions are too close for us to safely talk about them. I turn my gaze to the floor. Though I hate it, I sink to the ground on one knee, bend my head, and grit my teeth. By my side, Taryn does something similar. All around us, people are making obeisances.

Don't look at us, I think. *Don't look.*

As Valerian passes, he grabs one of my braided horns. The others move on through the throng as Valerian sneers down at me.

"Did you think I didn't see you there? You and your sister stand out in any crowd," he says, leaning in close. His breath is heavy with the scent of honey wine. My hand balls into a fist at my side, and I am conscious of the nearness of my knife. Still, I do not look him in the eye. "No other head of hair so dull, no other face so plain."

"Valerian," Prince Cardan calls. He is glowering already and when he sees me, his eyes narrow further.

Valerian gives my braid a hard tug. I wince, useless fury coiling in my belly. He laughs and moves on.

My fury curdles into shame. I wish I had smacked his hand away, even though it would have made everything worse.

Taryn sees something in my face. "What did he say to you?"

I shake my head.

Cardan has stopped beside a boy with long copper hair and a pair of small moth wings—a boy who isn't bowing. The boy laughs and Cardan lunges. Between one eyeblink and the next, the prince's balled fist strikes the boy hard across the jaw, sending him sprawling. As the boy falls, Cardan grabs one of his wings. It tears like paper. The boy's scream is thin and reedy. He curls up into himself on the ground, agony plain on his face. I wonder if faerie wings grow back; I know that butterflies that lose a wing never fly again.

The courtiers around us gape and titter, but only for a moment. Then they go back to their dancing and their songs, and the revel spirals on.

This is how they are. Someone gets in Cardan's way, and they're instantly and brutally punished. Driven from taking lessons at the palace, sometimes out of the Court entirely. Hurt. Broken.

As Cardan walks past the boy, apparently done with him, I am grateful that Cardan has five more worthy brothers and sisters; it's practically guaranteed that he'll never sit on the throne. I don't want to think of him with more power than he has.

Even Nicasia and Valerian share a weighted glance. Then Valerian shrugs and follows Cardan. But Locke pauses by the boy, bending down to help him to his feet.

The boy's friends come over to lead him away, and at that moment, improbably, Locke's gaze lifts. His tawny fox eyes meet mine and widen in surprise. I am immobilized, my heart speeding. I brace myself for more scorn, but then one corner of his mouth lifts. He winks, as if in acknowledgment of being caught out. As if we're sharing a secret. As if he thinks I am not loathly, as though he does not find my mortality contagious.

"Stop staring at him," Taryn demands.

"Didn't you see—" I start to explain, but she cuts me off, grabbing hold of me and hauling us toward the stairs, toward our landing of shimmering stone, where we can hide. Her nails sink into my skin.

"Don't give them any more reason to bother you than they've already got!" The intensity of her response surprises me into snatching back my hand. Angry red half moons mark where she grabbed me.

I look back toward where Locke was, but the crowd has swallowed him up.

CHAPTER 4

As dawn breaks, I open the windows to my bedroom and let the last of the cool night air flow in as I strip off my Court dress. I feel hot all over. My skin feels too tight, and my heart won't stop racing.

I've been to Court before many times. I've been witness to more awfulness than wings being torn or my person insulted. Faeries make up for their inability to lie with a panoply of deceptions and cruelties. Twisted words, pranks, omissions, riddles, scandals, not to mention their revenges upon one another for ancient, half-remembered slights. Storms are less fickle than they are, seas less capricious.

Like, for example, as a redcap, Madoc needs bloodshed the way a mermaid needs the salt spray of the sea. After every battle, he ritually dips his hood into the blood of his enemies. I've seen the hood, kept under glass in the armory. The fabric is stiff and stained a brown so deep it's almost black, except for a few smears of green.

Sometimes I go down and stare at it, trying to see my parents in the tide lines of dried blood. I want to feel something, something besides a vague queasiness. I want to feel *more*, but every time I look at it, I feel less.

I think about going to the armory now, but I don't. I stand in front of my window and imagine myself a fearless knight, imagine myself a witch who hid her heart in her finger and then chopped her finger off.

"I'm so tired," I say out loud. "So tired."

I sit there for a long time, watching the rising sun gild the sky, listening to the waves crash as the tide goes out, when a creature flies up to alight on the edge of my window. At first it seems like an owl, but it's got hob eyes. "Tired of what, sweetmeat?" it asks me.

I sigh and answer honestly for once. "Of being powerless."

The hob studies my face, then flies off into the night.

I sleep the day away and wake disoriented, battling my way out of the long, embroidered curtains around my bed. Drool has dried along one of my cheeks.

I find bathwater waiting for me, but it has gone tepid. Servants must have come and gone. I climb in anyway and splash my face. Living in Faerie, it's impossible not to notice that everyone else smells like verbena or crushed pine needles, dried blood or milkweed. I smell like pit sweat and sour breath unless I scrub myself clean.

When Tatterfell comes in to light the lamps, she finds me dressing for a lecture, which begins in the late afternoons and stretches on into some evenings. I wear gray leather boots and a tunic with Madoc's crest—a dagger, a crescent moon turned on its side so it rests like a cup, and a single drop of blood falling from one corner embroidered in silk thread.

Downstairs, I find Taryn at the banquet table, alone, nursing a cup of nettle tea and picking at a bannock. Today, she does not suggest anything will be fun.

Madoc insists—perhaps out of guilt or shame—that we be treated like the children of Faerie. That we take the same lessons, that we be given whatever they have. Changelings have been brought to the High Court before, but none of them has been raised like Gentry.

He doesn't understand how much that makes them loathe us.

Not that I am not grateful. I like the lessons. Answering the lecturers cleverly is something no one can take from me, even if the lecturers themselves occasionally pretend otherwise. I will take a frustrated nod in place of effusive praise. I will take it and be glad because it means I can belong whether they like it or not.

Vivi used to go with us, but then she became bored and didn't bother. Madoc raged, but since his approval of a thing only makes her despise it, all his railing just made her more determined to never, ever go back. She has tried to persuade us to stay home with her, but if Taryn and I cannot manage the machinations of the children of Faerie without quitting our lessons or running to Madoc, how will he ever believe we can manage the Court, where those same machinations will play out on a grander and more deadly scale?

Taryn and I set off, swinging our baskets. We don't have to leave Insmire to get to the High King's palace, but we do skirt the edge of two other tiny islands, Insmoor, Isle of Stone, and Insweal, Isle of Woe. All three are connected by half-submerged rocky paths and stones large enough that it's possible to leap your way from one to the next. A herd of stags is swimming toward Insmoor, seeking the best grazing. Taryn and I walk past the Lake of Masks and through the far corner of the Milkwood, picking our way past the pale, silvery trunks and bleached leaves. From there, we spot mermaids and merrows sunning themselves near craggy caves, their scales reflecting the amber glow of the late-afternoon sun.

All the children of the Gentry, regardless of age, are taught by lecturers from all over the kingdom on the grounds of the palace. Some afternoons we sit in groves carpeted with emerald moss, and other evenings we spend in high towers or up in trees. We learn about the movements of constellations in the sky, the medicinal and magical properties of herbs, the languages of birds and flowers and people as well as the language of the Folk (though it occasionally twists in my mouth), the composition of riddles, and how to walk soft-footed over leaves and brambles to leave neither trace nor sound. We are instructed in the finer points of the harp and the lute, the bow and the blade. Taryn and I watch them as they practice enchantments. For a break, we all play at war in a green field with a broad arc of trees.

Madoc trained me to be formidable even with a wooden sword. Taryn isn't bad, either, even though she doesn't bother practicing anymore. At the Summer Tournament, in only a few days, our mock war will take place in front of the royal family. With Madoc's endorsement, one of the princes or princesses might choose to grant me knighthood and take me into their personal guard. It would be a kind of power, a kind of protection.

And with it, I could protect Taryn, too.

We arrive at school. Prince Cardan, Locke, Valerian, and Nicasia are already sprawled in the grass with a few other faeries. A girl with deer horns—Poesy—is giggling over something Cardan has said. They do not so much as look at us as we spread our blanket and set out our notebooks and pens and pots of ink.

My relief is immense.

Our lesson involves the history of the delicately negotiated peace between Orlagh, Queen of the Undersea, and the various faerie kings and queens of the land. Nicasia is Orlagh's daughter, sent to be fostered in the High King's Court. Many odes have been composed to Queen Orlagh's beauty, although, if she's anything like her daughter, not to her personality.

Nicasia gloats through the lesson, proud of her heritage. When the instructor moves on to Lord Roiben of the Court of Termites, I lose interest. My thoughts drift. Instead, I find myself thinking through combinations—strike, thrust, parry, block. I grip my pen as though it were the hilt of a blade and forget to take notes.

As the sun dips low in the sky, Taryn and I unpack our baskets from home, which contain bread, butter, cheese, and plums. I butter a piece of bread hungrily.

Passing us, Cardan kicks dirt onto my food right before I put it into my mouth. The other faeries laugh.

I look up to see him watching me with cruel delight, like a raptor bird trying to decide whether to be bothered devouring a small mouse. He's wearing a high-collared tunic embroidered with thorns, his fingers heavy with rings. His sneer is well-practiced.

I grit my teeth. I tell myself that if I let the taunts roll off me, he will lose interest. He will go away. I can endure this a little longer, a few more days.

"Something the matter?" Nicasia asks sweetly, wandering up and draping her arm over Cardan's shoulder. "Dirt. It's what you came from, mortal. It's what you'll return to soon enough. Take a big bite."

"Make me," I say before I can stop myself. Not the greatest comeback, but my palms begin to sweat. Taryn looks startled.

"I *could*, you know," says Cardan, grinning as though nothing would please him more. My heart speeds. If I weren't wearing a string of rowan berries, he could ensorcell me so that I thought dirt was some kind of delicacy. Only Madoc's position would give him reason to hesitate. I do not move, do not touch the necklace hidden under the bodice of my tunic, the one that I hope will stop any glamour from working. The one I hope he doesn't discover and rip from my throat.

I glance in the direction of the day's lecturer, but the elderly phooka has his nose buried in a book.

Since Cardan's a prince, it's more than likely no one has ever cautioned him, has ever stayed his hand. I never know how far he'll go, and I never know how far our instructors will let him.

"You don't want that, do you?" Valerian asks with mock sympathy as he kicks more dirt onto our lunch. I didn't even see him come over. Once, Valerian stole a silver pen of mine, and Madoc replaced it with a ruby-studded one from his own desk. This threw Valerian into such a rage that he cracked me in the back of the head with his wooden practice sword. "What if we promise to be nice to you for the whole afternoon if you eat everything in your baskets?" His smile is wide and false. "Don't you want us for friends?"

Taryn looks down at her lap. *No*, I want to say. *We don't want you for friends.*

I don't answer, but I don't look down, either. I meet Cardan's gaze. There is nothing I can say to make them stop, and I know it. I have no power here. But today I can't seem to choke down my anger at my own impotence.

Nicasia pulls a pin from my hair, causing one of my braids to fall against my neck. I swat at her hand, but it happens too fast.

"What's this?" She's holding up the golden pin, with a tiny cluster of filigree hawthorn berries at the top. "Did you steal it? Did you think it would make you beautiful? Did you think it would make you as we are?"

I bite the inside of my cheek. Of course I want to be like them. They're beautiful as blades forged in some divine fire. They will live forever. Valerian's hair shines like polished gold. Nicasia's limbs are long and perfectly shaped, her mouth the pink of coral, her hair the color of the deepest, coldest part of the sea. Fox-eyed Locke, standing silently behind Valerian, his expression schooled to careful indifference, has a chin as pointed as the tips of his ears. And Cardan is even more beautiful than the rest, with black hair as iridescent as a raven's wing and cheekbones sharp enough to cut out a girl's heart. I hate him more than all the others. I hate him so much that sometimes when I look at him, I can hardly breathe.

"You'll never be our equal," Nicasia says.

Of course I won't.

"Oh, come on," Locke says with a careless laugh, his hand going around Nicasia's waist. "Let's leave them to their misery."

"Jude's sorry," Taryn says quickly. "We're both really sorry."

"She can show us how sorry she is," Cardan drawls. "Tell her she doesn't belong in the Summer Tournament."

"Afraid I'll win?" I ask, which isn't smart.

"It's not for mortals," he informs us, voice chilly. "Withdraw, or wish that you had."

I open my mouth, but Taryn speaks before I can. "I'll talk to her about it. It's nothing, just a game."

Nicasia gives my sister a magnanimous smile. Valerian leers at Taryn, his eyes lingering on her curves. "It's all just a game."

Cardan's gaze meets mine, and I know he isn't finished with me, not by a long shot.

"Why did you dare them like that?" Taryn asks when they've walked back to their own merry luncheon, all spread out for them. "Talking back to him—that's just stupid."

Make me.

Afraid I'll win?

"I know," I tell her. "I'll shut up. I just—I got angry."

"You're better off being scared," she advises. And then, shaking her head, she packs up our ruined food. My stomach growls, and I try to ignore it.

They want me to be afraid, I know that. During the mock war that very afternoon, Valerian trips me, and Cardan whispers foul things in my ear. I head home with bruises on my skin from kicks, from falls.

What they don't realize is this: Yes, they frighten me, but I have always been scared, since the day I got here. I was raised by the man who murdered my parents, reared in a land of monsters. I live with that fear, let it settle into my bones, and ignore it. If I didn't pretend not to be scared, I would hide under my owl-down coverlets in Madoc's estate forever. I would lie there and scream until there was nothing left of me. I refuse to do that. I will not do that.

Nicasia's wrong about me. I don't desire to do as well in the tournament as one of the fey. I want to win. I do not yearn to be their equal.

In my heart, I yearn to best them.

CHAPTER 5

On our way home, Taryn stops and picks blackberries beside the Lake of Masks. I sit on a rock in the moonlight and deliberately do not look into the water. The lake doesn't reflect your own face—it shows you someone else who has looked or will look into it. When I was little, I used to sit at the bank all day, staring at faerie countenances instead of my own, hoping that I might someday catch a glimpse of my mother looking back at me.

Eventually, it hurt too much to try.

"Are you going to quit the tournament?" Taryn asks, shoveling a handful of berries into her mouth. We are hungry children. Already we are taller than Vivi, our hips wider, and our breasts heavier.

I open my basket and take out a dirty plum, wiping it on my shirt. It's still more or less edible. I eat it slowly, considering. "You mean because of Cardan and his Court of Jerks?"

She frowns with an expression just like one I might make if she was being particularly thickheaded. "Do you know what they call us?" she demands. "*The Circle of Worms.*"

I hurl the pit at the water, watching ripples destroy the possibility of any reflections. My lip curls.

"You're littering in a magical lake," she tells me.

"It'll rot," I say. "And so will we. They're right. We are the Circle of Worms. We're mortal. We don't have forever to wait for them to let us do the things we want. I don't care if they don't like my being in the tournament. Once I become a knight, I'll be beyond their reach."

"Do you think Madoc's going to allow that?" Taryn asks, giving up on the bush after the brambles make her fingers bleed. "Answering to someone other than him?"

"What else has he been training us for?" I ask. Wordlessly, we fall into step together, making our way home.

"Not me." She shakes her head. "I am going to fall in love."

I am surprised into laughter. "So you've just decided? I didn't think it worked like that. I thought love was supposed to happen when you least expected it, like a sap to the skull."

"Well, I *have* decided," she says. I consider mentioning her last ill-fated decision—the one about having fun at the revel—but that will just annoy her. Instead, I try to imagine someone she might fall in love with. Maybe it will be a merrow, and he will give her the gift of breathing underwater and a crown of pearls and take her to his bed under the sea.

Actually, that sounds amazing. Maybe I am making all the wrong choices.

"How much do you like swimming?" I ask her.

"What?" she asks.

"Nothing," I say.

She, suspecting some sort of teasing, elbows me in the side.

We head through the Crooked Forest, with its bent trunks, since the Milkwood is dangerous at night. We have to stop to let some root men pass, for fear they might step on us if we didn't keep out of their way. Moss covers their shoulders and crawls up their bark cheeks. Wind whistles through their ribs.

They make a beautiful and solemn procession.

"If you're so sure Madoc is going to give you permission, why haven't you asked him yet?" Taryn whispers. "The tournament is only three days away."

Anyone can fight in the Summer Tournament, but if I want to be a knight, I must declare my candidacy by wearing a green sash across my chest. And if Madoc will not allow me that, then no amount of skill will help me. I will not be a candidate, and I will not be chosen.

I am glad the root men give me an excuse not to answer, because, of course, she's right. I haven't asked Madoc because I am afraid of what he will say.

When we get home, pushing open the enormous wooden door with its looping ironwork, someone is shouting upstairs, as though in distress. I run toward the sound, heart in my mouth, only to find Vivi in her room, chasing a cloud of sprites. They streak past me into the hall in a blast of gossamer, and she slams the book she was swinging at them into the door casing.

"Look!" Vivi yells at me, pointing toward her closet. "Look what they did."

The doors are open, and I see a sprawl of things stolen from the human world, matchbooks, newspapers, empty bottles, novels, and Polaroids. The sprites had turned the matchbooks into beds and tables, shredded all the paper, and ripped out the centers of the books to nest inside. It was a full-on sprite infestation.

But I am more baffled by the quantity of things Vivi has and how many of them don't seem to have any value. It's just junk. Mortal junk.

"What *is* all that?" Taryn asks, coming into the room. She bends down and extracts a strip of pictures, only gently chewed by sprites. The pictures are taken one right after the other, the kind you have to sit in a booth for. Vivi is in the photos, her arm draped over the shoulders of a grinning, pink-haired mortal girl.

Maybe Taryn isn't the only one who has decided to fall in love.

At dinner, we sit at a massive table carved along all four sides with images of piping fauns and dancing imps. Fat wax pillar candles burn at the center, beside a carved stone vase full of wood sorrel. Servants bring us silver plates piled with food. We eat fresh broad beans, venison with scattered pomegranate seeds, grilled brown trout with butter, a salad of bitter herbs, and, for after, raisin cakes smothered in apple syrup. Madoc and Oriana drink canary wine; we children mix ours with water.

Next to my plate and Taryn's is a bowl of salt.

Vivi pokes at her venison and then licks blood from her knife.

Oak grins across the table and starts to mimic Vivi, but Oriana snatches the cutlery from his grasp before he can slice his tongue open. Oak giggles and picks up his meat with his fingers, tearing at it with sharp teeth.

"You should know that the king will soon abdicate his throne in favor of one of his children," Madoc says, looking at all of us. "It is likely that he will choose Prince Dain."

It doesn't matter that Dain is third-born. The High Ruler chooses their successor—that's how the stability of Elfhame is ensured. The first High Queen, Mab, had her smith forge a crown. Lore has it that the blacksmith was a creature called Grimsen, who could shape anything from metal—birds that trill and necklaces that slither over throats, twin swords called Heartseeker and Heartsworn that never missed a strike. Queen Mab's crown was magically and wondrously wrought so that it passes only from one blood relation to another, in an unbroken line. With the crown passes the oaths of all those sworn to it. Although her subjects gather at each new coronation to renew their fealty, authority still rests in the crown.

"Why's he abdicating?" Taryn asks.

Vivi's smirk has turned nasty. "His children got impatient with him for remaining alive."

A wash of rage passes over Madoc's face. Taryn and I don't dare bait him for fear that his patience with us stretches only so far, but Vivi is expert at it. When he answers her, I can see the effort he's making to bite his tongue. "Few kings of Faerie have ruled so well for so long as Eldred. Now he goes to seek the Land of Promise."

As far as I can tell, the Land of Promise is their euphemism for death, although they do not admit it. They say it is the place that the Folk came from and to which they will eventually return.

"Are you saying he's leaving the throne because he's *old*?" I ask, wondering if I'm being impolite. There are hobs born with lined faces like tiny, hairless cats and smooth-limbed nixies whose true age shows only in their ancient eyes. I didn't think time mattered to them.

Oriana doesn't look happy, but she isn't actively shushing me, either, so maybe it's not *that* rude. Or maybe she doesn't expect any better than bad manners out of me.

"We may not die from age, but we grow weary with it," Madoc says with a heavy sigh. "I have made war in Eldred's name. I have broken Courts that denied him fealty. I have even led skirmishes against the Queen of the Undersea. But Eldred has lost his taste for bloodshed. He allows those under his banners to rebel in small and large ways even as other Courts refuse to submit to us. It's time to ride to battle. It's time for a new monarch, a hungry one."

Oriana furrows her brow in mild confusion. "By preference, your kin would have you safe."

"What good is a general with no war?" Madoc takes a large, restless swallow of wine. I wonder how often he needs to wet his cap with fresh blood. "The new king's coronation will be at the autumn solstice. Worry not. I have a plan to ensure our futures. Only concern yourselves with making ready for a great deal of dancing."

I am wondering what his plan might be when Taryn kicks me under the table. When I turn to glare at her, she raises both brows. "Ask him," she mouths.

Madoc looks in her direction. "Yes?"

"Jude wants to ask you something," Taryn says. The worst part is, I think she believes she's helping.

I take a deep breath. At least he seems to be in a good mood. "I've been thinking about the tournament." I imagined saying these words many, many times, but now that I am actually doing it, they don't seem to come out the way I planned. "I'm not bad with a sword."

"You do yourself too modest," Madoc says. "Your bladesmanship is excellent."

That seems encouraging. I look over at Taryn, who appears to be holding her breath. Everyone at the table has gone still except for Oak, who taps his glass against the side of his plate. "I am going to fight in the Summer Tournament, and I want to declare myself ready to be chosen for knighthood."

Madoc's brows go up. "That's what you want? It's dangerous work."

I nod. "I'm not afraid."

"Interesting," he says. My heart thuds dully in my chest. I have thought through every aspect of this plan except for the possibility that he won't allow it.

"I want to make my own way at the Court," I say.

"You're no killer," he tells me. I flinch, my gaze coming up to his. He looks back at me steadily with his golden cat eyes.

"I could be," I insist. "I've been training for a decade."

Since you took me, I do not say, although it must be in my eyes.

He shakes his head sadly. "What you lack is nothing to do with experience."

"No, but—" I begin.

"Enough. I have made my decision," he says, raising his voice to cut me off. After a moment when we both are silent, he gives me a conciliatory half smile. "Fight in the tournament if you like, for sport, but you will not put on the green sash. You're not ready to be a knight. You can ask me again after the coronation, if your heart's still set on it. And if it's a whim, that will be time enough for it to pass."

"This is no whim!" I hate the desperation in my voice, but I have been counting down the days to the tournament. The idea of waiting months, just so he can turn me down again, fills me with wild despair.

Madoc gives me an unreadable look. "After the coronation," he repeats.

I want to scream at him: Do you know how hard it is to always keep your head down? To swallow insults and endure outright threats? And yet I have done so. I thought it proved my toughness. I thought if you saw I could take whatever came at me and still smile, you would see that I was worthy.

You're no killer.

He has no idea what I am.

Maybe I don't know, either. Maybe I never let myself find out.

"Prince Dain will make a fine king," Oriana says, deftly shifting the conversation back to pleasant things. "A coronation means a month of balls. We will need new dresses." She seems to include Taryn and me in this sweeping statement. "Magnificent ones."

Madoc nods, smiling his toothy smile. "Yes, yes, as many as you like. I would have you look your finest and dance your hardest."

I try to breathe slowly, to concentrate on just one thing. The pomegranate seeds on my plate, shining like rubies, wet with venison blood.

After the coronation, Madoc said. I try to focus on that. It only feels like never.

I'd love to have a Court dress like the ones I have seen in Oriana's wardrobe, opulent patterns intricately stitched on skirts of gold and silver, each as beautiful as the dawn. I focus on that, too.

But then I go too far and imagine myself in that dress, sword at my hip, transformed, a true member of the Court, a knight in the Circle of Falcons. And Cardan watching me from across the room, standing beside the king, laughing at my pretension.

Laughing like he knows this is a fantasy that won't ever be real.

I pinch my leg until pain washes everything away.

"You'll have to wear out the soles of your shoes, just like the rest of us," Vivi says to me and Taryn. "I bet Oriana's sick with worry that since Madoc encouraged you to dance, she can't stop you. Horror of horrors, you might have a good time."

Oriana presses her lips together. "That's not fair, nor is it true."

Vivi rolls her eyes. "If it wasn't true, I couldn't say it."

"Enough, all of you!" Madoc slams his hand down on the table, making us all jump. "Coronations are a time when many things are possible. Change is coming, and there is no wisdom in crossing me."

I can't tell if he's talking about Prince Dain or ungrateful daughters or both.

"Are you afraid someone is going to try for the throne?" Taryn asks. Like me, she has been raised on strategy, moves and countermoves, ambushes and upper hands. But unlike me, she has Oriana's talent for asking the question that will steer a conversation toward less rocky shores.

"The Greenbriar line ought to worry, not me," Madoc says, but he looks pleased to be asked. "Doubtless some of their subjects wish there was no Blood Crown and no High King at all. His heirs ought to be particularly careful that the armies of Faerie are satisfied. A well-seasoned strategist waits for the right opportunity."

"Only someone with nothing to lose would attack the throne with you there to protect it," Oriana says primly.

"There's always something left to lose," Vivi says, and then makes a hideous face at Oak. He giggles.

Oriana reaches for him and then stops herself. Nothing bad is actually happening. And yet I see the gleam in Vivi's cat eyes, and I'm not sure Oriana's wrong to be nervous.

Vivi would like to punish Madoc, but her only power is to be a thorn in his side. Which means occasionally tormenting Oriana through Oak. I know Vivi loves Oak—he's our brother, after all—but that doesn't mean she's above teaching him bad things.

Madoc smiles at all of us, now the picture of contentment. I used to think he didn't notice all the currents of tension that ran through the family, but as I get older, I see that barely suppressed conflict doesn't bother him in the least. He likes it just as well as open war. "Perhaps none of our enemies are particularly good strategists."

"Let's hope not," Oriana says distractedly, her eyes on Oak, lifting her glass of canary wine.

"Indeed," says Madoc. "Let's have a toast. To the incompetence of our enemies."

I pick up my glass and knock it into Taryn's, then drain it to the very dregs.

There's always something left to lose.

I think about that all through the dawn, turning it over in my head. Finally, when I can toss and turn no more, I pull on a robe over my nightgown and go outside into the late-morning sun. Bright as hammered gold, it hurts my eyes when I sit down on a patch of clover near the stables, looking back at the house.

All of this was my mother's before it was Oriana's. Mom must have been young and in love with Madoc back then. I wonder what it was like for her. I wonder if she thought she was going to be happy here.

I wonder when she realized she wasn't.

I have heard the rumors. It is no small thing to confound the High King's general, to sneak out of Faerie with his baby in your belly and hide for almost ten years. She left behind the burned remains of another woman in the blackened husk of his estate. No one can say she didn't prove her toughness. If she'd just been a little luckier, Madoc would have never realized she was still alive.

She had a lot to lose, I guess.

I've got a lot to lose, too.

But so what?

"Skip our lessons today," I tell Taryn that afternoon. I am dressed and ready early. Though I have not slept, I do not feel at all tired. "Stay home."

She gives me a look of deep concern as a pixie boy, newly indebted to Madoc, braids her chestnut hair into a crown. She is sitting primly at her dressing table, clad all in brown and gold. "Telling me not to go means I should. Whatever you're thinking, stop. I know you're disappointed about the tournament—"

"It doesn't matter," I say, although, of course, it does. It matters so much that, now, without hope of knighthood, I feel like a hole has opened up under me and I am falling through it.

"Madoc might change his mind." She follows me down the stairs, grabbing up our baskets before I can. "And at least now you won't have to defy Cardan."

I turn on her, even though none of this is her fault. "Do you know why Madoc won't let me try for knighthood? Because he thinks I'm weak."

"Jude," she cautions.

"I thought I was supposed to be good and follow the rules," I say. "But I am done with being weak. I am done with being good. I think I am going to be something else."

"Only idiots aren't scared of things that are scary," Taryn says, which is undoubtedly true, but still fails to dissuade me.

"Skip lessons today," I tell her again, but she won't, so we go to school together.

Taryn watches me warily as I talk with the leader of the mock war, Fand, a pixie girl with skin the blue of flower petals. She reminds me that there's a run-through tomorrow in preparation for the tournament.

I nod, biting the inside of my cheek. No one needs to know that my hopes were dashed. No one needs to know I ever had any hope at all.

Later, when Cardan, Locke, Nicasia, and Valerian sit down to their lunch, they have to spit out their food in choking horror. All around them are the less awful children of faerie nobles, eating their bread and honey, their cakes and roasted pigeons, their elderflower jam with biscuits and cheese and the fat globes of grapes. But every single morsel in each of my enemies' baskets has been well and thoroughly salted.

Cardan's gaze catches mine, and I can't help the evil smile that pulls up the corners of my mouth. His eyes are bright as coals, his hatred a living thing, shimmering in the air between us like the air above black rocks on a blazing summer day.

"Have you lost your wits?" Taryn demands, shaking my shoulder so that I have to turn to her. "You're making everything worse. There's a reason no one stands up to them."

"I know," I say softly, unable to keep the smile off my lips. "A lot of reasons."

She's right to be worried. I just declared war.

CHAPTER 6

I've told this story all wrong. There are things I really ought to have said about growing up in Faerie. I left them out of the story, mostly because I am a coward. I don't even like to let myself think about them. But maybe knowing a few relevant details about my past will make more sense of why I'm the way I am. How fear seeped into my marrow. How I learned to pretend it away.

So here are three things I should have told you about myself before, but didn't:

1. When I was nine, one of Madoc's guards bit off the very top of the ring finger on my left hand. We were outside, and when I screamed, he pushed me hard enough that my head smacked into a wooden post in the stables. Then he made me stand there while he chewed the piece he'd bitten off. He told me exactly how much he hated mortals. I bled so

much—you wouldn't think that much blood could come out of a finger. When it was over, he explained that I better keep what happened secret, because if I didn't, he'd eat the rest of me. So, obviously, I didn't tell anyone. Until now, when I am telling you.

2. When I was eleven, I was spotted hiding under the banquet table at one of the revels by a particularly bored member of the Gentry. He dragged me out by one foot, kicking and squirming. I don't think he knew who I was—at least, I tell myself he didn't. But he compelled me to drink, and so I drank; the grass-green faerie wine slipping down my throat like nectar. He danced me around the hill. It was fun at first, the kind of terrifying fun that makes you screech to be put down half the time and feel dizzy and sick the rest. But when the fun wore off and I still couldn't stop, it was just terrifying. It turned out that my fear was equally amusing to him, though. Princess Elowyn found me at the end of the revel, puking and crying. She didn't ask me a single thing about how I got that way, she just handed me over to Oriana like I was a misplaced jacket. We never told Madoc about it. What would have been the point? Everyone who saw me probably thought I was having a grand old time.

3. When I was fourteen and Oak was four, he glamoured me. He didn't mean to—well, at least he didn't really understand why he shouldn't. I wasn't wearing any protective charms because I'd just come out of a bath. Oak didn't

> want to go to bed. He told me to play dolls with him, so we played. He commanded me to chase him, so we played chase through the halls. Then he figured out he could make me slap myself, which was very funny. Tatterfell came upon us hours later, took a good look at my reddened cheeks and the tears in my eyes, and then ran for Oriana. For weeks, a giggling Oak tried to glamour me into getting him sweets or lifting him above my head or spitting at the dinner table. Even though it never worked, even though I wore a strand of rowan berries everywhere after that, it was all I could do for months not to strike him to the floor. Oriana has never forgiven me for that restraint—she believes my not revenging myself on him then means I plan to revenge myself in the future.

Here's why I don't like these stories: They highlight that I am vulnerable. No matter how careful I am, eventually I'll make another misstep. I am weak. I am fragile. I am mortal.

I hate that most of all.

Even if, by some miracle, I could be better than them, I will never be one of them.

CHAPTER 7

They don't wait long to retaliate.

For the rest of the afternoon and early evening, we receive lessons in history. A cat-headed goblin named Yarrow recites ballads and asks us questions. The more correct answers I give, the angrier Cardan grows. He makes no secret of his displeasure, drawling to Locke about how boring these lessons are and sneering at the lecturer.

For once, we're done before dark has fully fallen. Taryn and I start for home, with her giving me concerned glances. The light of sunset filters through the trees, and I take a deep breath, drinking in the scent of pine needles. I feel a kind of weird calm, despite the stupidity of what I've done.

"This isn't like you," Taryn says finally. "You don't pick fights with people."

"Appeasing them won't help." I toe a stone with my booted foot. "The more they get away with, the more they believe they're entitled to have."

"So you're going to, what—teach them manners?" Taryn sighs. "Even if someone should do it, that someone doesn't have to be you."

She's right. I know she's right. The giddy fury of this afternoon will fade, and I will regret what I've done. Probably after a good, long sleep, I'll be as horrified as Taryn is. All I have bought myself is worse problems, no matter how good it felt to salve my pride.

You're no killer.

What you lack is nothing to do with experience.

And yet, I don't regret it now. Having stepped off the edge, what I want to do is fall.

I begin to speak when a hand claps down over my mouth. Fingers sink into the skin around my lips. I strike out, swinging my body around, and see Locke grabbing Taryn's waist. Someone has my wrists. I wrench my mouth free and scream, but screams in Faerie are like birdsong, too common to attract much attention.

They push us through the woods, laughing. I hear a whoop from one of the boys. I think I hear Locke say something about larks being over quickly, but it's swallowed up in the merriment.

Then a shove at my shoulders and the horrible shock of cold water closing over me. I sputter, trying to breathe. I taste mud and reeds. I shove myself up. Taryn and I are waist-high in the river, the current pushing us downstream toward a deeper, rougher part. I dig my feet into the muck at the bottom to keep from being swept away. Taryn is gripping a boulder, her hair wet. She must have slipped.

"There are nixies in this river," Valerian says. "If you don't get out before they find you, they'll pull you under and hold you there. Their sharp teeth will sink into your skin." He mimes taking a bite.

They're all along the riverbank, Cardan closest, Valerian beside him. Locke brushes his hand over the tops of cattails and bulrushes, looking abstracted. He does not seem kind now. He seems bored with his friends and with us, too.

"Nixies can't help what they are," Nicasia says, kicking the water so that it splashes my face. "Just like you won't be able to help drowning."

I dig my feet deeper into the mud. The water filling my boots makes it hard to move my legs, but the mud locks them in place when I manage to stand still. I don't know how I am going to get to Taryn without slipping.

Valerian is emptying our schoolbags onto the riverbank. He and Nicasia and Locke take turns hurling the contents into the water. My leather-bound notebooks. Rolls of paper that disintegrate as they sink. The books of ballads and histories make an enormous splash, then lodge between two stones and will not budge. My fine pen and nibs shimmer along the bottom. My inkpot shatters on the rocks, turning the river vermilion.

Cardan watches me. Although he doesn't lift a finger, I know this is all his doing. In his eyes, I see all the vast alienness of Faerie.

"Is this fun?" I call to the shore. I am so furious that there's no room for being scared. "Are you enjoying yourselves?"

"Enormously," says Cardan. Then his gaze slides from me to where shadows rest under the water. Are those nixies? I cannot tell. I just keep moving toward Taryn.

"This is just a game," Nicasia says. "But sometimes we play too hard with our toys. And then they break."

"It's not like we drowned you ourselves," Valerian calls.

My foot slips on slick rocks, and I am under, swept downstream helplessly, gulping muddy water. I panic, snorting into my lungs. I thrust out a hand, and it closes on the root of a tree. I get my balance again, gasping and coughing.

Nicasia and Valerian are laughing. Locke's expression is unreadable.

Cardan has one foot in the reeds, as though to get a better look. Furious and sputtering, I push my way back to Taryn, who comes forward to grab my hand and squeeze it hard.

"I thought you were going to drown," she says, the edge of hysteria in her voice.

"We're fine," I tell her. Digging my feet into the murk, I reach down for a rock. I find a large one and heft it up, green and slick with algae. "If the nixies come at us, I'll hold them off."

"Quit," Cardan says. He's looking directly at me. He does not even spare a glance for Taryn. "You should never have been tutored with us. Abandon thoughts of the tourney. Tell Madoc you don't belong with us, your betters. Do that and I'll save you."

I stare at him.

"All you have to do is give in," he says. "Easy."

I look over at my sister. It's my fault she's wet and scared. The river is cold, despite the heat of summer, the current strong. "And you'll save Taryn, too?"

"Oh, so you'll do what I say for her sake?" Cardan's gaze is hungry, devouring. "Does that feel noble?" He pauses, and in that silence, all I hear is Taryn's hitched breath. "Well, does it?"

I look at the nixies, watch them for any sign of movement. "Why don't you tell me how you want me to feel?"

"Interesting." He takes another step closer, squatting and regarding us from eye level. "There are so few children in Faerie that I've never seen one of us twinned. Is it like being doubled or more like being divided in half?"

I don't answer.

Behind him, I see Nicasia thread her arm through Locke's and whisper something to him. He gives her a scathing look, and she pouts. Maybe they're annoyed that we're not currently being eaten.

Cardan frowns. "Twin sister," he says, turning to Taryn. A smile returns to his mouth, as though a terrible new idea has come to delight him. "Would you make a similar sacrifice? Let's find out. I have a most generous offer for you. Climb up the bank and kiss me on both my cheeks. Once that's done, so long as you don't defend your sister by word or deed, I won't hold you accountable for her defiance. Now, isn't that a good bargain? But you get it only if you come to us now and leave her there to drown. Show her that she will always be alone."

For a moment, Taryn stands still, as if frozen.

"Go," I say. "I'll be fine."

It still hurts when she wades toward the bank. But of course she should go. She will be safe, and the price is nothing that matters.

One of the pale shapes detaches from the others and swims toward her, but my shadow in the water makes it hesitate. I mime throwing the rock, and it jolts a little. They like easy prey.

Valerian takes Taryn's hand and helps her out of the water as if she were a great lady. Her dress is soaked, dripping as she moves, like the dresses of water sprites or sea nymphs. She presses her bluish lips to Cardan's cheeks, one and then the other. She keeps her eyes closed, but his are open, watching me.

"Say 'I forsake my sister Jude,'" Nicasia tells her. "'I won't help her. I don't even like her.'"

Taryn looks in my direction, quick and apologetic. "I don't have to say that. That wasn't part of the bargain." The others laugh.

Cardan's boot parts the thistles and bulrushes. Locke starts to speak, but Cardan cuts him off. "Your sister abandoned you. See what we can do with a few words? And everything can get so much worse. We can enchant you to run around on all fours, barking like a dog. We can curse you to wither away for want of a song you'll never hear again or a kind word from my lips. We're not mortal. We will break you. You're a fragile little thing; we'd hardly need to try. Give up."

"Never," I say.

He smiles, smug. "Never? Never is like forever—too big for mortals to comprehend."

The shape in the water remains where it is, probably because the presence of Cardan and the others makes it seem like I have friends who might defend me if I were attacked. I wait for Cardan's next move, watching him carefully. I hope I look defiant. He scrutinizes me for a long, awful moment.

"Think on us," he says to me. "All through your long, sodden, shameful walk home. Think on your answer. This is the least of what we can do." With that, he turns away from us, and after a moment, the others turn, too. I watch him go. I watch them all go.

When they're out of sight, I pull myself onto the bank, flopping onto my back in the mud next to where Taryn is standing. I take big, gulping breaths of air. The nixies begin to surface, looking at us with hungry, opalescent eyes. They peer at us through a patch of foxtails. One begins to crawl onto land.

I throw my rock. It doesn't come close to hitting, but the splash startles them into not coming closer.

Grunting, I force myself up to begin walking. And all through our walk home, while Taryn makes soft, sobbing sounds, I think about how much I hate them and how much I hate myself. And then I don't think about anything but lifting my wet boots, one step after another carrying me past the briars and fiddleheads and elms, past bushes of red-lipped cherries, barberries and damsons, past the wood sprites who nest in the rosebushes, home to a bath and a bed in a world that isn't mine and might never be.

CHAPTER 8

My head is pounding when Vivienne shakes me awake. She jumps up onto the bed, kicking off the coverlets and making the frame groan. I press a cushion over my face and curl up on my side, trying to ignore her and go back to dreamless slumber.

"Get up, sleepyhead," she says, pulling back my blankets. "We're going to the mall."

I make a strangled noise and wave her away.

"Up!" she commands, leaping again.

"No," I moan, burrowing deeper in what's left of the blankets. "I've got to rehearse for the tournament."

Vivi stops bouncing, and I realize that it's no longer true. I don't have to fight. Except that I foolishly told Cardan I would never quit.

Which makes me remember the river and the nixies and Taryn.

How she was right, and I was magnificently, extravagantly wrong.

"I'll buy you coffee when we get there, coffee with chocolate and whipped cream." Vivi is relentless. "Come on. Taryn's waiting."

I half-stumble out of bed. Standing, I scratch my hip and glare. She gives me her most charming smile, and I find my annoyance fading, despite myself. Vivi is often selfish, but she's so cheerful about it and so encouraging of cheerful selfishness in others that it's easy to have fun with her.

I dress quickly in the modern clothes I keep in the very back of my wardrobe—jeans, an old gray sweater with a black star on it, and a pair of glittery silver Converse high-tops. I pull my hair into a slouchy knitted hat, and when I catch a glimpse of myself in the full-length mirror (carved so that it seems like a pair of bawdy fauns are on either side of the glass, leering), a different person is looking back at me.

Maybe the person I might have been if I'd been raised human.

Whoever that is.

When we were little, we used to talk about getting back to the human world all the time. Vivi kept saying that if she learned just a little more magic, we'd be able to go. We were going to find an abandoned mansion, and she was going to enchant birds to take care of us. They would buy us pizza and candy, and we would go to school only if we felt like it.

By the time Vivi learned how to travel there, though, reality had intruded on our plans. It turns out birds can't really buy pizza, even if they're enchanted.

I meet my sisters in front of Madoc's stables, where silver-shod faerie horses are penned up beside enormous toads ready to be saddled and bridled and reindeer with broad antlers hung with bells. Vivi is wearing black jeans and a white shirt, mirrored sunglasses hiding her cat eyes. Taryn has on pink jeggings, a fuzzy cardigan, and a pair of ankle boots.

We try to imitate girls we see in the human world, girls in magazines, girls we see on movie screens in air-conditioned theaters, eating candy so sweet it makes my teeth ache. I don't know what people think when they look at us. These clothes are a costume for me. I am playing dress-up in ignorance. I no more can guess the assumptions that go along with glittering sneakers than a child in a dragon costume knows what real dragons would make of the color of her scales.

Vivi picks stalks of ragwort that grow near the water troughs. After finding three that meet her specifications, she lifts the first and blows on it, saying, "Steed, rise and bear us where I command."

With those words, she tosses the stalk to the ground, and it becomes a raw-boned yellow pony with emerald eyes and a mane that resembles lacy foliage. It makes an odd keening neigh. She throws down two more stalks, and moments later three ragwort ponies snort the air and snuffle at the ground. They look a little like sea horses and will ride over land and sky, according to Vivi's command, keeping their seeming for hours before collapsing back into weeds.

It turns out that passing between Faerie and the mortal world isn't all that difficult. Faerie exists beside and below mortal towns, in the shadows of mortal cities, and at their rotten, derelict, worm-eaten centers. Faeries live in hills and valleys and barrows, in alleys and abandoned mortal buildings. Vivi isn't the only faerie from our islands to sneak across the sea and into the human world with some regularity, although most don mortal guises to mess with people. Less than a month ago, Valerian was bragging about campers he and his friends had tricked into feasting with them, gorging on rotten leaves enchanted to look like delicacies.

I climb onto my ragwort steed and wrap my hands around the creature's neck. There is always a moment when it begins to move that I can't help grinning. There is something about the sheer impossibility of it, the magnificence of the woods streaking by and the way the ragwort hooves kick up gravel as they leap up into the air, that gives me an electric rush of pure adrenaline.

I swallow the howl clawing up my throat.

We ride over the cliffs and then the sea, watching mermaids leap in the spangled waves and selkies rolling along the surf. Past the fog perpetually surrounding the islands and concealing them from mortals. And then on to the shoreline, past Two Lights State Park, a golf course, and a jetport. We touch down in a small tree-covered patch across the road from the Maine Mall. Vivi's shirt flutters in the wind as she lands. Taryn and I dismount. With a few words from Vivi, the ragwort steeds become just three half-wilted weeds among others.

"Remember where we parked," Taryn says with a grin, and we start toward the mall.

Vivi loves this place. She loves to drink mango smoothies, try on hats, and buy whatever we want with acorns she enchants to pass as money. Taryn doesn't love it the way Vivi does, but she has fun. When I am here, though, I feel like a ghost.

We strut through the JCPenney as though we're the most dangerous things around. But when I see human families all together, especially families with sticky-mouthed, giggling little sisters, I don't like the way I feel.

Angry.

I don't imagine myself back in a life like theirs; what I imagine is going over there and scaring them until they cry.

I would never, of course.

I mean, I don't think I would.

Taryn seems to notice the way my gaze snags on a child whining to her mother. Unlike me, Taryn is adaptable. She knows the right things to say. She'd be okay if she were thrust back into this world. She's okay now. She will fall in love, just as she said. She will metamorphose into a wife or consort and raise faerie children who will adore and outlive her. The only thing holding her back is me.

I am *so glad* she can't guess my thoughts.

"So," Vivi says. "We're here because you both could use some cheering up. So cheer up."

I look over at Taryn and take a deep breath, ready to apologize. I don't know if that's what Vivi had in mind, but it's what I've known I had to do since I got out of bed. "I'm sorry," I blurt out.

"You're probably mad," Taryn says at the same time.

"At you?" I am astonished.

Taryn droops. "I swore to Cardan that I wouldn't help you, even though I came with you that day to help."

I shake my head vehemently. "Really, Taryn, you're the one who should be angry that I got you tossed into the water in the first place. Getting yourself out of there was the smart thing to do. I would never be mad about that."

"Oh," she says. "Okay."

"Taryn told me about the prank you played on the prince," Vivi says. I see myself reflected in her sunglasses, doubled, quadrupled with Taryn beside me. "Pretty good, but now you're going to have to do something much worse. I've got ideas."

"No!" Taryn says with vehemence. "Jude doesn't need to do *anything*. She was just upset about Madoc and the tournament. If she goes back to ignoring them, they'll go back to ignoring her, too. Maybe not at first, but eventually."

I bite my lip because I don't think that's true.

"Forget Madoc. Knighthood would have been boring anyway," Vivi says, effectively dismissing the thing I've been working toward for years. I sigh. It's annoying, but also reassuring that she doesn't think it's that big a deal, when the loss has felt overwhelming to me.

"So what do you want to do?" I ask Vivi to avoid any more of this discussion. "Are we seeing a movie? Do you want to try on lipsticks? Don't forget you promised me coffee."

"I want you to meet my girlfriend," Vivienne says, and I remember the pink-haired girl in the strip of photos. "She asked me to move in with her."

"Here?" I ask, as though there could be any other place.

"The mall?" Vivi laughs at our expressions. "We're going to meet her here today but probably find a different place to *live*. Heather doesn't know Faerie exists, so don't mention it, okay?"

When Taryn and I were ten, Vivi learned how to make ragwort horses. We ran away from Madoc's house a few days later. At a gas station, Vivi enchanted a random woman to take us home with her.

I still remember the woman's blank face as she drove. I wanted to make her smile, but no matter what funny faces I pulled, her expression didn't change. We spent the night in her house, sick after having ice cream for dinner. I cried myself to sleep, clinging to a weeping Taryn.

After that, Vivi found us a motel room with a stove, and we learned how to cook macaroni and cheese from the package. We made coffee in the coffeepot because we remembered how our old house had smelled like it. We watched television and swam in the pool with other kids staying in the motel.

I hated it.

We lived that way for two weeks before Taryn and I begged Vivi to take us home, to take us back to Faerie. We missed our beds, we missed the food we were used to, we missed magic.

I think it broke Vivi's heart to return, but she did it. And she stayed. Whatever else I can say about Vivi, when it really mattered, she stuck by us.

I guess I shouldn't be surprised that she didn't plan to stay forever.

"Why didn't you tell us?" Taryn demands.

"I *am* telling you. I just did," Vivi says, leading us past stores with looping images of video games, past gleaming displays of bikinis and flowing maxi dresses, past cheese-injected pretzels and stores with counters full of gleaming, heart-shaped diamonds promising true love. Strollers stream past, groups of teenage boys in jerseys, elderly couples holding hands.

"You should have said something sooner," says Taryn, hands on her hips.

"Here's my plan to cheer you up," Vivi says. "We all move to the human world. Move in with Heather. Jude doesn't have to worry about knighthood, and Taryn doesn't have to throw herself away on some silly faerie boy."

"Does Heather know about this plan?" Taryn asks skeptically.

Vivi shakes her head, smiling.

"Sure," I say, trying to make a joke of it. "Except that I have no marketable skills other than swinging around a sword and making up riddles, neither of which probably pay all that well."

"The mortal world is where we grew up," Vivi insists, climbing onto a bench and walking the length of it, acting as though it were a stage. She pushes her sunglasses up onto her head. "You'd get used to it again."

"Where *you* grew up." She was nine when we were taken; she remembers so much more about being human than we do. It's unfair, since she's also the one with magic.

"The Folk are going to keep treating you like crap," Vivi says, and hops down in front of us, cat eyes flashing. A lady with a baby carriage swerves to avoid us.

"What do you mean?" I look away from Vivi, concentrating on the pattern of the tiles under my feet.

"Oriana acts like you two being mortal is some kind of awful surprise that gets sprung on her all over again every morning," she says. "And Madoc killed our parents, so that sucks. And then there are the jerks at school that you don't like to talk about."

"I was just talking about those jerks," I say, not giving her the satisfaction of being shocked by what she said about our parents. She acts like we don't remember, like there's some way I am ever going to forget. She acts like it's her personal tragedy and hers alone.

"And you didn't like it." Vivi looks immensely pleased with herself for that particular riposte. "Did you really think that being a knight would make everything better?"

"I don't know," I say.

Vivi swings on Taryn. "What about you?"

"Faerie is all we know." Taryn holds up a hand to forestall any more argument. "Here, we wouldn't have anything. There'd be no balls and no magic and no—"

"Well, I think *I'd* like it here," Vivi snaps, and stalks off ahead of us, toward the Apple Store.

We've talked about it before, of course, how Vivi thinks we're stupid for not being able to resist the intensity of Faerie, for desiring to stay in a place of such danger. Maybe growing up the way we have, bad things feel good to us. Or maybe we are stupid in the exact same way as every other idiot mortal who's pined away for another bite of goblin fruit. Maybe it doesn't matter.

A girl is standing in front of the entrance, playing around on her phone. *The* girl, I assume. Heather is small, with faded pink hair and brown skin. She's wearing a t-shirt with a hand-drawn design across the front. There are pen stains on her fingers. I realize abruptly that she might be the artist who drew the comics I've seen Vivi pore over.

I begin a curtsy before I remember myself and awkwardly stick out a hand. "I'm Vivi's sister Jude," I say. "And this is Taryn."

The girl shakes my hand. Her palm is warm, her grip nearly nonexistent.

It's funny how Vivi, who tried so hard to escape being anything like Madoc, wound up falling in love with a human girl, as Madoc did.

"I'm Heather," the girl says. "It's great to meet you. Vee almost never talks about her family."

Taryn and I glance at each other. *Vee?*

"You want to sit down or something?" Heather says, nodding toward the food court.

"Somebody owes me coffee," I say pointedly to Vivi.

We order and sit and drink. Heather tells us that she's in community college, studying art. She tells us about comics she likes and bands she's into. We dodge awkward questions. We lie. When Vivi gets up to throw away our trash, Heather asks us if she's the first girlfriend Vivi has let us meet.

Taryn nods. "That must mean she likes you a lot."

"So can I visit your place now? My parents are ready to buy a toothbrush for Vee. How come I don't get to meet hers?"

I almost snort my mocha. "Did she tell you anything about our family?"

Heather sighs. "No."

"Our dad is really conservative," I say.

A boy with spiky black hair and a wallet chain passes us, smiling in my direction. I have no idea what he wants. Maybe he knows Heather. She's not paying attention. I don't smile back.

"Does he even know Vee is bi?" Heather asks, astonished, but then Vivi returns to the table, so we don't have to keep making up stuff. Liking both girls and boys is the only thing in this scenario Madoc *wouldn't* be upset with Vivi about.

After that, the four of us wander the mall, trying on purple lipsticks and eating sour apple candy slices crusted in sugar that turn my tongue green. I delight in the chemicals that would doubtless sicken all the lords and ladies at the Court.

Heather seems nice. Heather has no idea what she's getting herself into.

We say polite farewells near Newbury Comics. Vivi watches three kids picking out bobblehead figurines, her gaze avid. I wonder what she thinks as she moves among humans. At moments like that, she seems like a wolf learning the patterns of sheep. But when she kisses Heather, she is entirely sincere.

"I am glad you lied for me," Vivi says as we retrace our steps through the mall.

"You're going to have to tell her eventually," I say. "If you're serious. If you're really moving to the mortal world to be with her."

"And when you do, she's still going to want to meet Madoc," Taryn says, although I can see why Vivi wants to avoid that for as long as possible.

Vivi shakes her head. "Love is a noble cause. How can anything done in the service of a noble cause be wrong?"

Taryn chews her lip.

Before we leave, we stop by CVS, and I pick up tampons. Every time I buy them, it's a reminder that while the Folk can look like us, they are a species apart. Even Vivi is a species apart. I divide the package in half and give the other portion to Taryn.

I know what you're wondering. No, they don't bleed once a month; yes, they do bleed. Annually. Sometimes less frequently than that. Yes, they have solutions—padding, mostly—and yes, those solutions suck. Yes, everything about it is embarrassing.

We start to cut across the parking lot toward our ragwort stalks when a guy about our age touches my arm, warm fingers closing just above my wrist.

"Hey, sweetheart." I have an impression of a too-big black shirt, jeans, a chain wallet, spiky hair. The glint of a cheap knife in his boot. "I saw you before, and I was just wondering—"

I am turning before I can think, my fist cracking into his jaw. My booted foot hits his gut as he falls, rolling him over the pavement. I blink and find myself standing there, staring down at a kid who is gasping for air and starting to cry. My boot is raised to kick him in the throat, to crush his windpipe. The mortals standing around him are staring at me in horror. My nerves are jangling, but it's an eager jangle. I am ready for more.

I think he was flirting with me.

I don't even remember deciding to hit him.

"Come on!" Taryn jerks my arm, and all three of us run. Someone shouts.

I look over my shoulder. One of the boy's friends has given chase. "Bitch!" he shouts. "Crazy bitch! Milo is bleeding!"

Vivi whispers a few words and makes a motion behind us. As she does, the crabgrass begins to grow, pushing gaps in the asphalt wider. The boy comes to a halt as something rushes by him, a look of confusion on his face. Pixie-led, they call it. He wanders through a row of cars as though he has no idea where he's going. Unless he turns his clothes inside out, which I am fairly confident he doesn't know to do, he'll never find us.

We stop near the edge of the lot, and Vivi immediately begins to giggle. "Madoc would be so proud—his little girl, remembering all her training," she says. "Staving off the terrifying possibility of romance."

I am too stunned to say anything. Hitting him was the most honest thing I've done in a long time. I feel better than great. I feel *nothing*, a glorious emptiness.

"See," I tell Vivi. "I can't go back to the world. Look what I would do to it."

To that, she has no response.

I think about what I did all the way home and then, again, at school. A lecturer from a Court near the coast explains how things wither and die. Cardan gives me a significant look as she explains decomposition, rot. But what I am thinking about is the stillness I felt when I hit that boy. That and the Summer Tournament tomorrow.

I dreamed of my triumph there. None of Cardan's threats would have kept me from wearing the gold braid and fighting as hard as I could. Now, though, his threats are the only reason I have to fight—the sheer perverse glory of not backing down.

When we break to eat, Taryn and I climb up a tree to eat cheese and oatcakes slathered with chokecherry jelly. Fand calls up to me, wanting to know why I didn't attend the rehearsal for the mock war.

"I forgot," I call back to her, which is not particularly believable, but I don't care.

"But you're going to fight tomorrow?" she asks. If I pull out, Fand will have to rearrange teams.

Taryn gives me a hopeful look, as though I may come to my senses.

"I'll be there," I say. My pride compels me.

Lessons are almost over when I notice Taryn, standing beside Cardan, near a circle of thorn trees, weeping. I must not have been paying attention, must have gotten too involved in packing up our books and things. I didn't even see Cardan take my sister aside. I know she would have gone, though, no matter the excuse. She still believes that if we do what they want, they'll get bored and leave us alone. Maybe she's right, but I don't care.

Tears spill over her cheeks.

There is such a deep well of rage inside me.

You're no killer.

I leave my books and cross the grass toward them. Cardan half-turns, and I shove him so hard that his back hits one of the trees. His eyes go wide.

"I don't know what you said to her, but don't you ever go near my sister again," I tell him, my hand still on the front of his velvet doublet. "You gave her your word."

I can feel the eyes of all the other students on me. Everyone's breath is drawn.

For a moment, Cardan just stares at me with stupid, crow-black eyes. Then one corner of his mouth curls. "Oh," he says. "You're going to regret doing that."

I don't think he realizes just how angry I am or how good it feels, for once, to give up on regrets.

CHAPTER 9

Taryn won't tell me what Prince Cardan said to her. She insists that it had nothing to do with me, that he wasn't actually breaking his promise not to hold her accountable for my bad behavior, that I should forget about her and worry about myself.

"Jude, give it up." She sits in front of the fire in her bedroom, drinking a cup of nettle tea from a clay mug shaped like a snake, its tail coiling to make the handle. She has on her dressing gown, scarlet to match the flames in the grate. Sometimes when I look at her, it seems impossible that her face is also mine. She looks soft, pretty, like a girl in a painting. Like a girl who fits inside her own skin.

"Just tell me what he said," I press.

"There's nothing to tell," Taryn says. "I know what I'm doing."

"And what's that?" I ask her, my eyebrows lifting, but she only sighs.

We've gone three rounds like this already. I keep thinking of the lazy blink of Cardan's lashes over his coal-bright eyes. He looked gleeful, gloating, as though my fist tightening on his shirt was exactly what he would have wished. As though, if I struck him, it would be because he had made me do it.

"I can annoy you in the hills and also the dales," I say, poking her in the arm. "I will chase you from crag to crag across all three islands until you tell me *something*."

"I think we could both bear it better if no one else had to see," she says, then takes a long pull of her tea.

"What?" I am surprised into not knowing what to say in return. "What do you mean?"

"I *mean*, I think I could stand being teased and being made to cry if you didn't know about it." She gives me a steady look, as though evaluating how much truth I can handle. "I can't just pretend my day was fine with you as a witness to what really happened. Sometimes it makes me not like you."

"That's not fair!" I exclaim.

She shrugs. "I know. That's why I'm telling you. But what Cardan said to me doesn't matter, and I want to pretend it didn't happen, so I need you to pretend along with me. No reminders, no questions, no cautions."

Stung, I stand and walk to her fireplace mantel, leaning my head against the carved stone. I can't count the number of times she's told me that messing with Cardan and his friends is stupid. And yet, given what she's saying now, whatever made her cry this afternoon has nothing to do with me. Which means she's gotten into some kind of trouble all on her own.

Taryn might have a lot of advice to give; I am not sure she's taking all of it.

"So what *do* you want me to do?" I ask.

"I want you to fix things with him," she says. "Prince Cardan's got all the power. There's no winning against him. No matter how brave or clever or even cruel you are, Jude. End this, before you get really hurt."

I look at her uncomprehendingly. Avoiding Cardan's wrath now seems impossible. That ship has sailed—and burned up in the harbor. "I can't," I tell her.

"You heard what Prince Cardan said by the river—he just wants you to *give up*. It's a blow to his pride, and it hurts his status, you acting like you're not afraid of him." She takes my arm at the wrist, pulling me close. I can smell the sharp scent of herbs on her breath. "Tell him that he's won and you've lost. They're just words. You don't have to mean them."

I shake my head.

"Don't fight him tomorrow," she continues.

"I'm not withdrawing from the tournament," I tell her.

"Even if it wins you nothing but more woe?" she asks.

"Even then," I say.

"Do something else," she insists. "Find a way. Fix it before it's too late."

I think of all the things she won't say, all the things I wish I knew. But since she wants me to pretend everything is fine, all I can do is swallow my questions and leave her to her fire.

In my room, I find my tournament outfit spread out on my bed, scented with verbena and lavender.

It's a slightly padded tunic stitched with metallic thread. The pattern is of a crescent moon turned on its side like a cup, with a droplet of red falling from one corner and a dagger beneath the whole. Madoc's crest.

I cannot put on that tunic tomorrow and fail, not without bringing disgrace on my household. And although embarrassing Madoc might give me a contrary pleasure, a small revenge for denying me knighthood, I'd embarrass myself, too.

What I should do is go back to keeping my head down. Be decent, but not memorable. Let Cardan and his friends show off. Save up my skill to surprise the Court when Madoc gives me permission to seek a knighthood. If that ever happens.

That's what I *should* do.

I knock the tunic to the floor and climb under the coverlets, pulling them up over my head so that I am slightly smothered. So that I breathe in my own warm breath. I fall asleep like that.

In the afternoon, when I rise, the garment is wrinkled, and I have no one to blame but myself.

"You are a foolish child," Tatterfell says, scraping my hair into tight warrior braids. "With a memory like that of a sparrow."

On my way to the kitchens, I pass Madoc in the hall. He is dressed all in green, his mouth pulled into a grim line.

"Hold a moment," he says.

I do.

He frowns. "I know what it is to be young and hungry for glory."

I bite my lip and say nothing. After all, he hasn't asked me a question. We stand there, watching each other. His cat eyes narrow. There are so many unsaid things between us—so many reasons we can only be something *like* father and daughter, but never fully inhabit our roles. "You will come to understand this is for the best," he says finally. "Enjoy your battle."

I make a deep bow and head for the door, my trip to the kitchens abandoned. All I want to do is get away from the house, from the reminder that there is no place for me at the Court, no place for me in Faerie.

What you lack is nothing to do with experience.

The Summer Tournament is being held on the edge of a cliff on Insweal, the Isle of Woe. It's far enough that I take a mount, a pale gray horse stabled beside a toad. The toad watches me with golden eyes as I saddle the mare and throw myself up onto her back. I arrive at the grounds out of sorts, slightly late, anxious, and hungry.

A crowd is already gathering around the tented box where the High King Eldred and the rest of the royals will sit. Long cream-colored banners whip through the air, flying Eldred's symbol—a tree that is half white flowers and half thorns, roots dangling beneath it and a crown atop. The uniting of the Seelie Courts, the Unseelie Courts, and the wild fey, under one crown. The dream of the Greenbriar line.

The decadent eldest son, Prince Balekin, is sprawled in a carved chair, three attendants around him. His sister Princess Rhyia, the huntress, sits beside him. Her eyes are all on the potential combatants, readying themselves on the grounds.

A wave of panicky frustration comes over me at the sight of her intent expression. I so badly wanted her to choose me to be one of her knights. And though she can't now, a sudden awful fear that I couldn't have impressed her comes over me. Maybe Madoc was right. Maybe I lack the instinct for dealing death.

If I don't try too hard today, at least I never need know if I would have been good enough.

My group is to go first because we are the youngest. Still in training, using wooden swords instead of live steel, unlike those who follow us. Bouts of fighting will last the whole day, broken up by bardic performances, a few feats of clever magic, displays of archery, and other skills. I can smell spiced wine in the air, but not yet that other perfume of tournaments—fresh blood.

Fand is organizing us into rows, handing out armbands in silver and gold. Her blue skin is even more blazingly cerulean under the bright sky. Her armor is varying shades of blue as well, from oceanic to berry, with her green sash cutting across the breastplate. She will stand out no matter how she fares, which is a calculated risk. If she does well, the audience cannot fail to notice. But she'd better do well.

As I approach the other students with their practice swords, I hear my name whispered. Unnerved, I look around, only to realize I am being scrutinized in a new way. Taryn and I are always noticeable, being mortal, but what makes us stand out is also what makes us unworthy of much regard. Today, however, that's not so. The children of Faerie seem to be holding a single indrawn breath, waiting to see what my punishment will be for putting hands on Cardan the day before. Waiting to see what I am going to do next.

I look across the field at Cardan and his friends, with silver on their arms. Cardan is wearing silver on his chest, too, a plate of gleaming steel that hooks over his shoulders and seems more ornamental than protective. Valerian smirks at me.

I do not give him the satisfaction of smirking back.

Fand gives me a gold band and tells me where to stand. There are to be three rounds in the mock war and two sides. Each side has a cloak of hide to protect—one, that of a yellow deer; the other, that of silvery fox fur.

I drink some water out of a pewter carafe set out for participants and begin to warm up. My stomach is sour with the lack of food, but I no longer feel hungry. I feel sick, eaten up with nerves. I try to ignore everything but the exercises I move through to limber up my muscles.

And then it is time. We troop onto the field and salute the seat of the High King, although Eldred has not yet arrived. The crowd is thinner than it will be closer to sunset. Prince Dain is there, though, with Madoc beside him. Princess Elowyn strums a lute thoughtfully. Vivi and Taryn have come to watch, although I see neither Oriana nor Oak. Vivi gestures with a kebab of glistening fruit, making Princess Rhyia laugh.

Taryn watches me intently, as though trying to warn me with her gaze.

Fix it.

All through the first battle, I fight defensively. I avoid Cardan. Nor do I come near Nicasia, Valerian, or Locke, even when Valerian knocks Fand to the dirt. Even when Valerian rips down our deer hide.

Still, I do nothing.

Then we are called to the field for the second battle.

Cardan walks behind me. "You are docile today. Did your sister admonish you? She desires our approval very much." One of his booted feet toes the clover-covered ground, kicking up a clod. "I imagine that if I asked, she'd roll with me right here until we turned her white gown green and then thank me for the honor of my favor." He smiles, going in for the kill, leaning toward me as if confiding a secret. "Not that I'd be the first to green gown her."

My good intentions evaporate on the wind. My blood is on fire, boiling in my veins. I do not have much power, but here is what I have—I can force his hand. Cardan might want to hurt me, but I can make him want to hurt me worse. We're supposed to play at war. When they call us to our places, I play. I play as viciously as possible. My practice sword cracks against Cardan's ridiculous chest plate. My shoulder bangs against Valerian's shoulder so hard that he staggers back. I attack again and again, knocking down anyone wearing a silver armband. When the mock war is over, my eye is blackened and both of my knees are skinned and the gold side has won the second and third battles.

You're no killer, Madoc said.

Right now I feel that I could be.

The crowd applauds, and it is as if I have suddenly woken from a dream. I forgot about them. A pixie tosses flower petals at us. From the stands, Vivi salutes me with a goblet of something as Princess Rhyia applauds politely. Madoc is no longer in the royal box. Balekin is gone, too. The High King Eldred is there, though, sitting on a slightly elevated platform, speaking with Dain, his expression remote.

I start to tremble all over, the adrenaline draining out of me. Courtiers, waiting for better battles, study my bruises and evaluate my prowess. No one seems particularly impressed. I have done my best, have fought my hardest, and it wasn't enough. Madoc didn't even stay to watch.

My shoulders slump.

Worse, Cardan is waiting for me when I get off the field. I am struck suddenly by his height, by the arrogant sneer he wears like a crown. He would seem like a prince even dressed in rags. Cardan grabs my face, fingers splayed against my neck. His breath is against my cheek. His other hand grabs my hair, winding it into a rope. "Do you know what mortal means? It means *born to die*. It means *deserving of death*. That's what you are, what defines you—dying. And yet here you stand, determined to oppose me even as you rot away from the inside out, you corrupt, corrosive mortal creature. Tell me how that is. Do you really think you can win against me? Against a prince of Faerie?"

I swallow hard. "No," I say.

His black eyes simmer with rage. "So you're not completely lacking in some small amount of animal cunning. Good. Now, beg my forgiveness."

I take a step back and tug, trying to wrench free of his grasp. He holds on to my braid, staring down into my face with hungry eyes and a small, awful smile. Then he opens his hand, letting me stagger free. Individual strands of hair flutter through the air.

On the periphery of my vision, I see Taryn standing with Locke, near where other knights are donning their armor. She looks at me pleadingly, as though she is the one who needs to be saved.

"Get down on your knees," Cardan says, looking insufferably pleased with himself. His fury has transmuted into gloating. "Beg. Make it pretty. Flowery. Worthy of me."

The other children of the Gentry are standing around in their padded tunics with their practice swords, watching, hoping my downfall will be amusing. This is the show they've been expecting since I stood up to him. This isn't a mock war; this is the real thing.

"Beg?" I echo.

For a moment, he looks surprised, but that's quickly replaced by even greater malice. "You *defied* me. More than once. Your only hope is to throw yourself on my mercy in front of everyone. Do it, or I will keep on hurting you until there is nothing left to hurt."

I think of the dark shapes of the nixies in the water and the boy at the revel, howling over his torn wing. I think of Taryn's tearstained face. I think of how Rhyia would never have chosen me, of how Madoc didn't even wait to see the conclusion of the battle.

There's no shame in surrender. As Taryn said, they're just words. I don't have to mean them. I can lie.

I start to lower myself to the ground. This will be over quickly, every word will taste like bile, and then it will be over.

When I open my mouth, though, nothing comes out.

I can't do it.

Instead, I shake my head at the thrill running through me at the sheer lunacy of what I'm about to do. It's the thrill of leaping without being able to see the ground below you, right before you realize that's called *falling*. "You think because you can humiliate me, you can control me?" I say, looking him in those black eyes. "Well, I think you're an idiot. Since we started being tutored together, you've gone out of your way to make me feel like I'm less than you. And to coddle your ego, I have made myself less. I have made myself small, I have kept my head down. But it wasn't enough to make you leave Taryn and me alone, so I'm not going to do that anymore.

"I am going to keep on defying you. I am going to shame you with my defiance. You remind me that I am a mere mortal and you are a prince of Faerie. Well, let me remind you that means you have much to lose and I have nothing. You may win in the end, you may ensorcell me and hurt me and humiliate me, but I will make sure you lose everything I can take from you on the way down. I promise you this"—I throw his own words back at him—"*this is the least of what I can do.*"

Cardan looks at me as though he's never seen me before. He looks at me as though no one has ever spoken to him like this. Maybe no one has.

I turn from him and begin walking, half-expecting Cardan to grab my shoulder and throw me to the ground, half-expecting him to find the rowan berry necklace at my throat, snap it, and speak the words that will make me crawl back to him, begging despite all my big talk. But he says nothing. I feel his gaze on my back, pricking the hairs on my neck. It is all I can do not to run.

I dare not look toward Taryn and Locke, but I catch a glimpse of Nicasia staring at me, openmouthed. Valerian looks furious, his hands fisted at his sides in mute rage.

I stagger past the tournament tents to a stone fountain, where I splash my face with water. I bend down, starting to clean the gravel from my knees. My legs feel stiff, and I am shaking all over.

"Are you all right?" Locke asks, gazing down with his tawny fox eyes. I didn't even hear him behind me.

I am not.

I am not all right, but he can't know that, and he shouldn't be asking.

"What do you care?" I say, spitting the words out. The way he's looking at me makes me feel more pathetic than ever.

He leans against the fountain, letting a slow, lazy smile grow on his mouth. "It's funny, that's all."

"Funny?" I echo, furious. "You think that was funny?"

He shakes his head, still smiling. "No. It's funny how you get under his skin."

At first, I'm not sure I heard him right. I almost ask whom he's talking about, because I can't quite believe he's admitting that high and mighty Cardan is affected by anything. "Like a splinter?" I say.

"Of iron. No one else bothers him quite the way that you do." He picks up a towel and wets it, then kneels down beside me and carefully wipes my face. I suck in a breath when the cold cloth touches the sensitive part of my eye, but he is far gentler than I would have been to myself. His face is solemn and focused on what he's doing. He doesn't seem to notice my studying him, his long face and sharp chin, his curling red-brown hair, the way his eyelashes catch the light.

Then he does notice. He's looking at me, and I'm looking back at him, and it's the strangest thing, because I thought Locke would never notice anyone like me. He is noticing, though. He's smiling like he did that night at the Court, as though we shared a secret. He's smiling as if we're sharing another one.

"Keep it up," he says.

I wonder at those words. Can he really mean them?

As I make my way back to the tournament and my sisters, I can't stop thinking of Cardan's shocked face, nor can I stop considering Locke's smile. I am not altogether sure which is more thrilling and which more dangerous.

CHAPTER 10

The rest of the Summer Tournament goes by in a blur. Swordsfolk go toe-to-toe against one another in single combat, fighting for the honor of impressing the High King and his Court. Ogres and foxkin, goblins and gwyllions, all engaged in the deadly dance of battle.

After a few rounds, Vivi wants us to push through the crowd and buy more fruit skewers. I keep trying to catch Taryn's eye, but she won't allow it. I want to know if she's angry. I want to ask what Locke said to her when they were standing together, although that might be the exact sort of question she would forbid.

But the conversation with Locke couldn't have been the humiliating kind, the kind she tries to pretend away, could it? Not when he practically told me he delighted in Cardan's being brought low. Which makes me think of the other question I can't ask Taryn.

Not that I'd be the first to green gown her. Faeries can't lie. Cardan couldn't have said it if he didn't believe it to be true—but why would he think that?

Vivi knocks her skewer against mine, bringing me out of my reverie. "To our clever Jude, who made the Folk remember why they stay in their barrows and hills, for fear of mortal ferocity."

A tall man with the floppy ears of a rabbit and a mane of walnut-brown hair turns to give Vivi a dirty look. She grins at him. I shake my head, pleased by her toast, even if it's wild exaggeration. Even if I impressed no one but her.

"Would that Jude was just a bit less clever," Taryn says under her breath.

I turn to her, but she has moved away.

When we get back to the arena, Princess Rhyia is readying herself for her bout. She holds a thin sword, very much like a long pin, and stabs at the empty air in preparation for an opponent. Her two lovers call out encouragements.

Cardan reemerges in the royal box, wearing loose white linen and a flower crown all of roses. He ignores the High King and Prince Dain and flops down in a chair beside Prince Balekin, with whom he exchanges a few sharp words that I dearly wish I were close enough to hear. Princess Caelia has arrived for her sister's bout and applauds wildly when Rhyia walks out onto the clover.

Madoc never returns.

I ride home alone. Vivi heads off with Rhyia after she wins her bout—they are going hunting in the nearby woods. Taryn agrees to accompany them, but I am too weary and too sore and too on edge.

In the kitchens of Madoc's house, I toast cheese over a fire and spread it on bread. Sitting on the stoop with that and a mug of tea, I watch the sun go down as I eat my lunch.

The cook, a trow named Wattle, ignores me and continues magicking the parsnips to chop themselves.

When I am done, I brush crumbs from my cheeks and head for my room.

Gnarbone, a servant with long ears and a tail that drags on the ground, stops in the hall when he sees me. He's carrying a tray of thimble-size acorn cups and a silvery decanter of what smells like blackberry wine in his large, clawed hands. His livery is pulled tight across his chest, and pieces of fur stick out of the gaps.

"Oh, you are at home," he says, a growl in his voice that makes him seem menacing no matter how benign the words he speaks. Despite myself, I can't help thinking of the guard who bit off the tip of my finger. Gnarbone's teeth could snap off my whole hand.

I nod.

"The prince is asking for you downstairs."

Cardan, here? My heartbeat speeds. I can't think. "Where?"

Gnarbone looks surprised by my reaction. "In Madoc's study. I was just bringing him this—"

I grab the tray out of his hands and head down the stairs, intent on getting rid of Cardan as quickly as I can, any way that I can. The last thing I need is for Madoc to overhear my being disrespectful and decide I'll never belong at the Court. He is a servant of the Greenbriar line, sworn as surely as anyone. He would not like my being at odds with even the least of the princes.

I fly down the stairs and kick open the door to Madoc's study. The knob crashes into a bookshelf as I stride into the room, plunking down the tray with enough force to make the cups dance.

Prince Dain has several books lying open on the library table in front of him. Golden curls fall over his eyes, and the collar of his pale blue doublet is open, showing a heavy silver torque at his throat. I halt, aware of the colossal mistake I have made.

He raises both eyebrows. "Jude. I didn't expect you to be in such a rush."

I sink into a low bow and hope he will think me only clumsy. Fear gnaws at me, sharp and sudden. Could Cardan have sent him? Is he here to punish me for my insolence? I can think of no other reason that honored and honorable Prince Dain, soon to be the ruler of Faerie, would ask for me.

"Uh," I say, panic tripping my tongue. With relief, I remember the tray and indicate the decanter. "Here. This is for you, my lord."

He picks up an acorn and pours a little of the thick black liquid into the cup. "Will you drink with me?"

I shake my head, feeling completely out of my depth. "It will go straight to my head."

That makes him laugh. "Well then, keep me company a time."

"Of course." That, I cannot possibly refuse. Alighting on an arm of one of the green leather chairs, I feel my heart thud dully. "May I get you anything else?" I ask, not sure how to proceed.

He lifts his acorn cup, as if in salute. "I have refreshment enough. What I require is conversation. Perhaps you can tell me what made you storm in here. Who did you think I was?"

"No one," I say quickly. My thumb rubs over my ring finger, over the smooth skin of the missing tip.

He sits up straighter, as though I am suddenly much more interesting. "I thought maybe one of my brothers was bothering you."

I shake my head. "Nothing like that."

"It's shocking," he says, as though he's giving me some great compliment. "I know humans can lie, but to watch you do it is incredible. Do it again."

I feel my face heat. "I wasn't . . . I . . ."

"Do it again," he repeats gently. "Don't be afraid."

Only a fool wouldn't be, despite his words. Prince Dain came here when Madoc was not at home. He asked for me specifically. He implied he knew about Cardan—perhaps he glimpsed us after the mock war, Cardan jerking my head by my braid. But what does Dain want?

I am breathing too shallowly, too fast.

Dain, about to be crowned the High King, has the power to grant me a place in the Court, the power to gainsay Madoc and make me a knight. If only I could impress him, he could give me everything I want. Everything I thought I lost my shot at.

I draw myself up and look into the silvered gray of his eyes. "My name is Jude Duarte. I was born on November thirteenth, 2001. My favorite color is green. I like fog and sad ballads and chocolate-covered raisins. I can't swim. Now tell me, which part was the lie? Did I lie at all? Because what's so great about lying is the not knowing."

I realize abruptly that he might not take any vow particularly seriously from me after that little performance. He looks pleased, though, smiling at me as if he'd found a rough ruby lying in the dirt. "Now," he says, "tell me how your father uses that little talent of yours."

I blink, confused.

"Really? He doesn't. What a shame." The prince tilts his head to study me. "Tell me what you dream of, Jude Duarte, if that's your true name. Tell me what you want."

My heart hammers in my chest, and I feel a little light-headed, a little dizzy. Surely it can't be this easy. Prince Dain, soon to be the High King of all Faerie, asking me what I want. I barely dare answer, and yet I must.

"I—I want to be your knight," I stammer.

His eyebrows go up. "Unexpected," he says. "And pleasing. What else?"

"I don't understand." I twist my hands together so he can't see how they are shaking.

"Desire is an odd thing. As soon as it's sated, it transmutes. If we receive golden thread, we desire the golden needle. And so, Jude Duarte, I am asking you what you would want next if I made you part of my company."

"To serve you," I say, still confused. "To pledge my sword to the crown."

He waves off my answer. "No, tell me what you *want*. Ask me for something. Something you've never asked from anyone."

Make me no longer mortal, I think, and then am horrified at myself. I don't want to want that, especially because there is no way to get it. I will never be one of the Folk.

I take a deep breath. If I could ask him for any boon, what would it be? I understand the danger, of course. Once I tell him, he is going to try to strike a bargain, and faerie bargains seldom favor the mortal. But the potential for power dangles before me.

My thoughts go to the necklace at my throat, the sting of my own palm against my cheek, the sound of Oak's laughter.

I think of Cardan: *See what we can do with a few words? We can enchant you to run around on all fours, barking like a dog. We can curse you to wither away for want of a song you'll never hear again or a kind word from my lips.*

"To resist enchantment," I say, trying to will myself to stillness. Trying not to fidget. I want to seem like a serious person who makes serious bargains.

He regards me steadily. "You already have True Sight, given to you as a child. Surely you understand our ways. You know the charms. Salt our food and you destroy any ensorcellment on it. Turn your stockings inside out and you will never find yourself led astray. Keep your pockets full of dried rowan berries and your mind won't be influenced."

The last few days have shown me how woefully inadequate those protections are. "What happens when they turn out my pockets? What happens when they rip my stockings? What happens when they scatter my salt in the dirt?"

He regards me thoughtfully. "Come closer, child," he says.

I hesitate. From all I have observed of Prince Dain, he has always seemed like a creature of honor. But what I have observed is painfully little.

"Come now, if you are going to serve me, you must trust me." He is leaning forward in the chair. I notice the small horns just above his brow, parting his hair on either side of his regal face. I notice the strength in his arms and the signet ring gleaming on one long-fingered hand, carved with the symbol of the Greenbriar line.

I slide from the chair arm and walk over to where he sits. I force myself to speak. "I didn't mean to be disrespectful."

He touches a bruise on my cheek, one I hadn't realized was there. I flinch, but I don't move away from him. "Cardan is a spoiled child. It is well-known in the Court that he squanders his lineage on drink and petty squabbles. No, don't bother to object."

I don't. I wonder how it was that Gnarbone came to tell me only that a prince was waiting for me downstairs, but not which prince. I wonder if Dain told him to give me that specific message. *A well-seasoned strategist waits for the right opportunity.*

"Although we are brothers, we are very different from each other. I will never be cruel to you for the sake of delighting in it. If you swear yourself into my service, you will find yourself rewarded. But what I want you for is not knighthood."

My heart sinks. It was too much to believe that a prince of Faerie had dropped by to make all my dreams come true, but it was nice while it lasted. "Then what do you want?"

"Nothing you haven't already offered. You wanted to give me your oath and your sword. I accept. I need someone who can lie, someone with ambition. Spy for me. Join my Court of Shadows. I can make you powerful beyond what you might ever hope. It's not easy for humans to be here with us. But I could make it easier for you."

I allow myself to sink into a chair. It feels a little bit like expecting a proposal of marriage, only to get offered the role of mistress.

A spy. A sneak. A liar and a thief. Of course that's what he thinks of me, of mortals. Of course that's what he thinks I am good for.

I consider the spies I have seen, like the parsnip-nosed and hunched figure Madoc consults with sometimes, or a shadowy, gray-shrouded figure whose face I've never managed to spot. All the royals probably have them, but doubtless part of their skill is in how well hidden they are.

And I would be well hidden, indeed, hidden in plain sight.

"It is perhaps not the future you imagined for yourself," Prince Dain says. "No shining armor or riding into battle, but I promise you that once I am the High King, if you serve well, you will be able to do as you like, for who can gainsay the High King? And I will put a geas on you, a geas of protection from enchantment."

I go very still. Usually given to mortals in exchange for their service, geases grant power, with a kick-in-the-teeth exception that comes upon you when you least expect it. Like, you're invulnerable, except to an arrow made of the heartwood of a hawthorn tree, which just so happens to be the exact kind of arrow that your worst enemy favors. Or you'll win every battle you're in, but you're not allowed to refuse invitations to dinner, so if someone invites you to dinner right before a battle, you're not going to be able to show up for that fight. Basically, like everything about Faerie, geases are awesome, and also they suck. Yet, it seems like that's what I am being offered.

"A geas," I echo.

His smile widens, and after a moment, I know why. I haven't said no. Which means I am thinking of saying yes.

"No geas can save you from the effects of our fruits and poisons. Think carefully. I could grant you the power to enrapture all who looked upon you instead. I could give you a spot right there." He touches my forehead. "And anyone who saw it would be struck with love. I could give you a magical blade that cuts through starlight."

"I don't want to be controlled," I say, my voice a whisper. I can't believe I am saying this out loud, to him. I can't believe I am doing this. "Magically, I mean. Give me that, and I will manage the rest."

He nods once. "So you accept."

It's frightening to have a choice like this in front of me, a choice that changes all future choices.

I want power so badly. And this is an opportunity for it, a terrifying and slightly insulting opportunity. But also an intriguing one. Would I have made a good knight? I have no way of knowing.

Maybe I would have hated it. Maybe it would have meant standing around in armor and going on dull quests. Maybe it would have meant fighting people I liked.

I nod and hope I make a good spy.

Prince Dain rises and touches my shoulder. I feel the shock of the contact, like a spark of static. "Jude Duarte, daughter of clay, from this day forward no Faerie glamour will addle your mind. No enchantment will move your body against your will. None save for that of the maker of this geas.

"Now no one will be able to control you," he says, and then pauses for a moment. "Except for me."

I suck in a breath. Of course there's a sting in the tail of this bargain. I cannot even be angry with him; I should have guessed.

And yet, it is still thrilling to have any protection at all. Prince Dain is only one faerie, and he has seen something in me, something Madoc wouldn't see, something I have yearned to have acknowledged.

Right then and there, I go down on one knee on the ancient rug in Madoc's study and swear myself into Prince Dain's service.

CHAPTER 11

All night, as I sit through dinner, I am conscious of the secret I hold. It makes me feel, for the first time, as though I have a power of my own, a power Madoc cannot take from me. Even thinking of it for too long—I am a spy! I am Prince Dain's spy!—gives me a thrill.

We eat little birds stuffed with barley and wild ramps, their skins crackling with fat and honey. Oriana delicately picks hers apart. Oak chews on the skin. Madoc does not bother to separate off the flesh, eating bones and all. I poke at the stewed parsnips. Although Taryn is at the table, Vivi has not returned. I suspect that hunting with Rhyia was a ruse and that she has gone to the mortal world after a brief ride through the woods. I wonder if she ate her dinner with Heather's family.

"You did well at the tournament," Madoc says between bites.

I do not point out that he left the grounds. He couldn't have been too impressed. I am not even sure how much he actually saw. "Does that mean you've changed your mind?"

Something in my voice makes him stop chewing and regard me with narrowed eyes. "About knighthood?" he asks. "No. Once there is a new High King in place, we will discuss your future."

My mouth curves into a secretive smile. "As you wish."

Down the table, Taryn watches Oriana and tries to copy her movements with the little bird. She does not look my way, even when she asks me to pass her a carafe of water.

She can't keep me from following her to her room when we're done, though.

"Look," I say on the stairs. "I tried to do what you wanted, but I couldn't, and I don't want you to hate me for it. It's my life."

She turns around. "Your life to squander?"

"Yes," I say as we come to the landing. I cannot tell her about Prince Dain, but even if I could, I am not sure it would help. I am not at all sure she'd approve of that, either. "Our lives are the only real thing we have, our only coin. We get to buy what we want with them."

Taryn rolls her eyes. Her voice is acid. "Isn't that pretty? Did you make it up yourself?"

"What is the matter with you?" I demand.

She shakes her head. "Nothing. Nothing. Maybe it would be better if I thought the way that you do. Never mind, Jude. You really were good out there."

"Thanks," I say, frowning in confusion. I wonder again over Cardan's words about her, but I do not want to repeat them and make her feel bad. "So have you fallen in love yet?" I ask.

All my question gets me is a strange look. "I am staying home from the lecture tomorrow," Taryn says. "I guess it is your life to squander, but I don't have to watch."

My feet feel like lead as I make my way to the palace, over ground strewn with windfall apples, their golden scent blowing in the air. I am wearing a long black dress with gold cuffs and a lacing of green braid, a comfortable favorite.

Afternoon birdsong trills above me, making me smile. I let myself have a brief fantasy of Prince Dain's coronation, of me dancing with a grinning Locke while Cardan is dragged away and thrown in a dark oubliette.

A flash of white startles me from my thoughts. It's a stag—a white stag, standing not ten feet from where I am. His antlers are threaded with a few thin cobwebs, and his coat is a white so bright that it seems silver in the afternoon light. We regard each other for a long moment, before he races off in the direction of the palace, taking my breath with him.

I decide to believe this is a good omen.

And, at least at first, it seems to be. Classes aren't too bad. Noggle, our instructor, is a kind but odd old Fir Darrig from up north, with huge eyebrows, a long beard into which he occasionally shoves pens or scraps of paper, and a tendency to maunder on about meteor storms and their meanings. As afternoon turns to evening, he has us counting falling stars, which is a dull but relaxing task. I lie back on my blanket and stare up at the night sky.

The only downside is that it is hard for me to note down numbers in the dark. Usually, glowing orbs hang from the trees or large concentrations of fireflies light our lessons. I carry extra stubs of candles for when even that is too dim, since human eyesight isn't nearly as keen as theirs, but I'm not allowed to light them when we study the stars. I try to write legibly and not get ink all over my fingers.

"Remember," Noggle says, "unusual celestial events often presage important political changes, so with a new king on the horizon, it's important for us to observe the signs carefully."

Some giggling rises out of the darkness.

"Nicasia," our instructor says. "Is there some difficulty?"

Her haughty voice is unrepentant. "None at all."

"Now, what can you tell me about falling stars? What would be the meaning of a shower of them in the last hour of a night?"

"A dozen births," Nicasia says, which is wrong enough to make me wince.

"*Deaths*," I say under my breath.

Noggle hears me, unfortunately. "Very good, Jude. I am glad someone has been paying attention. Now, who would like to tell me when those deaths are most likely to occur?"

There is no point in my holding back, not when I made a declaration that I was going to shame Cardan with my greatness. I better start being great. "It depends on which of the constellations they passed through and in which direction the stars fell," I say. Halfway through answering, I feel like my throat is going to close up. I am suddenly glad of the dark, so I don't have to see Cardan's expression. Or Nicasia's.

"Excellent," Noggle says. "Which is why our notes must be thorough. Continue!"

"This is dull," I hear Valerian drawl. "Prophecy is for hags and small folk. We should be learning things of a more noble mien. If I am going to pass a night on my back, then I'd wish to be lessoned in *love*."

Some of the others laugh.

"Very well," said Noggle. "Tell me what event might portend success in love?"

"A girl taking off her dress," he says to more laughter.

"Elga?" Noggle calls on a girl with silver hair and a laugh like shattering glass. "Can you answer for him? Perhaps he's had such little success in love that he truly doesn't know."

She begins to stammer. I suspect she knows the answer but doesn't want to court Valerian's ire.

"Shall I ask Jude again?" Noggle asks tartly. "Or perhaps Cardan. Why don't you tell us?"

"No," he says.

"What was that?" Noggle asks.

When Cardan speaks, his voice rings with sinister authority. "It is as Valerian says. This lesson is boring. You will light the lamps and begin another, more worthy one."

Noggle pauses for a long moment. "Yes, my prince," he says finally, and all the globes around us flare to life. I blink several times as my eyes try to adjust. I wonder if Cardan has ever had to do anything he didn't want to. I guess it is no surprise that he drowses during lectures. No surprise that he once, drunk as anything, rode a horse across the grass while we were having classes, trampling blankets and books and sending everyone scrambling to get out of his way. He can change our curriculum on a whim. How can anything matter to someone like that?

"Her eyesight is so poor," Nicasia says, and I realize she's standing over me. She has my notebook and waves it around so everyone can see my scrawls. "Poor, poor, Jude. It's so hard to overcome so many disadvantages."

There's ink all over my fingers and on the golden cuffs of my dress.

Across the grove, Cardan is talking with Valerian. Only Locke is watching us, his expression troubled. Noggle is flipping through a stack of thick, dusty books, probably trying to come up with a lesson that Cardan will like.

"Sorry if you can't read my handwriting," I say, grabbing the notebook. The page tears, leaving most of my night's work shredded. "But that's not exactly *my* disadvantage."

Nicasia slaps me in the face. I stumble, shocked, suddenly down on one knee, barely catching myself before I go sprawling. My cheek is hot, stinging. My head rings.

"You can't do that," I say to her nonsensically.

I thought I understood how this game worked. I thought wrong.

"I may do whatever I wish," she informs me, still haughty.

Our classmates stare. Elga has one delicate hand over her mouth. Cardan looks over, and I can tell from his expression that she has failed to please him. Embarrassment starts to creep over Nicasia's face.

For as long as I have been among them, there were lines they didn't cross. When they shoved us into the river, no one witnessed it. For better or worse, I am part of the general's household and under Madoc's protection. Cardan might dare to cross him, but I thought the others would at least strike in secret.

I seem to have angered Nicasia past caring about any of that.

I brush myself off. "Are you calling me out? Because then it's my right to choose the time and the weapon." How I would love to knock her down.

She realizes that my question actually demands a response. I might be lower than the ground, but that doesn't absolve her from obligations to her own honor.

Out of the corner of my eye, I see Cardan coming toward us. Jittery anticipation commingles with dread. On my other side, Valerian bumps my shoulder. I take a step away from him, but not fast enough to avoid being assailed with the smell of overripe fruit.

Above us, in the black dome of night, seven stars fall, streaking gloriously across the sky before guttering out. I look up automatically, too late to have seen their precise path.

"Did anyone note that down?" Noggle begins shouting, fumbling in his beard for a pen. "This is the celestial event we've been waiting for! Someone must have seen the exact origin point. Quickly! Set down everything you can remember."

Just then, as I am looking at the stars, Valerian shoves something soft against my mouth. An apple, sweet and rotten at the same time, honeyed juice running over my tongue, tasting of sunlight and pure heady, stupid joy. Faerie fruit, which muddles the mind, which makes humans crave it enough to starve themselves for another taste, which makes us pliant and suggestible and ridiculous.

Dain's geas protected me from enchantment, from anyone's control, but faerie fruit puts you out of even your own control.

Oh no. Oh no no no no no.

I spit it out. The apple rolls in the dirt, but I can already feel it working on me.

Salt, I think, fumbling for my basket. Salt is what I need. Salt is the antidote. It will clear the fog in my head.

Nicasia sees what I am going for and snatches up my basket, dancing out of the way, while Valerian pushes me to the ground. I try to crawl away from him, but he pins me, shoving the filthy apple back into my face.

"Let me sweeten that sour tongue of yours," he says, pressing it down. Pulp is in my mouth and up my nose.

I can't breathe. I can't breathe.

My eyes are open, staring up at Valerian's face. I'm choking. He's watching me with an expression of mild curiosity, as though he's looking forward to seeing what happens next.

Darkness is creeping in at the edges of my vision. I am choking to death.

The worst part is the joy blooming inside me from the fruit, blotting out the terror. Everything is beautiful. My vision is swimming. I reach up to claw at Valerian's face, but I am too dizzy to reach him. A moment later, it doesn't matter. I don't want to hurt him, not when I am so happy.

"Do something!" someone says, but in my delirium, I can't tell who is speaking.

Abruptly, Valerian is kicked off me. I roll onto my side, coughing. Cardan is looming there. Tears and snot are running down my face, but all I can do is lie in the dirt and spit out pieces of sweet, fleshy pulp. I have no idea why I am crying.

"Enough," Cardan says. He has an odd, wild expression on his face, and a muscle is jumping in his jaw.

I start to laugh.

Valerian looks mutinous. "Ruin my fun, will you?"

For a moment, I think they're going to fight, although I cannot think why. Then I see what Cardan's got in his hand. The salt from my basket. The antidote. (Why did I want that? I wonder.) He tosses it up into the air with a laugh, and I watch it scatter with the wind. Then he looks at Valerian, mouth curling. "What's wrong with you, Valerian? If she dies, your little prank is over before it begins."

"I'm not going to die," I say, because I don't want them to worry. I feel fine. I feel better than I have ever felt in my entire life. I'm glad the antidote is gone.

"Prince Cardan?" Noggle says. "She ought to be taken home."

"Everyone is so dull today," Cardan says, but he doesn't sound as if he's bored. He sounds as if he's barely keeping his temper in check.

"Oh, Noggle, she doesn't wish to go." Nicasia comes over to me and strokes my cheek. "Do you, pretty thing?"

The cloying taste of honey is in my mouth. I feel light. I am unwinding. I am unfurling like a banner. "I'd like to stay," I say, because here is wondrous. Because she is dazzling.

I'm not sure I feel good, but I know I feel great.

Everything is wondrous. Even Cardan. I didn't like him before, but that seems silly. I give him a wide, happy grin, although he doesn't smile in return.

I don't take it personally.

Noggle turns away from us, muttering something about the general and foolishness and princes getting their heads removed from their shoulders. Cardan watches him go, hands fisting at his sides.

A knot of girls flop down in the moss beside me. They're laughing, which makes me laugh again, too. "I've never seen a mortal take the fruits of Elfhame before," one of them, Flossflower, says to another. "Will she remember this?"

"Would that someone would enchant her to do otherwise," Locke says from somewhere behind me, but he doesn't sound angry like Cardan. He sounds nice. I turn toward him, and he touches my shoulder. I lean into the warmth of his skin.

Nicasia laughs. "She wouldn't want that. What she'd like is another bite of apple."

My mouth waters at the memory. I recall them strewn across my path, golden and glittering, on the way to school and curse my foolishness for not stopping to eat my fill.

"So we can ask her things?" Another girl—Moragna—wants to know. "Embarrassing things. And she'll answer?"

"Why should she find anything embarrassing when she's among friends?" says Nicasia, eyes slitted. She looks like a cat that has eaten all the cream and is ready for a nap in the sun.

"Which one of us would you most like to kiss?" Flossflower demands, coming closer. She's barely spoken to me before. I'm glad she wants to be friends.

"I'd like to kiss all of you," I say, which makes them scream with laughter. I grin up at the stars.

"You're wearing too many clothes," Nicasia says, frowning at my skirts. "And they've grown dirty. You should take them off."

My dress does seem abruptly heavy. I imagine myself naked in the moonlight, my skin turned as silvery as the leaves above us.

I stand. Everything feels as if it's going a bit sideways. I start pulling off my clothes.

"You're right," I say, delighted. My gown slides into a puddle of cloth that I can easily step out of. I am wearing mortal underclothes—a mint-and-black polka-dotted bra and underpants.

They're all staring at me oddly, as though wondering where I got my underwear. All of them so resplendent that it is difficult for me to look too long without my head hurting.

I am conscious of the softness of my body, of the calluses on my hands, and of the sway of my breasts. I am conscious of the soft tickle of grass underneath my feet and the warm earth.

"Am I beautiful like you are?" I ask Nicasia, genuinely curious.

"No," she says, darting a look toward Valerian. She picks up something from the ground. "You are nothing like us." I am sorry to hear it but not surprised. Beside them, anyone might as well be a shadow, a blurry reflection of a reflection.

Valerian points to the rowan necklace that dangles around my throat, dried red berries threaded onto a long silver chain. "You should take that off, too."

I nod conspiratorially. "You're right," I say. "I don't need it anymore."

Nicasia smiles, holding up the golden thing she has in her hand. The filthy, mashed remains of the apple. "Come lick my hands clean. You don't mind, do you? But you have to do it on your knees."

Gasping and tittering spread through our classmates like a breeze. They want me to do it. I want to make them happy. I want everyone to be as happy as I am. And I do want another taste of the fruit. I begin to crawl toward Nicasia.

"No," Cardan says, stepping in front of me, his voice ringing and a little unsteady. The others back off, giving him room. He toes off his soft leather shoe and puts one pale foot directly in front of me. "Jude will come here and kiss my foot. She said she wanted to kiss us. And I am her prince, after all."

I laugh again. Honestly, I don't know why I laughed so infrequently before. Everything is marvelous and ridiculous.

Looking up at Cardan, though, something strikes me wrong. His eyes are glittering with fury and desire and maybe even shame. A moment later, he blinks, and it's just his usual chilly arrogance.

"Well? Be quick about it," he says impatiently. "Kiss my foot and tell me how great I am. Tell me how much you admire me."

"Enough," Locke says sharply to Cardan. He's got his hands on my shoulders and is pulling me roughly to my feet. "I'm taking her home."

"Are you, now?" Cardan asks him, eyebrows raised. "Interesting timing. You like the savor of a little humiliation, just not too much?"

"I hate it when you get like this," Locke says under his breath.

Cardan pulls a pin from his coat, a glittering, filigree thing in the shape of an acorn with an oak leaf behind it. For a delirious moment, I think he's going to give it to Locke in exchange for leaving me there. That seems impossible, even to my wild mind.

Then Cardan takes hold of my hand, which seems even less possible. His fingers are overwarm against my skin. He stabs the point of his pin into my thumb.

"Ow," I say, pulling away from him and putting the injured digit into my mouth. My own blood is metallic against my tongue.

"Have a nice walk home," he tells me.

Locke guides me away, stopping to grab up someone's blanket, which he wraps around my shoulders. Faeries are staring at us as we pass out of the grove, me stumbling, him holding me up. The few teachers I see do not meet my gaze.

I suck on my injured thumb, feeling odd. My head is still swimming, but not like it was. Something's wrong. A moment later, I realize what. There's salt in my human blood.

My stomach lurches.

I look back at Cardan, who is laughing with Valerian and Nicasia. Moragna is on his arm. Another of our lecturers, a sinewy elf-woman from an island to the east, is trying to begin her talk.

I hate them. I hate them all so much. For a moment, there is only that, the heat of my fury turning my every thought to ash. With shaking hands, I clutch the blanket more tightly around my shoulders and let Locke lead me into the woods.

"I owe you a debt," I grit out after we walk for a little while. "For getting me out of there."

He gives me an appraising look. I am struck all over again by how handsome he is, by the soft curls falling around his face. It's awful to be alone with him, knowing he's seen me in my underwear and crawling around on the ground, but I am too angry for embarrassment.

He shakes his head. "You don't owe anyone anything, Jude. Especially not today."

"How can you stand them?" I ask, fury making me turn on Locke, even though he's the only one I'm not mad at. "They're horrible. They're monsters."

He doesn't answer me. We walk along, and when I come to the patch of windfall apples, I kick one so hard it ricochets off the trunk of an elm tree.

"There is a pleasure in being with them," he says. "Taking what we wish, indulging in every terrible thought. There's safety in being awful."

"Because at least they're not terrible to you?" I ask.

Again, he does not answer.

When we get close to Madoc's estate, I stop. "I should go alone from here." I give him a smile that probably wavers a little bit. It's hard to keep it on my face.

"Wait," he says, taking a step toward me. "I want to see you again."

I groan, too exasperated for surprise. I am standing here in a borrowed blanket, boots, and mall-bought underwear. I am smeared in soil, and I have just made a fool of myself. *"Why?"*

He looks at me as though he sees something else entirely. There's an intensity in his gaze that makes me stand up a little straighter, despite the dirt. "Because you're like a story that hasn't happened yet. Because I want to see what you will do. I want to be part of the unfolding of the tale."

I'm not sure if that's a compliment or not, but I guess I'll take it.

He lifts my hand—the same one Cardan stabbed with the pin—and kisses the very tips of my fingers. "Until tomorrow," he says, making a bow.

And so, in that borrowed blanket, boots, and mall-bought underwear, I walk on by myself, heading for home.

"Tell me who did this," Madoc insists, over and over again, but I won't. He stomps around, explaining in detail how he will find the faeries responsible and destroy them. He will rip out their hearts. He will cut off their heads and mount them on the roof of our house as a warning to others.

I know it's not me he's threatening, but it's still me he's yelling at.

When I am scared, I can't forget that no matter how well he plays the role of father, he will always and forever also be my father's murderer.

I don't say anything. I think about how Oriana was afraid that Taryn or I would misbehave at the Court and cause Madoc embarrassment. Now I wonder if she was more worried about how he'd react if something did happen. Cutting off Valerian's and Nicasia's heads is bad politics. Hurting Cardan amounts to treason.

"I did it myself," I say finally, to make this stop. "I saw the fruit and it looked good, so I ate it."

"How could you be so foolish?" Oriana says, whirling around. She doesn't look surprised; she looks as though I am confirming her worst suspicions. "Jude, you know better."

"I wanted to have fun. It's supposed to be fun," I tell her, playing the disobedient daughter for all it's worth. "And it *was*. It was like a beautiful dream—"

"Be quiet!" Madoc shouts, shocking us both into silence. "Both of you, *quiet*!"

I cringe involuntarily.

"Jude, stop trying to annoy Oriana," he says, giving me an exasperated look I am not sure he's ever given me before, but has turned it on Vivi plenty.

He knows I'm lying.

"And, Oriana, don't be so gullible." When she realizes what he means, a small, delicate hand comes up to cover her mouth.

"When I find out whom you're protecting," he tells me, "they will be sorry they ever drew breath."

"This is not helping," I say, leaning back in my chair.

He kneels down in front of me and takes my hand in his rough green fingers. He must be able to feel how I am trembling. He lets out a long sigh, probably discarding more threats. "Then tell me what will help, Jude. Tell me, and I will do it."

I wonder what would happen if I said the words: *Nicasia humiliated me. Valerian tried to murder me. They did it to impress Prince Cardan, who hates me. I am scared of them. I am more scared of them than I am of you, and you terrify me. Make them stop. Make them leave me alone.*

But I won't. Madoc's anger is fathomless. I have seen it in my mother's blood on the kitchen floor. Once summoned, it cannot be called back.

What if he murdered Cardan? What if he killed them all? His answer to so many problems is bloodshed. If they were dead, their parents would demand satisfaction. The wrath of the High King would fall on him. I would be worse off than I am now, and Madoc would likely be dead.

"Teach me more," I say instead. "More strategy. More bladework. Teach me everything you know." Prince Dain may want me for a spy, but that doesn't mean giving up my sword.

Madoc looks impressed, and Oriana, annoyed. I can tell she thinks that I am manipulating him and that I am doing a good job of it.

"Very well," he says with a sigh. "Tatterfell will bring you dinner, unless you feel up to joining us at the dining table. We will begin a more intensive training tomorrow."

"I'll eat upstairs," I say, and head to my room, still wrapped in someone else's blanket. On the way, I pass Taryn's closed door. Part of me wants to go in, fling myself on her bed, and weep. I want her to hold me and tell me that there wasn't anything I could have done differently. I want her to tell me that I am brave and that she loves me.

But since I am sure that's not what she'd do, I pass her door by.

My room has been tidied while I was gone, my bed made and my windows opened to let in the night air. And there, on the foot of my bed, is a folded-up dress of homespun with the royal crest that servants of the princes and princesses wear. Sitting on the balcony is the owl-faced hob.

It preens a bit, ruffling its feathers.

"You," I say. "You're one of his—"

"Go to Hollow Hall tomorrow, sweetmeat," it chirps, cutting me off. "Find us a secret the king won't like. Find treason."

Hollow Hall. That's the home of Balekin, the eldest prince.

I have my first assignment from the Court of Shadows.

CHAPTER 12

I go to sleep early, and when I wake, it is full dark. My head hurts—maybe from sleeping too long—and my body aches. I must have slept with all my muscles tensed.

The lectures of that day have already begun. It doesn't matter. I'm not going.

Tatterfell has left me a tray with coffee on it, spiced with cinnamon and cloves and a little bit of pepper. I pour a cup. It's lukewarm, which means it has been there for a while. There's toast, too, which softens up when I dunk it a few times.

Then I wash my face, which is still sticky with pulp, and then the rest of me. I brush my hair roughly, and then I pull it into a bun by knotting it around a twig.

I refuse to think about what happened the day before. I refuse to think about anything but today and my mission for Prince Dain.

Go to Hollow Hall. Find us a secret the king won't like. Find treason.

So Dain wants me to help ensure that Balekin isn't chosen to be the next High King. Eldred can choose any of his children for the throne, but he favors the three eldest: Balekin, Dain, and Elowyn—and Dain above the others. I wonder if spies help keep it that way.

If I can be good at this, then Dain will give me power when he ascends the throne. And after yesterday, I crave it. I crave it like I craved the taste of faerie fruit.

I put on the servant's dress without any of my mall-acquired underclothes to make sure I am as authentic as possible. For shoes, I dig out a pair of old leather slippers from the back of my closet. They have a hole through the toe that I tried to fix nearly a year ago, but my sewing skills are poor, and I wound up just making them ugly. They fit, though, and all my other shoes are too beautifully made.

We do not have human servants at Madoc's estate, but I have seen them in other parts of Faerie. Human midwives to deliver babies from human consorts. Human artisans cursed or blessed with tempting skill. Human wet nurses to suckle sickly faerie infants. Little human changelings, raised in Faerie, but not educated with the Gentry as we are. Cheerful magic-seekers who don't mind a little drudgery in exchange for some wish of their heart. When our paths cross, I try to talk to them. Sometimes they want to, and sometimes they don't. Most nonartisans have been at least slightly glamoured to smooth out their memories. They think they're in a hospital or at a rich person's house. And when they're returned home—and Madoc has assured me that they are—they're paid well and even given gifts, such as good luck or shiny hair or a knack for guessing the right lotto numbers.

But I know there are also humans who make bad bargains or offend the wrong faerie and who are not treated so well. Taryn and I hear things, even if no one means for us to—stories of humans sleeping on stone floors and eating refuse, believing themselves to be resting on feather beds and supping on delicacies. Humans drugged out of their minds on faerie fruit. Balekin's servants are rumored to be the latter, ill-favored and worse-treated.

I shudder at the thought of it. And yet I can see why a mortal would make a useful spy, beyond the ability to lie. A mortal can pass into low places and high without much notice. Holding a harp, we're bards. In homespun, we're servants. In gowns, we're wives with squalling goblin children.

I guess being beneath notice has advantages.

Next I pack a leather bag with a shift and a knife, throw a thick velvet cloak over my dress, and descend the stairs. The coffee churns in my gut. I am almost to the door when I see Vivi seated on the tapestry-covered window seat.

"You're up," she says, standing. "Good. Do you want to shoot things? I've got arrows."

"Maybe later." I keep my cloak clutched tightly around me and try to move past her, keeping a blandly happy expression on my face.

It doesn't work. Her arm shoots out to block me. "Taryn told me what you said to the prince at the tournament," she says. "And Oriana told me how you came home last night. I can guess the rest."

"I don't need another lecture," I say to her. This mission from Dain is the only thing keeping me from being haunted by what happened the day before. I don't want to lose focus. I am afraid that if I do, I will lose my composure, too.

"Taryn feels awful," Vivi says.

"Yeah," I say. "Sometimes it sucks to be right."

"Stop it." She grabs for my arm, looking at me with her split-pupiled eyes. "You can talk to me. You can trust me. What's going on?"

"Nothing," I say. "I made a mistake. I got angry. I wanted to prove something. It was stupid."

"Was it because of what I said?" Her fingers are gripping my arm hard.

The Folk are going to keep treating you like crap.

"Vivi, there's no way my deciding to mess up my life is your fault," I tell her. "But I will make them regret crossing me."

"Wait, what do you mean?" Vivi asks.

"I don't know," I say, pulling free. I head toward the door, and this time she doesn't stop me. Once I'm out, I rush across the lawn to the stables.

I know I am not being fair to Vivi, who hasn't done anything. She just wanted to help.

Maybe I don't know how to be a good sister anymore.

At the stables, I have to stop and lean against a wall while I take deep breaths. For more than half my life, I've been fighting down panic. Maybe it's not the best thing for a constant rattle of nerves to seem normal, even necessary. But at this point, I wouldn't know how to live without it.

The most important thing is to impress Prince Dain. I can't let Cardan and his friends take that from me.

To get to Hollow Hall, I decide to take one of the toads, since only the Gentry ride silver-shod horses. Although a servant would probably not have a mount of any kind, at least the toad is less conspicuous.

Only in Faerieland is a giant toad the *less* conspicuous choice.

I saddle and bridle a spotted one and lead her out onto the grass. Her long tongue lashes one of her golden eyes, making me take an involuntary step back.

I hook my foot in the stirrup and swing up onto the seat. With one hand, I pull on the reins, and with the other, I pat the soft, cool skin of her back. The spotted toad launches us into the air, and I hang on.

Hollow Hall is a stone manor with a tall, crooked tower, the whole thing half-covered in vines and ivy. There's a balcony on the second floor that seems to have a rail of thick roots in place of iron. A curtain of thinner tendrils hangs down from it, like a scraggly beard clotted with dirt. There is something misshapen about the estate that ought to make it charming but instead makes it ominous. I tie up the toad, stuff my cloak into her saddlebags, and start toward the side of the manor, where I believe I will find a servants' door. On the way, I stop to pick mushrooms, so it will seem as though I had a reason for being out in the woods.

As I get close, my heart speeds anew. Balekin won't hurt me, I tell myself. Even if I'm caught, he'll simply turn me over to Madoc. Nothing bad is going to happen.

I'm not entirely sure that's true, but I manage to persuade myself enough to approach the servants' entrance and slip inside.

A hallway goes to the kitchens, where I deposit the mushrooms on a table beside a brace of bloody rabbits, a pigeon pie, a bouquet of garlic scapes and rosemary, a few cloudy-skinned plums, and dozens of bottles of wine. A troll stirs a large pot alongside a winged pixie. And cutting up vegetables are two sunken-cheeked humans, a boy and a girl, both of them with small, stupid smiles on their faces and glazed-over looks in their eyes. They don't even look down as they chop, and I'm surprised they don't cut off their own fingers by accident. Worse, if they did, I am not sure they'd notice.

I think of how I felt yesterday, and the echo of faerie fruit comes unbidden into my mouth. I feel my gorge rise, and I hurry past, down the hall.

I am stopped by a pale-eyed faerie guard, who grabs my arm. I look up at him, hoping I can school my expression to be as blank and pleasant and dreamy as that of the mortals in the kitchens.

"I haven't seen you before," he tells me, making it an accusation.

"You're lovely," I say, trying to sound awed and a little confused. "Pretty eye mirrors."

He makes a disgusted sound, which I guess means I am doing a good enough job of pretending to be an ensorcelled human servant, although I feel I went weird and over the top in my nervousness. I am not as good at improvising as I had hoped I would be.

"Are you new?" he asks, saying the words slowly.

"New?" I echo, trying to figure out what someone brought here might think about the experience. I cannot stop remembering the sickly sweet taste of faerie fruit on my tongue, but instead of getting me deeper into character, I just want to throw up. "Before I was somewhere else," I blurt out, "but now I have to clean the great hall with polish until every inch of it shines."

"Well, I guess you best, then," he says, letting me go.

I try to control the shudder building up under my skin. I don't flatter myself that my acting convinced him; he was convinced because I'm human and he expects humans to be servants. Again, I can see why Prince Dain thought I would be useful. After the guard, it is fairly easy to move around Hollow Hall. There are dozens of humans drifting through their chores, lost in sickly dreams. They sing little songs to themselves and whisper words out loud, but it's obviously just snatches of a conversation happening in their dreams. Their eyes are shadowed. Their mouths, chapped.

No wonder the guard thought I was new.

Besides the servants, however, are the fey. Guests of some fete that seems to have ebbed rather than ended. They sleep in various states of undress, draped over couches and entwined on the floors of the parlors I pass through, their mouths stained gold with nevermore, a glittering golden powder so concentrated that it stupefies faeries and gives mortals the ability to glamour one another. Goblets lie on their side, mead pooling to run over the uneven floor like tributaries into great honey-wine lakes. Some of the Folk are so still I worry that they have debauched themselves into death.

"Excuse me," I say to a girl about my age carrying a tin bucket. She passes me without even seeming to notice I have spoken.

With no idea what else to do, I decide to follow. We pad up a wide stone staircase without rails. Three more of the Folk lie in a dissipated stupor beside a thimble-sized bottle of spirits. Above, from the other end of the hall, I hear an odd cry, like someone in pain. Something heavy hits the ground. Rattled, I try to school my face back to dreamy nonchalance, but it isn't easy. My heart beats like a trapped bird.

The girl opens a door to a bedroom suite, and I slip in behind her.

The walls are stone and hung with no paintings or tapestries. A massive half-tester bed takes up most of the space in the first room, the headboard panel carved with various animals with women's heads and bare breasts—owls and snakes and foxes—doing some kind of weird dance.

I guess I shouldn't be surprised, since Balekin heads the profligate Circle of Grackles.

The books piled up on the wooden desk are ones I recognize—the same books Taryn and I study for our classes. These are spread out, with a few pieces of paper scattered over the wood between them, beside an open inkpot. One of the books has careful notations along one side, while the other is covered in blots. A broken pen, snapped in half deliberately—or at least I can't think of a way it could have happened that's not deliberate—is lying in the hinge of the ink-stained book.

Nothing that looks treasonous.

Prince Dain gifted me the uniform, knowing I could walk in as I had done. He was counting on my ability to lie for the rest. But now that I am inside, I hope there is something in Hollow Hall to find.

Which means that no matter how frightened I am, I must pay attention.

Along the wall are more books, some of them familiar from Madoc's library. I pause in front of a shelf, frowning, and kneel down. Stuffed into a corner is a copy of a book I know but didn't expect to see here in this place—*Alice's Adventures in Wonderland* and *Through the Looking Glass*, bound together in one volume. Mom read to us from one a lot like that back in the mortal world.

Opening the book, I see the familiar illustrations and then the words:

"But I don't want to go among mad people," Alice remarked.

"Oh, you can't help that," said the Cat: "we're all mad here. I'm mad. You're mad."

"How do you know I'm mad?" said Alice.

"You must be," said the Cat, "or you wouldn't have come here."

A bubble of scary laughter threatens to rise up my throat, and I have to bite my cheek to keep it from coming.

The human girl is kneeling in front of a huge fireplace, sweeping up ash from the grate. The andirons, shaped like enormous curling serpents, flank her, their glass eyes ready to glow with lit flames.

Although it's ridiculous, I can't bear to put the book back. It isn't one Vivi packed, and I haven't seen it since my mother read it at bedtime. I stuff it down the front of my dress.

Then I go to the wardrobe and open it, seeking some clue, some valuable piece of information. But as soon as I look inside, a wild panic starts in my chest. I am instantly sure whose room I am in. Those are Prince Cardan's extravagant doublets and breeches, Prince Cardan's gaudy, fur-edged capelets and spider-silk shirts.

Done sweeping up ash in the fireplace, the servant girl stacks new wood into a pyramid with aromatic pine for kindling resting on top.

I want to push by her and run from Hollow Hall. I had assumed that Cardan lived in the palace with his father, the High King. It didn't occur to me that he might live with one of his brothers. I remember Dain and Balekin drinking together at the last Court revel. I hope desperately that this wasn't arranged to humiliate me further, to give Cardan another excuse—or worse, opportunity—to punish me more.

I will not believe it. Prince Dain, about to be crowned the High King, does not have time to indulge in the petty sport of pretending to take me into his service just because a callow younger brother wishes it. He would not set a geas on me or bargain with me just for that. I must continue to believe it, because the alternative is too awful.

All this means is that besides Prince Balekin, I must avoid Prince Cardan on my way through the house. Either of them might recognize me if they glimpsed my face. I must make sure they do not glimpse it.

Probably they will not look too closely. No one looks too closely at human servants.

Realizing I am not so different, I force myself to notice the pattern of moles on the human girl's skin and the split ends of her blond hair and the roughness of her knees. I watch how she sways a little as she pushes to her feet; her body's clearly exhausted, even if her brain doesn't know it.

If I see her again, I want to know I would recognize her.

But it does no good, undoes no spell. She continues her tasks, smiling the same awful, contented smile. When she leaves the room, I head in the opposite direction. I must find Balekin's private rooms, find his secrets, and then get out.

I open doors carefully, peering inside. I discover two bedrooms, both under a thick layer of dust, one with a figure lying under a cobwebby shroud on the bed. I pause for a moment, trying to decide if it's a statue or a corpse or even some kind of living thing, then I realize this has nothing to do with my mission and back out quickly. I open another door to find several faeries twined together on a bed, asleep. One of them blinks drowsily at me, and I catch my breath, but he just slumps back down.

The seventh room enters into a hallway with stairs spiraling up and up into what must be the tower. I take them quickly, my heart racing, my leather shoes soft on the stone.

The circular room I come to is paneled in bookshelves, filled with manuscripts, scrolls, golden daggers, thin glass vials with jewel-colored liquids inside, and the skull of some deerlike creature with massive antlers supporting thin taper candles. Two large chairs rest near the only window. There's a huge table dominating the middle of the room, and on it are maps weighed down on the corners by chunks of glass and metal objects. Beneath them is correspondence. I shuffle through the papers until I come to this letter:

I know the provenance of the blusher mushroom that you ask after, but what you do with it must not be tied to me. After this, I consider my debt paid. Let my name be stricken from your lips.

Although the letter is unsigned, the writing is in an elegant, feminine hand. It seems important. Could it be the proof Dain is looking for? Might it be useful enough to please him? And yet I cannot possibly take it. If it were to go missing, then Balekin would know for certain that someone had been here. I find a sheet of blank paper and press it over the note. As quickly as I can, I trace the letter, trying to capture the precise hand in which it was written.

I am almost done when I hear a sound. People are coming up the stairs.

I panic. There's nowhere to hide. There's practically nothing even in the room; it's mostly open space, exempting the shelves. I fold up the note, knowing it's unfinished, knowing the fresh ink will smear.

As quickly as I can, I scuttle underneath one of the large leather chairs, folding myself into a tight ball. I wish I'd left the stupid book where I'd found it because one sharp corner of the cover is digging into my underarm. I wonder what I was thinking, believing myself clever enough to be a spy in Faerieland.

I squeeze my eyes shut, as though somehow not seeing whoever is coming into the room will keep them from seeing me.

"I hope you've been practicing," Balekin says.

My eyes open into slits. Cardan is standing beside the bookshelves, a bland-faced male servant holding a court sword with gold engraving along the hilt and metal wings making the shape of the guard. I have to bite my tongue to keep from making some sound.

"Must we?" Cardan asks. He sounds bored.

"Show me what you've learned." Balekin lifts a single staff from a vessel beside his desk that holds an assortment of staves and canes. "All you have to do is get a single hit in. Just one, little brother."

Cardan just stands there.

"Pick up the sword." Balekin's patience is worn thin already.

With a long-suffering sigh, Cardan lifts the blade. His stance is terrible. I can see why Balekin is annoyed. Surely Cardan must have been given fighting tutors since he was old enough to hold a stick in his hands. I was taught from the time I got to Faerie, so he'd have had years on me, and the first thing I learned was where to put my feet.

Balekin raises his staff. "Now, attack."

For a long moment, they stand still, regarding each other. Cardan swings his sword in a desultory manner, and Balekin brings down his staff hard, smacking him in the side of the head. I wince at the sound of the wood against his skull. Cardan staggers forward, baring his teeth. His cheek and one of his ears is red, all the way to the point.

"This is ridiculous," Cardan says, spitting on the floor. "Why must we play this silly game? Or do you like this part? Is this what makes it fun for you?"

"Swordplay isn't a game." Balekin swings again. Cardan tries to jump back, but the staff catches the edge of his thigh.

Cardan winces, bringing up his sword defensively. "Then why call it sword*play*?"

Balekin's face darkens, and his grip on the staff tightens. This time he jabs Cardan in the stomach, striking suddenly and with enough force for Cardan to sprawl on the stone floor. "I have tried to improve you, but you insist on wasting your talents on revels, on being drunk under the moonlight, on your thoughtless rivalries and your pathetic romances—"

Cardan pushes himself to his feet and rushes at his brother, swinging his sword wildly. He wields it like a club. The sheer frenzy of the attack makes Balekin fall back a step.

Cardan's technique finally shows. He becomes more deliberate, attacking from new angles. He's never shown much interest in swordsmanship at school, and, although he knows the basics, I am not sure he practices. Balekin disarms him ruthlessly and efficiently. Cardan's sword flies from his hand, clattering across the floor toward me.

I scuttle back deeper into the shadows of the chair. For a moment, I think that I am going to be caught, but the servant is the one to pick up the blade, and his gaze does not waver.

Balekin cracks his staff against the back of Cardan's legs, sending him to the ground.

I am delighted. There's a part of me that wishes I were the one wielding that staff.

"Don't bother to rise." Balekin unbuckles his belt and hands it over to the servant. The human man wraps it twice around his palm. "You have failed the test. Again."

Cardan doesn't speak. His eyes are glittering with a familiar rage, but for once it isn't directed at me. He's on his knees, but he doesn't appear in any way cowed.

"Tell me." Balekin's voice has gone silky, and he paces around his younger brother. "When will you cease being a disappointment?"

"Maybe when you stop pretending that you don't do this for your own pleasure," Cardan answers. "If you want to hurt me, it would save us both a lot of time if you got right down to—"

"Father was old and his seed weak when he sired you. That's why you're weak." Balekin puts one hand on his brother's neck. It looks affectionate, until I see Cardan's flinch, the shifting of his balance. That's when I realize Balekin is pressing down hard, pinning Cardan in place on the floor. "Now, take off your shirt and receive your punishment."

Cardan begins to strip off his shirt, showing an expanse of moon-pale skin and a back with a delicate tracery of faded scars.

My stomach lurches. They're going to beat him.

I should be glorying in seeing Cardan like this. I should be glad that his life sucks, maybe worse than mine, even though he's a prince of Faerie and a horrible jerk and probably going to live forever. If someone had told me that I'd get an opportunity to see this, I would have thought the only thing I'd have to stifle was applause.

But watching, I cannot help observing that beneath his defiance is fear. I know what it is to say the clever thing because you don't want anyone to know how scared you are. It doesn't make me like him any better, but for the first time he seems real. Not good, but real.

Balekin nods. The servant strikes twice, the slap of the leather echoing loudly in the still air of the room.

"I don't order this because I am angry with you, brother," Balekin tells Cardan, causing me to shudder. "I do it because I love you. I do it because I love our family."

When the servant lifts his arm to strike a third time, Cardan lunges for his blade, resting on Balekin's desk where the servant put it. For a moment, I think Cardan is going to run the human man straight through.

The servant does not cry out or lift his hands to protect himself. Maybe he is too ensorcelled for that. Maybe Cardan could stab him right through the heart and he wouldn't do a single thing to defend himself. I am weak with horror.

"Go ahead," Balekin says, bored. He makes a vague gesture toward the servant. "Kill him. Show me you don't mind making a mess. Show me that at least you know how to land a killing blow on such a pathetic target as this."

"I am no murderer," says Cardan, surprising me. I would not have thought that was something to be proud of.

In two strides, Balekin is in front of his brother. They look so alike, standing close. Same inky hair, matching sneers, devouring eyes. But Balekin shows his decades of experience, wrenching the sword from Cardan's hands and knocking him to the ground with the crossbar.

"Then take your punishment like the pathetic creature that you are." Balekin nods to the servant, who rouses from somnolence.

I watch every blow, every flinch. I have little choice. I can shut my eyes, but the sounds are just as terrible. And worst of all is Cardan's empty face, his eyes as dull as lead.

Truly, he has come by his cruelty honestly in Balekin's care. He has been raised up in it, instructed in its nuances, honed through its application. However horrible Cardan might be, I now see what he might become and am truly afraid.

CHAPTER 13

Disturbingly, it is even easier to gain entrance to the Palace of Elfhame in my servant's gown than it was to enter Balekin's household. Everyone, from goblin to the Gentry to the High King's mortal Court Poet and Seneschal, barely gives me a passing look as I find my clumsy way through the labyrinthine halls. I am nothing, no one, a messenger no more worthy of attention than an animated twig woman or an owl. My pleasant, placid expression, combined with forward momentum, gets me to Prince Dain's chambers without so much as a second look, even though I lose my way twice and have to retrace my steps.

I rap on his door and am relieved when the prince himself opens it.

He raises both brows, taking in the sight of me in the homespun dress. I make a formal curtsy, as any servant might. I do not alter my expression, for fear of his not being alone. "Yes?" he asks.

"I am here with a message for you, Your Highness," I say, hoping that sounds right. "I beg for a moment of your time."

"You're a natural," he tells me, grinning. "Come inside."

It's a relief to relax my face. I drop the inane smile as I follow him into his parlor.

Furnished in elaborate velvets, silks, and brocades, it's a riot of scarlet and deep blues and greens, everything rich and dark, like overripe fruit. The patterns on the material are the sorts of things I have become accustomed to—intricate braids of briars, leaves that might also be spiders when you looked at them from another angle, and a depiction of a hunt where it is unclear which of the creatures is hunting the other.

I sigh and sit down in the chair he is pointing me toward, fumbling in my pocket.

"Here," I say, drawing out the folded-up note and smoothing it against the top of a cunning little table with carved bird feet for legs. "He came in while I was copying it, so it's kind of a mess." I had left the stolen book with the toad; the last thing I want Prince Dain to know is that I took something for myself.

Dain squints to see the shapes of the letters past my smudges. "And he didn't see you?"

"He was distracted," I say truthfully. "I hid."

He nods and rings a small bell, probably to summon a servant. I will be glad of anyone not ensorcelled. "Good. And did you enjoy it?"

I am not sure what to make of that question. I was frightened pretty much the whole time—how is that enjoyable? But the longer I think about it, the more I realize that I *did* sort of enjoy it. Most of my life is dreadful anticipation, a waiting for the other shoe to drop—at home, in classes, with the Court. Being afraid I would be caught spying was an entirely new sensation, one where I felt, at least, as though I knew exactly what to be scared of. I knew what it would take to win.

Sneaking through Balekin's house had been less frightening than some revels.

At least until I'd watched Cardan get beaten. Then I'd felt something I don't want to examine too closely.

"I liked doing a good job," I say, finally finding an honest answer.

That makes Dain nod. He's about to tell me something else when another faerie enters the room. A male goblin, scarred, his skin the green of ponds. His nose is long and twists fully around, before bending back toward his face like a scythe. His hair is a black tuft at the very crown of his head. His eyes are unreadable. He blinks several times, as though trying to focus on me.

"They call me the Roach," he says, his voice melodious, completely at odds with his face. He bows and then cocks the side of his head toward Dain. "At his service. I guess we both are. You're the new girl, right?"

I nod. "Am I supposed to tell you my name, or am I supposed to come up with something clever?"

The Roach grins, which twists his whole face up even more hideously. "I am supposed to take you to meet the troupe. And don't worry about what we're going to call you. We decide that for ourselves. You think anyone in their right mind would want to be called the Roach?"

"Great," I say, and sigh.

He gives me a long look. "Yeah, I can see how that's a real talent. Not having to say what you mean."

He's dressed in an imitation of a court doublet, except his doublet is made from scraps of leather. I wonder what Madoc would say if he knew where I was and with whom. I do not think he would be pleased.

I don't think he'd be pleased by anything I did today. Soldiers have a peculiar kind of honor, even those who dip their caps in the blood of their enemies. Sneaking around houses and stealing papers is not at all in line with it. Even though Madoc has spies of his own, I don't think he'd like my being one.

"So he's been blackmailing Queen Orlagh," Dain says, and the Roach and I look over at him.

Prince Dain is frowning over the letter, and suddenly I understand—he recognizes my copy of the handwriting. Nicasia's mother, Queen Orlagh, must be the woman who obtained poison for Balekin. She wrote that she was repaying a debt, although knowing Nicasia, I would guess a little nastiness wouldn't give her mother much pause. But the Queen of the Undersea's kingdom is vast and mighty. It is hard to imagine what Balekin could have over her.

Dain hands my letter to the Roach. "So do you still believe he will use it before the coronation?"

The goblin's nose quivers. "That's the smart move. Once the crown is on your head, nothing's going to get it off."

Until that moment, I hadn't been sure whom the poison was for. I open my mouth and then bite the side of my cheek to stop myself from saying something foolish. Of course it must be for Prince Dain. Whom else would Balekin need some special poison to kill? If he were going to put regular people to death, he'd probably use some kind of cheap, regular-person poison.

Dain seems to notice my surprise. "We have never gotten along, my brother and I. He has always been too ambitious for that. And yet I had hoped..." He waves his hand around, dismissing whatever he was about to say. "Poison may be a coward's weapon, but it is an effective one."

"What about Princess Elowyn?" I ask, and then wish I could take back the question. Poison for her, too, probably. Queen Orlagh must have a cartload of it.

This time, Dain doesn't answer me.

"Maybe Balekin plans on marrying her," the Roach says, surprising us both. At our expressions, he shrugs. "What? If he makes things too obvious, he's going to be the next one to get a knife in the back. And he wouldn't be the first member of the Gentry to wed a sister."

"If he marries her," Dain says, laughing for the first time in this conversation, "he'll get a knife in the front."

I had always thought of Elowyn as the gentle sister. Again, I am aware of how little I really know about the world I am trying to navigate.

"Come," says the Roach, waving me to my feet. "It's time you met the others."

I cast a plaintive look in Dain's direction. I don't want to go with the Roach, whom I have just met and whom I am not at all sure I trust. Even I, who have grown up in the house of a redcap, fear goblins.

"Before you go." Dain walks over until he's standing directly in front of me. "I promised that none might compel you, save for me. I am afraid I am going to have to use that power. Jude Duarte, I forbid you from speaking aloud about your service to me. I forbid you from putting it into writing or into song. You will never tell anyone of the Roach. You will never tell anyone of any of my spies. You will never reveal their secrets, their meeting places, their safe houses. So long as I live, you will obey this."

I am wearing my necklace of rowan berries, but they are no protection against the magic of the geas. This is no regular glamour, no simple sorcery.

The weight of the geas slams down on me, and I know that if I tried to speak, my mouth wouldn't be able to form those forbidden words. I hate it. It's an awful, out-of-control feeling. It makes me scramble around in my head, trying to imagine my way around his commandment, but I cannot.

I think of my first ride to Faerie and the sound of Taryn and Vivi wailing. I think of Madoc's grim expression, jaw locked, doubtlessly unused to children, no less human ones. His ears must have been ringing. He must have wanted us to shut up. It's hard to think anything good about Madoc in that moment, with our parents' heartsblood on his hands. But I will say this for him—he never enchanted away our grief or took our voices. He never did any of the things that might have made the trip easier for him.

I try to convince myself that Prince Dain is only doing the smart thing, the necessary thing, in binding me. But it makes my skin crawl.

For a moment, I am unsure of my decision to serve him.

"Oh," Dain says as I am about to leave. "One more thing. Do you know what mithridatism is?"

I shake my head, not sure I am interested in anything he has to say right now.

"Look into it." He smiles. "That's not a command, only a suggestion."

I follow the Roach through the palace, keeping back from him a few steps so it doesn't seem like we're together. We pass a general Madoc knows, and I make sure to keep my head bowed. I don't think he would look closely enough to recognize me, but I cannot be sure.

"Where are we going?" I whisper after several minutes of walking through the halls.

"Just a little farther," he says gruffly, opening a cupboard and climbing inside. His eyes reflect orange, like a bear's. "Well, come on, get in and close the door."

"I can't see in the dark," I remind him, because that is one of the many things the Folk never remember about us.

He grunts.

I get in, folding myself up tightly so that no part of me touches him, and then I close the cabinet door behind me. I hear the slide of wood and feel the rush of cold, damp air. The scent of wet stone fills the space.

His hand on my arm is careful, but I can feel his claws. I let him pull me forward, allow him to press my head so I know when to duck. When I straighten out, I am on a narrow platform above what appears to be the palace's wine cellars.

My eyes are still adjusting, but from what I can see, there is a network of passageways worming below the palace. I wonder how many people know about them. I smile at the thought of having a secret about this place. Me, of all people.

I wonder if Madoc knows.

I bet Cardan doesn't.

I grin, wider than before.

"Enough gawping?" the Roach asks. "I can wait."

"Are you ready to tell me anything?" I ask him. "Like, where we're going or what's going to happen when we get there?"

"Figure it out," he says, the growl in his voice. "Go on."

"You said we were going to meet the others," I tell him, starting with what I know, trying to keep up and avoid stumbling on the uneven ground. "And Prince Dain made me promise not to reveal any hidden locations, so obviously we're going to your lair. But that doesn't tell me what we're going to do when we get there."

"Maybe we're going to show you secret handshakes," the Roach says. He's doing something I can't quite see, but a moment later, I hear a click—as though a lock was tripped or a trap disarmed. A gentle shove against the small of my back and I am heading down a new, even more dimly lit tunnel.

I know when we come to a door because I walk straight into it, much to the Roach's amusement. "You really can't see," he says.

I rub my forehead. "I told you I couldn't!"

"Yes, but you're the liar," he reminds me. "I'm not supposed to believe anything you say."

"Why would I lie about something like that?" I demand, still annoyed.

He lets my question hang in the air. The answer is obvious—so I could retrace my steps. So he might accidentally show me something he wouldn't show someone else. So that he would be incautious.

I really need to stop asking stupid questions.

And maybe he really needs to be less paranoid, since Dain put a geas on me so I can't tell anyone no matter what.

The Roach opens the door, and light floods the hallway, causing me to throw my arm up in front of my face. Blinking, I look into the secret lair of Prince Dain's spies. It's packed earth on all four sides, with walls that curve inward and a rounded ceiling. A large table dominates the room, and sitting at it are two faeries I've never met—both of them gazing at me unhappily.

"Welcome," says the Roach, "to the Court of Shadows."

CHAPTER 14

The two other members of Dain's spy troupe also have code names. There's the lean, handsome faerie that looks at least part human, who winks and tells me to call him the Ghost. He has sandy-colored hair, which is normal for a mortal but is unusual for a faerie, and ears that come to very subtle points.

The other is a tiny, delicate girl, her skin the dappled brown of a doe, her hair a cloud of white around her head, and a miniature pair of blue-gray butterfly wings on her back. She's got at least some pixie in her, if not some imp.

I recognize her now from the High King's full moon revel. She's the one who stole a belt from an ogre, weapons and pouches attached.

"I'm the Bomb," she says. "I like blowing things up."

I nod. It's the kind of blunt thing I don't expect faeries to say, but I am used to being around Court faeries with their baroque etiquette.

I am not used to the solitary fey. I am at a loss as to how to speak with them. "So is it just the three of you?"

"Four now," says the Roach. "We make sure Prince Dain stays alive and well informed about the doings of the Court. We steal, sneak, and deceive to secure his coronation. And when he is king, we will steal, sneak, and deceive to make sure he stays on the throne."

I nod. After seeing what Balekin is like, I want Dain on the throne more than ever. Madoc will be by his side, and if I can make myself useful enough, maybe they'll get the rest of the Gentry off my back.

"You can do two things the rest of us can't," the Roach says. "One, you can blend in with the human servants. Two, you can move among the Gentry. We're going to teach you some other tricks. So until you get another mission directly from the prince, your job is what I say it is."

I nod. I expected something like that. "I can't always get away. I skipped classes today, but I can't do that all the time or someone will notice and ask where I've been. And Madoc expects me to have dinner with him and Oriana and the rest of the family around midnight."

The Roach looks over at the Ghost and shrugs. "This is always the problem with infiltrating the Court. Lots of etiquette taking up time. When *can* you get away?"

"I could sneak out after I'm supposed to be in bed," I tell them.

"Good enough," the Roach says. "One of us will meet you near the house and either train you or give you assignments. You need not always come here, to the nest." The Ghost nods, as though my problems are reasonable, part of the job, but I feel childish. They are a child's problems.

"So let's initiate her," the Bomb says, walking up to me.

I catch my breath. Whatever happens next, I can endure it. I have endured more than they can guess.

But the Bomb only starts laughing, and the Roach gives her a playful shove.

The Ghost gives me a sympathetic look and shakes his head. His eyes, I notice, are a shifting hazel. "If Prince Dain says you are part of the Court of Shadows, then you are. Try not to be too much of a disappointment and we'll have your back."

I let out my breath. I am not sure that I wouldn't have preferred some ordeal, some way to prove myself.

The Bomb makes a face. "You'll know you're really one of us when you get your name. Don't expect it anytime soon."

The Ghost goes over to a cabinet and takes out a half-empty bottle of a pale greenish liquid and a stack of polished acorn cups. He pours out four shots. "Have a drink. And don't worry," he tells me. "It won't befuddle you any more than any other drink."

I shake my head, thinking of the way I felt after having the golden apple mashed into my face. Never do I want to feel out of control like that again. "I'll pass."

The Roach knocks back his drink and makes a face, as though the liquor is scorching his throat. "Suit yourself," he manages to choke out before he starts to cough.

The Ghost barely winces at the contents of his acorn. The Bomb is taking tiny sips of hers. From her expression, I am extra glad I passed on it.

"Balekin's going to be a problem," the Roach says, explaining what I found.

The Bomb puts down her acorn. "I mislike everything about this. If he was going to go to Eldred, he would have done it already."

I had not considered that he might poison his father.

The Ghost stretches his lanky body as he gets up. "It's getting late. I should take the girl home."

"Jude," I remind him.

He grins. "I know a shortcut."

We go back into the tunnels, and following him is a challenge because, as his name suggests, he moves almost completely silently. Several times, I think he's left me alone in the tunnels, but just when I am about to stop walking, I hear the faintest exhalation of breath or shuffle of dirt and persuade myself to go on.

After what feels like an agonizingly long time, a doorway opens. The Ghost is standing in it, and beyond him is the High King's wine cellar. He makes a small bow.

"This is your shortcut?" I ask.

He winks. "If a few bottles happen to fall into my satchel as we pass through, that's hardly my fault, is it?"

I force out a laugh, the sound creaky and false in my ears. I'm not used to one of the Folk including me in their jokes, at least not outside my family. I like to believe that I am doing okay here in Faerie. I like to believe that even though I was drugged and nearly murdered at school yesterday, I am able to put that behind me today. I'm fine.

But if I can't laugh, maybe I'm not so fine after all.

I change into the blue shift I packed in the woods outside Madoc's grounds, despite being so tired that my joints hurt. I wonder if the Folk are ever tired like that, if they ever ache after a long evening. The toad seems exhausted, too, although maybe she's just full. As far as I can tell, most of what she did today was snap her tongue at passing butterflies and a mouse or two.

It's full deep dark when I get back to the estate. The trees are lit with tiny sprites, and I see a laughing Oak racing through them, pursued by Vivi and Taryn and—*oh hell*—Locke. It's disorienting to see him here, impossibly out of context. Has he come because of me?

With a shriek, Oak dashes over, clamoring up the saddlebags and onto my lap.

"Chase me!" he yells, out of breath, full of the wriggling ecstasy of childhood.

Even faeries are young once.

Impulsively, I hug him to my chest. He's warm and smells of grass and deep woods. He lets me do it for a moment, small arms twining around my neck, small horned head butting against my chest. Then, laughing, he slides down and away, throwing a puckish glance back to see if I'll follow.

Growing up here, in Faerie, will he learn to scorn mortals? When I am old and he is still young, will he scorn me, too? Will he become cruel like Cardan? Will he become brutal like Madoc?

I have no way of knowing.

I step off the toad, foot in the stirrup as I swing my body down. I pat just above her nose, and her golden eyes drift shut. In fact, she seems a little like she might be asleep until I yank on the reins, leading her back toward the stables.

"Hello," Locke says, jogging up to me. "Now, where might you have gone off to?"

"None of your business," I tell him, but I soften the words with a smile. I can't help it.

"Ah! A lady of mystery. My very favorite kind." He's wearing a green doublet, with slits to show his silk shirt underneath. His fox eyes are alight. He looks like a faerie lover stepped out of a ballad, the kind where no good comes to the girl who runs away with him. "I hope you'll consider returning to classes tomorrow," he says.

Vivi continues to chase Oak, but Taryn has stopped near a large elm tree. She watches me with the same expression she had on the tournament field, as though if she concentrates hard enough, she can will me into not offending Locke.

"You mean so your friends know they haven't chased me off?" I say. "Does it matter?"

He looks at me oddly. "You're playing the great game of kings and princes, of queens and crowns, aren't you? Of course it matters. Everything matters."

I am not sure how to interpret his words. I didn't think I was playing that kind of game at all. I thought I was playing the game of pissing off people who hated me already and eating the consequences.

"Come back. You and Taryn both should return. I told her so." I turn my head, looking for my twin in the yard, but she is no longer by the elm. Vivi and Oak are disappearing over a hill. Perhaps she has gone with them.

We get to the stables, and I return the toad to her pen. I fill her water station from a barrel in the center of the room, and a fine mist appears, raining down on her soft skin. The horses nicker and stamp as we leave. Locke watches this all in silence.

"May I ask you something else?" Locke says, glancing in the direction of the manor.

I nod.

"Why haven't you told your father what's been happening?" Madoc's stables are very impressive. Maybe standing in them, Locke was reminded of just how much power and influence the general has. But that doesn't mean I am the inheritor of that power. Maybe Locke should also remember that I am merely one of the by-blow children of Madoc's human wife. Without Madoc and his honor, no one would care about me.

"You mean so he can go stomping into our classes with a broadsword, killing everyone in sight?" I ask, instead of correcting Locke about my station in life.

Locke's eyes widen. I guess that wasn't what he meant. "I thought that your father would pull you out—and that if you didn't tell him, it was because you wanted to stay."

I give a short laugh. "That's not what he'd do at all. Madoc is not a fan of surrender."

In the cool dark of the stables, with the snorting of faerie horses all around us, he takes my hands. "Nothing there would be the same without you."

Since I never intended to quit, it's nice to have someone making all this effort to get me to do something I would have done anyway. And the way he's looking at me, the intensity of it, is so nice that I am embarrassed. No one has ever looked at me this way.

I can feel the heat of my cheeks and wonder if the shadows help cover it up at all. Right then, I feel as though he sees everything—every hope of my heart, every stray thought I've had before falling into an exhausted sleep each dawn.

He brings one of my hands up to his mouth and presses his lips against my palm. My whole body tenses. I am suddenly too warm, too everything. His breath is a soft susurration against my skin.

With a gentle tug, he pulls me closer. His arm is around me. He leans in for a kiss and my thoughts slide away.

This can't be happening.

"Jude?" I hear Taryn call uncertainly from nearby, and I stagger away from Locke. "Jude? Are you still in the stable?"

"Here," I say, my face hot. We emerge into the night to find Oriana on the steps of the house, hauling Oak inside. Vivi is waving to him as he tries to squirm free from his mother's grip. Taryn has her hands on her hips.

"Oriana has called everyone in to dinner," Taryn informs us both grandly. "She wants Locke to stay and eat with us."

He makes a bow. "You may inform your lady mother that though I am honored to be asked to her table, I would not so impose myself on her. I only wanted to speak with you both. I will, however, call again. You may be sure of that."

"You talked to Jude about school?" There is trepidation in Taryn's voice. I wonder what they spoke about before I returned. I wonder if he persuaded her to attend the lectures again, and if so, how he did it.

"Until tomorrow," he says to us with a wink.

I watch him walk off, still overwhelmed. I don't dare look at Taryn, for fear she will see all of it on my face, the whole day's events, the almost kiss. I am not ready to talk, so I am the one who avoids her for once. Skipping up the steps with as much nonchalance as I can muster, I head to my room to change for dinner.

I forgot that I asked Madoc to teach me swordplay and strategy, but after dinner he gives me a stack of military history books from his personal library.

"When you're done reading these, we will talk," he informs me. "I will set you a series of challenges, and you will tell me how you might overcome them with the resources I give you."

I think he expects me to object and insist on more swordplay, but I am too tired to even think of it.

Flopping down on my bed an hour later, I decide that I am not going to even take off the blue silk dress I am wearing. My hair is still disarranged, although I tried to improve it with a few pretty pins. I should take those out, at least, I tell myself, but I can't seem to make any movement toward doing so.

My door opens, and Taryn comes in, hopping up onto my bed.

"Okay," she says, poking me in the side. "What did Locke want? He said he had to talk to you."

"He's nice," I say, rolling over and folding my arms behind my head, staring up at the folds of fabric gathered above me. "Not totally Cardan's puppet like the rest of them."

Taryn has an odd expression on her face, like she wants to contradict me but is holding herself back. "Whatever. Spill."

"About Locke?" I ask.

She rolls her eyes. "About what happened with him and his friends."

"They're never going to respect me if I don't fight back," I tell her.

She sighs. "They're never going to respect you, period."

I think of crawling across the grass, my knees dirty, the savor of the fruit in my mouth. Even now I can taste the echo of it, the emptiness it would fill, the giddy, delirious joy it promises.

Taryn goes on. "You came home practically naked yesterday, smeared with faerie fruit. Isn't that bad enough? Don't you care?" Taryn has pulled her whole body back against one of the posts of my bed.

"I am tired of caring," I say. "Why should I?"

"Because they could kill you!"

"They better," I say to her. "Because anything less than that isn't going to work."

"Do you have a plan for stopping them?" she asks. "You said you were going to defy Cardan by being your awesome self and if he tried to take you down, you'd take him down with you. How are you going to manage that?"

"I don't know exactly," I admit.

She throws up her hands in frustration.

"No, look," I say. "Every day that I don't beg Cardan for forgiveness over a feud he started is a day I win. He can humiliate me, but every time he does and I don't back down, he makes himself less powerful. After all, he's throwing everything he's got at someone as weak as I am and it's not working. He's going to take himself down."

She sighs and comes over to me, laying her head against my chest, putting her arms around me. Against my shoulder she whispers, "He's flint, you're tinder."

I hug her closer and make no promises.

We stay like that for a long moment.

"Did Locke threaten you?" she asks softly. "It was so odd that he came here looking for you, and then you had such a weird expression when I walked into the stables."

"No, nothing bad," I tell her. "I don't know exactly what he came for, but he kissed my hand. It was nice, like out of a storybook."

"Nice things don't happen in storybooks," Taryn says. "Or when they do happen, something bad happens next. Because otherwise the story would be boring, and no one would read it."

It's my turn to sigh. "I know it's stupid, thinking well of one of Cardan's friends, but he really did help me. He stood up to Cardan. But I'd rather talk about you. There's someone, isn't there? When you said you were going to fall in love, you were talking about someone in particular."

Not that I'd be the first to green gown her.

"There's a boy," she says slowly. "He's going to declare himself at Prince Dain's coronation. He's going to ask for my hand from Madoc, and then everything is going to change for me."

I think of her weeping, standing beside Cardan. I think of how angry she's been that I am feuding with him. I think of that, and a cold and terrible dread creeps over me. "*Who?*" I demand.

Please not Cardan. Anyone but Cardan.

"I promised not to tell anyone," she says. "Even you."

"Our promises don't matter," I say, thinking of Prince Dain's geas still freezing my tongue, of how little any of them trust us. "No one expects us to have any honor. Everyone knows we lie."

She gives me a stern, disapproving look. "It's a faerie prohibition. If I break it, he'll know. I need to show him I can live like one of the Folk."

"Okay," I say slowly.

"Be happy for me," she says, and I feel cut to the quick. She has found her place in Faerie, and I guess I have found mine. But I can't help worrying.

"Just tell me something about him. Tell me that he is kind. Tell me that you love him and that he's promised to be good to you. Tell me."

"He's a faerie," she says. "They don't love the way we do. And I think you would like him—there, that's something."

That doesn't sound like Cardan, whom I despise. But I am not sure I find her answer reassuring, either.

What does it mean, I would like him? Does that mean we've never met? What does it mean that he doesn't love the way we do?

"I *am* happy for you. Honest," I say, although I am more worried than anything. "This is exciting. When Oriana's dressmaker comes, you're going to have to make sure you get an extra-pretty gown."

Taryn relaxes. "I just want everything to be better. For both of us."

I reach over to my bedside table to retrieve the book I stole from Hollow Hall. "Remember this?" I ask, lifting up the collected *Alice's Adventures in Wonderland* book. When I do, a folded piece of paper slips out and flutters to the floor.

"We used to read that when we were little," she says, grabbing for the book. "Where did you get it?"

"I found it," I say, not able to explain whose bookshelf it had come from or why I had been in Hollow Hall in the first place. To test the geas, I try to say the words: *Spying for Prince Dain*. My mouth will not move. My tongue stays still. A wave of panic washes over me, but I push it back. This is a small price for what he's given me.

Taryn doesn't press for more information. She's too busy flipping through the pages and reading bits of it aloud. While I can't quite remember the cadence of my mother's voice, I think I hear an echo of it in Taryn's.

"*Now,* here, *you see, it takes all the running* you *can do, to keep in the same place,"* she reads. *"If you want to get somewhere else, you must run at least twice as fast as that!"*

I reach down surreptitiously and shove the fallen paper under my pillow. I plan to unfold it once she returns to her room, but instead I fall asleep, long before the story is over.

I wake in the early morning, alone, needing to pee. I pad into my bath area, lift my skirts, and do my business in the copper basin left there for this purpose, shame heating my face even though I am alone. It is one of the most humbling aspects of being human. I know that faeries are not gods—maybe I know that better than any mortal alive—but neither have I ever seen one hunched over a bedpan.

Back in bed, I push aside the curtain and let the sunlight spill in, brighter than any lamp. I take the folded-up paper from behind my pillow.

Smoothing it out, I see Cardan's furious, arrogant handwriting scrawled over the page, taking up all available space. In some places he pressed the nib so angrily that the paper tore.

Jude, it reads, each hateful rendering of my name like a punch to the gut.

Jude Jude Jude Jude Jude Jude Jude Jude Jude Jude Jude Jude
Jude Jude Jude Jude Jude Jude Jude Jude Jude Jude Jude Jude
Jude Jude Jude Jude Jude Jude Jude Jude Jude Jude Jude
Jude Jude Jude Jude Jude Jude Jude Jude Jude Jude Jude

Jude Jude Jude Jude Jude Jude Jude Jude Jude Jude Jude
Jude Jude Jude Jude Jude Jude Jude Jude Jude Jude Jude
Jude Jude Jude Jude Jude Jude Jude Jude Jude Jude
Jude Jude Jude Jude Jude Jude Jude Jude Jude Jude
Jude Jude Jude Jude Jude Jude Jude Jude Jude Jude
Jude Jude Jude Jude Jude Jude Jude Jude Jude Jude
Jude Jude Jude Jude Jude Jude Jude Jude Jude Jude
Jude Jude Jude Jude Jude Jude Jude Jude Jude Jude
Jude Jude Jude Jude Jude Jude Jude Jude Jude
Jude Jude Jude Jude Jude Jude Jude Jude Jude
Jude Jude Jude Jude Jude Jude Jude Jude Jude
Jude Jude Jude Jude Jude Jude Jude Jude Jude
Jude Jude Jude Jude Jude Jude Jude Jude Jude
Jude Jude Jude Jude Jude Jude Jude Jude Jude
Jude Jude Jude Jude Jude Jude Jude Jude
Jude Jude Jude Jude Jude Jude Jude Jude

CHAPTER 15

The dressmaker comes early the next afternoon, a long-fingered faerie called Brambleweft. Her feet are turned backward, giving her an odd gait. Her eyes are like those of a goat, brown with a horizontal line of black just at the center. She is wearing an example of her work, a woven dress with embroidered lines of thorns making a striped pattern down the length of it.

She has brought with her bolts of fabric, some of it stiff gold, one that changes color like iridescent beetle wings. Beside that, she tells us, is a spider silk so fine that it could have fit through the eye of a needle three times over and yet strong enough to have to be cut with silver scissors magicked to never lose their edge. The purple fabric shot through with gold and silver is so bright that it seems like moonlight itself puddling over the cushions.

All the fabrics are draped onto the couch in Oriana's parlor for us to inspect. Even Vivi is drawn to run her fingers over the cloth, an absent smile on her face. There is nothing like this in the mortal world, and she knows it.

Oriana's current maid, a hairy, wizened creature named Toadfloss, brings tea and cakes, meat and jam, all piled on a massive silver tray. I pour myself tea and drink it without cream, hoping it will settle my stomach. The terror of the last few days is at my heels, making me shudder without warning. The memory of the faerie fruit keeps rising unbidden to my tongue, along with the cracked lips of the servants in Balekin's palace and the sound of the leather as it struck Prince Cardan's bare back.

And my own name, written over and over and over. I thought I knew how much Cardan hated me, but looking at that paper, I realized I had no idea. And he'd hate me even more still if he knew I had seen him on his knees, beaten by a human servant. A mortal, for an extra bit of humiliation, an extra dose of rage.

"Jude?" Oriana says, and I realize that I've been staring off toward the window and the fading light.

"Yes?" I put on a bright, false smile.

Taryn and Vivienne begin to laugh.

"And just who are you thinking about with a dreamy expression like that on your face?" Oriana asks, which makes Vivi laugh again. Taryn doesn't, probably because she thinks I am an idiot.

I shake my head, hoping I have not gone red-faced. "No, it wasn't anything like that. I was just—I don't know. It doesn't matter. What were we talking about?"

"The seamstress wishes to measure you first," Oriana says. "Since you're the youngest."

I look over at Brambleweft, who holds a string between her hands. I hop up onto the box she has set before her, holding out my arms. I am a good daughter today. I am going to get a pretty gown. I will dance at Prince Dain's coronation until my feet bleed.

"Don't scowl," the seamstress says. Before I can stammer apologies, she continues, voice pitched low. "I was told to sew this dress with pockets that can conceal weapons and poisons and other little necessities. We'll make sure that's done while still showing you to great advantage."

I almost stumble off the box, I am so surprised. "That's wonderful," I whisper back, knowing better than to thank her. Faeries don't believe in dismissing gratitude with a few words. They believe in debts and bargains, and the person I am meant to be most indebted to is not here. Prince Dain is the one who expects to be repaid.

She smiles, pins in her mouth, and I grin back at her. I will repay him, although it seems I will have much to repay him for. I will make him proud of me. Everyone else, I will make very, very sorry.

When I look up, Vivi is watching me suspiciously. Taryn is next to be measured. As she gets on the box, I go and drink more tea. Then I eat three sugary cakes and a strip of ham.

"Where did you go the other day?" Vivi asks as I gulp down the meat like some kind of raptor bird. I have woken ravenous.

I think of how I fled from our conversation on my way to Hollow Hall. I can't exactly deny that, not without explaining more about where I was going than my geased tongue will allow. I shrug, one-shouldered.

"I made one of the other Gentry kids describe what happened to you at that lecture," Vivi says. "You could have died. The only reason you're alive is that they didn't want their game to be over."

"That's the way they are," I remind her. "That's the way things are. Do you want the world to be different than it is? Because this is the world we get, Vivi."

"It's not the only world," she says softly.

"It's *my* world," I say, my heart hammering in my chest. I stand before she can tell me otherwise. My hands are shaking, though, and my palms are sweaty when I go to finger the fabrics.

Ever since I staggered home through the woods in my underwear, I have been trying to feel nothing about what happened. I am afraid that if I begin to feel, I won't be able to bear it. I am afraid that the emotion will be like a wave sucking me under.

It's not the first awful thing I have endured and pushed into the back of my brain. That's how I've been coping, and if there's another, better way, I do not know it.

I focus my attention on the cloth until I can breathe evenly again, until the panic dissipates. There's a velvet blue-green, reminding me of the lake at dusk. I find an amazing, fantastical fabric embroidered with moths and butterflies and ferns and flowers. I lift it up, and underneath is a bolt of beautiful fog-gray cloth that ripples like smoke. They're so very pretty. The kind of fabrics that princesses in fairy tales wear.

Of course, Taryn is right about stories. Bad things happen to those princesses. They are pricked with thorns, poisoned by apples, married to their own fathers. They have their hands cut off and their brothers turned into swans, their lovers chopped up and planted in basil pots. They vomit up diamonds. When they walk, it feels as though they're walking on knives.

They still manage to look nice.

"I want that one," Taryn says, pointing to the bolt of fabric I'm holding, the one with the embroidery. She's done being measured. Vivi is up there, holding out her arms, watching me in that unnerving way she has, as though she knows my very thoughts.

"Your sister found it first," Oriana says.

"Pleeeeeeeease," Taryn says to me, bending her head and looking up through her eyelashes. She's joking, but she's not. She needs to look nice for this boy who is supposed to declare himself at the coronation. She doesn't understand what use my looking nice would be, me with my grudges and feuds.

With a half smile, I set down the bolt. "Sure. All yours."

Taryn kisses me on the cheek. I guess we're back to normal. If only everything in my life were so easily resolved.

I choose a different cloth, the dark blue velvet. Vivienne chooses a violet that seems to be a silvery gray when she turns it over her hand. Oriana chooses a blush pink for herself and a cricket green for Oak. Brambleweft starts to sketch—billowing skirts and cunning little capes, corsets stitched with fanciful creatures. Butterflies alighting along arms and in elaborate headpieces. I am charmed at the alien vision of myself—my corset will have two golden beetles stitched in what looks like a breastplate, with Madoc's moon crest and elaborate swirls of shining thread continuing down my front, and tiny sheer drop sleeves of more gold.

It will certainly be clear to what household I belong.

We are still making small changes when Oak runs in, being chased by Gnarbone. Oak spots me first and scrambles onto my lap, throwing his arms around my neck and giving me a small bite just beneath my shoulder.

"Ow!" I say in surprise, but he just laughs. It makes me laugh, too. He's kind of a weird kid, maybe because he's a faerie or maybe because all kids, human or inhuman, are equally weird. "Do you want me to tell you a story about a little boy who bit a stone and lost all his pearly white teeth?" I ask him in what I hope is a menacing fashion, sticking my fingers under his armpits to tickle him.

"Yes," he says immediately between breathless giggles and shrieks.

Oriana strides over to us, her face full of trouble. "That's very kind of you, but we ought to begin dressing for dinner." She pulls him off my lap and into her arms. He begins screaming and kicking his legs. One of the kicks lands against my stomach hard enough to bruise, but I don't say anything.

"Story!" he shouts. "I want the story!"

"Jude is busy right now," she says, carrying his squirming body toward the door, where Gnarbone is waiting to take him back to the nursery.

"Why don't you ever trust me with him?" I shout, and Oriana wheels around, shocked that I said a thing we don't say. I am shocked, too, but I can't stop. "I'm not a monster! I've never done anything to either of you."

"I want the story," Oak whines, sounding confused.

"That's enough," Oriana says sternly, as though we've all been arguing. "We will speak about this later with your father."

With that, she strides from the room.

"I don't know whose father you're talking about, because he's sure not mine," I call after her.

Taryn's eyes go saucer-wide. Vivienne has a small smile on her face. She takes a minute sip of tea, and then she raises the cup in my direction in salute. The seamstress is looking down and away, leaving us to our private family moment.

I cannot seem to contort myself back into the shape of a dutiful child.

I am coming unraveled. I am coming undone.

The next day at school, Taryn walks beside me, swinging her lunch basket. I keep my head high and my jaw set. I have my little knife with me, cold iron, tucked into one of the pockets of my skirt, and more salt than I reasonably need. I even have a new necklace of rowan berries, sewn by Tatterfell and worn because there was no way she could know I didn't need it.

I dally in the palace garden to gather a few more things.

"Are you allowed to pick those?" Taryn asks, but I do not answer her.

In the afternoon, we attend a lecture in a high tower, where we are taught about birdsongs. Every time I feel as though my courage will falter, I let my fingers brush the cool metal of the blade.

Locke looks over, and when he catches my eye, he winks.

From the other side of the room, Cardan scowls at the lecturer but does not speak. When he moves to take an inkpot from a satchel, I see him wince. I think about how sore his back must be, how it must hurt to move. But if he holds himself a little more stiffly as he sneers, that seems to be the only difference in his manner.

He looks well practiced in hiding pain.

I think of the note I found, of the press of his nibbed pen hard enough to send flecks of ink spattering as he wrote my name. Hard enough to dig through the page, maybe to scar the desk beneath.

If that's what he did to the paper, I shudder to think what he wants to do to me.

After school, I practice with Madoc. He shows me a particularly clever block, and I do it over and over again, better and faster, surprising even him. When I go inside, covered in sweat, I pass Oak, who is running somewhere, dragging my stuffed snake after him on a dirty rope. He's clearly stolen the snake from my room.

"Oak!" I call after him, but he's up the stairs and away.

I sluice off in my bath and then, alone in my room, unpack my schoolbag. Tucked down in the bottom, wrapped in a leftover piece of paper, is a single worm-eaten faerie fruit I picked up on the way home. I set it on a tray and pull on leather gloves. Then I take out my knife and cut it into pieces. Tiny slivers of squishy golden fruit.

I have researched faerie poisons in dusty, hand-scribed books in Madoc's library. I read about the blusher mushroom, a pale fungus that blooms with beads of a red liquid that looks uncomfortably like blood. Small doses cause paralysis, while large doses are lethal, even for the Folk. Then there is deathsweet, which causes a sleep that lasts a hundred years. And wraithberry, which makes your blood race until your heart stops. And faerie fruit, of course, which one book called everapple.

I take out a flask of pine liquor, nicked from the kitchens, thick and heavy as sap. I drop the fruit into it to keep it fresh.

My hands are shaking.

The final piece, I put on my tongue. The rush of it hits me hard, and I grit my teeth against it. Then, while I am feeling stupid, I take out the other things. A leaf of wraithberry from the palace garden. A petal from a flower of deathsweet. The tiniest bead of juice from the blusher mushroom. From each, I cut away a tinier portion and swallow.

Mithridatism, it's called. Isn't that a funny name? The process of eating poison to build up immunity. So long as I don't die from it, I'll be harder to kill.

I do not make it downstairs for dinner. I am too busy retching, too busy shivering and sweating.

I fall asleep in the bath area of my room, spread out on the floor. That's where the Ghost finds me. I wake to his poking me in the stomach with the foot of his boot. It's only grogginess that keeps me from crying out.

"Rise, Jude," the Ghost says. "The Roach wants you to train tonight."

I push myself up, too exhausted to disobey. Outside, on the dewy grass, with the first rays of sun creeping across the island, the Ghost shows me how to climb trees silently. How to put down a foot without snapping a branch or crackling a dried leaf. I thought I'd learned how in my lessons at the palace, but he shows me mistakes my teachers didn't bother correcting. I try, over and over. Mostly, I fail.

"Good," he says, once my muscles are shaking. He's spoken so little that his voice startles me. He could more easily pass for human than Vivi, with the subtler point on his ears, light brown hair, and hazel eyes. And yet he seems unknowable to me, both calmer and colder than she is. The sun is almost up. The leaves are turning to gold. "Keep practicing. Sneak up on your sisters." When he grins, with sandy hair falling over his face, he seems younger than I am, but I'm sure he's not.

And when he goes, he does it in such a way that it appears like vanishing. I head back home and use what I've just learned to slyfoot my way past the servants on the stairs. I make it to my room, and this time when I collapse, I manage to do it in my bed.

Then I get up the next day and do everything all over again.

CHAPTER 16

Attending lectures is harder than ever. For one thing, I am sick, my body fighting the effects of the fruit and the poisons I am forcing down. For another, I am exhausted from training with Madoc and training with Dain's Court of Shadows. Madoc gives me puzzles—twelve goblin knights to storm a fortress, nine untrained Gentry to defend one—and then asks for my answers each evening after dinner. The Roach orders me to practice moving through the crowds of courtiers without being noticed, to eavesdrop without seeming interested. The Bomb teaches me how to find the weak spot in a building, the pressure point on a body. The Ghost teaches me how to hang from rafters and not be seen, to line up a shot with a crossbow, to steady my shaking hands.

I am sent on two more missions to get information. First, I steal a letter addressed to Elowyn from a knight's desk in the palace. The next time, I wear the clothing of a faerie bride and walk through a party to the private chambers of the lovely Taracand, one of Prince Balekin's consorts, where I take a ring from a desk. In neither case am I allowed to know the significance of what I stole.

I attend lectures beside Cardan, Nicasia, Valerian, and all the Gentry children who laughed at my humiliation. I do not give them the satisfaction of my withdrawing, but since the incident with the faerie fruit, there are no more skirmishes. I bide my time. I can only assume they are doing the same. I am not foolish enough to think we are done with one another.

Locke continues his flirtation. He sits with Taryn and me when we take our lunch, spread out on a blanket, watching the sun set. Occasionally he walks me home through the woods, stopping to kiss me near a copse of fir trees just before Madoc's estate. I only hope he doesn't taste the bitterness of poison on my lips.

I do not understand why he likes me, but it is exciting to be liked.

Taryn doesn't seem to understand it, either. She regards Locke with suspicion. Perhaps since I am worried over her mysterious paramour, it is fitting that she seems equally worried over mine.

"Are you enjoying yourself?" I overhear Nicasia ask Locke once, as he joins them for a lecture. "Cardan won't forgive you for what you're doing with her."

I pause, unable to pass by without listening for his answer.

But Locke only laughs. "Is he more angry that you chose me over him or that I chose a mortal over you?"

I startle, not sure I heard him right.

She's about to answer when she spots me. Her mouth curls. "Little mousie," she says. "Don't believe his sugared tongue."

The Roach would despair of me if he saw how badly I fumbled

my newfound skills. I did nothing he taught me—I neither concealed myself nor blended in with others to avoid notice. At least no one would suspect me of knowing much about spycraft.

"So has Cardan forgiven *you*?" I ask her, pleased by her stricken look. "Too bad. I hear a prince's favor is a really big deal."

"What need have I for princes?" she demands. "My mother is a queen!"

There's much I could say about her mother, Queen Orlagh, who is planning a poisoning, but I bite my tongue. In fact, I bite it so hard that I don't say anything at all. I just walk to where Taryn is sitting, a small, satisfied smile on my face.

More weeks pass, until the coronation is mere days away. I am so tired that I fall asleep whenever I put my head down.

I even fall asleep in the tower during a demonstration of moth summoning. The susurration of their wings lulls me, I guess. It doesn't take much.

I wake on the stone floor. My head is ringing, and I am scrambling for my knife. I don't know where I am. For a moment, I think that I must have fallen. For a moment, I think I am paranoid. Then I see Valerian, grinning down at me. He has pushed me out of my chair. I know it just from the look on his face.

I have not yet become paranoid enough.

Voices sound from outside, the rest of our classmates having their luncheon on the grass as evening rolls in. I hear the shrieks of the youngest children, probably chasing one another over blankets.

"Where's Taryn?" I ask, because it wasn't like her not to wake me.

"She promised not to help you, remember?" Valerian's golden hair hangs over one eye. As usual, he's clad entirely in red, a tone so deep that it might appear black at first glance. "Not by word or by deed."

Of course. Stupid me to forget I was on my own.

I push myself up, noticing a bruise on my calf as I do. I am not sure how long I was sleeping. I brush off my tunic and trousers. "What do you want?"

"I'm disappointed," he says slyly. "You bragged about how you were going to best Cardan, and yet you've done nothing, sulking after one little prank."

My hand slides automatically to the hilt on my knife.

Valerian lifts my necklace of rowan berries from his pocket and smirks at me. He must have cut it from my throat while I slept. I shudder at the thought that he was so close to me, that instead of slicing the necklace, he could have sliced skin. "Now you will do what I say." I can practically smell the glamour in the air. He's weaving magic with his words. "Call down to Cardan. Tell him he's won. Then jump from the tower. After all, being born mortal is like being born already dead."

The violence of it, the awful finality of his command, is shocking. A few months ago, I would have done it. I would have said the words, I would have leapt. If I hadn't made that bargain with Dain, I would be dead.

Valerian may have been planning my murder since the day he choked me. I remember the light in his eyes then, the eagerness with which he watched me gasp. Taryn had warned me I was going to get myself killed, and I bragged that I was ready for it, but I am not.

"I think I'll take the stairs," I tell Valerian, hoping I don't seem half as shaken as I am. Then, acting as though everything is normal, I go to move past him.

For a moment, he just looks confused, but his confusion quickly morphs into rage. He blocks my escape, moving in front of the steps. "I commanded you. Why don't you obey me?"

Looking him dead in the eye, I force myself to smile. "You had the advantage of me twice, and twice you gave it away. Good luck getting it again."

He's sputtering, furious. "You're nothing. The human species pretends it is so resilient. Mortal lives are one long game of make-believe. If you couldn't lie to yourselves, you'd cut your own throats to end your misery."

I am struck by the word *species*, by the idea that he thinks I am something entirely else, like an ant or a dog or a deer. I am not sure he's wrong, but I don't like the thought. "I don't feel particularly miserable right at the moment." I can't show him I'm afraid.

His mouth curls. "What happiness do you have? Rutting and breeding. You'd go mad if you accepted the truth of what you are. You are nothing. You barely exist at all. Your only purpose is to create more of your kind before you die some pointless and agonizing death."

I look him in the eye. "And?"

He seems taken aback, although the sneer doesn't leave his face.

"Yeah, yeah, sure. I am going to die. And I am a big liar. So what?"

He pushes me against the wall, hard. "So *you lose*. Admit that you lost."

I try to shrug him off, but he grabs for my throat, fingers pressing hard enough to cut off my airflow. "I could kill you right now," he says. "And you would be forgotten. It would be as though you'd never been born."

There is no doubt in my mind that he means it, no doubt at all. Gasping, I pull the knife from my little pocket and stab him in the side. Right between his ribs. If my knife had been longer, I would have punctured his lung.

His eyes go wide with shock. His grip on me loosens. I know what Madoc would say—to push the blade higher. Go for an artery. Go for his heart. But if I manage it, I will have murdered one of the favored sons of Faerie. I cannot even guess my punishment.

You're no killer.

I balk and pull the knife free, running out of the room. I shove the bloody blade into my pocket. My boots clatter on the stone as I head for the stairs.

Looking back, I see him on his knees, pressing a hand to his side to stanch the blood. He lets out a hiss of pain that makes me recall my knife is cold iron. Cold iron hurts faeries a lot.

I could not be gladder of carrying it.

I round the corner and nearly run down Taryn.

"Jude!" she exclaims. "What happened?"

"Come on," I tell her, dragging her toward the other students. There's blood on my knuckles, blood on my fingers, but not much. I rub it off on my tunic.

"What did he do to you?" Taryn cries as I hustle her along.

I tell myself that I don't mind that she left me. It wasn't her job to stick out her neck, especially when she made it abundantly clear she didn't want any part of this fight. Is there a treacherous part of me that's pissed off and sad that she didn't kick me awake and damn the consequences? Sure. But even I didn't guess how far Valerian would go or how fast he'd get there.

We're crossing the lawn when Cardan veers in our direction. He's wearing loose clothes and carrying a practice sword.

His eyes narrow at the blood, and he points the wooden stick at me. "You seem to have cut yourself." I wonder if he's surprised that I'm alive. I wonder if he watched the tower the whole time during his luncheon, waiting for the amusing spectacle of me jumping to my death.

I take the knife out from under my tunic and show it to him, stained a flinty red. I smile. "I could cut you, too."

"Jude!" Taryn says. She's clearly shocked by my behavior. She should be. My behavior is shocking.

"Oh, *go* already," Cardan tells her, waving her off with one hand. "Stop boring us both."

Taryn takes a step back. I'm surprised, too. Is this part of the game?

"Are your dirty blade and even dirtier habits supposed to mean something?" His words are airy, drawling. He is looking at me as though I'm being *uncouth* by pointing a weapon at him—even though he's the one with the minion who assaulted me. Twice. He's looking at me as though we're going to share some kind of witty repartee, but I am not sure what to say.

Is he really not worried about what I might have done to Valerian?

Could he possibly not know Valerian attacked me?

Taryn spots Locke and takes off toward him, hurrying across the field. They converse for a moment, then Taryn departs. Cardan notices my noticing. He sniffs, as though the very smell of me offends him.

Locke starts toward us, all loose limbs and shining eyes. He gives me a wave. For a moment, I feel almost safe. I am immensely grateful to Taryn, for sending him over. I am immensely grateful to Locke, for coming.

"You think I don't deserve him," I say to Cardan.

He smiles slowly, like the moon slipping beneath the waves of the lake. "Oh no, I think you're perfect for each other."

A few moments later, Locke has an arm thrown around my shoulders. "Come on," he says. "Let's get out of here."

And so, without a backward glance at any of them, we do.

We walk through the Crooked Forest, where all the trees are bowed in the same direction as though they've been blown by a strong wind since they were saplings. I stop to pick a few blackberries from prickly stems of bushes growing between them. I have to blow tiny sugar ants from each before putting it in my mouth.

I offer a berry to Locke, but he demurs.

"So, in short, Valerian tried to kill me," I say, finishing my story. "And I stabbed him."

His fox eyes are steady on me. "You *stabbed* Valerian."

"So I might be in some trouble." I take a deep breath.

He shakes his head. "Valerian won't tell anyone he was bested by a mortal girl."

"What about Cardan? Won't he be disappointed his plan didn't work?" I gaze out at the sea, visible between the trunks of the trees. It seems to stretch on to forever.

"I doubt he even knew about it," Locke says, and smiles at my surprise. "Oh, he'd like to make you believe he's our leader, but it's more that Nicasia likes power, I like dramatics, and Valerian likes violence. Cardan can provide us with all three, or at least excuses for all three."

"Dramatics?" I echo.

"I like for things to happen, for stories to unfold. And if I can't find a good enough story, I make one." He looks every inch the trickster in that moment. "I know you overheard Nicasia talking about what was between us. She had Cardan, but only in leaving him for me did she gain power over him."

I ponder that for a moment, and while I do, I realize we're not taking our usual path to Madoc's grounds. Locke has been leading me another way. "Where are we going?"

"My demesne," he says with a grin, happy to be caught out. "It's not far. I think you'll like the hedge maze."

I have never been to one of their estates, save for Hollow Hall. In the human world, we children were always in the neighbors' yards, swinging and swimming and jumping, but the rules here are nothing the same. Most of the children in the High King's Court are royals, sent from smaller Courts to gain influence with the princes and princesses, and have no time for much else.

Of course, in the mortal world, there are such things as backyards. Here, there are forest and sea, rocks and mazes, and flowers that are red only when they get fresh blood. I don't much like the idea of getting lost deliberately in a hedge maze, but I smile as though nothing could ever delight me more. I don't want to disappoint him.

"There will be a gathering later," Locke continues. "You should stay. I promise it will be diverting."

At that, my stomach clenches. I doubt he's having a party without his friends. "That seems foolish," I say, to avoid refusing the invitation outright.

"Your father doesn't like you to stay out late?" Locke gives me a pitying look.

I know he's just trying to make me feel childish when he knows perfectly well why I shouldn't be there, but even though I am aware of what he's doing, it works.

Locke's estate is more modest than Madoc's and less fortified. Tall spires covered in shingles of mossy bark rise between the trees. The spiraling vines of ivy and honeysuckle that twine up the sides turn the whole thing green and leafy.

"Wow," I say. I have ridden by here and seen those spires in the distance, but I never knew to whose house they belonged. "Beautiful."

He gives me a quick grin. "Let's go inside."

Although there is a pair of grand doors in the front, he takes me around to a small door on the side that leads directly to the kitchens. A fresh loaf of bread rests on the counter, along with apples, currants, and a soft cheese, but I do not see any servants who might have prepared this.

I think, involuntarily, of the girl in Hollow Hall cleaning Cardan's fireplace. I wonder where her family thinks she is and what bargain she made. I wonder how easily I could have been her.

"Is your family home?" I ask, pushing that thought away.

"I have none," he tells me. "My father was too wild for the Court. He liked the deep, feral woods far better than my mother's intrigues. He left, and then she died. Now it's just me."

"That's terrible," I say. "And lonely."

He shakes off my words. "I've heard the story of your parents. A tragedy suitable for a ballad."

"It was a long time ago." The last thing I want to talk about is Madoc and murder. "What happened to your mother?"

He makes a dismissive gesture in the air. "She got involved with the

High King. In this Court, that's enough. There was a child—*his* child, I suppose—and someone didn't want it born. Blusher mushroom." Although he began his speech airily, it doesn't end that way.

Blusher mushroom. I think of the letter I found in Balekin's house from Queen Orlagh. I try to convince myself that the note could not have referred to the poisoning of Locke's mother, that Balekin had no motive when Dain was already the High King's chosen heir. But no matter how I try to convince myself, I cannot stop thinking about the possibility, of the horror, of Nicasia's mother having had a hand in Locke's mother's death. "I shouldn't have asked—that was rude of me."

"We are children of tragedy." He shakes his head and then smiles. "This is not how I meant to begin. I meant to give you wine and fruit and cheese. I meant to tell you how your hair is as beautiful as curling woodsmoke, your eyes the exact color of walnuts. I thought I could compose an ode about it, but I am not very good at odes."

I laugh, and he covers his heart as though stung by cruelty. "Before I show you the maze, let me show you something else."

"What's that?" I ask, curious.

He takes my hand. "Come," he says, prankish, leading me through the house. We come to spiraling stairs. Up we go, up and up and up.

I feel dizzy. There are no doors and no landings. Just stone and steps and my heart beating loud in my chest. Just his slanted smiles and amber eyes. I try not to stumble or slip as I climb. I try not to slow down, no matter how light-headed I feel.

I think of Valerian. *Jump from the tower.*

I keep climbing, taking shallow breaths.

You are nothing. You barely exist at all.

When we get to the top, there's a small door—half our height. I lean against the wall, waiting for my balance to return, and watch Locke turn the elaborate silver knob. He ducks as he goes in. I steel myself, push off the wall, and follow.

And gasp. We're on a balcony at the very top of the tallest tower, one higher than the tree line. From here, lit by starlight, I can see the maze below and the folly in the center. I can see the aboveground parts of the Palace of Elfhame and Madoc's estate and Balekin's Hollow Hall. I can see the sea that encircles the island and beyond it, the bright lights of human cities and towns through the ever-present mist. I have never looked directly from our world into theirs.

Locke puts his hand against my back, between my shoulder blades. "At night, the human world looks as though it's full of fallen stars."

I lean into his touch, pushing away the awfulness of the climb, trying not to stand too close to the edge. "Have you ever been there?"

He nods. "My mother took me when I was a child. She said our world would grow stagnant without yours."

I want to tell him that it's not mine, that I barely understand it, but I get what he's trying to say, and the correction would make it seem as though I didn't. His mother's sentiment is kind, certainly kinder than most views of the mortal world. She must have been kind herself.

He turns me toward him and then slowly brings his lips to mine. They're soft, and his breath is warm. I feel as distant from my body as the lights of the faraway city. My hand reaches for the railing. I grip it hard as his arm goes around my waist, to ground myself in what's happening, to convince myself that I am here and that this moment, high above everything, is real.

He draws back. "You really are beautiful," he says.

I am never so glad to know they cannot lie.

"This is incredible," I say, looking down. "Everything looks so small, like on a strategy board."

He laughs, as though I cannot possibly be serious. "I take it you spend a lot of time in your father's study?"

"Enough," I say. "Enough to know what my odds are against Cardan. Against Valerian and Nicasia. Against you."

He takes my hand. "Cardan is a fool. The rest of us don't matter." His smile turns slanted. "But maybe this is part of your plan—persuade me to take you to the very heart of my stronghold. Maybe you're about to reveal your evil scheme and bend me to your will. Just so you know, I don't think it will be very hard to bend me to your will."

I laugh despite myself. "You're nothing like them."

"Aren't I?" he asks.

I give him a long look. "I don't know. Are you going to order me off this balcony?"

His eyebrows go up. "Of course not."

"Well then, you're not like them," I say, poking him hard in the center of his chest. My hand flattens, almost unconsciously, letting the warmth of him seep up through my palm. I hadn't realized how cold I'd become, standing in the wind.

"You're not the way they said you would be," he says, bending toward me. He kisses me again.

I don't want to think about the things they must have said, not now. I want his mouth on mine, blotting out everything else.

It takes us a long time to wend our way back down the stairs. My hands are in his hair. His mouth is on my neck. My back is against the ancient stone wall. Everything is slow and perfect and makes no sense at all. This can't be my life. This feels nothing like my life.

We sit at the long, empty banquet table and eat cheese and bread. We drink pale green wine that tastes of herbs out of massive goblets that Locke finds in the back of a cabinet. They're so thick with dust he has to wash them twice before we can use them.

When we're done, he presses me back against the table, lifting me so that I am seated on it, so that our bodies are pressed together. It's exhilarating and terrifying, like so much of Faerie.

I am not sure I am very good at kissing. My mouth is clumsy. I am shy. I want to pull him closer and push him away at the same time. Faeries do not have a lot of taboos around modesty, but I do. I am afraid that my mortal body stinks of sweat, of decay, of fear. I am not sure where to put my hands, how hard to grab, how deep to sink my nails into his shoulders. And while I know what comes after kissing, while I know what it means to have his hands slide up over my bruised calf to my thigh, I have no idea how to hide my inexperience.

He pulls back to look at me, and I try to keep the panic out of my eyes.

"Stay tonight," he murmurs.

For a moment, I think he means with him, like *with him*, and my heart speeds with some combination of desire and dread. Then, abruptly, I remember there's going to be a party—that's what he's asking me to stay for. Those unseen servants, wherever they are, must be preparing the estate. Soon Valerian, my would-be murderer, might be dancing in the garden.

Well, maybe not *dancing*. He'll probably be leaning against a wall stiffly, with a drink in his hand, bandages around his ribs, and a new plan to murder me in his heart. If not new *orders* to murder me from Cardan.

"Your friends won't like it," I say, sliding off the table.

"They'll quickly be too drunk to notice. You can't spend your life locked up in Madoc's glorified barracks." He gives me a smile that is clearly meant to charm me. It kind of works. I think about Dain's offer to give me a love mark on my brow and wonder idly if Locke might have one, because, despite everything, I am tempted.

"I don't have the right clothes," I say, gesturing to the tunic I have on, stained with Valerian's blood.

He looks me up and down longer than an inspection of my garments requires. "I can find you a gown. I can find you anything you'd like. You asked me about Cardan, Valerian, and Nicasia—come see them outside of school, come see them be foolish and drunk and debased. See their vulnerabilities, the cracks in their armor. You've got to know them to beat them, right? I don't say you'll like them any better, but you don't need to like them."

"I like *you*," I tell him. "I like playing pretend with you."

"Pretend?" he echoes, as though he's not sure if I'm insulting him.

"Of course," I say, going to the windows of the hall and looking out. Moonlight streams onto the leafy entrance to the maze. Torches are burning nearby, the flames flickering and wavering in the wind. "Of course we're pretending! We don't belong together, but it's fun anyway."

He gives me an evaluating, conspiratorial look. "Then let's keep doing it."

"Okay," I say helplessly. "I'll stay. I'll go to your party." I have had little fun in my life so far. The promise of more is difficult to resist.

He leads me through several rooms until we come to double doors. For a moment, he hesitates, glancing back at me. Then he pushes them open, and we're in an enormous bedroom. A thick, oppressive layer of dust blankets everything. There are footprints—two sets. He's come in here before, but not many times.

"The dresses in the closet were my mother's. Borrow whatever you like," he says, taking my hand.

Looking around this untouched room at the heart of the house, I understand the grief that made him lock it up for so long. I am glad to be let in. If I had a room full of my mother's things, I do not know if I would let anyone inside. I don't even know if I would brave it myself.

He opens one of the closets. Much of the clothing is moth-eaten, but I can see what they once were. A skirt with a beaded pattern of pomegranates, another that pulls up, like a curtain, to show a stage with jeweled mechanical puppets underneath. There is even one stitched with the silhouette of dancing fauns as tall as the skirt itself. I've admired Oriana's dresses for their elegance and opulence, but these awaken in me a hunger for a dress that's riotous. They make me wish I'd seen Locke's mother in one of her gowns. They make me think she must have liked to laugh.

"I don't think I've ever seen a dress like any of these," I tell him. "You really want me to wear one?"

He brushes a hand over a sleeve. "I guess they're a bit rotted."

"No," I say. "I like them."

The one with the fauns is the least damaged. I dust it off and tug it on behind an old screen. I struggle, because it's the sort of dress that's difficult to put on without Tatterfell's help. I have no idea how to arrange my hair any differently, so I leave it as is—braided in a crown around my head. When I wipe off a silver mirror with my hand and see myself dressed in a dead faerie's clothes, a shudder goes through me.

Suddenly, I do not know why I am here in this place. I am not sure of Locke's intentions. When he tries to drape me in his mother's jewels, I refuse them.

"Let's go out to the garden," I say. I no longer want to be in this empty, echoing room.

He puts away the long string of emeralds he was holding. As we leave, I look back at the closet of moldering clothes. Despite my feelings of unease, there's a part of me that can't help imagining what it would be like to be the mistress of this place. Imagining Prince Dain with the crown. Imagining entertaining at the long table we kissed against, my classmates all drinking the pale green wine and pretending they had never tried to murder me. Locke, with his hand in mine.

And me, spying on them all for the king.

The hedge maze is taller than the height of an ogre and formed of dense, glossy leaves in a deep green. Apparently, Cardan's circle meets here often. I can hear them laughing at the center of the maze when I walk outside with Locke, late to his own gathering. The smell of pine liquor is alive in the air. The firelight of the torches makes long shadows and limns everything in scarlet. My steps slow.

Reaching into the pocket of the borrowed dress, I touch my knife, still stained with Valerian's blood. When I do, my fingers light on something else, something Locke's mother must have left years before. I pull out her bauble—a golden acorn. It doesn't look like jewelry—there is no chain—and I cannot imagine what purpose it might have had other than to be pretty. I drop it back into my pocket.

Locke holds my hand as we move through the turns of the hedge maze. It does not seem as though there are many. I try to map it in my mind as I go, in case I have to find my way out alone. The simplicity of the maze makes me nervous rather than confident. I do not believe there are many simple things in Faerie. At home, dinner will be coming to a close without me. Taryn will be whispering to Vivi how I went somewhere with Locke. Madoc will be frowning and stabbing his meat, annoyed with me for missing his lessons.

I have braved worse things.

At the center of the maze, a piper is playing a lilting, wild song. White rose petals blow through the air. Folk are gathered, eating and drinking from a long banquet table that seems mostly piled with different distillations—cordials in which mandrake roots float, sour plum wine, a clear liquor infused with handfuls of red clover. And beside those, vials of golden nevermore.

Cardan is lying on a blanket, his head tipped back and his loose white shirt unbuttoned. Although it is still early in the night, he appears to be very drunk. His mouth is flaked with gold. A horned girl I don't know is kissing his throat, and another, this one with daffodil hair, presses her mouth against the calf of his leg, just above the top of his boot.

To my relief, I do not see Valerian. I hope he's home, nursing that wound I gave him.

Locke brings me a thimbleful of liquor, and I take a tiny scalding sip for the sake of politeness. I start coughing immediately. At that moment,

Cardan's gaze goes to me. His eyes are barely open, but I can see the shine of them, wet as tar. He watches me as the girl kisses his mouth, watches me as she slides her hand beneath the hem of his silly, ruffly shirt.

My cheeks heat. I look away and then am angry with myself for giving him the satisfaction of seeming uncomfortable. He's the one who's making a spectacle of himself.

"I see a member of the *Circle of Worms* has chosen to grace us with her presence tonight," Nicasia says, swanning up to us in a dress with all the colors of the sunset in it. She peers into my face. "But which one is it?"

"The one you don't like," I tell her, ignoring her jibe.

That makes her give a high, false laugh. "Oh, you might be surprised how some of us feel about both of you."

"I promised you better amusements than this," Locke says stiffly, taking my elbow. I am grateful when he pulls me toward a low table with pillows strewn haphazardly around it, but I can't help giving Nicasia a small, antagonizing wave as I go. I pour out my thimble of liquor onto the grass when Locke isn't looking. The piper finishes, and a naked boy, shining with gold paint, takes out a lyre and sings a filthy song about broken hearts: "*O lady fair! O lady cruel! How I miss your sweet misrule. I miss your hair. I miss your eyes. But most of all, I miss your thighs.*"

Locke kisses me again, in front of the fire. Everyone can see it, but I don't know if they're looking, because I close my eyes as tightly as they will go.

CHAPTER 17

I wake in Locke's house on a bed covered in tapestries. My mouth tastes of sour plums and is swollen from kissing. Locke is beside me on the bed, eyes shut, still in his party clothes. I pause in the act of rising to study him, his sharp ears and fox-fur hair, the softness of his mouth, his long limbs spread out in sleep. His head is pillowed on one ruffle-covered wrist.

The night comes back in a rush of memory. There was dancing and a chase through the maze. I remember falling on my hands in the dirt and laughing, totally unlike myself. Indeed, when I look down at the borrowed ball gown I slept in, there are grass stains on it.

Not that I'd be the first to green gown her.

Prince Cardan watched me all night, a shark restlessly circling, waiting for the right moment to bite. Even now I can conjure the memory of the scorched black of his eyes. And if I laughed louder for the sake of angering him, if I smiled wider, and kissed Locke longer, that is a kind of deceit that even the Folk cannot condemn.

Now, however, the night feels like one long, impossible dream.

Locke's bedroom is messy—books and clothes scattered on divans and low couches. I wade through to the door and pad over the empty halls of the house. Finding my way back to the dusty room of his mother's, I take off her gown and tug on yesterday's clothes. I reach to take my knife from her pocket, and when I do, the golden acorn comes out with it.

Impulsively, I tuck both knife and acorn into my tunic. I want some memento of the night, something to recall it, should nothing like it ever happen again. Locke told me I could borrow anything in the room, and I am borrowing this.

On my way out, I pass the long dining table. Nicasia is there, sectioning an apple with a little knife.

"Your hair looks like a thicket," she says, popping a slice of fruit into her mouth.

I glance at a silver plate on the wall, which shows only a distorted and blurred image of myself. Even in that, I can tell she's right—a halo of brown surrounds my head. Reaching up, I begin undoing my braid, combing it out with my fingers.

"Locke's asleep," I say, assuming that she's waiting to see him. I expect to feel as though I have something over her, being the one that came from his bedroom, but what I actually feel is a little bit of panic.

I don't know how to do this. I don't know how to wake up in a boy's house and talk to the girl with whom he had a relationship. That she's also a girl who probably wants me dead is, oddly, the only part of this that feels at all normal.

"My mother and his brother thought we were to be wed," she says, seeming as though she might be talking to the air and not to me at all. "It was going to be a useful alliance."

"With Locke?" I ask, confused.

She gives me an annoyed look, my question seeming to bring her briefly out of her story. "Cardan and me. He ruins things. That's what he likes. To ruin things."

Of course Cardan likes to ruin things. I wonder how that could be something she only just realized. I would have thought that would be something they had in common.

I leave her to her apple and her reminiscences and head toward the palace. A cool breeze blows through the trees, lifting my loose hair and bringing me the scent of pine. In the sky, I hear the call of gulls. I am grateful for the lecture today, glad to have an excuse for not going home and hearing whatever Oriana has to say to me.

Today the lecture is in the tower, my least favorite location. I climb the steps and settle myself. I am late, but I find a spot on a bench near the back. Taryn is sitting on the other side. She looks at me once, raising her brows. Cardan is beside her, dressed in green velvet, with golden stitching picking out thorns tipped in blue thread. He lounges in his seat, long fingers tapping restlessly against the wood of the bench beside him.

Looking at him makes me feel equally restless.

At least Valerian hasn't shown up. It is too much to hope that he never returns, but at least I have today.

A new instructor, a knight named Dulcamara, is talking about rules of inheritance, probably in anticipation of the coming coronation.

The coronation, which will mark my rise to power as well. Once

Prince Dain is the High King, his spies can haunt the shadows of Elfhame with only Dain himself to keep us in check.

"In some of the lower Courts, a king or queen's murderer can take the throne," Dulcamara says. She goes on to tell us that she is part of the Court of Termites, which has not yet joined Eldred's banner.

Although she is not wearing armor, she stands as though she's used to the weight of it. "And that is why Queen Mab bargained with the wild fey to make the crown King Eldred wears, which can only be passed down to her descendants. It would be tricky to get it by force." She grins wickedly.

If Cardan were to try to stop her lesson, she looks like she would eat him alive and crack his bones for marrow.

The Gentry children look at Dulcamara uncomfortably. Rumor has it that Lord Roiben, her king, is planning to swear to the new High King, bringing with him his large Court, one that has held off Madoc's forces for years. Roiben's joining the High Court of Elfhame is widely considered to be a masterstroke of diplomacy, negotiated by Prince Dain against Madoc's wishes. I suppose she's come for the coronation.

Larkspur, one of the youngest of us, pipes up. "What happens when there are no more children in the Greenbriar line?"

Dulcamara's smile gentles. "Once there are fewer than two descendants—one to wear the crown and the other to place it on the ruler's head—the High Crown and its power crumble. All of Elfhame will be free from their oaths to it.

"Then, who knows? Maybe a new ruler will make a new crown. Maybe you'll return to warring with smaller Seelie and Unseelie Courts. Maybe you will join our banners in the Southwest." Her smile makes it clear which of those she would prefer.

I stick my hand up. Dulcamara nods in my direction. "What if someone *tries* to take the crown?"

Cardan gives me a look. I want to glare, but I can't help thinking of him sprawled out on the ground with those girls. My cheeks heat all over again. I drop my gaze.

"An interesting question," Dulcamara says. "Legend has it that the crown will not allow itself to be placed on the brow of anyone who isn't an heir of Mab, but Mab's line has been very fruitful. So long as a pair of descendants try to take the crown, it could be done. But the most dangerous part of a coup would be this: The crown is cursed so that a murder of its wearer causes the death of the person responsible."

I think of the note I found in Balekin's house, about blusher mushrooms, about vulnerability.

After the lecture, I go down the steps carefully, remembering taking them at a run after stabbing Valerian. My vision blurs, and I feel dizzy for a moment, but the moment passes. Taryn, coming behind me, all but pushes me into the woods once we're outside.

"First of all," she says, tugging me over patches of curling ferns, "no one knows you weren't home all last night except for Tatterfell, and I gave her one of your nicest rings to make sure she wouldn't say anything. But you have to tell me where you were."

"Locke had a party at his house," I say. "I stayed—but it wasn't, I mean, nothing much happened. We kissed. That was it."

Her chestnut braids fly as she shakes her head. "I don't know if I believe that."

I let out my breath, perhaps a little dramatically. "Why would I lie? I'm not the one hiding the identity of the person courting me."

Taryn frowns. "I just think that sleeping in someone's room, in someone's bed, is more than kissing."

My cheeks heat, thinking of the way it had felt to wake up with his body stretched out beside mine. To get the attention off me, I start speculating about her. "Ooooh, maybe it's Prince Balekin. Are you going to marry Prince Balekin? Or perhaps it's Noggle and you can count the stars together."

She smacks me in the arm, a little too hard. "Stop guessing," she says. "You know I'm not allowed to say."

"Ow." I pick a white campion flower and stick it behind my ear.

"So you like him?" she asks. "Really like him?"

"Locke?" I ask. "Of course I do."

She gives me a look, and I wonder how much I worried her, not coming home the night before.

"Balekin I like less well," I say, and she rolls her eyes.

When we get back to the stronghold, I find that Madoc has left word he will be out until late. With little else to do for once, I look for Taryn, but although I saw her go upstairs just minutes before, she's not in her room. Instead, her dress is on the bed and her closet open, a few gowns hanging roughly, as though she pulled them out before finding them wanting.

Has she gone to meet her suitor? I take a turn around the room, trying to see it as a spy might, alert for signs of secrets. I notice nothing unusual but a few rose petals withering on her dressing table.

I go to my room and lie on my bed, going over my memories of the night before. Reaching into my pocket, I remove my knife to finally clean it. When I bring it out, I am holding the golden acorn, too. I turn the bauble over in my hand.

It's a solid lump of metal—a beautiful object. At first I take it only for that, before I notice the tiny lines running across it, tiny lines that seem to indicate moving parts. As though it were a puzzle.

I can't screw off the top, although I try. I can't seem to do anything else with it, either. I am about to give up and toss it onto my dressing table when I glimpse a tiny hole, so small as to be nearly invisible, right at the bottom. Hopping off my bed, I rattle through my desk, looking for a pin. The one I find has a pearl on one end. I try to fit the point into the acorn. It takes a moment, but I manage, pushing past resistance until I feel a click and it opens.

Mechanized steps swing out from a shining center, where a tiny golden bird rests. Its beak moves, and it speaks in a creaky little voice. *"My dearest friend, these are the last words of Liriope. I have three golden birds to scatter. Three attempts to get one into your hand. I am too far gone for any antidote, and so if you hear this, I leave you with the burden of my secrets and the last wish of my heart. Protect him. Take him far from the dangers of this Court. Keep him safe, and never, ever tell him the truth of what happened to me."*

Tatterfell comes into the room, bringing with her a tray with tea things. She tries to peek at what I am doing, but I cup my hand over the acorn.

When she goes out, I set down the bauble and pour myself a cup of tea, holding it to warm my hands. Liriope is Locke's mother. This seems like a message asking someone—her dearest friend—to spirit him—Locke—away. She calls the message her "last words," so she must have known she was about to die. Perhaps the acorns were to be sent to Locke's father, in the hopes Locke might spend the rest of his life exploring wild places with him rather than be caught up in intrigues.

But since Locke is still here, it seems as if none of the three acorns were found. Maybe none of them even left her bower.

I should give it to him, let him decide for himself what to do with it. But all I keep thinking about is the note on Balekin's desk, the note that seemed to implicate Balekin in Liriope's murder. Should I tell Locke everything?

I know the provenance of the blusher mushroom that you ask after, but what you do with it must not be tied to me.

I turn the words over in my mind the way I turned the acorn in my hand, and I feel the same seams.

There's something odd about that sentence.

I copy it out again on a piece of paper to be sure I remember it correctly. When I first read it, the note seemed to imply that Queen Orlagh had located a deadly poison for Balekin. But blusher mushrooms—while rare—grow wild, even on this island. I picked blusher mushrooms in the Milkwood, beside the black-thorned bees, who build their hives high in the trees (an antidote can be made with their honey, I learned recently from all my reading). Blusher mushrooms aren't dangerous if you don't drink the red liquid.

What if Queen Orlagh's note didn't mean that she'd *found* blusher mushrooms and she was going to give them to Balekin? What if by "know the provenance," Orlagh literally just meant that she *knew* where *particular* blusher mushrooms had come from? After all, she says "what you do with *it*" and not "what you do with *them*." She's cautioning him about what he's going to do with the knowledge, not the actual mushrooms.

Which means he's not going to poison Dain.

It also means that Balekin may have uncovered who'd caused Locke's mother's death, if he found out who had the blusher mushrooms that killed her. The answer could have been there, among the other papers that I, in my eagerness, had overlooked.

I have to go back. I have to get back into the tower. Today, before the coronation is any closer. Because maybe Balekin isn't going to try to kill Dain at all and the Court of Shadows has the wrong idea. Or, if they have the right idea, he isn't going to do it with blusher mushrooms.

Gulping down my tea, I find the servant garb in the back of my closet. I take down my hair and arrange it in an approximation of the rough braid that the girls in Balekin's house wore. I tuck my knife high on my thigh and shake out some of my silver box of salt into my pocket. Then I grab for my cloak, toe on my leather shoes, and am out the door, palms starting to sweat.

I have learned a lot more since my first foray into Hollow Hall, enough to make me understand better the risks I was taking. That does nothing for my nerves. Given what I saw of him with Cardan, I am not at all confident I could endure what Balekin would do to me if he caught me.

Taking a deep breath, I remind myself not to get caught.

That's what the Roach says a spy's real job is. The information is secondary. The job is not to get caught.

In the hall, I pass Oriana. She looks me up and down. I have to resist the urge to pull the cloak more tightly around myself. She is wearing a gown the color of unripe mulberries, and her hair is pulled slightly back. The very tips of her pointed ears are covered in shimmering crystal cuffs. I am a little envious of them. If I wore them, they'd disguise the human roundness of my own ears.

"You came home very late last night," she says, annoyance pulling at her mouth. "You missed dinner, and your father was expecting you to spar with him."

"I'll do better," I say, then instantly regret the declaration because I am probably not going to be back for dinner tonight, either. "Tomorrow. I'll start doing better tomorrow."

"Faithless creature," Oriana says, looking at me as though through the sheer intensity of her gaze she might ferret out my secrets. "You're scheming."

I am so tired of her suspicion, so very tired.

"You always think that," I say. "It's just that for once you're right." Leaving her to worry what that might mean, I go down the stairs and out onto the grass. This time, there's no one in my way, no one to make me reconsider what I am about to do.

I don't bring the toad this time; I am more careful. As I walk through the woods, I see an owl circling overhead. I pull the hood of my cape to cover my face.

At Hollow Hall, I stow my cloak outside between the logs of a woodpile and enter through the kitchens, where supper is being prepared. Squabs are lacquered with rose jelly, the smell of their crackling skin enough to make my mouth water and my stomach clench.

I open a cabinet and am greeted by a dozen candles, all of them the color of buffed leather and accented with a gold stamp of Balekin's personal crest—three laughing black birds. I take out nine candles and, trying to move as mechanically as possible, carry them past the guards. One guard gives me an odd look. I am sure there is something off about me, but he's seen my face before, and I am more sure-footed than last time.

At least until I see Balekin coming down the stairs.

He glances in my direction, and it is all I can do to keep my head down, my step even. I carry the candles into the room in front of me, which turns out to be the library.

To my immense relief, he doesn't seem to truly see me. My heart is speeding, though, my breaths coming too fast.

The servant girl who was cleaning the grate in Cardan's room is blurrily putting books back onto the shelves. She is as I remember her—cracked lips, thin, and bruise-eyed. Her movements are slow, as if the air were as thick as water. In her drugged dream, I am no more interesting than the furniture and of less consequence.

I scan the shelves impatiently, but I can see nothing useful. I need to get up to the tower, to go through all of Prince Balekin's correspondence and hope I find something to do with Locke's mother or Dain or the coronation, something I overlooked.

But I can't do anything with Balekin between me and the stairs.

I look at the girl again. I wonder what her life is like here, what she dreams of. If she ever, for a moment, had a chance to get away. At least, thanks to the geas, if Balekin did catch me, this could not be my fate.

I wait, counting to a thousand, while piling my candles on a chair. Then I look out. Thankfully, Balekin is gone. Quickly, I head up the stairs toward the tower. I hold my breath as I pass Cardan's door, but luck is with me. It is shut tight.

Then I am up the stairs and into Balekin's study. I note the herbs in the jars around the room, herbs I see with new eyes. A few are poisonous, but most are just narcotic. Nowhere do I see blusher mushrooms. I go to his desk and wipe my hands against the rough cloth of my dress, trying to leave no trace of sweat, trying to memorize the pattern of papers.

There are two letters from Madoc, but they just seem to be about which knights will be at the coronation and in what pattern around the central dais. There are others that seem to be about assignations, about revels and parties and debauches. Nothing about blusher mushrooms, nothing about poisons at all. Nothing about Liriope or murder. The only thing that seems even a little surprising is a bit of doggerel, a love poem in Prince Dain's hand, about a woman who remains unidentified, except by her "sunrise hair" and "starlit eyes."

Worse, nothing I can find tells me anything about a plan to move against Prince Dain. If Balekin is going to murder his brother, he's smart enough not to leave evidence lying around. Even the letter about the blusher mushroom is gone.

I have risked coming to Hollow Hall for nothing.

For a moment, I just stand there, trying to corral my thoughts. I need to leave without drawing attention to myself.

A messenger. I will disguise myself as a messenger. Messages run in and out of estates all the time. I take a blank sheet of paper and scrawl *Madoc* on one side, then seal the other with wax. The sulfur of the match hangs in the air for a moment. As it dissipates, I descend the steps, faked message in hand.

When I pass the library, I hesitate. The girl is still inside, mechanically lifting books from a pile and placing them on shelves. She will keep doing that until she's told to do something else, until she collapses, until she fades away, unremembered. As if she were nothing.

I cannot leave her here.

I don't have anything to go back to in the mortal world, but she might. And yes, it's a betrayal of Prince Dain's faith in me, a betrayal of Faerie itself. I know that. But all the same, I can't leave her.

There is a kind of relief in realizing it.

I walk into the library, setting down the note on a table. She does not turn, does not react at all. I reach into my pocket and cup a little salt in the center of my palm. I hold it out to her, the way I would if I were coaxing a horse with sugar.

"Eat this," I tell her in a low voice.

She turns toward me, although her gaze doesn't focus. "I'm not allowed," she says, voice rough with disuse. "No salt. You're not supposed to—"

I clap my hand over her mouth, some of the salt tipping out onto the ground, the rest pressed against her lips.

I am an idiot. An impulsive idiot.

Locking my arm around her, I drag her deeper into the library. She's alternating between trying to shout and trying to bite me. She keeps scratching at my arms, her nails digging into my skin. I hold her there, against the wall, until she sags, until the fight goes out of her.

"I'm sorry," I whisper as I hold on. "I'm winging it. I don't want to hurt you. I want to save you. Please, let me do this. Let me save you."

Finally, she has been still long enough that I take a chance and pull my hand away. She's panting, breaths coming fast. She doesn't scream, though, which seems like a good sign.

"We're getting out of here," I tell her. "You can trust me."

She gives me a look of blank incomprehension.

"Just act like everything's normal." I pull her to her feet and realize the impossibility of what I'm asking. Her eyes are rolling in her head like a mad pony. I don't know how long we have until she completely loses it.

Still, there is nothing for me to do but march her out of Hollow Hall as fast as I can. I stick my head into the main chamber. It's still empty, so I drag her from the library. She's looking around as though she's seeing the heavy wooden staircase and the gallery above for the first time. Then I remember I left my fake note on the table in the library.

"Hold on," I say. "I have to go back and—"

She makes a plaintive sound and pulls against my grip. I drag her along with me anyway and grab the message. I crumple it up and stuff it into my pocket. It's useless now, when the guards could recall it and connect a servant girl's disappearance to the household of the person who stole her. "What's your name?"

The girl shakes her head.

"You must remember it," I insist. It's terrible that instead of being sympathetic, I am annoyed. *Buck up*, I think. *Stop feeling your feelings. Let's go.*

"Sophie," she says in a kind of sob. Tears are starting in her eyes. I feel worse and worse still for how cruel I am about to be.

"You're not allowed to cry," I tell her as harshly as I can, hoping my tone will scare her into listening. I try my best to sound like Madoc, to sound as if I am used to having my commands obeyed. "You *must not cry*. I will slap you if I have to."

She cringes but subsides into silence. I wipe her eyes with the back of my hand. "Okay?" I ask her.

When she doesn't answer, I figure there's no more point in conversation. I steer her toward the kitchens. We'll have to pass by guards;

there's no other way out. She has pasted on a horrible rictus of a smile, but at least she has enough self-possession for that. More worrying is the way she can't stop staring at things. As we walk toward the guards, the intensity of her gaze is impossible to disguise.

I improvise, trying to sound as though I am reciting a memorized message, without inflection in the words. "Prince Cardan says we are to attend him."

One of the guards turns to the other. "Balekin won't like that."

I try not to react, but it's hard. I just stand there and wait. If they lunge at us, I am going to have to kill them.

"Very well," the first guard says. "Go. But inform Cardan that his brother demands he bring both of you back this time."

I don't like the sound of that.

The second guard glances over at Sophie and her wild eyes. "What do you see?"

I can feel her trembling beside me, her whole body shaking. I need to say something fast, before she does. "Lord Cardan told us to be more observant," I say, hoping that the plausible confusion of an ambiguous command will help to explain the way she's acting.

Then I walk on with Sophie through the kitchens, past the human servants I am not saving, aware of the futility of my actions. Does helping one person really matter, on balance?

Once I have power, I will find a way to help them all, I tell myself. And once Dain is in power, I will have power.

I make sure to keep my movements slow. I let myself breathe only when we've finally stepped outside.

And it turns out, even that's too soon. Cardan is riding toward us on a tall, dappled gray horse. Behind him is a girl on a palfrey—Nicasia. As soon as he gets inside, the guards will ask him about us. As soon as he gets inside, he will know something is wrong.

If he doesn't see me and know sooner than that.

What would be the punishment for stealing a prince's servant? I don't know. A curse perhaps, such as being turned into a raven and forced to fly north and live for seven times seven years in an ice palace—or worse, no curse at all. An execution.

It takes everything I've got not to break and run. It's not as though I think I could make it to the woods, especially not hauling a girl with me. He would ride us both down. "Stop staring," I hiss at Sophie, harsher than I mean to. "Look at your feet."

"Stop scolding me," she says, but at least she's not crying. I keep my head down and, looping her arm through mine, walk toward the woods.

Out of the corner of my eye, I see Cardan swing down from his saddle, black hair blown by the wind. He looks in my direction and pauses for a moment. I suck in my breath and don't run.

I can't run.

There is no thundering of hoofbeats, no racing to catch and punish us. To my immense relief, he seems to see only two servants heading toward the forest, perhaps to gather wood or berries or something.

The closer we get to the edge of the woods, the more each step feels fraught.

Then Sophie sinks to her knees, turning to look back at Balekin's manor. A keening sound comes from deep in her throat. "No," she says, shaking her head. "No no no no no. No. This isn't real. This didn't happen."

I jerk her up, digging my fingers into her armpit. "Move," I say. "Move or I will leave you here. Do you understand me? I will leave you, and Prince Cardan will find you and drag you back inside."

Cheating a glance back, I see him. He's off his horse and leading it to the stables. Nicasia still sits atop hers, her head tipped back, laughing at something he said. He's smiling, too, but it's not his usual sneer. He doesn't look like the wicked villain from a story. He looks like an inhuman boy out for a walk with his friend in the moonlight.

Sophie staggers onward. We can't get caught now, not when we're so close.

The moment when I cross into the pine-needle-strewn woods, I let out an enormous breath. I keep her moving until we reach the stream. I make her walk through it, though the cold water and sucking mud slows us down. Any way of hiding our tracks is worth doing.

Eventually, she sinks down on the bank and gives over to weeping. I watch her, wishing I knew what to do. Wishing I was a better, more sympathetic person, instead of being annoyed and worried that any delay is going to get us caught. I make myself sit on the remains of a termite-eaten log on the bank of the stream and let her cry, but when minutes have passed and her tears haven't stopped, I go over and kneel in the muddy grass.

"It's not far to my house," I say, trying to sound persuasive. "Just a little more walking."

"Shut up!" she shouts, lifting her hand to ward me off.

Frustration flares. I want to scream at her. I want to shake her. I bite my tongue and fist my hands to make myself stop.

"Okay," I say, taking a deep breath. "This is happening fast, I know. But I really do want to help you. I can get you out of Faerie. Tonight."

The girl is shaking her head again. "I don't know," she says. "I don't know. I was at Burning Man, and there was this guy who said he had this gig passing hors d'oeuvres for a rich weirdo in one of the air-conditioned tents. *Just don't take anything*, he told me. *If you do, you'll have to serve me for a thousand years. . . .*"

Her voice trails off, but now I see how she was trapped. It must have sounded like he was making a joke. She must have laughed, and he must have smiled. And then, whether she ate a single shrimp puff or pocketed some of the silverware—it would all be the same.

"It's okay," I say nonsensically. "It's going to be okay."

She looks at me and seems to see me for the first time, takes in that I am dressed like her, like a servant, but that there's something off about me. "Who are you? What is this place? What happened to us?"

I asked for her name, so I guess I should give her mine. "I'm Jude. I grew up here. One of my sisters, she can take you over the sea to the human town near here. From there, you can call someone to get you or you can go to the police and they'll find your people. This is almost over."

Sophie takes this in. "Is this some kind of—what happened? I remember things, impossible things. And I wanted. No, I couldn't have wanted . . ."

Her voice trails off, and I don't know what to say. I cannot guess the end of her sentence.

"Please, just tell me this isn't real. I don't think I can live with any of this being real." She's looking around the forest, as though if she can prove it isn't magic, then nothing else is, either. Which is stupid. All forests are magic.

"Come on," I say, because while I don't like the way she's talking, there's no point in lying for the sake of making her feel better. She's going to have to accept that she's been trapped in Faerie. It's not as if I have a boat to take her across the water; all I have are Vivi's ragwort steeds. "Can you walk a little farther now?" The faster she's back in the human world, the better.

As I get closer to Madoc's, I remember my cloak, still bunched up and hidden in a woodpile outside Hollow Hall, and curse myself all over again. Leading Sophie to the stables, I seat her in an empty stall. She slumps on the hay. I think the glimpse of the giant toad undid the last of her trust in me.

"Here we are," I say with forced cheerfulness. "I'm going inside to get my sister, and I want you to wait right here. Promise me."

She gives me a terrible look. "I can't do this. I can't face this."

"You have to." My voice comes out harsher than I intended. I stalk into the house and go up the steps as quickly as I can, hoping against hope that I don't run into anyone else on the way. I fling open the door to Vivienne's room without bothering to knock.

Vivi, thankfully, is lying on her bed, writing a letter in green ink with drawings of hearts and stars and faces in the margins. She looks up when I come in, tossing back her hair. "That's an interesting outfit you've got on."

"I did something really stupid," I say, out of breath.

That makes her push herself up, sliding off the bed and onto her feet. "What happened?"

"I stole a human girl—a human servant—from Prince Balekin, and I need you to help me get her back to the mortal world before anyone finds out." As I say this, I realize all over again how ridiculous it was for me to do that—how risky, how foolish. He will just find another human willing to make a bad bargain.

But Vivi doesn't chide me. "Okay, let me put on my shoes. I thought you were going to tell me you'd killed someone."

"Why would you think that?" I ask.

She snorts as she searches around for boots. Her eyes meet mine as she does up the laces. "Jude, you keep smiling a pleasant smile in front of Madoc, but all I can see anymore is bared teeth."

I am not sure what to say to that.

She puts on a long, fur-trimmed green coat with frog clasps. "Where is the girl?"

"In the stables," I say. "I'll take you—"

Vivi shakes her head. "Absolutely not. You have to get out of those clothes. Put on a dress and go down to dinner and make sure you act like everything's normal. If someone comes to question you, tell them you've been in your room this whole time."

"No one saw me!" I say.

Vivi gives me her best fish-eyed look. "No one? You're sure."

I think of Cardan, riding up as we made our escape, and of the guards, whom I'd lied to. "Probably no one," I amend. "No one who noticed anything." If Cardan had, he would never have let me get away. He would never have given up having that much power over me.

"Yeah, that's what I thought," she says, holding up a forbidding, long-fingered hand. "Jude, it isn't safe."

"I'm going," I insist. "The girl's name is Sophie, and she's really freaked out—"

Vivi snorts. "I bet."

"I don't think she'll go with you. You look like one of them." Maybe I am more afraid of my nerve running out than anything else. I worry about the adrenaline ebbing out of my body, leaving me to face the mad thing I have done. But given Sophie's suspicion of me, I absolutely think that Vivi's cat eyes would be enough to send her over the edge. "Because you *are* one of them."

"Are you telling me in case I forgot?" Vivi asks.

"We've got to go," I say. "And I am coming. We don't have time to debate this."

"Come, then," she says. Together, we go down the stairs, but as we are about to go out the door, she grabs my shoulder. "You can't save our mother, you know. She's already dead."

I feel as though she has slapped me.

"That's not—"

"Isn't it?" she demands. "Isn't that what you're doing? Tell me this girl isn't some stand-in for Mom. Some surrogate."

"I want to help Sophie," I say, shrugging off her grip. "Just Sophie."

Outside, the moon is high in the sky, turning the leaves silver. Vivi goes out to pick a bouquet of ragwort stalks. "Fine, then go get this Sophie."

She is where I left her, hunched in the hay, rocking back and forth and talking softly to herself. I am relieved to see her, relieved she didn't run off and we weren't even now tracking her through the forest, relieved that someone from Balekin's household hadn't ferreted out her location and hauled her away.

"Okay," I say with forced cheerfulness. "We're ready."

"Yes," she says, standing up. Her face is tearstained, but she's no longer crying. She looks like she's in shock.

"It's going to be okay," I tell her again, but she doesn't answer. She follows me mutely out behind the stables, where Vivi is waiting, along with two rawboned ponies with green eyes and lacy manes.

Sophie looks at them and then at Vivi. She begins to back away, shaking her head. When I come near her, she backs away from me, too.

"No, no, no," she says. "Please, no. No more. No."

"It's only a very little bit of magic," Vivi says reasonably, but it's still coming from someone with lightly furred points on her ears and eyes that flash gold in the dark. "Just a smidgen, and then you won't ever have to see another magical thing. You'll be back in the mortal world, the daylight world, the normal world. But this is the only way to get you there. We're going to fly."

"No," Sophie says, her voice coming out broken.

"Let's walk to the cliffside near here," I say. "You'll be able to see the lights—maybe even a few boats. You'll feel better when you can see a destination."

"We don't have a lot of time," Vivi reminds me with a significant look.

"It's not far," I argue. I don't know what else to do. The only other choices I can think of are knocking her unconscious or asking Vivi to glamour her; both are terrible.

And so we walk through the woods, ragwort steeds following. Sophie doesn't balk. The walk seems to calm her. She picks up rocks as we go, smooth stones that she dusts the dirt from and then puts in her pockets.

"Do you remember your life from before?" I ask her.

She nods and doesn't speak for a little while, but then she turns back to me. She gives a weird croaking laugh. "I always wanted there to be magic," she says. "Isn't that funny? I wanted there to be an Easter

Bunny and a Santa Claus. And Tinker Bell, I remember Tinker Bell. But I don't want it. I don't want it anymore."

"I know," I say. And I do. I have wished for many things over the years, but the first wish of my heart was that none of this was real.

At the water's edge, Vivi mounts one of the steeds and puts Sophie up before her. I swing up onto the back of the other. Sophie gives the forest a trembling look and then glances over at me. She doesn't seem afraid. She seems as though maybe she's starting to believe that the worst is behind her.

"Hold on tight," Vivi says, and her steed kicks up off the cliff and into the air. Mine follows. The wild exhilaration of flying hits me, and I grin with familiar delight. Beneath us are the whitecapped waves and ahead the shimmering lights of mortal towns, like a mysterious land strewn with stars. I glance over at Sophie, hoping to give her a reassuring smile.

Sophie isn't looking at me, though. Her eyes are closed. And then, as I am watching, she tilts to one side, lets go of the steed's mane, and lets herself fall. Vivi grabs for her, but it's too late. She is plunging soundlessly through the night sky, toward the mirrored darkness of the sea.

When she hits, there is barely even a splash.

I cannot speak. Everything seems to slow around me. I think of Sophie's cracked lips, think of her saying, *Please, just tell me this isn't real. I don't think I can live with any of this being real.*

I think of the stones she filled her pockets with.

I hadn't been listening. I hadn't wanted to hear her; I'd just wanted to save her.

And now, because of me, she is dead.

CHAPTER 18

I wake up groggy. I cried myself to sleep, and now my eyes are swollen and red, my head pounding. The whole previous night feels like a feverish, terrible nightmare. It doesn't seem possible that I snuck into Balekin's house and stole one of his servants. It seems even less possible that she preferred to drown than to live with the memories of Faerie. As I drink fennel tea and shrug on a doublet, Gnarbone comes to my door.

"Your pardon," he says with a short bow. "Jude must come immediately—"

Tatterfell waves him off. "She's not fit to see anyone right at the moment. I'll send her down when she's dressed."

"Prince Dain awaits her downstairs in General Madoc's parlor. He commanded me to fetch her and not to mind whatever state of dishabille she was in. He said to carry her if I had to." Gnarbone seems repentant at having to say that, but it's clear that none of us can refuse the Crown Prince.

Cold dread coils in my stomach. How did I not think that he of all people, with his spies, would find out what I'd done? I wipe my hands against my velvet top. Despite his order, I pull on pants and boots before I go. No one stops me. I am vulnerable enough; I will keep what dignity I can.

Prince Dain is standing near the window, behind Madoc's desk. His back is to me, and my gaze goes automatically to the sword hanging from his belt, visible beneath his heavy wool cloak. He does not turn when I come in.

"I have done wrong," I say. I am glad he stays where he is. It's easier to speak when he's not looking at me. "And I will repent in whatever way—"

He turns, his face full of a wild rage that makes me suddenly see his resemblance to Cardan. His hand comes down hard on Madoc's desk, rocking everything atop it. "Have I not taken you into my service and given you a great boon? Did I not promise you a place in my Court? And yet—*and yet*, you use what I have taught you to endanger my plans."

My gaze goes to the floor. He has the power to do anything to me. Anything. Not even Madoc could stop him—nor do I think he would try. And not only have I disobeyed him, I have declared my loyalty to something completely separate from him. I have helped a mortal girl. I have acted like a mortal.

I bite my bottom lip to keep from begging for his forgiveness. I cannot allow myself to speak.

"The boy wasn't as badly hurt as he might have been, but with the right knife—a longer knife—the strike would have been lethal. Do not think I don't know you were going for that worse strike."

I look up, suddenly, too surprised to hide it. We look at each other for several uncomfortable moments. I stare into the silvered gray of his eyes, taking note of the way his brows furrow, forming deep, displeased lines. I note all this to avoid thinking of how I almost gave away an even greater crime than the one he's discovered.

"Well?" he demands. "Had you no plan for being found out?"

"He tried to glamour me into jumping out of the tower," I say.

"And so he knows you can't be glamoured. Worse and worse." He comes around the desk toward me. "You are my creature, Jude Duarte. You will strike only when I tell you to strike. Otherwise, stay your hand. Do you understand?"

"No," I say automatically. What he's asking is ridiculous. "Was I supposed to just let him hurt me?"

If he knew all the things I'd really done, he would be even angrier than he is.

He slams a dagger down on Madoc's desk. "Pick it up," he says, and I feel the compulsion of a glamour. My fingers close on the hilt. A kind of haziness comes over me. I both know and don't know what I am doing.

"In a moment, I am going to ask you to put the blade through your hand. When I ask you to do that, I want you to remember where your bones are, where your veins are. I want you to stab through your hand doing the least damage possible." His voice is lulling, hypnotic, but my heart speeds anyway.

Against my will, I aim the sharp point of the knife. I press it lightly against my skin. I am ready.

I hate him, but I am ready. I hate him, and I hate myself.

"Now," he says, and the glamour releases me. I take a half step back.

I am in control of myself again, still holding the knife. He was about to make—

"Do not disappoint me," Prince Dain says.

I realize all at once that I have not gotten a reprieve. He hasn't released me because he wants to spare me. He could glamour me again, but he won't because he wants me to stab myself willingly. He wants me to prove my devotion, blood and bone. I hesitate—of course I hesitate. This is absurd. This is awful. This isn't how people show loyalty. This is epic, epic bullshit.

"Jude?" he asks. I cannot tell if this is a test he expects me to pass or one he wants me to fail. I think of Sophie at the bottom of the sea, her pockets full of stones. I think of the satisfaction on Valerian's face when he told me to jump from the tower. I think of Cardan's eyes, daring me to defy him.

I have tried to be better than them, and I have failed.

What could I become if I stopped worrying about death, about pain, about anything? If I stopped trying to belong?

Instead of being afraid, I could become something to fear.

My eyes on him, I slam the knife into my hand. The pain is a wave that rises higher and higher but never crashes. I make a sound low in my throat. I may not deserve punishment for this, but I deserve punishment.

Dain's expression is odd, blank. He takes a step back from me, as though I am the one who did the shocking thing instead of merely doing what he ordered. Then he clears his throat. "Do not reveal your skill with a blade," he says. "Do not reveal your mastery over glamour. Do not reveal all that you can do. Show your power by appearing powerless. That is what I need from you."

"Yes," I gasp, and draw the blade out again. Blood runs over Madoc's desk, more than I expect. I feel suddenly dizzy.

"Wipe it up," he says. His jaw is set. Whatever surprise he felt seems gone, replaced by something else.

There is nothing to clean the desk with but the hem of my doublet.

"Now give me your hand." Reluctantly, I hold it out to him, but all he does is take it gently and wrap it in a green cloth from his pocket. I try to flex my fingers and nearly pass out from pain. The fabric of the makeshift bandage is already turning dark. "Once I am gone, go to the kitchens and put moss on it."

I nod again. I am not sure I can translate my thoughts into speech. I am afraid I am not going to be able to stand much longer, but I lock my knees and stare at the notch of chipped wood on Madoc's desk where the tip of the blade hit, stained a bright but fading red.

The door to the study swings open, startling us both. Prince Dain drops my hand, and I shove it into my pocket, the pain of which nearly staggers me. Oriana stands there, a wooden tray in her hands with a steaming pot and three clay cups atop it. She is dressed in a day gown the vivid hue of unripe persimmons. "Prince Dain," she says, making a pretty bow. "The servants said you were sequestered with Jude, and I told them they had to be mistaken. Surely, with your coronation so close, your time is too valuable for a silly girl to take up so much of it. You do her too much credit, and no doubt the weight of your regard is quite overwhelming."

"No doubt," he says, giving her a tooth-gritting smile. "I have tarried too long."

"Take some tea before you leave us," she says, putting down the tray on Madoc's desk. "We could all have a cup and speak together. If Jude has done something to offend you..."

"Your pardon," he says, not particularly kindly. "But your reminder of my duties spurs me to immediate action."

He brushes past Oriana, looking back at me once before stalking off. I have no idea whether I passed the test or not. But either way, he does not trust me as he once did. I have thrown that away.

I don't trust him as much, either.

"Thank you," I say to Oriana. I am shivering all over.

She doesn't scold me, for once. She doesn't say anything. Her hands come down lightly on my shoulders, and I lean against her. The scent of crushed verbena is in my nose. I close my eyes and drink in the familiar smell. I am desperate. I will take any comfort there is, any comfort at all.

I do not think of lessons or lectures. Shaking all over, I go straight back to my room and climb into bed. Tatterfell strokes my hair briefly, as though I am a drowsy cat, and then returns to the task of sorting my dresses. My new gown is scheduled to arrive later today, and the coronation will begin the day after. Dain's being named as the High King will kick off a month of revelry, while the moon wanes and then swells anew.

My hand hurts so much that I cannot bear to put moss on it. I just cradle it against my chest.

It throbs, the pain coming in staggering pulses, like a second, ragged heartbeat. I cannot bring myself to do more than lie there and wait for it to ebb. My thoughts drift dizzily.

Somewhere out there, all the lords and ladies and lieges ruling over far-flung Courts are arriving to pay their respects to the new High King. Night Courts and Bright Courts, Free Courts, and Wild Courts. The High King's subjects and the Courts with which there are truces, however wobbly. Even Orlagh's Court of the Undersea will be in attendance. Many will pledge themselves to faithfully accept the new High King's judgment in exchange for his wisdom and protection. Pledge to defend him and avenge him, if need be. Then all will show their respect by partying their hardest.

I'll be expected to party along with them. A month of dancing and feasting and boozing and riddling and dueling.

For that, each of my best dresses must be dusted off, pressed, and refreshed. Tatterfell sews on cunning cuffs made from the scales of pinecones around the edges of frayed sleeves. Small tears in skirts are stitched over with embroidery in the shape of leaves and pomegranates and—on one—a cavorting fox. She has stitched dozens of leather slippers for me. I will be expected to dance so fiercely that I wear through a pair every night.

At least Locke will be there to dance with me. I try to concentrate on the memory of his amber eyes instead of the pain in my hand.

As Tatterfell moves around the room, my eyes close, and I fall into a strange, fitful sleep. When I wake, it's full night, and I am sweaty all over. I feel oddly calm, though, tears and panic and pain somehow smoothed over. The agony of my hand has turned into a dull throb.

Tatterfell is gone. Vivi is sitting at the end of my bed, her cat eyes catching moonlight and shining chartreuse.

"I came to see if you were well," she says. "Except that of course you're not."

I force myself to sit up again, using only one of my hands. "I'm sorry—what I asked you to do. I shouldn't have. I put you in danger."

"I am your elder sister," she says. "You don't need to protect me from my own decisions."

After Sophie plunged into the water, Vivi and I spent the hours until dawn diving into the icy sea, calling for Sophie, trying to find some trace of her. We swam under the black water and screamed her name until our throats were hoarse.

"Still," I say.

"*Still*," she echoes fiercely. "I wanted to help. I wanted to help that girl."

"Too bad we didn't." The words catch in my throat.

Vivienne shrugs, and I am reminded of how, despite her being my sister, we differ in ways that are hard to comprehend. "You did a brave thing. Be glad of that. Not everyone can be brave. I'm not always."

"What do you mean? The whole 'not telling Heather what's really going on'?"

She makes a face at me but smiles, clearly grateful I am speaking of something less dire—and yet both of our thoughts went from one dead mortal girl to her beloved, also mortal. "We were lying in bed together a few days ago," Vivi says. "And she started tracing the shape of my ear. I thought she was going to ask something that would give me an opening, but she just told me my ear modding was really good. Did you know there are mortals who cut human ears and sew them so they heal pointed?"

I am not surprised. I understand longing for ears like hers. I feel like I have spent half my life wanting them, with their delicate, furred points.

What I do not say is this: No one could touch those ears and believe they were made by anything other than nature. Heather is either lying to Vivi or lying to herself.

"I don't want her to be afraid of me," Vivi says.

I think of Sophie, and I am sure Vivi is thinking of her, too, pockets full of stones. Sophie at the bottom of the sea. Perhaps she is not so unaffected by what happens as she wants to seem.

From downstairs, I hear Taryn's voice. "They're here! Our dresses! Come look!"

Slipping off my bed, Vivi smiles at me. "At least we had an adventure. And now we're going to have another one."

I let her go ahead, as I need to cover my bandaged hand with a glove before I follow her down the stairs. I press a button, ripped from a coat, over the wound to divert direct pressure. Now I have to hope that the bulge on my palm isn't too noticeable.

Our gowns have been spread out over three chairs and a sofa in Oriana's salon. Madoc is patiently listening to her rhapsodize over the perfection of their garments. Her ball gown is the exact pink of her eyes, deepening to red, and seems to be made of enormous petals that spread into a train. The fabric of Taryn's is gorgeous, the cut of her mantua and stomacher perfect. Beside them is Oak's sweet little suit of clothes, and there are a doublet and cape for Madoc in his favorite shade of crusted-blood red. Vivi holds up her silvery gray dress, with its tattered edges, sparing a smile for me.

Across the room, I see my gown. Taryn gasps when I lift it up.

"That's not what you ordered," she says, accusatory. As though somehow I have deliberately deceived her.

It's true that the dress I am holding is not the one that Brambleweft sketched for me. It's something else entirely, something that reminds me of the mad, amazing garments that Locke's mother's closet was stuffed with. An ombré ball gown, its color deepening from white near my throat, through palest blue to deepest indigo at my feet. Over that is stitched the stark outlines of trees, the way I see them from my window as dusk is falling. The seamstress has even sewn on little crystal beads to represent stars.

This is a dress I could never have imagined, one so perfect that for a moment, looking at it, I can think of nothing but its beauty.

"I—I don't think this is mine," I say. "Taryn's right. It doesn't look anything like the sketches."

"It's still lovely," Oriana says consolingly, as though I am displeased. "And it had your name pinned to it."

I am glad no one is making me give it back. I do not know why I was given such a dress, but if there's any way I can fit into it, I will.

Madoc raises his brows. "We will all look magnificent." When he walks past, departing the salon, he ruffles my hair. In moments like these, it is almost possible to think there is no river of spilled blood between us all.

Oriana claps her hands together. "Girls, come here for a moment. Attend me."

We three arrange ourselves on the couch beside her, waiting, puzzled.

"Tomorrow, you will be among the Gentry from many different Courts. You've been under Madoc's protection, but that protection will be unknown to most of the Folk in attendance. You must not allow yourselves to be lured into making bargains or promises that can be used against you. And, above all, give no insult that might excuse a trespass of hospitality. Do not be foolish, and do not put yourself in anyone's power."

"We are never foolish," Taryn says, a blatant lie if ever there was one.

Oriana makes a pained face. "I would keep you from the revels, but Madoc has specifically instructed that you participate in them. So heed my advice. Be careful, and perhaps you will find ways to be pleasing."

I should have expected this—more cautions, another lecture. If she does not trust us to behave at a revel, she certainly will not trust us at a coronation. We rise, dismissed, and she takes each of us in turn, pressing her chilly mouth against our cheeks. My kiss comes last.

"Do not aspire above your station," she says softly to me.

For a moment, I don't understand why she would say that. Then, horrified, I get her meaning. After this afternoon, she thinks I am Prince Dain's lover.

"I'm not," I blurt out. Of course, Cardan would say that *everything* I've got is above my station.

She takes my hand, her expression pitying.

"I am only thinking of your future," Oriana says, voice still soft. "Those close to the throne are seldom truly close to anyone else. A mortal girl would have even fewer allies."

I nod as though giving in to her wise advice. If she doesn't believe me, then the easiest thing is to go along with her. I guess it makes more sense than the truth—that Dain has selected me to be part of his nest of thieves and spies.

Something about my expression causes her to catch both of my hands. I wince at the pressure on my wound. "Before I was Madoc's wife, I was one of the consorts to the King of Elfhame. Hear me, Jude. It is no easy thing to be the lover of the High King. It is to always be in danger. It is to always be a pawn."

I must be gaping at her, as shocked as I am. I never wondered about her life before she came to us. Suddenly, Oriana's fears for us make a different kind of sense; she was used to playing by an entirely different set of rules. The floor seems to have tilted beneath my feet. I do not know the woman in front of me, do not know what she suffered before coming to this house, no longer even know how she really came to be Madoc's wife. Did she love him, or was she making a clever marriage, to gain his protection?

"I didn't know," I say stupidly.

"I never gave Eldred a child," she tells me. "But another of his lovers nearly did. When she died, rumor pointed to one of the princes poisoning her, just to prevent competition for the throne." Oriana watches my face with her pale pink eyes. I know she's talking about Liriope. "You don't need to believe me. There are a dozen more rumors just as terrible. When there is a lot of power concentrated in one place, there are plenty of scraps to fight over. If the Court isn't busy drinking poison, then it's drinking bile. You wouldn't be well suited to it."

"What makes you think that?" I ask, her words annoyingly close to Madoc's when he dismissed my chances at knighthood. "Maybe it would suit me just fine."

Her fingers brush my face again, stroking back my hair. It should be a tender gesture, but it's an evaluating one instead. "He must have loved your mother very much," she says. "He's besotted with you girls. If I were him, I would have sent you away a long time ago."

I don't doubt that.

"If you go to Prince Dain despite my warning, if he gets his heir on you, tell no one before you tell me. Swear it on your mother's grave." I feel her nails as her hand comes to rest against the back of my neck and wince. "No one. Do you understand?"

"I promise." This is one vow I should have no trouble keeping. I try to give the words weight, so she'll believe I mean it. "Seriously. I promise."

She releases me. "You may go. Rest well, Jude. When you rise, the coronation will be upon us, and there will be little time left for resting."

I curtsy and take my leave.

In the hall, Taryn is waiting for me. She sits on a bench carved with coiled serpents and swings her feet. As the door closes, she looks up. "What was going on with her?"

I shake my head, trying to rid myself of a jumble of feelings. "Did you know she used to be the High King's consort?"

Taryn's eyebrows go up, and she snorts, delighted. "No. Is that what she told you?"

"Pretty much." I think of Locke's mother and the singing bird in the acorn, of Eldred on his throne, head bowed by his own crown. It is hard for me to picture him taking lovers, no less the quantity he must have taken to have so many children, an unnatural number for a Faerie. And yet, perhaps that's just a failure of my imagination.

"Huh." Taryn looks as though she's having the same failure of imagination. She frowns, puzzling for a moment, then seems to remember what she'd waited to ask me. "Do you know why Prince Balekin was here?"

"He was here?" I am not sure I can weather more surprises. "Here, in the house?"

She nods. "He arrived with Madoc, and they were shut up in his office for hours."

I wonder how long they arrived after Prince Dain's departure. Hopefully, long enough for Prince Dain not to overhear anything about a missing servant. My hand throbs whenever I move it, but I am just glad I can move it at all. I am not eager to face any more punishment.

And yet Madoc didn't seem angry with me just now when he saw me with my dress. He seemed normal, pleased even. Perhaps they were conferring about other things.

"Weird," I say to Taryn, because I am commanded not to tell her about being a spy and I cannot bring myself to tell her about Sophie.

I am glad that the coronation is nearly here. I want it to come and sweep everything else away.

That night, I drowse in my bed, fully dressed, waiting for the Ghost. I have bagged out on lessons for two nights straight—the night of Locke's party and last night, searching the water for Sophie. He's bound to be annoyed when he comes.

I put that as far out of my head as I can and concentrate on resting. Breathing in and out.

When I first came to Faerie, I had trouble sleeping. You'd think I'd have had nightmares, but I don't remember many. My dreams struggled to rival the horror of my actual life. Instead, I couldn't calm down enough to rest. I would toss and turn all night and all morning, my heart racing, finally falling into a headachy sleep in the late afternoon, when the rest of Faerie was just rising. I took to wandering the corridors of the house like a restless spirit, thumbing through ancient books, moving around the game pieces on the Fox and Geese board, toasting cheese in the kitchens, and staring at Madoc's blood-soaked cap, as though it contained the answers to the universe in its tide lines. One of the hobs who used to work here, Nell Uther, would find me and guide me back to my room, telling me that if I couldn't sleep, then I ought to just close my eyes and lie still. That at least my body could rest, even if my mind wouldn't.

I am lying like that when I hear a rustling on the balcony. I turn, fully expecting to see the Ghost. I am about to tease him for actually making a sound when I realize the person rattling the doors isn't the Ghost at all. It's Valerian, and he has a long, curving knife in one hand and a smile every bit as sharp pulling at his mouth.

"What…" I scramble into a sitting position. "What are you doing here?"

I realize that I am whispering, as though *I* am afraid of *his* being discovered.

You are my creature, Jude Duarte. You will strike only when I tell you to strike. Otherwise, stay your hand.

At least Prince Dain didn't glamour me to obey those orders.

"Why shouldn't I be here?" Valerian asks me, striding closer. He smells like pinesap and burned hair, and there is a light dusting of golden powder streaked over one cheek. I am not sure where he's been before this, but I don't think he's sober.

"This is my home." I am prepared for training with the Ghost. I have a knife in my boot and another at my hip, but thinking of Dain's command, thinking of how not to disappoint him further, I reach for neither. I am flummoxed by Valerian's being here, in my room.

He walks up to my bed. He's holding the knife well enough, but I can tell he's not particularly practiced with it. He is no general's son. "*None of this is your home,*" he tells me, voice shaking with anger.

"If Cardan put you up to this, you should really rethink your relationship," I say, finally, now, afraid. By some miracle, my voice stays steady. "Because if I scream, there are guards in the hall. They'll come. They've got big, pointy swords. Huge. Your friend is going to get you killed."

Show your power by appearing powerless.

He doesn't seem to be absorbing my words. His eyes are wild, red-rimmed, and not entirely focused on me. "Do you know what he said when I told him you'd stabbed me? He told me it was no more than I deserved."

That's impossible; Valerian must have misunderstood. Cardan must have been mocking him for letting me under his guard.

"What did you expect?" I ask him, trying to hide my surprise. "I don't know if you noticed, but the guy is a real jerk."

If Valerian wasn't sure he wanted to stab me before, he's sure now. With a leap, he slams the blade into the mattress as I roll out of the way and onto my feet. Goose feathers fly up when he draws back the blade, drifting through the air like snow. He scrambles to his feet as I pull out a dagger of my own.

Do not reveal your skill with a blade. Do not reveal your mastery over glamour. Do not reveal all that you can do.

Little did Prince Dain know that my real skill lies in pissing people off.

Valerian advances on me again. He's intoxicated and furious and not all that well trained, but he's one of the Folk, born with their cat reflexes and blessed with height that gives him better reach. My heart is hammering in my chest. I should scream for help. I should scream.

I open my mouth, and he lunges at me. The scream comes out as a whuff of breath as I lose my balance. My shoulder hits the floor hard as I roll again. I am practiced enough that despite my surprise, I kick his knife hand when he comes toward me. The blade skitters across the floor.

"Okay," I say, as though I am trying to calm us both down. "Okay."

He doesn't pause. Even though I am holding a knife, even though I've avoided his attacks twice and disarmed him, even though I've stabbed him once before, he grabs for my throat again. His fingers sink into the flesh of my neck, and I remember how it felt to have fruit jammed into my mouth, soft flesh parting against my teeth. I remember choking on nectar and pulp as the horrible bliss of the everapple stole over me, robbing me of caring even that I was dying. He'd wanted to watch me die, wanted to watch me fight for breath the way I am fighting for it now. I look into his eyes and find the same expression there.

You are nothing. You barely exist at all. Your only purpose is to create more of your kind before you die.

He's wrong about me. I am going to make my mayfly life count for something.

I won't be afraid of him or of Prince Dain's censure. If I cannot be better than them, I will become so much worse.

Despite his fingers against my windpipe, despite the way my vision has begun to go dark around the edges, I make sure of my strike before I drive my knife into his chest. Into his heart.

Valerian rolls off me, making a gurgling sound. I suck in lungfuls of air. He tries to stand, sways, and falls back to his knees. Looking over at him dizzily, I see the hilt of my knife is sticking out of his chest. The red velvet of his doublet is turning a deeper, wetter red.

He reaches for the blade as though to draw it out.

"Don't," I say automatically, because that will only make the wound worse. I grab for anything nearby—there is a discarded petticoat on the floor that I can use to stanch the blood. He slides down onto his side, away from me, and sneers, although he can barely open his eyes.

"You've got to let me—" I start.

"I curse you," Valerian whispers. "I curse you. Three times, I curse you. As you've murdered me, may your hands always be stained with blood. May death be your only companion. May you—" He breaks off abruptly, coughing. When he stops, he doesn't stir. His eyes stay as they are, half-lidded, but the gleam has gone out of them.

My wounded hand flies to cover my mouth in horror at the curse, as though to stop a scream, but I don't scream. I haven't screamed this whole time, and I am not going to start now, when there's nothing more to scream about.

As minutes slip by, I just sit there beside Valerian, watching the skin of his face grow paler as the blood no longer pumps to it, watching his lips go a kind of greenish blue. He doesn't die very differently than mortals, although I am sure it would gall him to know that. He might have lived for a thousand years, if it wasn't for me.

My hand hurts worse than ever. I must have banged it in the fight.

I look around and catch my own reflection in the mirror across the room: a human girl, hair tousled, eyes feverish, a pool of blood forming at her feet.

The Ghost is coming. He'd know what to do with a dead body. He has certainly killed people before. But Prince Dain is already angry with me just for stabbing the child of a well-favored member of his Court. Killing that same child the night before Dain's coronation won't go over well. The last people I need to know about this are the Court of Shadows.

No, I need to hide the body myself.

I scan the room, hoping for inspiration, but the only place I can think of that will even conceal him temporarily is beneath my bed. I spread the petticoat next to Valerian's body and then roll him onto it. I feel a little queasy. His body is still warm. Ignoring that, I drag him over to the bed and push him and all the skirts under, first with my hands and then with my feet.

Only a smear of blood remains. I get the pitcher of water near the bedpan and splash some on the wooden planks of the floor and then some on my face. My good hand is shaking as I finish wiping up, and I sink to the floor, both hands in my hair.

I am not okay.

I am not okay.

I am not okay.

But when the Ghost arrives on my balcony, he can't tell, and that's the important thing.

CHAPTER 19

That night, the Ghost shows me how to climb far higher than the landing where Taryn and I tarried the last time. We climb all the way up to the rafters above the great hall and perch on heavy wooden beams. They are coiled around with a lattice of roots, which sometimes form the shapes of cages, sometimes balconies, and sometimes what appear more like tightropes. Beneath us, the preparations for the coronation go on. Blue velvet and hammered silver and braided gold tablecloths are rolled out, each one decorated with the House of Greenbriar's standard, a tree of flowers, thorns, and roots.

"Do you think things will be better after Prince Dain becomes the High King?" I ask him.

The Ghost gives me a vague smile and shakes his head sadly. "Things will be as they always are," he tells me. "Only more so."

I don't know what that means, but it's a fey enough answer that I figure I am unlikely to get more out of him. I think of Valerian's body under my bed. The Folk do not rot the way mortals do. Sometimes their bodies grow over with lichen or bloom with mushrooms. I've heard stories about battlefields turning into green hills. I wish I could go back and find that he'd turned into mulch, but I doubt I will be that lucky.

I shouldn't be thinking about his body; I should be thinking about *him*. I should be worrying over more than getting caught.

We walk across roots and beams, unnoticed, jumping silently high above swarms of liveried servants. I turn to the Ghost, watching his calm face and the expert way he places each foot. I try to do the same. I try not to use my sore hand for anything more than balance. He seems to notice, but he doesn't ask. Maybe he already knows what happened.

"Now wait," he says as we settle onto a heavy beam.

"For anything in particular?" I ask.

"I have word that a messenger is coming from Balekin's estate, disguised in the High King's livery," he says. "We're to kill it before it enters the royal quarters."

The Ghost says this without particular emotion. I wonder how long he has worked for Dain. I wonder if Dain ever asked him to drive a knife through his palm, if he tested them all that way, or if that was a special test, just for mortals.

"Is the messenger going to assassinate Prince Dain?" I ask.

"Let's not find out," he says.

Below me, spun-sugar creations are being finished off with high crystalline spires. Apples painted with nevermore are piled on the banquet tables in such quantity as to send half the Court dreaming.

I think of Cardan's mouth, flaked with gold. "Are you sure they're coming this way?"

"I am," he says, and no more than that.

So we wait, and I try not to fidget as minutes slide into hours, moving just enough to keep my muscles from stiffening. This is part of my training—probably the aspect the Ghost thinks is most essential, after slyfooting. He has told me again and again that most of being a killer and a thief is waiting. The hardest thing, according to him, is not letting your mind drift to other things. He seems to be right. Up here, watching the ebb and flow of the servants, my thoughts turn to the coronation, to the drowned girl, to Cardan riding up on his horse as I fled Hollow Hall, to Valerian's frozen, dying smile.

I wrench my thoughts back to the present. Beneath me, a creature with a long, hairless tail that drags in the dirt scuttles across the ground. For a moment, I think it is part of the kitchen staff. But the bag it carries is too filthy, and there is something subtly wrong with its livery. It isn't dressed like one of Balekin's servants, and neither is its uniform the same as the other palace staff.

I glance over at the Ghost.

"Good," he says. "Now shoot."

My hands feel sweaty as I draw out the miniature crossbow, seeking to steady it against my arm. I have grown up in a house of butchery. I have trained for this. My principal childhood memory is of bloodshed. I have killed already tonight. And yet, for a moment, I am not sure I can do it.

You're no killer.

I take a breath and loose the bolt. My arm spasms from the recoil. The creature topples over, a flailing arm sending a pyramid of golden apples spilling to the dirt. I press myself down against a thick cluster of roots, camouflaging myself as I've been taught. Servants scream, looking around for the shooter.

Next to me, the Ghost has a smile on the corner of his mouth. "Was that your first?" he asks me. And then when I look at him blankly, he clarifies. "Have you ever killed anyone before?"

May death be your only companion.

I shake my head, not trusting myself to speak the lie out loud convincingly.

"Sometimes mortals throw up. Or cry," he says, clearly pleased I am doing neither of those things. "It shouldn't shame you."

"I feel fine," I say, taking a deep breath and fitting a new bolt into the bow.

What I feel is a kind of nervous adrenaline-soaked readiness. I seem to have passed some kind of threshold. Before, I never knew how far I would go. Now I believe I have the answer. I will go as far as there is to go. I will go way too far.

He raises both brows. "You're good at this. Nice marksmanship and a stomach for violence."

I am surprised. The Ghost is not given to compliments.

I have vowed to become worse than my rivals. Two murders completed in a single night mark a descent I should be proud of. Madoc could not have been more wrong about me.

"Most of the children of the Gentry don't have the patience," he says. "And they're not used to getting their hands dirty."

I do not know what to say to that, with Valerian's curse fresh in my mind. Maybe there's something broken in me from watching my parents being murdered. Maybe my messed-up life turned me into someone capable of doing messed-up things. But another part of me wonders if I was raised by Madoc in the family business of bloodshed. Am I like this because of what he did to my parents or because he was my parent?

May your hands always be stained with blood.

The Ghost reaches out to grab my wrist, and before I can snatch it back, he points to the pale half moons at the base of my nails. "Speaking of hands, I can see what you've been doing in the discoloration of your fingers. The blue cast. I can smell it in your sweat, too. You've been poisoning yourself."

I swallow, and then, because there's no reason to deny it, I nod.

"Why?" The thing I like about the Ghost is that I can tell he's not asking to set me up for a lecture. He just seems curious.

I am not sure how to explain it. "Being mortal means I have to try harder."

The Ghost studies my face. "Someone's really sold you a bill of goods. Plenty of mortals are better at plenty of stuff than the Folk. Why do you think we steal them away?"

It takes me a moment to realize he's serious. "So I could be…?" I can't finish the sentence.

He snorts. "Better than me? Don't press your luck."

"That's not what I was going to say," I protest, but he only grins. I look down. The body is still lying there. A few knights have gathered around it. As soon as they move the body, we will move, too. "I just need to be able to vanquish my enemies. That's all."

He looks surprised. "Do you have a lot of enemies, then?" I am sure he imagines me among the children of the Gentry, with their soft hands and velvet skirts. He thinks of little cruelties, small slights, minor snubs.

"Not many," I say, thinking of the lazy, hateful look Cardan gave me by torchlight in the hedge maze. "But they're quality."

When the knights finally bear the body away and no one is searching for us anymore, the Ghost leads me across the roots again. We slip through corridors until he can get close enough to the messenger bag to light-finger the papers inside. Up close, though, I realize something that chills my blood. The messenger was disguised. The creature is female, and while her tail is fake, her long parsnip nose is entirely real. She's one of Madoc's spies.

The Ghost tucks the note into his jacket and doesn't unroll it until we're out in the woods, with only moonlight to see by. When he looks, though, his expression turns stony. He's gripping the paper so hard it's crinkling in his fingers.

"What does it say?" I ask.

He turns the page toward me. There, six words are scrawled: KILL THE BEARER OF THIS MESSAGE.

"What does that mean?" I ask, feeling sick.

The Ghost shakes his head. "It means that Balekin set us up. Come on. We need to go."

He pulls me along into the shadows, and together we slink away. I do not tell the Ghost that I thought she worked for Madoc. Instead, I try to puzzle through things myself. But I have too few pieces.

What does the murder of Liriope have to do with the coronation? What does Madoc have to do with any of this? Could his spy have been a double agent, working for Balekin as well as Madoc? If so, does that mean she was stealing information from my household?

"Someone is trying to distract us," the Ghost says. "While they set their trap. Be alert tomorrow."

The Ghost doesn't give me any more specific orders, doesn't even tell me to stop taking my tiny doses of poison. He doesn't direct me to do anything differently; he leads me home to catch scraps of sleep just after dawn. As we're about to part, I want to stop and throw myself on his mercy. *I've done a terrible thing,* I want to say. *Help me with the body. Help me.*

But we all want stupid things. That doesn't mean we should have them.

I bury Valerian near the stables, but outside the paddock, so that even the most carnivorous of Madoc's sharp-toothed horses are unlikely to dig him up and gnaw on his bones.

It's not easy to bury a body. It's especially not easy to bury a body without your whole household finding out. I must roll Valerian onto my balcony and hurl him into the brush below. Then, one-handed, I must drag him away from the house. I am straining and sweating by the time I get to a likely plot of dew-covered grass. Newly woken birds call to one another beneath the brightening sky.

For a moment, all I want to do is lie down myself.

But I still have to dig.

The next afternoon is a sleep-deprived blur of being painted and braided, corseted and cinched. Three fat gold earrings run up the side of one of Madoc's green ears, and he wears long gold claws over his fingers. Oriana looks like a rose in bloom beside him, wearing a massive necklace of rough-cut green emeralds at her throat, large enough to nearly count as armor.

In my room, I unwrap my hand. It looks worse than I had hoped—wet and sticking instead of scabbed over. Swollen. I finally take Dain's advice and get some moss from the kitchens, wash the wound, and rewrap it with my makeshift button brace. I wasn't planning to wear gloves to the coronation, but I don't have much choice. Hunting around in my drawers, I find a set in a dark blue silk and draw them on.

I imagine Locke taking my hands tonight, imagine him sweeping me around the hill. I hope I can avoid flinching if he presses on my palm. I can never let him guess what happened to Valerian. No matter how much he likes me, he wouldn't like kissing the person who put his friend in the ground.

My sisters and I pass one another in the hall as we dart around, grabbing stray things we need. Vivienne goes through my jewelry cabinet, finding nothing adequately matching her ghostly dress in her own.

"You're actually coming with us," I say. "Madoc will be stunned."

I am wearing a choker to cover the bruises blooming on my throat where Valerian's fingers sank into my skin. When Vivi gets down on her knees to sort through a tangle of earrings, I have a terror that she will glance beneath my bed and see some smear of blood I have missed cleaning. I am so worried that I barely register her smile.

"I like to keep everyone on their toes," she says. "Besides, I want to gossip with Princess Rhyia and see the spectacle of so many rulers of faerie Courts in one place. But most of all, I want to meet Taryn's mysterious suitor and see what Madoc makes of his proposal."

"Do you have any idea who he is?" I ask. With everything that's happened, I had nearly forgotten about him.

"Not even a guess. Do you?" She finds what she is looking for—iridescent gray labradorite drops given to me by Taryn for my sixteenth birthday, forged by a goblin tinker with whom she traded three kisses.

In idle moments, I have turned over and over who might ask for her hand. I think of the way Cardan pulled her aside and made her cry. I think of Valerian's leer. Of the way she shoved me too hard when I teased her about Balekin, although I am almost certain it isn't him. My head swims, and I want to lie back down on the bed and close my eyes. Please, please let it be none of them. Let it be someone nice we don't know.

I remind myself of what she said: *I think you would like him.*

Turning to Vivi, I am about to start making a list of safer possibilities when Madoc comes into the room. He's holding a slim silver-sheathed blade in one hand.

"Vivienne," he says with a little dip of his head. "Could you give me a moment with Jude here?"

"Sure, *Daddy*," she says with small, poisonous emphasis as she slips out with my earrings.

He clears his throat a little awkwardly and holds the silver sword out to me. The guard and pommel are unadorned, elegantly shaped. The blade is etched along the fuller with a barely visible pattern of vines. "I have something I'd like you to wear tonight. It's a gift."

I think I make a little gasp. It's a really, really, really pretty sword.

"You've been training so diligently that I knew it should be yours. Its maker called it Nightfell, but of course you are welcome to call it anything you like or nothing at all. It's said to bring the wielder luck, but everyone says that about swords, don't they? It's something of a family heirloom."

Oriana's words come back to me: *He's besotted with you girls. He must have loved your mother very much.* "But what about Oak?" I blurt out. "What if he wants it?"

Madoc gives me a small smile. "Do *you* want it?"

"Yes," I say, unable to help myself. When I pull it from its sheath, it comes as though made for my hand. The balance is perfect. "Yes, of course I do."

"That's good, because this is your sword by right, forged for me by your father, Justin Duarte. He's the one who crafted it, the one who named it. It's *your* family heirloom."

I am momentarily robbed of breath. I have never heard my father's name spoken aloud by Madoc before. We do not talk about the fact that he murdered my parents; we talk around it.

We certainly don't talk about when they were alive.

"My father made this," I say carefully, to be sure. "My father was here, in Faerie?"

"Yes, for several years. I only have a few pieces of his. I found two, one for you and one for Taryn." He grimaces. "This is where your mother met him. Then they ran away together, back to the mortal world."

I take a shuddering breath, finding the courage to ask a question I have often wondered but never dared voice aloud. "What were they like?" I flinch as the words leave my mouth. I don't even know if I want him to tell me. Sometimes I just want to hate her; if I can hate her, then it won't be so bad that I love him.

But, of course, she's still my mother. The only thing I can truly be angry with her for is being gone, and that's certainly not her fault.

Madoc sits down on the goat-footed stool in front of my dressing table and stretches out his bad leg, looking for all the world as though he's about to tell me a bedtime story. "She was clever, your mother. And young. After I brought her to Faerie, she drank and danced weeks away at a time. She was at the center of every revel.

"I could not always accompany her. There was a war in the East, an Unseelie king with a lot of territory and no desire to bend his knee to the High King. But I drank in her happiness when I was here. She had a way of making everyone around her feel as though every impossible thing was possible. I suppose I put it down to her mortality, but I don't think I was being fair. It was something else. Her daring, perhaps. She never seemed cowed, not by any of the magic, not by anything."

I thought he might be angry, but he obviously isn't. In fact, his voice holds a totally unexpected fondness. I sit down on the bench in front of my bed, holding on to my new silver sword for support.

"Your father was interesting. I imagine you think I didn't know him, but he came to my house—my old house, the one they burned down—many times. We drank honey wine in the gardens, the three of us. He loved swords, he said, from the time he was a child. When he was around your age, he persuaded his parents to allow him to build his first forge in their backyard.

"Instead of going to college, he found a master swordsmith to take him on as an apprentice. From there, he got himself introduced to an assistant curator in a museum. She snuck him in after hours, allowing him to see ancient swords up close and honing his craft. But then he heard about the kinds of blades that could be wrought only by the fey, so he came looking for us.

"He was a master smith when he came here and even better when he left. But he couldn't resist bragging about stealing our secrets along with his bride. Eventually, the tale came to Balekin, who gave it to me."

If my father had really talked with Madoc, he ought to have known better than to brag about stealing from him. But I have stood on the streets of the mortal world and felt how far it seems from Elfhame. As the years passed, his time in Faerie must have seemed like a distant dream.

"There is little good in me," Madoc says. "But I owe you a debt, and I have sworn to do the best by you that I know how."

I rise, crossing the room to put one gloved hand against the pallid green skin of his face. He closes his cat eyes. I cannot forgive him, but I cannot hate him, either. We stand like that for a long moment, then he looks up, takes my unbandaged hand, and kisses the back of it, mouth against cloth.

"After today, things will be different," he tells me. "I will wait for you in the carriage."

He leaves me. I hold my head. My thoughts will not focus. When I rise, though, I strap on my new sword. It is cold and solid in my hands, heavy as a promise.

CHAPTER 20

Oak is in cricket green, dancing around in front of the carriage. When he sees me, he runs over, wanting me to carry him, then he runs off to pet the horses before I can. He is a faerie child, with a faerie child's whims.

Taryn is beautiful in her heavily embroidered dress, and Vivi radiant in soft violet gray with artfully sewn moths seeming to fly from her shoulder across her chest to gather in another group on one side of her waist. I realize how rarely I've seen her in truly splendid clothes. Her hair is up, and my earrings glitter in her lightly furred ears. Her cat eyes gleam in the half light, twin to Madoc's. For once, that makes me smile. I take Taryn's hand with my undamaged one, and she squeezes it, hard. We grin at each other, conspirators for once.

In the carriage, there is a hamper of things to eat, which was smart of someone, because none of us has remembered to eat enough all day. I remove a glove and eat two small rolls of bread so light and filled with air that they seem to dissolve on my tongue. At the center of each is a mass of honeyed raisins and nuts, their sweetness enough to bring tears to my eyes. Madoc passes me a slab of pale yellow cheese and a still-bloody slice of juniper-and-pepper-crusted venison. We make quick work of the food.

I spot Madoc's red cap, half in and half out of his front pocket. His version of a medal, I suppose, to be worn on state occasions.

None of us really speaks. I do not know what the others dwell on, but abruptly, I realize I am going to have to dance. I am terrible at dancing, since I have no practice in it other than humiliating lessons at school, partnered with Taryn.

I think of the Ghost and the Roach and the Bomb, trying to safeguard Dain against whatever Balekin has planned. I wish I knew what to do, how to help them.

KILL THE BEARER OF THIS MESSAGE.

I look over at Madoc, drinking spiced wine. He seems entirely comfortable, totally unaware of—or unconcerned with—the loss of one of his spies.

My heartbeat drums faster. I keep remembering not to wipe my hand on my skirts for fear of smearing them with food. Eventually, Oriana pulls out some handkerchiefs soaked in rose and mint water for us to wipe ourselves down with. This sets off a chase, with Oak trying to avoid being washed. There isn't far for him to run in the carriage, but he keeps it going longer than you'd think, stepping on all of us in the process.

I am so distracted I don't even automatically brace when we go straight through the rock and into the palace. We're lurching to a stop before I even notice we've arrived. A footman opens the door, and I see the whole courtyard, filled with music and voices and merriment. And candles, forests of them, the wax melting to create an effect like termite-eaten wood. Candles rest atop tree branches, flames flickering with the whoosh of dresses sweeping below. They line the walls like sentries and clump in tight arrangements on stones, lighting up the hill.

"Ready?" Taryn whispers to me.

"Yes," I say a little breathlessly.

We pile out of the carriage. Oriana has a little silver leash she attaches to Oak's wrist, which strikes me as not the worst idea, although he whines and sits in the dirt in protest, like a cat.

Vivienne looks around the courtyard. There's something feral in her gaze. Her nose flares. "Are we supposed to present ourselves to the High King one last time?" she asks Madoc.

He gives a half shake of his head. "No. We will be called forth when it is time to take our oaths. Until then, I must stand beside Prince Dain. The rest of you should go enjoy yourselves until the bells chime and Val Moren begins the ceremony. Then, come to the throne room to witness the coronation. I'd have you close to the dais, where my knights can look after you."

I turn toward Oriana, expecting another speech about not getting into trouble or even a new speech about keeping my legs closed around royalty, but she is too busy pleading with Oak to get out of the road.

"Let's party," Vivi says, sweeping Taryn and me along with her. We escape into the crowd, and moments later, we are drowning in it.

The Palace of Elfhame is packed with bodies. The unallied wild fey, courtiers, and monarchs mingle together. Selkies from Queen Orlagh's Court of the Undersea speak together in their own language, skins slung from their shoulders like capes. I spot the lord of the Court of Termites,

Roiben, who is said to have killed his own lover to win a throne. He stands near one of the long trestle tables, and even in the cramped hall, there is space around him, as though no one dares get too close. His hair is the color of salt, his garments entirely black, and a deadly curved sword sits at his hip. Incongruously, beside him, a green-skinned pixie girl is dressed in what appears to be a pearl-gray slip dress and heavy lace-up boots—obviously mortal clothes. And standing on either side of the pixie are two knights in his livery, one with scarlet hair braided into a crown on her head. Dulcamara, who lectured us on the crown.

There are others, figures I have heard of in ballads: Rue Silver of New Avalon, who cut her island out of the California coast, is talking to the exiled Alderking's son, Severin, who might try to ally with the new High King or might join Lord Roiben's Court. He's with a red-haired human boy about my age, which makes me pause to study them. Is the boy his servant? Is he enchanted? I can't tell just from the way he looks around the room, but when he sees me staring, he grins.

I turn quickly away.

As I do, the selkies shift, and I spot someone else with them. Gray-skinned and blue-lipped, hair hanging around her sunken-eyed face. But despite all that, I recognize her. Sophie. I had heard stories about the merfolk of the Undersea keeping drowned sailors, but I didn't believe them. When her mouth moves, I see that she has sharp teeth. A shudder ripples across my shoulders.

I stumble along after Vivi and Taryn. When I look back, I don't see Sophie, and I am not entirely sure I didn't imagine her.

We slide past a shagfoal and a barghest. Everyone is laughing too loudly, dancing too fiercely. As I pass one reveler in a goblin mask, he lifts it and winks at me. It's the Roach.

"Heard about the other night. Good work," he says. "Now keep your eyes out for anything that seems amiss. If Balekin's going to move against Dain, he's going to do it before the ceremony starts."

"I will," I say, pulling free of my sisters to tarry with him a moment. In a crowd this size, it's easy to be briefly lost.

"Good. Came to see Prince Dain win the crown with my own eyes." He reaches into his leaf-brown jacket and pulls out a silver flask, popping the top and taking a swig. "Plus watching the Gentry cavort and make fools out of themselves."

He holds the flask out to me with one gray-green clawed hand. Even from there, I can smell whatever is inside, pungent and strong and a little swampy. "I'm okay," I say, shaking my head.

"You sure are," he tells me, laughing, and then pulls down his mask again.

I am left grinning after him as he sweeps away into the crowd. Just seeing him has filled me with a sense of finally belonging to this place. He and the Ghost and the Bomb are not precisely my friends, but they actually seem to like me, and I am not inclined to split hairs. I have a place with them and a purpose.

"Where have you been?" Vivienne asks, grabbing hold of me. "You need a leash like Oak's. Come on, we're going to dance."

I eddy along with them. There's music everywhere, urging a lightness of step. They say the pull of faerie music is impossible to resist, which isn't quite true. What's impossible is to stop dancing once you've begun, so long as the music goes on. And it does, all night, one dance bleeding into the next, one song becoming another without a pause to catch your breath. It's exhilarating to be caught up in the music, to be swept away in the tide of it. Of course, Vivi, being one of them, can stop whenever she wants. She can also yank us out, so dancing with her is almost safe. Not that Vivi always remembers to do the safe thing.

But really, I am the last person to judge anyone for that.

We clasp hands and join the circle dance, leaping and laughing. The song feels as though it is calling my blood, moving it through my veins to the same ragged beat, with the same sweet chords. The circle breaks up, and somehow I am holding Locke's hands. He sweeps me around in a giddy whoosh.

"You are very beautiful," he says. "Like a winter night."

He smiles down at me with his fox eyes. His russet hair curls around his pointed ears. From one lobe, a golden earring dangles, catching the candlelight like a mirror. He's the one who's beautiful, a kind of breathless, inhuman beauty.

"I'm glad you like the dress," I manage.

"Tell me, could you love me?" he asks, seemingly out of nowhere.

"Of course." I laugh, not sure of the answer I am supposed to give. But the question is so oddly phrased that I can hardly deny him. I love my parents' murderer; I suppose I could love anyone. I'd *like* to love him.

"I wonder," he says. "What would you do for me?"

"I don't know what you mean." This riddling figure with flinty eyes isn't the Locke who stood on the rooftop of his estate and spoke so gently to me or who chased me, laughing, through its halls. I am not quite sure who this Locke is, but he has put me entirely off balance.

"Would you forswear a promise for me?" He is smiling at me as though he's teasing.

"What promise?" He sweeps me around him, my leather slippers pirouetting over the packed earth. In the distance, a piper begins to play.

"Any promise," he says lightly, although it is no light thing he is asking.

"I guess it depends," I say, because the real answer, a flat no, isn't what anyone wants to hear.

"Do you love me enough to give me up?" I am sure my expression is stricken. He leans closer. "Isn't that a test of love?"

"I—I don't know," I say. All this must be leading up to some declaration on his part, either of affection or of a lack of it.

"Do you love me enough to weep over me?" The words are spoken against my neck. I can feel his breath, making the tiny hairs stand up, making me shudder with an odd combination of desire and discomfort.

"You mean if you were hurt?"

"I mean if I hurt you."

My skin prickles. I don't like this. But at least I know what to say. "If you hurt me, I wouldn't cry. I would hurt you back."

His step falters as we sweep over the floor. "I'm sure you'd—"

And then he breaks off speaking, looking behind him. I can barely think. My face is hot. I dread what he will say next.

"Time to change partners," a voice says, and I look to see that it's the worst person possible: Cardan. "Oh," he says to Locke. "Did I steal your line?"

His tone is unfriendly, and as I turn his words over in my mind, they do little to comfort me.

Locke relinquishes me to the youngest prince, as is expected out of deference. I see out of the corner of my eye that Taryn is watching us. She's standing frozen in the middle of the revel, looking lost, as faeries swarm around her, swinging their partners in dizzying spirals. I wonder if Cardan bothered her before he bothered me.

He takes my wounded hand in his. He's wearing black gloves, the leather warm even through the silk over my fingers, and a black suit of clothes. Raven feathers cover the upper half of his doublet, and his boots have excessively pointed metal toes that make me conscious of how easy it will be to kick me savagely once we've begun dancing. At his brow, he wears a crown of woven metal branches, cocked slightly askew. Dark silver paint streaks over his cheekbones, and black lines run along his lashes. The left one is smeared, as though he forgot about it and wiped his eye.

"What do you want?" I ask him, forcing the words out. I am still thinking about Locke, still reeling from what he said and what he didn't. "Go ahead. Insult me."

His eyebrows go up. "I don't take commands from mortals," he says with his customary cruel smile.

"So you're going to say something nice? I don't think so. Faeries can't lie." I want to be angry, but what I feel right now is gratitude. My face is no longer flaming and my eyes aren't stinging. I am ready to fight, which is far better. Though I am sure it's the last thing he meant, he did me an enormous favor when he whisked me away from Locke.

His hand slides lower on my hip. I narrow my eyes at him.

"You really hate me, don't you?" he asks, his smile growing.

"Almost as much as you hate me," I say, thinking of the page with my name scratched on it. Thinking of the way he looked at me when he was drunk in the hedge maze. The way he's looking at me now.

He lets go of my hand. "Until we spar again," he says, making a bow that I cannot help feel is nothing but mockery.

I look after him as he weaves unsteadily through the crowd, not sure what to make of that conversation.

Bells begin to ring, signaling the start of the ceremony. The musicians quiet their fiddles and harps. For a long moment, the hill is silent, listening, and then people move to their places. I push toward the front, where the rest of the Gentry of the High King's Court are assembling. Where my family will be. Oriana is there already, standing beside one of Madoc's best knights and looking as though she wishes she could be anywhere else. Oak is off his leash and on Taryn's shoulders. She is whispering something to a laughing Locke.

I stop moving. The crowd surges around me, but I am rooted to the spot as Taryn leans in and tucks a stray bit of hair behind Locke's ear.

There is so much in that small gesture. I try to make myself believe it means nothing, but after the strange conversation we had, I can't. But Taryn has a lover, one who is going to ask for her hand tonight. And she knows that Locke and I are... whatever we are.

Do you love me enough to give me up? Isn't that a test of love?

Vivienne has come out of the crowd, cat eyes agleam, hair loose around her face. She takes Oak in her arms and swings him around and around until they both fall in a whoosh of Vivi's skirts. I should go over, but I don't.

I can't face Taryn yet, not when I cannot get such a disloyal thought out of my head.

Instead, I hang back, watching the royal family assemble on the dais. The High King is seated on his throne of woven branches, wearing the heavy circlet, looking out from his deeply lined face with alert bronze eyes, like those of an owl. Prince Dain sits on a humble wooden stool beside him, dressed in all-white robes, his feet and hands bare. And behind the throne stands the rest of the royal family—Balekin and Elowyn, Rhyia and Caelia. Even Taniot, Prince Dain's mother, is present, in a garment of shining gold. The only family member missing is Cardan.

The High King Eldred stands, and the entire hill goes quiet. "Long has been my rule, but today I take my leave of you." His voice echoes through the hill. Rarely has he ever spoken this way, to a great assemblage of us, and I am struck both by the power of his voice and the frailness of his person. "When first I felt the call to search out the Land of Promise, I believed it would pass. But I can resist it no longer. Today, I will be king no more, but wanderer."

Although everyone here must know this was what we've gathered for, still there are cries from all around me. A sprite begins to weep into the hair of a goat-headed phooka.

The Court Poet and Seneschal, Val Moren, steps from the side of the dais. He is stooped, spindly, his long hair full of sticks, with a scald crow perched on one shoulder. He leans heavily on a staff of smooth wood that has begun to bud at the very top, as though it were still alive. He is rumored to have been lured away from the mortal lands to Eldred's bed in his youth. I wonder what he will do now, without his king.

"We are loath to let you go, my lord," he says, and the words seem to take on a special, bittersweet resonance coming from his mouth.

Eldred cups his hands, and the branches of the throne shudder and begin to grow, sending up new green shoots to spiral into the air, leaves unfurling and flower buds bursting along the length of them. The roots of the ceiling begin to worm, lengthening like vines and crawling across the underside of the hill. There is a scent in the air, like a summer breeze, heavy with the promise of apples. "Another will stand in my place. I ask of you, release me."

The assembled Folk speak as one, surprising me. "*We release you,*" they say, words echoing around me.

The High King lets his heavy robe of state fall from his shoulders. It crumples on the stone in a jewel-encrusted pile. He takes the oak-leaf crown from his own head. Already, he stands up straighter. There is an unnerving eagerness in him. Eldred has been the High King of Elfhame longer than the memories of many of the Folk; he has always seemed ancient to me, but the years seem to fall from him along with the mantle of rule.

"Whom will you put in your stead, to be our High King?" Val Moren asks.

"My third-born, my son Dain," says Eldred. "Come forward, child."

Prince Dain rises from his humble place on the stool. His mother removes the white cloth covering him, leaving him naked. I blink once. I am used to a certain amount of nakedness in Faerie, but not among the royal family. Standing next to the rest of them in their heavy brocade and embroidered magnificence, he looks exquisitely vulnerable.

I wonder if he's cold. I think of my hurt hand and hope so.

"Will you accept?" Val Moren asks. The scald crow on his shoulder lifts black-tipped wings and beats the air. I am not sure if that's supposed to be part of the ceremony.

"I will assume the burden and the honor of the crown," Dain says gravely, and in that moment, his nakedness becomes something else, some sign of power. "I will have it."

"Unseelie Court, night host, come forward and anoint your prince," Val Moren says.

A boggan makes her hulking way to the raised dais. Her body is covered in thick golden hair, her arms long enough to drag on the ground if she didn't bend them. She looks strong enough to break Prince Dain in half. Around her waist she wears a skirt of patchwork furs, and in one massive hand she carries what looks like an inkpot.

She paints his left arm with long spirals of clotting blood, paints it over his stomach, down his left leg. He does not flinch. When she is done, she steps back to admire her grisly handiwork and then gives a shallow bow to Eldred.

"Seelie Court, twilight folk, come forward and anoint your prince," Val Moren says.

A diminutive boy in a wrapper of what looks like birch bark, his wild hair sticking up at odd angles, walks to the dais. Small pale green wings sit on his back. When he anoints Dain's other side, he paints it in thick swaths of pollen, yellow as butter.

"Wild fey, Shy Folk, come forward and anoint your prince," says Val Moren.

It is a hob who comes forward this time, in a dapper little suit, carefully sewn. He carries with him a handful of mud, which he smears over the center of Prince Dain's chest, just above his heart.

I finally spot Cardan in the crowd, unsteady on his feet and with a wineskin in one hand. He appears to have gotten himself riotously drunk. When I think of the smear of silver paint on his face and the way his hand had slid on my hip, I guess he was well on his way there when I saw him. I feel an immense, mean satisfaction that he is not standing with the royal family at the most important moment for the Court in centuries.

He's going to be in so much trouble.

"Who will clothe him?" Val Moren asks, and in turn, each of his sisters and then his mother bring him a white tunic and pants made from hide, a collar of gold, and high kidskin boots. He looks like a storybook king, one who will have a wise and just rule. I imagine the Ghost in the rafters, and the Roach in his mask, watching proudly. I feel some of that same pride, being sworn to him.

But I cannot forget his words to me: *You are my creature, Jude Duarte.*

I touch my wounded hand to the hilt of my silver sword, the sword my father forged. After tonight, I will be the High King's spy and a true member of his Court. I will lie to his enemies and, if that doesn't work, I will find a way to do something worse. And if he crosses me, well, then I will find a way around that, too.

Val Moren brings the end of his staff down hard against the ground, and I feel the reverberation to my teeth. "And who will crown him?"

Eldred wears an expression of pride. The crown gleams in his gnarled hands, glowing as if sunlight emanated from the metal itself. "I will."

The guards are changing configuration subtly, perhaps preparing to escort Eldred out of the palace. There are more knights at the edges of the crowd than there were when the coronation ceremony began.

The High King speaks. "Come, Dain. Kneel before me."

The Crown Prince bends down in front of his father and the assemblage.

My gaze cuts to Taryn, who is still standing with Locke. Oriana has a protective arm around Oak, one of Madoc's lieutenants bending to speak with her. He gestures toward a doorway, and she says something to Vivi and then starts toward it. Taryn and Locke follow. I grit my teeth and start to push my way through the crowd to them. I don't want to disgrace myself like Cardan, by not being where I'm supposed to be.

Val Moren's voice cuts through my thoughts. "And will you, the Folk of Elfhame, accept Prince Dain as your High King?"

The cry rose up from the crowd, in chirping voices and bellows: "We will."

My gaze goes to the knights surrounding the dais. In another life, I would have been one of them. But as my eyes rest there, I notice familiar faces. Madoc's best commanders. Warriors who are fiercely loyal.

They are not dressed in their uniforms. Over shining armor, they wear the Greenbriar livery. Perhaps Madoc is only being careful, only putting his best people in place. But the spy I killed, the one with the taunting message, was Madoc's as well.

And Oriana, Oak, and my sisters are gone. Escorted out of the hill by one of Madoc's lieutenants just as the dais became more heavily guarded.

I have a plan to ensure our futures.

I need to find the Roach. I need to find the Ghost. I need to tell them that something's wrong.

A well-seasoned strategist waits for the right opportunity.

I push past a trio of goblins and a troll and one of the Still Folk. A spriggan growls at me, but I don't pay any mind. The end of the coronation is in sight. I see goblets and tankards being refilled.

Up on the dais, Balekin has left his place with the other princes and princesses. For a moment, I think it's part of the ceremony—until he draws a long, thin blade, one I recognize from his horrible duel with Cardan. I stop moving.

"Brother," Prince Dain admonishes.

"I will not accept you," Balekin says. "I have come to challenge you for the crown." All around the dais, I see knights unsheathing blades.

But neither Elowyn nor Eldred, nor any of the rest of them—not Val Moren nor Taniot nor Rhyia—is equipped. Only Caelia pulls out a knife from her bodice, the blade too small to be of much use.

I want to draw my own sword, but everyone is pressed in too tightly.

"Balekin," Eldred says sternly. "Child. The High Court cannot be like the lower Courts. We have no blood inheritance. No duel with your brother will induce me to place a crown on your unworthy head. Content yourself with my choice. Do not humiliate yourself before all of Faerie."

"This ought only be between us," Balekin says to Dain, not acknowledging that his father had even spoken. "There is no High Monarch now. There is no one but us and a crown."

"I need not fight you," Dain says, gesturing out toward the knights grouped thickly around the dais, waiting for an order. Madoc is among them, but I am not close enough to see more than that. "And you are not worthy of even that much regard."

"Then have this on your conscience." Balekin walks two steps and thrusts out his arm. He doesn't even look in the direction he's thrusting, but his blade pierces Elowyn's throat. Someone shrieks, then everyone does. For a moment, the wound is just a blotch against her skin, and then blood pours out, a river of red. She staggers forward, going to her hands and knees. Gold fabric and glittering gems are drowning in scarlet.

It was a mere flick of Balekin's blade, an almost nonchalant gesture.

Eldred's hand comes up. I think he means to conjure up the same magic that made the roots grow, made the branches of the throne bloom and twine. But that power is gone; he gave it up with his kingdom. Instead, the newly budded flowers of the throne brown and wither.

The crow on Val Moren's shoulder takes to wing, cawing as it flies toward the roots hanging down from the hollow roof of the hill.

"*Guards*," Dain says, in a voice that expects to be obeyed. None of the knights advance toward the dais, though. As one, they turn so their backs are to the royal family and their swords to the assemblage. They're allowing this to happen, allowing Balekin to stage his coup.

But I cannot believe that this is Madoc's plan. Dain is his friend. Dain campaigned with him. Dain is going to reward him once he's the High King.

The crowd surges, carrying me with it. Everyone is moving, pushing forward or away from the gruesome tableau. I see the salt-haired king of the Court of Termites try to wade toward the fight, but his own knights get in front of him, holding him back. My family is gone. I look around for Cardan, but he is lost in the crowd.

It is all happening so fast. Caelia has run to the High King's side. She has her small knife, barely long enough to be a weapon, but she holds it bravely. Taniot crouches over Elowyn's body, trying to stem the tide of blood with the skirts of her dress.

"What do you say now, Father?" Balekin demands. "Brother?"

Two bolts fly from the shadows, thudding into Balekin's side. He staggers forward. The cloth of his doublet appears ripped, a gleam of metal underneath. Armor. I scan the rafters for the Ghost.

I am an agent of the prince as surely as he is. It's my duty to get to Dain. I shove forward again. In my head I can see a vision of the future, like a story I am telling myself, a clear, shining narrative to contrast with the chaos around me. Somehow, I will get to the prince and defend him against Balekin's treachery until the loyal members of his guard reach us. I will be the hero, the one who put herself between the traitors and her king.

Madoc gets there before I do.

For a brief moment, I am relieved. His commanders' loyalty might be bought, but Madoc would never—

Then Madoc thrusts his sword through Dain's chest with such force that the blade emerges on the other side. He drags it up, through his rib cage, to his heart.

I stop moving and let the crowd flow around me. I am still as stone.

I see a flash of white bone, of wet red muscle. Prince Dain, who was almost the High King, falls on top of the gem-crusted red cloak of state, his spilling blood lost in the jumble of jewels.

"Traitors," Eldred whispers, but his voice is amplified by the space. The word feels as though it rings through the hall.

Madoc pauses and then sets his jaw, as though he is doing some grim duty. He is wearing his red cap now, the one I saw sticking out of his pocket, the one I have studied in its case. Tonight he will freshen it. There will be new tide lines. But I cannot believe he is doing this on anyone's orders.

He must have allied with Balekin, misdirected Dain's spies. Put his own commanders in place, to keep the royal family isolated from anyone who would help them. Urged Balekin to orchestrate a strike at the one time no one would expect it. Even figured out that the only way not to trigger the crown's death curse was to move when it rested on no one's head. Knowing him as I do, I am sure he planned this coup.

Madoc has betrayed Eldred, and Dain is gone, taking all my hopes and plans with him.

Coronations are a time when many things are possible.

Balekin looks insufferably satisfied with himself. "Give me the crown."

Eldred drops the circlet from his hand. It rolls a little ways across the floor. "Take it yourself if it's what you so desire."

Caelia is making a terrible keening sound. Rhyia stares at the crowd in horror. Val Moren stands beside Eldred, his narrow poet's face pale. With the knights circling it, the dais is like a terrible stage, where all the players are doomed to run through their roles to the same bloody end.

Madoc's hands are gloved in red. I cannot stop staring at them.

Balekin lifts the High Crown. The golden oak leaves glitter with the light of candle flame. "You waited too long to depart the throne, Father. You have become weak. You let traitors rule little fiefdoms, the power of the low Courts goes unchecked, and the wild fey do as they like. Dain would have been the same, a coward who hid behind intrigues. But I am not afraid of bloodshed."

Eldred does not speak. He makes no move toward the crown or toward a weapon. He simply waits.

Balekin orders a knight to bring him Taniot. A female redcap in armor steps onto the dais to grab the struggling consort. Taniot's head lashes back and forth, her long black horns cutting into the redcap knight's shoulder. It doesn't matter. None of it matters. There are too many knights. Two more step forward, and there is no more struggling.

Balekin draws himself up before his father. "Declare me the High King, put the crown on my head, and you may go from this place, free and unharmed. My sisters will be protected. Your consort will live. Otherwise, I will kill Taniot. I will kill her here in front of everyone, and they will all know that you allowed it."

My gaze goes to Madoc, but he is on the steps, speaking in low tones to one of his commanders, a troll who has eaten at our table, has teased Oak and made him laugh. I laughed, too, then. Now my hands are shaking, my whole body trembling.

"Balekin, firstborn, no matter whose blood you spill, you will never rule Elfhame," Eldred says. "You are unworthy of the crown."

I close my eyes and think of Oriana's words to me: *It is no easy thing to be the lover of the High King. It is to always be a pawn.*

Taniot goes to her death with grace. She is still. Her bearing is regal and doomed, as though she has already passed into the realm of ballads. Her fingers are laced together. She makes no sound as one of the knights—the redcap knight with the slashed shoulder—beheads her with a single swift and brutal strike of her blade. Taniot's horned head rolls a short ways until it hits Dain's corpse.

I feel something wet on my face, like rain.

There are plenty of the Folk who delight in murder and plenty more who delight in spectacle. A kind of giddy madness seems to come upon the crowd, a kind of hunger for even greater slaughter. I fear they may have a surfeit of satisfaction. Two of the knights have seized Eldred.

"I will not ask you again," Balekin says.

But Eldred only laughs. He keeps laughing when Balekin runs him through. He doesn't fall like the others. Instead of blood pouring from his wound, red moths stream out, into the air. They rush out of him so quickly that in a moment, the High King's body is gone and there are just those red moths, swirling up into the air in a vast cloud, a tornado of soft wings.

But whatever magic made them does not last. They begin to fall until they are scattered across the dais like blown leaves. The High King Eldred is, impossibly, dead.

The dais is strewn with bodies and blood. Val Moren is on his knees.

"Sisters," Balekin says, striding toward them. Some of the arrogance is gone from his voice, replaced with a horrible softness. He sounds like a man in the midst of a terrible dream from which he refuses to wake. "Which of you will crown me? Crown me and live."

I think of Madoc telling my mother not to run.

Caelia steps forward, dropping her knife. She is dressed in a stomacher of gold and a skirt of blue, a circlet of berries in her loose hair.

"I will do it," she says. "It is enough. I will make you the High King, although the stain of what you have done will forever taint your rule."

Never is like forever, I think, and then am angry to be reminded of anything Cardan has ever said, especially now. There's a part of me that is glad she has given in, despite the awfulness of Balekin, the inevitable horror of his rule. At least this is over.

A bolt comes from the shadows of the rafters—in a completely different trajectory than the last. It strikes her in the chest. Her eyes go wide, her hands flutter over her heart, as though the wound is immodest and she needs to cover it. Then her eyes roll back, and she goes down without a sigh. It is Balekin who cries out with frustration. Madoc gives orders to his men, pointing toward the ceiling. A phalanx breaks off from the others and rushes up the stairs. A few guards fly up into the air on pale green wings, blades drawn.

He killed her. The Ghost killed her.

I push my way blindly toward the dais, past a sluagh howling for more blood. I don't know what I think I am going to do when I get there.

Rhyia picks up her sister's knife, holds it in one shaking hand. Her blue dress makes her look like a bird, caught before she could take flight. She's Vivi's only real friend in Faerie.

"Are you really going to fight me, sister?" Balekin says. "You have neither sword nor armor. Come, it is too late for that."

"It is too late," she says, and brings the knife to her own throat, pressing the point just below her ear.

"No!" I shout, although my voice is drowned out by the crowd, drowned out by Balekin shouting, too. And then, because I can't stand to see any more death, I close my eyes. I keep them closed through being jostled by something heavy and furred. Balekin starts calling for someone to find Cardan, to bring him Cardan, and my eyes automatically fly open. But there's no Cardan in sight. Only Rhyia's crumpled body and more horror.

Winged archers take aim at the cluster of roots where the Ghost was hiding. A moment later, he drops down into the crowd. I hold my breath, afraid he has been hit. But he rolls, stands, and takes off up the stairs, with guards hot on his heels.

He has no chance. There are too many of them, and the brugh is too packed, leaving nowhere to run. I want to help him, want to go to him, but I am hemmed in. I can do nothing. I can save no one.

Balekin turns on the Court Poet, pointing at him. "You will crown me. Speak the words of the ceremony."

"I cannot," Val Moren says. "I am no kin to you, no kin to the crown."

"You will," Balekin says.

"Yes, my liege," the Court Poet answers in a quavering voice. He stumbles through a quick version of the coronation as the hill goes silent. But when the crowd is asked to accept Balekin as the new High King, no one speaks. The golden oak-leaf crown is in Balekin's hand, but not yet on his head.

Balekin's gaze sweeps over the audience, and though I know it will not settle on me, I still flinch. His voice booms. "Pledge yourselves to me."

We do not. The monarchs do not bend their knees. The Gentry are silent. The wild faeries watch and measure. I see Queen Annet of the southmost Unseelie Court, the Court of Moths, signal to her courtiers to leave the hall. She turns away with a sneer.

"You are sworn to the High King," Balekin booms. "And I am king now." Balekin lifts the crown and sets it on his own head. But a moment later, he howls, knocking it off. A burn is on his brow, the red shadow of a circlet.

"We do not swear to the king, but to the crown," someone cries. It is Lord Roiben of the Court of Termites. He has made his way to stand in front of the knights. And although there are more than a dozen directly between him and Balekin, Roiben does not seem particularly concerned. "You have three days to get it onto your head, kin slayer. Three days before I will depart here, unsworn, unchecked in power, and unimpressed. And I am certain not to be the only one."

There is a smattering of laughter and whispers as his words spread. A motley group still fills the hall: glittering Seelie and terrifying Unseelie; the wild fey that seldom leave their hills, rivers, or grave mounds; goblins and hags; pixies and phookas. They have watched nearly all the royal family be slaughtered in a single night. I wonder how much more violence will spring up if there is no new monarch to caution them. I wonder who would welcome it.

Sprites glitter in air that stinks of freshly spilled blood. The revel will go on, I realize. Everything will go on.

But I am not sure that I can.

Book Two

Empty your heart of its mortal dream.
The winds awaken, the leaves whirl round,
Our cheeks are pale, our hair is unbound,
Our breasts are heaving, our eyes are a-gleam,
Our arms are waving, our lips are apart;
And if any gaze on our rushing band,
We come between him and
the deed of his hand,
We come between him and
the hope of his heart.

—William Butler Yeats,
"The Hosting of the Sidhe"

CHAPTER 21

I am a child again, hiding under a table, with the revel spinning around above me.

Pressing my hand to my heart, I feel the speeding thud of it. I cannot think. I cannot think. I cannot think.

There is blood on my dress, little dots of it sinking into the blue sky.

I thought I could not be shocked by death, but—there was just so *much* of it. An embarrassing, ridiculous excess. My mind keeps going back over Prince Dain's white ribs, the spray of blood from Elowyn's throat, and the High King's denying Balekin over and over as he died. Over poor Taniot and Caelia and Rhyia, who were forced to discover, each in turn, how the crown of Faerie mattered more than their lives.

I think of Madoc, who had been at Dain's right hand all these years. Faeries might not be able to lie outright, but Madoc had lied with every laugh, every clap on the back, every shared cup of wine. Madoc, who'd let us all get dressed up and given me a beautiful sword to wear tonight, as though we were really going to some fun party.

I knew what he was, I try to tell myself. *I saw the blood crusted on his red cap. If I let myself forget, then more fool me.*

At least knights had led my family away before the killing started. At least none of the others had to watch, although, unless they were very far away, they could not have failed to hear the screams. At least Oak would not grow up as I have, with death as my birthright.

I sit there until my heart slows again. I need to get out of the hill. This revel is going to turn wilder, and with no new High Monarch on the throne, there is little holding any of the revelers back from any entertainment they can devise. It's probably not the best time to be a mortal here.

I try to remember looking down on the layout of the throne room from above with the Ghost. I try to recall the entrances into the main part of the castle.

If I could find one of the guards and make them believe that I was part of Madoc's household, they might take me to the rest of my family. But I don't want to go. I don't want to see Madoc, covered in blood, sitting beside Balekin. I don't want to pretend that what happened is anything other than horrific. I don't want to disguise my disgust.

There's another way out. I can crawl under the tables to the steps and go up them to the ledge near Madoc's strategy room. I think from there I can climb directly through and be in the part of the castle most likely to be deserted—and the part with access to secret tunnels. From there, I can get out without worrying about knights or guards or anyone else. Adrenaline makes my whole body sing with the desire to move, but although what I have feels like a plan, it's not one yet. I can get out of the palace, but I have nowhere to go after that.

Figure it out later, instinct urges.

Okay, half a plan is good enough.

On my hands and knees, heedless of my dress, heedless of the way the sheath of my sword drags against the packed-earth floor, heedless of the pain in my hand, I crawl. Above me I hear music. I hear other things, too—the snap of what might be bones, a whimper, a howl. I ignore all of it.

Then the tablecloth lifts, and as my eyes adjust to the brightness of the candlelight, a masked figure grabs for my arm. There's no easy way to draw my sword, crouched as I am under a table, so I grab for the knife inside my bodice. I am about to strike when I recognize those ridiculous spike-tipped shoes.

Cardan. The only one who can legitimately crown Balekin. The only other descendant of the Greenbriar line left. Everyone in Faerie must be looking for him, and here he is, wandering around in a flimsy silver fox half mask, blinking at me with drunken confusion and swaying a bit on his feet. I almost laugh outright. Imagine my luck to be the one to find him.

"You're mortal," he informs me. In his other hand, he's carrying an empty goblet, tipped over absently, as though he's forgotten he still carries it. "It's not safe for you here. Especially if you go around stabbing everyone."

"Not safe for *me*?" Absurdity of the statement aside, I have no idea why he's acting as though he's ever thought about my safety for a moment, except to endanger it. I try to remind myself he must be in shock and grieving, and that might make him behave strangely, but it's hard to think of him as a person who could care about anyone enough to mourn. Right now, he doesn't even seem to care about himself. "Get down here before you're recognized."

"Playing hide-and-seek under the table? Crouching in the dirt? Typical of your kind, but far beneath my dignity." He laughs unsteadily, like he expects I am going to laugh, too.

I don't. I ball up my fist and punch him in the stomach, right where I know it will hurt. He staggers to his knees. The goblet drops to the dirt, making a hollow clanking sound. "Ow!" he shouts, and lets me tug him under the table.

"We'll get out of here without anyone noticing," I tell him. "We stay under the tables and make our way to the steps to the upper levels of the palace. And don't tell me it's beneath your dignity to crawl. You're so drunk you can barely stand anyway."

I hear him snort. "If you insist," he says. It's too dark to see his expression, and even if it wasn't, he's masked.

We make our way through the underside of the tables, with ballads and drinking songs sung above us, screams and whispers in the air, and the soft footfalls of dancers echoing around us like rain. My heart is hammering from the bloodshed, from Cardan being so close, from striking him without consequences. I concentrate on him shuffling behind me. Everything smells of packed earth, spilled wine, and blood. I can feel my thoughts spiraling away, can feel myself start to tremble. I bite the inside of my lip to give myself a fresh pain to focus on.

I must keep it together. I can't lose it now, not where Cardan will see.

And not when a plan is starting to form in my mind. A plan requiring this last prince.

I glance back and see that he has stopped moving. He's sitting on the ground, looking at his hand. Looking at his ring. "He despised me." His voice sounds light, conversational. Like he's forgotten where he is.

"Balekin?" I ask, thinking of what I saw at Hollow Hall.

"My father." Cardan snorts. "I didn't much know the others, my brothers and sisters. Isn't that funny? Prince Dain—he didn't want me in the palace, so he forced me out."

I wait, not sure what to say. It's disturbing to see him like this, behaving as though he might have emotions.

After a moment, he seems to come back to himself. His eyes focus on me, glittering in the dark. "And now they're all dead. Thanks to Madoc. Our honorable general. They never should have trusted him. But your mother discovered that a long time ago, didn't she?"

I narrow my eyes. "Crawl."

The corner of his mouth lifts. "You first."

We go from table to table, until finally we're as close as we're likely to get to the steps. Cardan pushes back the tablecloth and reaches out his hand toward me, in the gallant manner of someone helping up the person they've been trysting with. Maybe Cardan would say he was doing it for the benefit of onlookers, but we both know he's mocking me. I stand without touching him.

The only thing that matters is getting out of the hall before the revel gets bloodier, before the wrong creature decides I am an amusing plaything, before Cardan is gutted by someone who doesn't want any High Monarch in power.

I start toward the steps, but he stops me. "Not like that. Your father's knights will recognize you."

"I'm not the one they're looking for," I remind him.

He frowns, although his mask hides most of it. Still, I can see it in the turn of his mouth. "If they see your face, they may pay too much attention to whom you're with."

Annoyingly, he's right. "If they knew me at all, they'd know I'd never be with you." Which is ridiculous, since I am currently standing beside him, although it makes me feel better to say it. With a sigh, I take down my braids, rubbing my hands through my hair until it hangs wild in my face.

"You look..." he says, and then trails off, blinking a few times, not seeming able to finish. I am guessing the hair thing worked better than he had expected.

"Give me a second," I say, and I plunge into the crowd. I don't like risking this, but covering my face is safer than not. I spot a nixie in a black velvet mask eating a tiny sparrow's heart off a long pin. Slyfooting up behind her, I cut the ribbons and catch the mask before it hits the floor. She turns, searching for where it fell, but I am already away. Soon she will abandon looking and eat another delicacy—or at least I hope she will. It is just a mask, after all.

When I return, Cardan is swilling down more wine, his gaze burning into me. I have no idea what he sees, what he's even looking for. A thin rivulet of green liquid pours over his cheek. He reaches for the heavy silver pitcher as if to pour himself another cup.

"Come on," I say, grabbing for his gloved hand with mine.

We're to the steps out of the hall when three knights move to block our way. "Look elsewhere for your pleasure," one informs us. "This is the way to the palace, and it is barred to common Folk."

I feel Cardan stiffen beside me, because he's an idiot and cares more about being called common than anyone's safety, sadly even his own. I tug his arm. "We will do as we are bid," I assure the knight, trying to move Cardan away before he does something we will both regret.

Cardan, however, will not be moved. "You are much mistaken in us."

Shut up. Shut up. Shut up.

"The High King Balekin is a friend to my lady's Court," Cardan says, silver-tongued in his silver fox mask. He wears an easy half smile. He's speaking the language of privilege, speaking it with his drawling tone, with the looseness of his limbs, as though he thinks he owns everything he can see. Even drunk, he's convincing. "You may have heard of Queen Gliten in the Northwest. Balekin sent a message about the missing prince. He is waiting for an answer."

"I don't suppose you have any proof of that?" one of the knights asks.

"Of course." Cardan holds out a fisted hand and opens it to reveal a royal ring gleaming in the center of his palm. I have no idea when he took it off his finger, a neat bit of sleight of hand that I had no idea he could do, no less while inebriated. "I was given this token so you would know me."

At the sight of the ring, they step back.

With an obnoxious, too-charming smile, Cardan grabs my arm and hauls me past them. Although I have to grit my teeth, I let him. We're on the steps, and it's because of him.

"What about the mortal?" one of the guards calls. Cardan turns.

"Oh, well, you aren't *entirely* mistaken in me. I intended to keep some of the delights of the revel for myself," he says, and they all smirk.

It is all I can do not to knock him to the ground, but there's no dispute he's clever with words. According to the baroque rules that govern fey tongues, everything he said was true enough, so long as you concentrate only on the words. Balekin is Madoc's friend, and I am part of Madoc's Court, if you squint a little. So I am the "lady." And the knights probably *have* heard of Queen Gliten; she's famous enough. I'm sure Balekin *is* waiting for an answer about the missing prince. He's probably desperate for one. And no one can claim that Cardan's ring isn't meant to be a token by which he's known.

As for what he wants to keep from the revel, it could be anything.

Cardan is clever, but it's not a nice kind of cleverness. And it's a little too close to my own propensity for lying to be comfortable. Still, we're free. Behind us, what should have been a celebration of a new High King continues: the shrieking, the feasting, the whirling around in endless looping dances. I glance back once as we climb, taking in the sea of bodies and wings, inkdrop eyes and sharp teeth.

I shudder.

We climb the steps together. I let him keep his possessive grip on my arm, guiding me. I let him open the doors with his own keys. I let him do whatever he wants. And then, once we're in the empty hall in the upper level of the palace, I turn and press the point of my knife directly underneath his chin.

"Jude?" he asks, up against the wall, pronouncing my name carefully, as though to avoid slurring. I am not sure I have ever heard him use my actual name before.

"Surprised?" I ask, a fierce grin starting on my face. The most important boy in Faerie and my enemy, finally in my power. It feels even better than I thought it would. "You shouldn't be."

CHAPTER 22

I press the tip of the knife against his skin so he can feel the bite. His black eyes focus on me with new intensity. "Why?" he asks. Just that.

Seldom have I felt such a rush of triumph. I have to concentrate on keeping it from going to my head, stronger than wine. "Because your luck is terrible and mine is great. Do what I say and I'll delay the pleasure of hurting you."

"Planning to spill a little more royal blood tonight?" He sneers, moving as if to shrug off the knife. I move with him, keeping it against his throat. He keeps talking. "Feeling left out of the slaughter?"

"You're drunk," I say.

"Oh, indeed." He leans his head back against the stone, closing his eyes. Nearby torchlight turns his black hair to bronze. "But do you really believe I am going to let you parade me in front of the general, as though I am some lowly—"

I press the knife harder. He sucks in a breath and bites off the end of that sentence. "Of course," he says, a moment later, with a laugh full of self-mockery. "I was passed out cold while my family was murdered; it's hard to fall more lowly than that."

"Stop talking," I tell him, pushing aside any twinge of sympathy. He never had any for me. "Move."

"Or what?" he asks, still not opening his eyes. "You're not really going to stab me."

"When was the last time you saw your dear friend Valerian?" I whisper. "Not today, despite the insult implied by his absence. Did you wonder at that?"

His eyes open. He looks as though I slapped him awake. "I did. Where is he?"

"Rotting near Madoc's stables. I killed him, and then I buried him. So believe me when I threaten you. No matter how unlikely it seems, you are the most important person in all of Faerie. Whosoever has you, has power. And I want power."

"I suppose you were right after all." He studies my face, giving nothing away on his own. "I suppose I didn't know the least of what you could do."

I try not to let him know how much his calmness rattles me. It makes me feel as though the knife in my hand, which should lend me authority, isn't enough. It makes me want to hurt him just to convince myself he can be frightened. He's just lost his whole family; I shouldn't be thinking like this.

But I can't help thinking that he will exploit any pity on my part, any weakness.

"Time to move," I say harshly. "Go to the first door and open it. When we're inside, we're going to the closet. There's a passageway through there."

"Yes, fine," he says, annoyed, trying to push my blade away.

I hold it steady, so that the knife cuts into his skin. He swears and puts a bleeding finger in his mouth. "What was that for?"

"For fun," I say, and then ease the blade from his throat, slowly and deliberately. My lip curls, but otherwise I keep my expression as mask-like as I know how, as cruel and cold as the face that reoccurs in my nightmares. It is only as I do it that I realize who I am aping, whose face frightened me into wanting it for my own.

His.

My heart is hammering so hard I feel sick.

"Will you at least tell me where we're going?" he asks as I shove him ahead of me with my free hand.

"No. Now move." The growl in my voice is all mine.

Unbelievably, he does, swaying as he makes his way down the hall and then into the study I indicate. When we get to the hidden passageway, he crawls in with only a single inscrutable glance back at me. Maybe he's even drunker than I thought.

It doesn't matter. He'll sober up soon enough.

The first thing I do when I get to the nest of the Court of Shadows is tie Prince Cardan to a chair with shredded pieces of my own dirty dress. Then I remove both of our masks. He lets me do it all, an odd look on his face. No one else is there, and I have no idea when anyone might come back, if they will at all.

It doesn't matter. I can manage without them.

I have made it this far, after all. When Cardan found me, I knew that having control of him was the only path to having some control over the fate of my world.

I think of all the vows I made to Dain, including the one I never spoke out loud: *Instead of being afraid, I will become something to fear.* If Dain isn't going to give me power, then I am going to take it for myself.

Not having spent much time in the Court of Shadows, I don't know its secrets. I walk through rooms, opening heavy wooden doors, opening cabinets, taking inventory of my supplies. I discover a pantry that is as full of poisons as it is of cheeses and sausages; a training room with sawdust on the floor, weapons on the wall, and a new wooden dummy in the center, its face crudely painted with a disturbing grin. I go into the back room with four pallets on the ground and a few mugs and discarded clothing spread out near them. I touch none of it, until I come to the map room with a desk. Dain's desk, stuffed with scrolls and pens and sealing wax.

For a moment, I am overwhelmed by the enormity of what has happened. Prince Dain is gone, gone forever. And his father and sisters are gone with him.

I go back to the main room and drag Cardan and the chair into Dain's office, propping it against the open door so I can keep an eye on him. I take down a handheld crossbow from the wall in the training room, along with a few bolts. Weapon beside me, cocked and ready, I sit down in Dain's chair and rest my head in my hands.

"Will you tell me where exactly we are, now that I am trussed up to your satisfaction?" I want to strike Cardan over and over until I slap that smugness off his face. But if I did, he'd know just how much he scares me.

"This is where Prince Dain's spies meet," I inform him, trying to shake off my fear. I need to concentrate. Cardan is nothing, an instrument, a gambling marker.

He fixes me with an odd, startled look. "How do you know that? What possessed you to bring me here?"

"I'm trying to figure out what to do next," I say with uncomfortable honesty.

"And if one of the spies returns?" he asks me, rousing from his stupor enough to actually seem concerned. "They're going to discover you in their lair and..."

He trails off at the smirk on my face and subsides into stunned silence. I can see the moment he arrives at the realization that I'm one of them. That I belong here.

Cardan lapses back into silence.

Finally. Finally, I've made him flinch.

I do something I would never dare to do before. I go through Prince Dain's desk. There are mounds of correspondence. Lists. Notes neither to Dain nor from him, probably stolen. More in his hand—movements, riddles, proposals for laws. Formal invitations. Informal and innocuous letters, including a few from Madoc. I am not sure what I am looking for. I am just scanning everything as quickly as I can for something, anything, that might give me some idea of why he was betrayed.

All my life, I grew up thinking of the High King and Prince Dain as our unquestioned rulers. I believed Madoc to be entirely loyal to them; I was loyal, too. I knew Madoc was bloodthirsty. I guess I knew he wanted more conquest, more war, more battle. But I thought he considered wanting war to be part of his role as the general, while part of the High King's role was to keep him in check. Madoc talked about honor, about obligation, about duty. He'd raised Taryn and me in the name of those things; it seemed logical he was willing to put up with other unpleasantness.

I didn't think Madoc even *liked* Balekin.

I recall the dead messenger, shot by me, and the note in the scroll: KILL THE BEARER OF THIS MESSAGE. It was a piece of misdirection, all meant to keep Dain's spies busy chasing our tails while Balekin and Madoc planned to strike in the one place no one looked—right out in the open.

"Did you know?" I ask Cardan. "Did you know what Balekin was going to do? Is that why you weren't with the rest of your family?"

He barks out a laugh. "If you think that, why do you suppose I didn't run straight into Balekin's loving arms?"

"Tell me anyway," I say.

"I didn't know," he says. "Did you? Madoc is your father, after all."

I take out a long bar of wax from Dain's desk, one end blackened. "What does it matter what I say? I could lie."

"Tell me anyway," he says, and yawns.

I really want to slap him.

"I didn't know, either," I admit, not looking at him. Instead, I am staring at the pile of notes, at the soft wax impressions, an intaglio in reverse. "And I should have."

My gaze cuts toward Cardan. I walk over to him, squat down, and begin to prize off his royal ring. He tries to pull his hand out of my grasp, but he's tied in such a way that he can't. I yank it off his finger.

I hate how I feel around him, the irrational panic when I touch his skin.

"I'm just borrowing your stupid ring," I say. The signet fits perfectly into the impression on the letter. All the rings of all the princes and princesses must be identical. That means a seal from one looks much like the seal of another. I pull out a fresh piece of paper and begin to write.

"I don't suppose you have anything to drink around here?" Cardan asks. "I don't imagine that whatever happens next is going to be particularly comfortable for me, and I would like to stay drunk in order to face it."

"Do you really think I care if you're comfortable?" I demand.

I hear a footfall and stand up from the desk. From the common room comes the sound of smashing glass. I shove Cardan's ring into my bodice, where it rests heavily against my skin, and head into the hall. The Roach has knocked a line of jars off the bookshelf and cracked the wood of a cabinet. Jagged glass and spilled infusions carpet the stone floor. Mandrake. Snakeroot. Larkspur. The Ghost is grabbing the Roach's arm, hauling him back from smashing more things. Despite the line of blood streaking down his leg, the stiffness of his movements. The Ghost has been in a fight.

"Hey," I say.

Both look surprised to see me. They are even more surprised when they notice Prince Cardan tied to a chair in the doorway of the map room.

"Shouldn't you be with your father, celebrating?" the Ghost spits. I take a step back. Before, he's always been a model of perfect, unnatural calm. Neither of them seems calm now. "The Bomb is still out there, and both of them nearly gave their lives to free me from Balekin's dungeon, only to find you here, gloating."

"No!" I say, holding my ground. "Think about it. If I knew what was going to happen, if I was on Madoc's side, the only way I would be here is with a retainer of knights. You'd have been shot coming in the door. I would hardly have come alone, dragging along a prisoner that my father would dearly love to have."

"Peace, both of you. We're all of us reeling," the Roach says, looking at the damage he has done. He shakes his head, then his attention goes to Cardan. He walks toward him, studying the prince's face. The Roach's black lips pull back from his teeth in a considering grimace. When he turns back to me, he's obviously impressed. "Although it seems that one of us kept her head."

"Hello," Cardan says, raising his brows and regarding the Roach as though they were sitting down to tea together.

Cardan's clothes are disarranged, from crawling under tables or being captured and tied, and his infamous tail is showing under the white lawn of his shirt. It is slim, nearly hairless, with a tuft of black fur at the tip. As I watch, the tail forms one wavering curve after another, snaking back and forth, betraying his cool face, telling its own story of uncertainty and fear.

I can see why he hides that thing away.

"We should kill him," says the Ghost, slouching in the hallway, light brown hair blown across his forehead. "He's the only member of the royal family who can crown Balekin. Without Cardan, the throne will be forever lost, and we will have avenged Dain."

Cardan draws a sharp breath and then lets it out slowly. "I'd prefer to live."

"We don't work for Dain anymore," the Roach reminds the Ghost, the nostrils of his long green knife of a nose flaring. "Dain's dead and beyond caring about thrones or crowns. We sell the prince back to

Balekin for everything we can get and leave. Go among the low Courts or the free Folk. There's fun to be had, and gold. You could come along, Jude. If you want."

The offer is tempting. Burn it all down. Run. Start over in a place where no one knows me except the Ghost and the Roach.

"I don't want Balekin's money." The Ghost spits on the ground. "And other than that, the boy prince is useless to us. Too young, too weak. If not for Dain, then let's kill him for all of Faerie."

"Too young, too weak, too mean," I put in.

"Wait," Cardan says. I have imagined him afraid many times, but the reality outstrips those imaginings. Seeing the quickening of his breath, the way he pulls against my careful knots, delights me. "Wait! I could tell you what I know, everything I know, anything about Balekin, anything you'd like. If you want gold and riches, I could get them for you. I know the way to Balekin's treasury. I have the ten keys to the ten locks of the palace. I could be useful."

Only in my dreams has Cardan ever been like this. Begging. Miserable. Powerless.

"What did you know about your brother's plan?" the Ghost asks him, peeling himself off the wall. He limps over.

Cardan shakes his head. "Only that Balekin despised Dain. I despised him as well. He was despicable. I didn't know he'd managed to convince Madoc of that."

"What do you mean, despicable?" I ask, indignant, even with the still-healing wound on my hand. Dain's death washed away the resentment I had for him.

Cardan gives me an indecipherable look. "Dain poisoned his own child, still in the womb. He worked on our father until he trusted no one but Dain. Ask them—surely Dain's spies know how he made Eldred believe that Elowyn was plotting against him, convinced him that Balekin was a fool. Dain orchestrated my being thrown out of the palace, so that I had to be taken in by my elder brother or go without any home at the Court. He even persuaded Eldred to step down after poisoning his wine so that he became tired and ill—the curse on the crown doesn't prevent that."

"That can't be true." I think of Liriope, of the letter, of how Balekin wanted proof of who got the poison. But Eldred couldn't have been poisoned with blusher mushroom.

"Ask your friends," Cardan says, with a nod to the Roach and the Ghost. "It was one of them who administered the poison that killed the child and its mother."

I shake my head, but the Ghost doesn't meet my gaze. "Why would Dain do that?"

"Because he'd fathered the child with Eldred's consort and was afraid Eldred would find out and choose another of us for his heir." Cardan seems pleased with himself at having surprised me—surprised *us*, from the looks on the faces of the Roach and the Ghost. I do not like the way they watch him now, as though he might have value after all. "Even the King of Faerie doesn't like to think of his son taking his place in a lover's bed."

It shouldn't shock me that the Court of Faerie is corrupt and kind of gross. I knew that, just as I knew Madoc could do gruesome things to people he cared about. Just as I knew Dain was never kind. He made me stab my own hand, clean through. He took me on for my usefulness, nothing more.

Faerie might be beautiful, but its beauty is like a golden stag's carcass, crawling with maggots beneath his hide, ready to burst.

I feel sick from the smell of blood. It's on my dress, under my fingers, in my nose. How am I supposed to be worse than the Folk?

Sell the prince back to Balekin. I turn the idea over in my mind. Balekin would be in my debt. He'd make me a member of the Court, just as I once wanted. He'd give me anything I asked for, any of the things Dain offered and more: land, knighthood, a love mark on my brow so all who looked upon me would be sick with desire, a sword that wove charms with every blow.

And yet none of those things seems all that valuable anymore. None of those are true power. True power isn't granted. True power can't be taken away.

I think of what it will be like to have Balekin for a High King, for the Circle of Grackles to devour all the other circles of influence. I think of his starveling servants, of his urging Cardan to kill one of them for training, of the way he ordered Cardan beaten while professing his love for their family.

No, I cannot see myself serving Balekin.

"Prince Cardan is *my* prisoner," I remind them, pacing back and forth. I'm not good at much, and I've been good at being a spy for only a very short time. I am not ready to give that up. "I get to decide what happens to him."

The Roach and the Ghost exchange glances.

"Unless we're going to fight," I say, because they're not my friends, and I need to remember that. "But I have access to Madoc. I have access to Balekin. I'm our best shot at brokering a deal."

"Jude," Cardan cautions me from the chair, but I am beyond caution, especially from him.

There's a tense moment, but then the Roach cracks a grin. "No, girl, we're not fighting. If you've got a plan, then I'm glad of it. I'm not really much of a planner, unless it's how to prize out a gem from a nice setting. You stole the boy prince. This is your play, if you think you can make it."

The Ghost frowns but doesn't contradict him.

What I must do is put the puzzle pieces together. Here's what doesn't make sense—why is Madoc backing Balekin? Balekin is cruel and volatile, two qualities not preferable in a monarch. Even if Madoc believes Balekin will give him the wars he wants, it seems as though he could have gotten those some other way.

I think of the letter I found on Balekin's desk, the one to Nicasia's mother: *I know the provenance of the blusher mushroom that you ask after.* Why, after all this time, would Balekin want proof that Dain orchestrated Liriope's murder? And if he had it, why hadn't he taken it to Eldred? Unless he *had* and Eldred hadn't believed him. Or cared. Or... unless the proof was for someone else.

"When was Liriope poisoned?" I ask.

"Seven years ago, in the month of storms," the Ghost says with a twist in his mouth. "Dain told me that he'd been given a foresight about the child. Is this important or are you just curious?"

"What was the foresight?" I ask.

He shakes his head, as if he doesn't want the memory, but he answers. "If the boy was born, Prince Dain would never be king."

What a typical faerie prophecy—one that gives you a warning about what you'll lose but never promises you anything. The boy is dead, but Prince Dain will never be king.

Let me not be that kind of fool, to base my strategies on riddles.

"So it's true," the Roach says quietly. "You're the one who killed her." The Ghost's frown deepens. It didn't occur to me until then that they might not know one another's assignments.

Both of them look uncomfortable. I wonder if the Roach would have done it. I wonder what it means that the Ghost did. When I look at him now, I don't know what I see.

"I'm going to go home," I say. "I'll pretend I got lost at the coronation revel. I should be able to figure out what Cardan is worth to them. I'll come back tomorrow and run the particulars by you both and the Bomb, if she's here. Give me a day to see what I can do and your oath to make no decisions until then."

"If the Bomb has better sense than we do, she's already gone to ground." The Roach points to a cabinet. Wordlessly, the Ghost goes and gets out a bottle, placing it on the worn wooden table. "How do we know you won't betray us? Even if you think you're on our side now, you might get back to that stronghold of Madoc's and reconsider."

I eye the Roach and the Ghost speculatively. "I'll have to leave Cardan in your care, which means trusting you. I promise not to betray you, and you promise that the prince will be here when I get back."

Cardan looks relieved at the idea that there will be a delay, whatever happens next. Or perhaps he's just relieved by the presence of the bottle.

"You could be a kingmaker," the Ghost says. "That's seductive. You could make Balekin even more deeply indebted to your father."

"He's not my father," I say sharply. "And if I decide that I want to throw in with Madoc, well then, so long as you get paid, it won't matter, will it?"

"I guess not," the Ghost says grudgingly. "But if you come back here with Madoc or anyone else, we'll kill Cardan. And then we'll kill you. Understood?"

I nod. If it wasn't for Prince Dain's geas, they might have compelled me. Of course, whether Prince Dain's geas lasted past his death, I do not know and am afraid to find out.

"And if you take more than the day you asked for to get back, we'll kill him and cut our losses," the Ghost continues. "Prisoners are like damson plums. The longer you keep them, the less valuable they become. Eventually, they spoil. One day and one night. Don't be late."

Cardan flinches and tries to catch my eye, but I ignore him.

"I'll agree to that," I say, because I am no fool. None of us is feeling all that trusting at the moment. "So long as you swear Cardan will be here and hale when I return tomorrow, alone."

And because they're not fools, either, they swear it.

CHAPTER 23

I don't know what I expect to find when I get home. It's a long walk through the woods, longer because I give the encampments of the Folk here for the coronation a wide berth. My dress is dirty and tattered at the hem, my feet are sore and cold. When I arrive, Madoc's estate looks the way it always does, familiar as my own step.

I think of all the other dresses hanging in my closet, waiting to be worn, the slippers waiting to be danced in. I think of the future I thought I was going to have and the one yawning in front of me like a chasm.

In the hall, I see that there are more knights here than I am used to, coming in and out of Madoc's parlor. Servants rush back and forth, bringing tankards and inkpots and maps. Few spare me a look.

There's a cry from across the hall. Vivienne. She and Oriana are in the parlor. Vivi runs toward me, throws her arms around me.

"I was going to kill him," she says. "I was going to kill him if his stupid plan got you hurt."

I realize I have not moved. I bring one hand up to touch her hair, let my fingers slip to her shoulder. "I'm fine," I say. "I just got swept up in the crowd. I'm fine. Everything's fine."

Everything is, of course, not at all fine. But no one tries to contradict me. "Where are the others?"

"Oak is in bed," Oriana says. "And Taryn is outside Madoc's study. She'll be along in a moment."

Vivi's expression shifts at that, although I am not sure how to read it.

I go up the stairs to my room, where I wash the paint off my face and the mud off my feet. Vivi follows me, perches on a stool. Her cat eyes are bright gold in the sunlight streaming in from my balcony. She doesn't speak as I take a comb to my hair, raking through the tangles. I dress myself in dark colors, in a deep blue tunic with a high collar and tight sleeves, in shiny black boots, with new gloves to cover my hands. I strap Nightfell onto a heavier belt and surreptitiously put the ring with the royal seal into my pocket.

It feels so surreal to be in my room, with my stuffed animals and my books and my collection of poisons. With Cardan's copy of *Alice's Adventures in Wonderland* and *Through the Looking Glass* sitting on my bedside table. A new wave of panic passes over me. I'm supposed to figure out how to turn the capture of the missing prince of Faerie to my advantage. Here, in my childhood home, I want to laugh at my daring. Just who do I think I am?

"What happened to your throat?" Vivi asks, frowning at me. "And what's wrong with your left hand?"

I forgot how carefully I had concealed those injuries. "They're not important, not with everything that happened. Why did he do it?"

"You mean, why did Madoc help Balekin?" she says, lowering her voice. "I don't know. Politics. He doesn't care about murder. He doesn't care that it's his fault Princess Rhyia is dead. He doesn't care, Jude. He's never cared. That's what makes him a monster."

"Madoc can't really want Balekin to rule Elfhame," I say. Balekin would influence how Faerie interacts with the mortal world for centuries, how much blood is shed, and whose. All of Faerie will be like Hollow Hall.

That's when I hear Taryn's voice float up the stairwell. "Locke has been in with Madoc for ages. He doesn't know anything about where Cardan is hiding."

Vivi goes still, watching my face. "Jude—" she says. Her voice is mostly breath.

"Madoc's probably just trying to frighten him," Oriana says. "You know he's not keen on arranging a marriage in the middle of all this turmoil."

Before Vivi can say anything else, before she can stop me, I've gone to the top of the stairs.

I recall the words Locke said to me after I'd fought in the tournament and pissed off Cardan: *You're like a story that hasn't happened yet. I want to see what you will do. I want to be part of the unfolding of the tale.* When he said that he wanted to see what I would do, did he mean to find out what would happen if he broke my heart?

If I can't find a good enough story, I make one.

Cardan's words when I asked if he thought I didn't deserve Locke echo in my head. *Oh no,* he'd said with a smirk. *You're perfect for each other.* And at the coronation: *Time to change partners. Oh, did I steal your line?*

He knew. How he must have laughed. How they all must have laughed.

"So I suppose I know who your lover is now," I call to my twin sister.

Taryn looks up and blanches. I descend the stairs slowly, carefully.

I wonder if, when Locke and his friends laughed, she laughed with them.

All the odd looks, the tension in her voice when I talked about Locke, her concern about what he and I were doing in the stables, what we'd done at his house—all of it makes sudden, awful sense. I feel the sharp stab of betrayal.

I draw Nightfell.

"I challenge you," I tell Taryn. "To a duel. For my honor, which was grievously betrayed."

Taryn's eyes widen. "I wanted to tell you," she says. "There were so many times I started to say something, but I just couldn't. Locke said if I could endure, it would be a test of love."

I remember his words from the revel: *Do you love me enough to give me up? Isn't that a test of love?*

I guess she passed the test, and I failed.

"So he proposed to you," I say. "While the royal family got butchered. That's so romantic."

Oriana gives a little gasp, probably afraid that Madoc would hear me, that he'd object to my characterization. Taryn looks a little pale, too. I suppose since none of them actually saw it, they could have been told nearly anything. One doesn't have to lie to deceive.

My hand tightens on the hilt of Nightfell. "What did Cardan say that made you cry the day after we came back from the mortal world?" I remember my hands buried in his velvet doublet, his back hitting the tree when I shoved him. And then later, how she denied it had anything to do with me. How she wouldn't tell me what it did have to do with.

For a long moment, she doesn't answer. By her expression, I know she doesn't want to tell me the truth.

"It was about this, wasn't it? He knew. They all knew." I think of Nicasia sitting at Locke's dining table, seeming for a moment to take me into her confidence. *He ruins things. That's what he likes. To ruin things.*

I thought she'd been talking about Cardan.

"He said it was because of me that he kicked dirt onto your food," Taryn says, voice soft. "Locke tricked them into thinking it was you who stole him away from Nicasia. So it was you they were punishing. Cardan said you were suffering in my place and that if you knew why, you'd back down, but I couldn't tell you."

For a long moment, I do nothing but take in her words. Then I throw my sword down between us. It clangs on the floor. "Pick it up," I tell her.

Taryn shakes her head. "I don't want to fight you."

"You sure about that?" I stand in front of her, in her face, annoyingly close. I can feel how much she itches to take my shoulders and shove. It must have galled her that I kissed Locke, that I slept in his bed. "I think maybe you do. I think you'd love to hit me. And I know I want to hit you."

There's a sword hung high on the wall over the hearth, beneath a silken banner with Madoc's turned-moon crest. I climb onto a nearby chair, step up onto the mantel, and lift it from its hook. It will do.

I hop down and walk toward her, pointing steel at her heart.

"I'm out of practice," she says.

"I'm not." I close the distance between us. "But you'll have the better sword, and you can strike the first blow. That's fair and more than fair."

Taryn looks at me for a long moment, then picks up Nightfell. She steps back several paces and draws.

Across the room, Oriana springs to her feet with a gasp. She doesn't come toward us, though. She doesn't stop us.

There are so many broken things that I don't know how to fix. But I know how to fight.

"Don't be idiots!" Vivi shouts from the balcony. I cannot give her much of my attention. I am too focused on Taryn as she moves across the floor. Madoc taught us both, and he taught us well.

She swings.

I block her blow, our swords slamming together. The metal rings out, echoing through the room like a bell. "Was it fun to deceive me? Did you like the feeling of having something over me? Did you like that he was flirting and kissing me and all the while promising you would be his wife?"

"No!" She parries my first series of blows with some effort, but her muscles remember technique. She bares her teeth. "I hated it, but I'm not like you. I want to belong here. Defying them makes everything worse. You never asked me before you went against Prince Cardan—maybe he started it because of me, but you kept it going. You didn't care what it brought down on either of our heads. I had to show Locke I was different."

A few of the servants have gathered to watch.

I ignore them, ignore the soreness in my arms from digging a grave only a night before, ignore the sting of the wound through my palm. My blade slices Taryn's skirt, cutting nearly to her skin. Her eyes go wide, and she stumbles back.

We trade a series of fast blows. She's breathing harder, not used to being pushed like this, but not backing down, either.

I beat my blade against hers, not giving her time to do more than defend herself. "So this was *revenge*?" We used to spar when we were younger, with practice sticks. And since then we've engaged in hair pulling, shouting matches, and ignoring each other—but we've never fought like this, never with live steel.

"Taryn! Jude!" Vivi yells, starting toward the spiral stair. "Stop or I will stop you."

"You hate the Folk." Taryn's eyes flash as she spins her sword in an elegant strike. "You never cared about Locke. He was just another thing to take from Cardan."

That staggers me enough that she's able to get under my guard. Her blade just kisses my side before I whirl away, out of her reach.

She goes on. "You think I'm weak."

"You *are* weak," I tell her. "You're weak and pathetic and I—"

"I'm a mirror," she shouts. "I'm the mirror you don't want to look at."

I swing toward Taryn again, putting my whole weight into the strike. I am so angry, angry at so many things. I hate that I was stupid. I hate that I was tricked. Fury roars in my head, loud enough to drown out my every other thought.

I swing my sword toward her side in a shining arc.

"I said stop," Vivi shouts, glamour shimmering in her voice like a net. "Now, *stop*!"

Taryn seems to deflate, relaxing her arms, letting Nightfell hang limply from suddenly loose fingers. She has a vague smile on her face, as though she's listening to distant music. I try to check my swing, but it's too late. Instead, I let the sword go. Momentum sends it sailing across the room to slam into a bookshelf and knock a ram's skull to the ground. Momentum sends me sprawling on the floor.

I turn to Vivi, aghast. "You had no right." The words tumble out of my mouth, ahead of the more important ones—I could have sliced Taryn in half.

She looks as astonished as I am. "Are you wearing a charm? I saw you change your clothes, and you didn't have one."

Dain's geas. It outlasted his death.

My knees feel raw. My hand is throbbing. My side stings where Nightfell grazed my skin. I am furious she stopped the fight. I am furious she tried to use magic on us. I push myself to my feet. My breath comes hard. There's sweat on my brow, and my limbs are shaking.

Hands grab me from behind. Three more servants pitch in, getting between us and grabbing my arms. Two have Taryn, dragging her away from me. Vivi blows in Taryn's face, and she comes to sputtering awareness.

That's when I see Madoc outside his parlor, lieutenants and knights crowded around him. And Locke.

My stomach drops.

"What is wrong with you two?" Madoc shouts, as angry as I have ever seen him. "Have we not already had a surfeit of death today?"

Which seems like a paradoxical thing to say since he was the cause of so much of it.

"Both of you will wait for me in the game room." All I can think of is him up on the dais, his blade cracking through Prince Dain's chest. I cannot meet his gaze. I am shaking all over. I want to scream. I want to run at him. I feel like a child again, a helpless child in a house of death.

I want to do something, but I do nothing.

He turns to Gnarbone. "Go with them. Make sure they stay away from each other."

I am led into the game room and sit on the floor with my head in my hands. When I bring them away, they are wet with tears. I wipe my fingers quickly against my pants, before Taryn can see.

We wait at least an hour. I don't say a single thing to Taryn, and she doesn't say anything to me, either. She sniffles a little, then wipes her nose and doesn't weep.

I think of Cardan tied to a chair to cheer myself. Then I think of the way he looked up at me through the curtain of his crow-black hair, of the curling edges of his drunken smile, and I don't feel in the least bit comforted.

I feel exhausted and utterly, completely defeated.

I hate Taryn. I hate Madoc. I hate Locke. I hate Cardan. I hate everyone. I just don't hate them enough.

"What did he give you?" I ask Taryn, finally tiring of the silence. "Madoc gave me the sword Dad made. That's the one we were fighting with. He said he had something for you, too."

She's quiet long enough that I don't think she's going to answer. "A set of knives, for a table. Supposedly, they cut right through bone. The sword is better. It has a name."

"I guess you could name your steak knives. Meaty the Elder.

Gristlebane," I say, and she makes a little snorting noise that sounds like the smothering of a laugh.

But after that, we lapse back into silence.

Finally, Madoc enters the room, his shadow preceding him, spreading across the floor like a carpet. He tosses a scabbarded Nightfell onto the ground in front of me, and then settles himself on a couch with legs in the shape of bird feet. The couch groans, unused to taking so much weight. Gnarbone nods at Madoc and sees himself out.

"Taryn, I would talk with you of Locke," Madoc says.

"Did you hurt him?" There is a barely contained sob in her voice. Unkindly, I wonder if she's putting it on for Madoc's benefit.

He snorts, as though maybe he's wondering the same thing. "When he asked for your hand, he told me that although, as I knew, the Folk are changeable people, he'd still like to take you to wife—which is to mean, I suppose, that you will not find him particularly constant. He said nothing about a dalliance with Jude then, but when I asked a moment ago, he told me, 'mortal feelings are so volatile that it's impossible to help toying with them a little.' He told me that you, Taryn, had shown him that you could be like us. No doubt whatever you did to show him that was the source of conflict between you and your sister."

Taryn's dress is pillowed around her. She looks composed, although she has a shallow slash on her side and a cut skirt. She looks like a lady of the Gentry, if one does not stare overmuch at the rounded curves of her ears. When I allow myself to truly think on it, I cannot fault Locke for choosing her. I am violent. I've been poisoning myself for weeks. I am a killer and a liar and a spy.

I get why *he* chose her. I just wish *she* had chosen me.

"What did you say to him?" Taryn asks.

"That I have never found myself particularly changeable," Madoc says. "And that I found him to be unworthy of both of you."

Taryn's hands curl into fists at her side, but there is no other sign that she's angry. She has mastered a kind of courtly composure that I have not. While I have studied under Madoc, her tutor has been Oriana. "Do you forbid me from accepting him?"

"It will not end well," Madoc says. "But I will not stand in front of your happiness. I will not even stand in front of misery that you choose for yourself."

Taryn says nothing, but the way she lets out her breath shows her relief.

"Go," he tells her. "And no more fighting with your kin. Whatever pleasure you find with Locke, your loyalty is to your family."

I wonder what he means by that, by loyalty. I thought he was loyal to Dain. I thought he was sworn to him.

"But she—" Taryn begins, and Madoc holds up a hand, with the menace of his curved black fingernails.

"Was the challenger? Did she thrust a sword into your hand and make you swing it? Do you really think that your sister has no honor, that she would chop you into pieces while you stood by, unarmed?"

Taryn glowers, putting her chin up. "I didn't want to fight."

"Then you ought not do so in the future," Madoc says. "There's no point in fighting if you're not intending to win. You may go. Leave me to talk with your sister."

Taryn stands and walks to the door. With her hand on the heavy brass latch, she turns back, as though to say something else. Whatever camaraderie we found when he wasn't there is gone. I can see in her face that she wants him to punish me and is half-sure that he won't.

"You should ask Jude where Prince Cardan is," she says, narrow-eyed. "The last time I saw him, he was dancing with her."

With that, she sweeps out the door, leaving me with a thundering heart and the royal seal burning in my pocket. She doesn't know. She's just being awful, just trying to get me in trouble with a parting shot. I cannot believe she would say that if she knew.

"Let's talk about your behavior tonight," says Madoc, leaning forward.

"Let's talk about *your* behavior tonight," I return.

He sighs and rubs one large hand over his face. "You were there, weren't you? I tried to get you all out, so you wouldn't have to see it."

"I thought you loved Prince Dain," I say. "I thought you were his friend."

"I loved him well enough," Madoc says. "Better than I will ever love Balekin. But there are others who have a claim on my loyalty."

I think again of my puzzle pieces, of the answers I came back home to get. What could Balekin have given or promised Madoc that would have persuaded him to move against Dain?

"Who?" I demand. "What could be worth this much death?"

"Enough," he growls. "You are not yet on my war council. You will know what there is to know in the fullness of time. Until then, let me assure you that although things are in disarray, my plans are not overturned. What I need now is the youngest prince. If you know where Cardan is, I could get Balekin to offer you a handsome reward. A position in his Court. And the hand of anyone you wanted. Or the still-beating heart of anyone you despised."

I look at him in surprise. "You think I'd take Locke from Taryn?"

He shrugs. "You seemed like you wanted to take Taryn's head from her shoulders. She played you false. I don't know what you might consider a fitting punishment."

For a moment, we just look at each other. He's a monster, so if I want to do a very bad thing, he's not going to judge me for it. Much.

"If you want my advice," he says slowly, "love doesn't grow well, fed on pain. Grant me that I know that at least. I love you, and I love Taryn, but I don't think she's suited for Locke."

"And I am?" I cannot help thinking that Madoc's idea of love doesn't seem like a very safe thing. He loved my mother. He loved Prince Dain. His love for us is likely to afford us no more protection than it afforded either of them.

"I don't think *Locke* is suited for *you*." He smiles his toothy smile. "And if your sister is right and you do know where Prince Cardan is, give him to me. He's a foppish sort of boy, no good with a sword. He's charming, in a way, and clever, but nothing worth protecting."

Too young, too weak, too mean.

I think again of the coup that Madoc had planned with Balekin, wondering how it was supposed to go. Kill the two elder siblings, the ones with influence. Then surely the High King would relent and put the crown on the head of the prince with the most power, the one with the military on his side. Perhaps grudgingly, but once threatened, Eldred would crown Balekin. Except he didn't. Balekin tried to force his hand, and then everyone died.

Everyone but Cardan. The board swept nearly clear of players.

That can't be how Madoc thought things would play out. But, still, I remember his lessons on strategy. Every outcome of a plan should lead to victory.

No one can really plan for every variable, though. That's ridiculous.

"I thought you were supposed to lecture me about not sword fighting in the house," I say, trying to steer the conversation away from the whereabouts of Cardan. I've gotten what I promised the Court of Shadows—an offer. Now I just have to decide what to do with it.

"Must I tell you that if your blade had struck true and you'd hurt Taryn, you would have regretted it all your days? Of all the lessons I imparted to you, I would have thought that was the one I taught you best." His gaze is steady on mine. He's talking about my mother. He's talking about murdering my mother.

I can say nothing to that.

"It is a shame you didn't take out that anger on someone more deserving. In times like these, the Folk go missing." He gives me a significant look.

Is he telling me it's okay to kill Locke? I wonder what he'd say if he knew I'd already killed one of the Gentry. If I showed him the body. Apparently, maybe, *congratulations.*

"How do you sleep at night?" I ask him. It's a crappy thing to say, and I am only saying it, I know, because he has shown me just how close I am to being everything I have despised in him.

His eyebrows furrow, and he looks at me as though he's evaluating what sort of answer to give. I imagine myself as he must see me, a sullen girl sitting in judgment of him. "Some are good with pipes or paint. Some have skill in love," he says finally. "My talent is in making war. The only thing that has ever kept me awake was denying it."

I nod slowly.

He gets up. "Think about what I've said, and then think about where your own talents lie."

We both know what that means. We both know what I am good at, what I am—I just chased my sister around the downstairs with a sword. But what to do with that talent is the question.

As I exit the game room, I realize that Balekin must have arrived with his retainers. Knights with his livery—three laughing birds emblazoned on their tabards—stand at attention in the hall. I slink past them and up the stairs, dragging my sword behind me, too exhausted to do anything else.

I am hungry, I realize, but I feel too sick to eat. Is this what it is to be brokenhearted? I am not sure it is Locke I am sick over, so much as the world the way it was before the coronation began. But if I could undo the passing of the days, why not unwind them to before I killed Valerian, why not unwind them until my parents are alive, why not unwind them all the way to the beginning?

There's a knock on my door, and then it opens without my signaling anything. Vivi comes in, carrying a wooden plate with a sandwich on it, along with a stoppered bottle of amber glass.

"I'm a jerk. I'm an idiot," I say. "I admit it. You don't have to lecture me."

"I thought you were going to give me a hard time about the glamour," she says. "You know, the one you resisted."

"You shouldn't magic your sisters." I draw the cork on the bottle and take a long swig of water. I didn't realize how thirsty I was. I guzzle more, nearly draining the whole container in one continuous gulping swallow.

"And you shouldn't try to chop yours in half." She settles back against my pillows, against my worn stuffed animals. Idly, she picks up the snake and flicks the forks of its felt tongue. "I thought all of it—swordplay, knighthood—I thought it was a game."

I remember how angry she was when Taryn and I gave in to Faerie and started having fun. Crowns of flowers on our heads, shooting bows and arrows at the sky. Eating candied violets and falling asleep with our heads pillowed on logs. We were children. Children can laugh all day and still cry themselves to sleep at night. But to hold a blade in my hand, a blade like the one that killed our parents, and think it was a toy, she'd have to believe I was heartless.

"It's not," I say finally.

"No," Vivi says, wrapping the stuffed snake around the stuffed cat.

"Did she tell you about him?" I ask, climbing onto my bed next to her. It feels good to lie down, maybe a little too good. I am instantly drowsy.

"I didn't know Taryn was with Locke," Vivi says, deliberately giving me the whole sentence so I won't have to wonder if she's trying to trick me. "But I don't want to talk about Locke. Forget him. I want us to leave Faerie. Tonight."

That makes me sit upright. "What?"

She laughs at my reaction. It's such a normal sound, so completely out of step with the high drama of the last two days. "I thought that would surprise you. Look, whatever happens next here, it's not going to be good. Balekin's an asshole. And he's dumb on top of it. You should have heard Dad swearing on our way home. Let's just go."

"What about Taryn?" I ask.

"I've already asked her, and I'm not going to tell you if she agreed to come or not. I want you to answer for *you*. Jude, listen. I know you're keeping secrets. Something is making you sick. You're paler and thinner, and your eyes have a weird shine."

"I'm fine," I say.

"Liar," she says, but the accusation has no heat. "I know that you're stuck here in Faerie because of me. I know that the shittiest things that have happened in your whole life are because of me. You've never said it, which is kind of you, but I know. You've had to turn yourself into something else, and you've done it. Sometimes, when I look at you, I'm not sure if you'd even know how to be human anymore."

I don't know what to do with that—compliment and insult all at once. But behind it is a feeling of prophecy.

"You fit in better here than I do," Vivi says. "But I bet it cost you something."

I mostly don't like to imagine the life I could have had, the one without magic in it. The one where I went to a regular school and learned regular things. The one where I had a living father and mother. The one where my older sister was the weirdo. Where I wasn't so angry. Where my hands weren't stained with blood. I picture it now, and I feel strange, tense all over, my stomach churning.

What I feel is panic.

When the wolves come for that Jude, she'll be eaten up in an instant—and wolves always come. It frightens me to think of myself so vulnerable. But as I am now, I am well on my way to becoming one of the wolves. Whatever essential thing the other Jude has, whatever part that's unbroken in her and broken in me, that thing might be unrecoverable. Vivi is right; it cost me something to be the way I am. But I do not know what. And I don't know if I can get it back. I don't even know if I want it.

But maybe I could try.

"What would we do in the mortal world?" I ask her.

Vivi smiles and pushes the plate with the sandwich toward me. "Go to movies. Visit cities. Learn to drive a car. There are lots of the Folk who don't live in the Courts, don't play at politics. We could live any way we like. In a loft. In a tree. Whatever you want."

"With Heather?" I pick up the food and take a huge bite. Sliced mutton and pickled dandelion greens. My stomach growls.

"Hopefully," she says. "You can help me explain things to her."

It occurs to me for the first time that, whether she knows it or not, she isn't suggesting running away to be *human*. She's suggesting we live like the wild fey, among mortals, but not of them. We'd steal the cream from their cups and the coins from their pockets. But we wouldn't settle down and get boring jobs. Or at least she wouldn't.

I wonder what Heather is going to think of that.

Once Prince Cardan is dealt with in some way, then what? Even if I figure out the mystery of Balekin's letters, there's still no good place for me. The Court of Shadows will be disbanded. Taryn will be wed. Vivi will be gone. I could go with her. I could try to figure out what's broken in me, try to start over.

I think of the Roach's offer, to go with them to another court. To start over in Faerie. Both feel like giving up, but what else is there to do? I thought that once I was home, I'd come up with a plan, but so far I haven't.

"I couldn't leave tonight," I say hesitatingly.

She gasps, hand to her heart. "You're seriously thinking about it."

"There are some things I need to finish. Give me a day." I keep bargaining for the same thing over and over: time. But in a day I will have squared things with the Court of Shadows. Arrangements will be made for Cardan. One way or another, everything will be settled. I will wring whatever payment I can from Faerie. And if I still don't have a plan, it will be too late to make one. "What's a single day in your eternal, everlasting, interminable life?"

"One day to decide or one day to pack your bags?"

I take another bite of sandwich. "Both."

Vivi rolls her eyes. "Just remember, in the mortal world, it won't be the way it is here." She goes to the door. "*You* wouldn't have to be the way you are here."

I hear Vivi's steps in the hall. I take another bite of my sandwich. I chew and swallow it, but I don't taste anything.

What if the way I am is the way I am? What if, when everything else is different, I'm not?

I take Cardan's royal ring out of my pocket and hold it in the center of my palm. I shouldn't have this. Mortal hands shouldn't hold it. Even looking closely seems wrong, yet I do anyway. The gold is full of a deep rich redness, and the edges are smoothed by constant wear. There is a little bit of wax stuck in the impression, and I try to root it out with the edge of my nail. I wonder how much the ring would be worth out in the world.

Before I can persuade myself not to, I slip it onto my unworthy finger.

CHAPTER 24

I wake up the next afternoon with the taste of poison in my mouth. I had gone to sleep in my clothes, curled around Nightfell's scabbard.

Although I don't really want to, I pad down to Taryn's door and knock on it. I have to say something to her before the world turns upside down again. I have to make things right between us. But no one answers, and when I turn the knob and enter, I find her chamber is empty.

I head down to Oriana's rooms, hoping she might know where I can find Taryn. I peek in through the open door and find her out on her balcony, looking at the trees and the lake beyond. The wind whips her hair behind her like a pale banner. It balloons her filmy dress.

"What are you doing?" I ask, coming in.

She turns, surprised. And well she might be. I am not sure that I have ever sought her out before. "My people had wings once," she says, the longing clear in her voice. "And though I've never had a pair of my own, sometimes I feel the lack of them."

I wonder if, when she imagines having wings, she pictures herself flying up into the sky and away from all this.

"Have you seen Taryn?" Vines curl around the posts of Oriana's bed, their stems a vivid green. Blue flowers hang down in clumps over where she sleeps, making for a richly perfumed bower. There is nowhere to sit that doesn't seem crawling with plants. It's hard for me to picture Madoc comfortable here.

"She's gone to the house of her betrothed, but they'll be at the High King Balekin's manor tomorrow. You will be there, too. He's throwing a feast for your father and some of the Seelie and Unseelie rulers. You'll be expected to be less hostile to each other."

I cannot even imagine the horror, the awkwardness, of being dressed in gossamer, the smell of faerie fruit heavy in the air, while I am supposed to pretend that Balekin is anything but a murdering monster.

"Will Oak go?" I ask her, and feel the first real pang of regret. If I leave, I won't get to see Oak grow up.

Oriana clasps her hands together and walks over to her dressing table. Her jewelry hangs there—slices of agate on long chains of raw crystal beads, collars set with moonstones, deep green bloodstones strung together, and an opal pendant, bright as fire in the sunlight. And on a silver tray, beside a pair of ruby earrings in the shape of stars, is a golden acorn.

A golden acorn, twin to the one I found in the pocket of the gown that Locke gave me. The dress that had belonged to his mother. Liriope. Locke's mother. I think of her madcap, joyful dresses, of her dust-covered bedroom. Of how the acorn in her pocket opened to show a bird inside.

"I tried to convince Madoc that Oak was too young and that this dinner will be too dull, but Madoc insisted that he come. Perhaps you can sit beside him and keep him amused."

I think about the story of Liriope, of how Oriana told it to me when she believed I was getting too close to Prince Dain. Of how Oriana had been a consort to the High King Eldred before she was Madoc's wife. I think about why she might have needed to make a swift marriage, what she might have had to hide.

I think about the note I found on Balekin's desk, the one in Dain's hand, a sonnet to a lady with *sunrise hair* and *starlit eyes.*

I think about what the bird said: *My dearest friend, these are the last words of Liriope. I have three golden birds to scatter. Three attempts to get one into your hand. I am too far gone for any antidote, and so if you hear this, I leave you with the burden of my secrets and the last act of my heart. Protect him. Take him far from the dangers of this Court. Keep him safe, and never, ever tell him the truth of what happened to me.*

I think again about strategy, about Dain and Oriana and Madoc. I recall when Oriana first came to us. How quickly Oak was born and how we weren't allowed to see him for months because he was so sickly. About how she has always been protective of him around us, but maybe that was for one reason, when I had assumed another.

Just as I'd assumed the child Liriope wanted her friend to take was Locke. But what if the baby she had been carrying didn't die with her?

I feel as though I've been robbed of breath, as if getting out words is a struggle against the very air in my lungs. I cannot quite believe what I am about to say, even as I know it's the conclusion that makes sense. "Oak isn't Madoc's child, is he? Or, at least, no more Madoc's than I am."

If the boy is born, Prince Dain will never be king.

Oriana claps a hand over my mouth. Her skin smells like the air after a snowfall. "Don't say that." She speaks close to my face, voice trembling. "Do not ever say that again. If you ever loved Oak, do not say those words."

I push her hand away. "Prince Dain was his father and Liriope his mother. Oak is the reason Madoc backed Balekin, the reason he wanted Dain dead. And now he's the key to the crown."

Her eyes widen, and she takes my chilly hand in hers. She has never not seemed strange to me, like a creature from a fairy tale, pale as a ghost. "How could you know that? How could you know any of this, human child?"

I had thought Prince Cardan was the most valuable individual in all of Faerie. I had no idea.

Swiftly, I shut the door and close up her balcony. She watches me and doesn't protest. "Where is he now?" I ask her.

"Oak? With his nurse," she whispers, drawing me toward the little divan in one corner, patterned with a snake brocade and covered in a fur. "Talk quickly."

"First, tell me what happened seven years ago."

Oriana takes a deep breath. "You might think that I would have been jealous of Liriope for being another of Eldred's consorts, but I wasn't. I loved her. She was always laughing, impossible not to love—even though her son has come between you and Taryn, I cannot help loving him a little, for her sake."

I wonder what it was like for Locke to have his mother be the lover of the High King. I am torn between sympathy and a desire for his life to have been as miserable as possible.

"We were confidantes," Oriana says. "She told me when she began her affair with Prince Dain. She didn't seem to take any of it seriously. She had loved Locke's father very much, I think. Dain and Eldred were dalliances, distractions. Our kind do not worry overmuch about children, as you know. Faerie blood is thin. I don't think it occurred to her that she might have a second son, a mere decade after she bore Locke. Some of us have centuries between children. Some of us never carry any at all."

I nod. That's why human men and women are the unacknowledged necessity they are. Without their strengthening the bloodline, Faerie would die out, despite the endless span of their lives.

"Blusher mushroom is a terrible way to die," Oriana says, hand to her throat. "You begin to slow, your limbs tremble until you can move no more. But you are still conscious until everything inside you stops, like frozen clockwork. Imagine the horror of that, imagine hoping that you might yet move, imagine straining to move. By the time she got me the message, she was dead. I cut…" Her voice falters. I know what the rest of the sentence must be. She must have cut the child out of Liriope's belly. I cannot picture prim Oriana doing such a brutal, brave thing—pressing the point of her knife into flesh, finding the right spot and slicing. Prizing a child from a womb, holding its wet body against her. And yet who else could have done it?

"You saved him," I say, because if she doesn't want to talk about that part, she doesn't have to.

"I named him for Liriope's acorn," she tells me, her voice barely more than a whisper. "My little golden Oak."

I wanted so badly to believe that being in Dain's service was an honor, that he was someone worth following. That's what comes of hungering for something: You forget to check if it's rotten before you gobble it down. "Did you know it was Dain who poisoned Liriope?"

Oriana shakes her head. "Not for a long time. It could have been another of Eldred's lovers. Or Balekin—there were rumors he was the one responsible. I even wondered if it could have been Eldred, if he had poisoned her for dallying with his son. But then Madoc discovered Dain had obtained the blusher mushroom. He insisted I never let Oak be anywhere near the prince. He was furious—angry in a frightening way I had never seen before."

It's not hard to see why Madoc would be furious with Dain. Madoc, who once thought his own wife and child were dead. Madoc, who loved Oak. Madoc, who reminded us over and over that family came before all else.

"And so you married Madoc because he could protect you?" I have only blurry memories of his courting Oriana, and then they were sworn, with a child on the way. Maybe I thought it was unusual, but anyone can have good fortune. And it had seemed like bad fortune to me at the time, since Taryn and I worried what the new baby would mean for us. We thought Madoc might tire of us and drop us somewhere with a pocket full of gold and riddles pinned to our shirts. No one finds bad fortune suspicious.

Oriana looks out the glass doors at the wind blowing the trees. "Madoc and I have an understanding. We do not pretend with each other."

I have no idea what that means, but it sounds like it makes for a cold and careful marriage.

"So what's his play?" I ask her. "I don't imagine he intends for Balekin to keep the throne long. I think he would consider it some kind of crime against strategy to leave such an obvious move unexploited."

"What do you mean?" She looks honestly baffled. They don't pretend with each other, my ass.

"He's going to put Oak on the throne," I tell her, as though it's obvious. Because it is obvious. I don't know how he intends to do it—or when—but I am sure he does. Of course he does.

"Oak," she says. "No, no, no. Jude, no. He's just a child."

Take him far from the dangers of this Court. That's what Liriope's note had said. Maybe Oriana should have listened.

I remember what Madoc told us at the dinner table ages ago, about how the throne was vulnerable during a change in power. Whatever he intended to happen with Balekin—and now I am wondering if what he imagined was for Dain to die and Balekin to die, too, for the High King to suspend the coronation, for Madoc to make a different play—he had to see the opportunity in front of him, with only three royals left. If Oak was the High King, then Madoc could be the regent. He would rule over Faerie until Oak came of age.

And then, who knew what might happen? If he could keep Oak in check, he might rule over Faerie forever.

"I was just a child once, too," I tell her. "I don't think Madoc was enormously concerned about what I could handle then, and I don't think he will be too worried about Oak now."

It's not like I don't think he loves Oak. Of course he loves him. He loves me, too. He loved my mother. But he is what he is. He cannot be other than his nature.

Oriana grabs my hand, squeezing it tightly enough that her nails sink into my skin. "You don't understand. Child kings do not survive long, and Oak is a frail boy. He was too little when he was brought into this world. No king or queen from any Court will bow their heads to him. He wasn't raised for this burden. You must stop it."

What might Madoc do with so much power unchecked? What might I do with a brother on the throne? And I could put him there. I have the winning card to play, because while Balekin would resist crowning Oak, I bet Cardan wouldn't. I could make my brother the

High King and myself a princess. All that power is right there for the taking. All I have to do is reach out my hand.

The odd thing about ambition is this: You can acquire it like a fever, but it is not so easy to shed. Once, I was content to hope for knighthood and the power to force Cardan and his friends to leave me alone. All I wanted was to find some place to fit in here in Faerie.

Now I wonder what it would be like to choose the next king.

I think of the tide of blood running over the stone dais to drip down onto the packed-earthen floor of the hill. Running over the bottom edge of the crown so that when Balekin had lifted it, his hands had been smeared red. I imagine that crown on Oak's brow and flinch from the image.

I remember, too, what it had felt like to be glamoured by Oak. Over and over I'd slapped myself until my cheek was red and hot and sore. A bruise bloomed the next morning, a bruise that didn't fade for a week. That's what children do with power.

"What makes you think I can stop it?" I demand.

Oriana doesn't release my hand. "You once said that I was wrong about you, that you would never hurt Oak. Tell me, *can* you do anything? Is there a chance?"

I'm not a monster, I'd told her, back when I said I would never hurt Oak. But maybe being a monster was my calling. "Maybe," I tell her, which is no answer at all.

On my way out, I spot my little brother. He is out in the garden, picking a bouquet of foxgloves. He's laughing, sunlight turning his brown hair gold. When his nurse comes toward him, he darts away from her.

I bet he doesn't even know that those flowers are poison.

CHAPTER 25

Laughter greets me when I return to the Court of Shadows. I am expecting to find Cardan as I left him, cowed and quiet, perhaps even more miserable than before. Instead, his hands have been untied, and he is at the table, playing cards with the Roach, the Ghost—and the Bomb. At the center are a pile of jewels and a jug of wine. Two empty bottles rest beneath the table, green glass catching the candlelight.

"Jude," the Bomb calls happily. "Sit down! We'll deal you in."

I am relieved to see her, here and unscathed. But nothing else about this tableau is any good.

Cardan grins at me as though we've been great friends all our lives. I forgot how charming he can be—and how dangerous that is.

"What are you doing?" I burst out. "He's supposed to be tied up! He's our *prisoner*."

"Worry not. Where's he going to go?" the Roach asks. "You really think he can get past all three of us?"

"I don't mind being one-handed," Cardan interjects. "But if you're going to restrain both of my hands, then you'll have to pour the wine directly into my mouth."

"He told us where the old king kept the really good bottles," says the Bomb, pushing back her white hair. "Not to mention a stash of jewelry that belonged to Elowyn. He figured that in the confusion, no one would notice if it got lifted, and so far, no one has. Easiest job the Roach has ever done."

I want to scream. They weren't supposed to like him, but why wouldn't they? He's a prince who's treating them with respect. He's Dain's brother. He's Folk, like them.

"Everything is spiraling into chaos anyway," says Cardan. "Might as well have some fun. Don't you think, Jude?"

I take a deep breath. If he undermines my position here, if he manages to make me an outsider, then I am never going to get the Court of Shadows to go along with the plan that is still jumbled up in my head. I can't seem to figure out how to help anyone. The last thing I need is him making everything worse.

"What did he offer you?" I ask, like we're all in on the same joke. Yes, it's a gamble. Maybe Cardan didn't offer them anything at all.

I try not to seem like I'm holding my breath. I try not to show how small Cardan makes me feel.

The Ghost gives me one of his rare smiles. "Mostly gold, but also power. Position."

"A lot of things he hasn't got," said the Bomb.

"I thought we were friends," Cardan says halfheartedly.

"I'm going to take him in the back," I say, putting my hand on the top of the chair in a proprietary fashion. I need to get him out of the room before he gets the better of me in front of them. I need to get him away now.

"And do what?" asks the Roach.

"He's *my* prisoner," I remind them, squatting down and slicing through the strips of my dress still tying his legs to the chair. I realize he must have slept this way, sitting upright, if he slept at all. But he doesn't look tired. He smiles down at me, as if the reason I'm on my knees is because I am curtsying.

I want to wipe that smile off his face, but maybe I can't. Maybe he'll go on smiling that way to his grave.

"Can't we stay out here?" Cardan asks me. "There's wine out here."

That makes the Roach snicker. "Something bothering you, princeling? You and Jude don't get along after all?"

Cardan's expression shifts into something that appears to resemble worry. Good.

I lead him into Dain's office, which I guess I've just commandeered for my own. He walks unsteadily, his legs stiff from being bound. Also possibly because he has helped my crew down several bottles of wine. No one stops me from taking him, though. I close the door and turn the lock.

"Sit down," I tell him, pointing to a chair.

He does.

I walk around, settling myself on the other side of the desk.

It occurs to me that if I kill him, I can finally stop thinking about him. If I kill him, I won't have to feel like this anymore.

Without him, there's no clear path to putting Oak on the throne. I'd have to trust that Madoc had some way of forcing Balekin into crowning him. Without him, I have no cards to play. No plan. No helping my brother. No nothing.

Maybe it would be worth it.

The crossbow is where I left it, in the drawer of Dain's desk. I draw it out, cock it back, and point it at Cardan. He draws a ragged breath.

"You're going to shoot me?" He blinks. "Right now?"

My finger caresses the trigger. I feel calm, gloriously calm. This is weakness, to put fear above ambition, above family, above love, but it feels good. It feels like being powerful.

"I can see why you'd want to," he says, as though reading my face and coming to some decision. "But I'd really prefer if you didn't."

"Then you shouldn't have smirked at me constantly—you think I am going to stand being mocked, here, now? You still so sure you're better than me?" My voice shakes a little, and I hate him even more for it. I have trained every day to be dangerous, and he is entirely in my power, yet I'm the one who is afraid.

Fearing him is a habit, a habit I could break with a bolt to his heart.

He holds up his hands in protest, long bare fingers splayed. I am the one with the royal ring. "I'm nervous," he says. "I smile a lot when I'm nervous. I can't help it."

That is not at all what I expected him to say. I lower the crossbow momentarily.

He keeps talking, as though he doesn't want to leave me too much time to think. "You are *terrifying.* Nearly my whole family is dead, and while they never had much love for me, I don't want to join them. I've spent all night worrying what you're going to do, and I know exactly what I deserve. I have a reason to be nervous." He's talking to me as though we're friends instead of enemies. It works, too: I relax a little.

When I realize that, I am nearly freaked out enough to shoot him outright.

"I'll tell you whatever you want," he says. "Anything."

"No word games?" The temptation is enormous. Everything Taryn told me is still rattling around in my head, reminding me how little I know.

He puts a hand over where his heart should be. "I swear it."

"And if I shoot you anyway?"

"You might well," he says, wry. "But I want your word that you won't."

"My word isn't worth much," I remind him.

"So you keep saying." He raises his brows. "It's not comforting, I've got to tell you."

I give a surprised laugh. The crossbow wavers in my hand. Cardan's gaze is locked on it. With deliberate slowness, I set it down on the wood of the desk. "You tell me whatever I want to know—all of it—and I won't shoot you."

"And what can I do to persuade you not to turn me over to Balekin and Madoc?" He lifts a single eyebrow. I am not used to the force of his attention being on me like this. My heart speeds.

All I can do is glower in return. "How about you concentrate on staying alive?"

He shrugs. "What do you want to know?"

"I found a piece of paper with my name on it," I say. "Over and over, just my name."

He flinches a little but doesn't say anything.

"Well?" I prompt.

"That's not a question," he groans, as though exasperated. "Ask me a proper question, and I'll give you an answer."

"You're terrible at this whole 'telling me whatever I want to know' thing." My hand goes to the crossbow, but I don't pick it up.

He sighs. "Just ask me something. Ask about my tail. Don't you want to see it?" He raises his brows.

I have seen his tail, but I am not going to give him the satisfaction of telling him that. "You want me to ask you something? Fine. When did Taryn start whatever it is she has with Locke?"

He laughs with delight. This appears to be a discussion he isn't interested in avoiding. Typical. "Oh, I wondered when you would ask about that. It was some months ago. He told us all about it—throwing stones at her window, leaving her notes to meet him in the woods, wooing her by moonlight. He swore us to silence, made it all seem like a lark. I think, in the beginning, he did it to make Nicasia jealous. But later..."

"How did he know it was her room?" I ask, frowning.

That makes his smile grow. "Maybe he didn't. Maybe either of you would have done as his first mortal conquest. I believe his goal is to have both of you in the end."

I don't like any of this. "What about you?"

He gives me a quick, odd look. "Locke hasn't gotten around to seducing me yet, if that's what you're asking. I suppose I should be insulted."

"That's not what I mean. You and Nicasia were..." I don't know what to call them. *Together* isn't quite the word for an evil and beautiful team, ruining people and enjoying it.

"Yes, Locke stole her from me," Cardan says with a tightness in his jaw. He doesn't smile, doesn't smirk. Clearly, it costs him something to tell me this. "And I don't know if Locke wanted her to make some other lover jealous or to make me angry or just because of Nicasia's magnificence. Nor do I know what fault in me made her choose him. Now do you believe I am giving you the answers you were promised?"

The thought of Cardan being brokenhearted is almost beyond my imagining. I nod. "Did you love her?"

"What kind of question is that?" he demands.

I shrug. "I want to know."

"Yes," he says, his gaze on the desk, on my hand resting there. I am suddenly conscious of my fingernails, bitten to the quick. "I loved her."

"Why do you want me dead?" I ask, because I want to remind us both that answering embarrassing questions is the least of what he deserves. We're enemies, no matter how many jokes he tells or how friendly he seems. Charmers are charming, but that's all they are.

He lets out a long breath and puts his head down on his hands, not paying nearly enough attention to the crossbow. "You mean with the nixies? You were the one who was thrashing around and throwing things at them. They're extremely lazy creatures, but I thought you might actually annoy them into taking a bite out of you. I may be rotten, but my one virtue is that I'm not a killer. I wanted to frighten you, but I never wanted you *dead*. I never wanted anyone dead."

I think of the river and how, when one nixie detached from the others, Cardan waited until it paused and then left so we could get out of the water. I stare at him, at the traces of silver on his face from the party, at the inky black of his eyes. I suddenly remember how he pulled Valerian off me when I was choking on faerie fruit.

I never wanted anyone dead.

Against my will, I recall the way he held that sword in the study with Balekin and the sloppiness of his technique. I thought he'd been doing that deliberately, to annoy his brother. Now, for the first time, I consider the possibility that he just doesn't much like sword fighting. That he'd never learned it particularly well. That if we ever fought, I would win. I consider all the things I have done to become a worthy adversary of him, but maybe I haven't been fighting Cardan at all. Maybe I've been fighting my own shadow.

"Valerian tried to murder me outright. Twice. First in the tower, then in my room at my house."

Cardan lifts his head, and his whole posture stiffens as though some uncomfortable truth just came home to him. "I thought when you said you killed him you meant that you tracked him down and..." His voice trails off, and he starts over. "Only a fool would break into the general's house."

I draw down the collar of my shirt so he can see where Valerian tried to strangle me. "I have another on my shoulder from where he knocked me into the floor. Believe me yet?"

He reaches toward me, as though he's going to run his fingers over the bruises. I bring up the crossbow, and he thinks better of it. "Valerian liked pain," he says. "Anyone's. Mine, even. I knew he wanted to hurt you." He pauses, seeming to actually have heard his own words. "And he had. I thought he'd be satisfied with that."

It never occurred to me to wonder what it was like to be Valerian's friend. It sounds like it wasn't so different from being his enemy.

"So it doesn't matter that Valerian wanted to hurt me?" I ask. "So long as he wasn't going to kill me."

"You have to admit, being alive is better," Cardan returns, that faintly amused tone back in his voice.

I put both of my hands on the desk. "Just tell me why you hate me. Once and for all."

His long fingers smooth over the wood of Dain's desk. "You really want honesty?"

"I am the one with the crossbow, not shooting you because you promised me answers. What do you think?"

"Very well." He fixes me with a spiteful look. "I hate you because your father loves you even though you're a human brat born to his unfaithful wife, while mine never cared for me, though I am a prince of Faerie. I hate you because you don't have a brother who beats you. And I hate you because Locke used you and your sister to make Nicasia cry after he stole her from me. Besides which, after the tournament, Balekin never failed to throw you in my face as the mortal who could best me."

I didn't think Balekin even knew who I was.

We stare at each other across the desk. Lounging in the chair, Cardan looks every bit the wicked prince. I wonder if he expects to be shot.

"Is that all?" I demand. "Because it's ridiculous. You can't be jealous of me. You don't have to live at the sufferance of the same person who murdered your parents. You don't have to stay angry because if you don't, there's a bottomless well of fear ready to open up under you." I stop speaking abruptly, surprised at myself.

I said I wasn't going to be charmed, but I let him trick me into opening up to him.

As I think that, Cardan's smile turns into a more familiar sneer. "Oh, really? I don't know about being angry? I don't know about being afraid? You're not the one bargaining for your life."

"That's really why you hate me?" I demand. "Only that? There's no better reason?"

For a moment, I think he's ignoring me, but then I realize he's not answering because he can't lie and he doesn't want to tell me the truth.

"Well?" I say, lifting the crossbow again, glad to have a reason to reassert my position as the person in charge. "Tell me!"

He leans in and closes his eyes. "Most of all, I hate you because I think of you. Often. It's disgusting, and I can't stop."

I am shocked into silence.

"Maybe you should shoot me after all," he says, covering his face with one long-fingered hand.

"You're playing me," I say. I don't believe him. I won't fall for some silly trick, because he thinks I am some fool to lose my head over beauty; if I was, I couldn't last a single day in Faerie. I stand, ready to call his bluff.

Crossbows aren't great at close range, so I trade mine for a dagger.

He doesn't look up as I walk around the desk to him. I place the tip of the blade against the bottom of his chin, as I did the day before in the hall, and I tilt his face toward mine. He shifts his gaze with obvious reluctance.

The horror and shame on his face look entirely too real. Suddenly, I am not so sure what to believe.

I lean toward him, close enough for a kiss. His eyes widen. The look in his face is some commingling of panic and desire. It is a heady feeling, having power over someone. Over *Cardan*, who I never thought had any feelings at all.

"You really do want me," I say, close enough to feel the warmth of his breath as it hitches. "And you *hate* it." I change the angle of the knife, turning it so it's against his neck. He doesn't look nearly as alarmed by that as I might expect.

Not nearly as alarmed as when I bring my mouth to his.

CHAPTER 26

I don't have a lot of experience with kisses. There was Locke, and before him, no one. But kissing Locke never felt the way that kissing Cardan does, like taking a dare to run over knives, like an adrenaline strike of lightning, like the moment when you've swum too far out in the sea and there is no going back, only cold black water closing over your head.

Cardan's cruel mouth is surprisingly soft, and for a long moment after our lips touch, he's still as a statue. His eyes close, lashes brushing my cheek. I shudder, as you're supposed to when someone walks over your grave. Then his hands come up, gentle as they glide over my arms. If I didn't know better, I'd say his touch was reverent, but I do know better. His hands are moving slowly because he is trying to stop himself. He doesn't want this. He doesn't want to want this.

He tastes like sour wine.

I can feel the moment he gives in and gives up, pulling me to him despite the threat of the knife. He kisses me hard, with a kind of devouring desperation, fingers digging into my hair. Our mouths slide together, teeth over lips over tongues. Desire hits me like a kick to the stomach. It's like fighting, except what we're fighting for is to crawl inside each other's skin.

That's the moment when terror seizes me. What kind of insane revenge is there in exulting in his revulsion? And worse, far worse, *I like this.* I like everything about kissing him—the familiar buzz of fear, the knowledge I am punishing him, the proof he wants me.

The knife in my hand is useless. I throw it at the desk, barely registering as the point sinks into the wood. He pulls back from me at the sound, startled. His mouth is pink, his eyes dark. He sees the knife and barks out a startled laugh.

Which is enough to make me stagger back. I want to mock him, to show up his weakness without revealing mine, but I don't trust my face not to show too much.

"Is that what you imagined?" I ask, and am relieved to find that my voice sounds harsh.

"No," he says tonelessly.

"Tell me," I say.

He shakes his head, somewhat chagrined. "Unless you're really going to stab me, I think I won't. And I might not tell you even if you were going to stab me."

I get up on Dain's desk to put some distance between us. My skin feels too tight, and the room seems suddenly too small. He almost made me laugh there.

"I am going to make a proposal," Cardan says. "I don't want to put the crown on Balekin's head just to lose mine. Ask whatever you want for yourself, for the Court of Shadows, but ask something for me. Get him to give me lands far from here. Tell him I will be gloriously irresponsible, far from his side. He never needs to think of me again. He can sire some brat to be his heir and pass the High Crown to it. Or perhaps it will slit his throat, a new family tradition. I care not."

I am grudgingly impressed that he's managed to come up with a fairly decent bargain, despite having been tied to a chair for most of the night and probably quite drunk.

"Get up," I tell him.

"So you're not worried I'm going to run for it?" he asks, stretching out his legs. His pointy boots gleam in the room, and I wonder if I should confiscate them since they're potential weapons. Then I remember how bad he is with a sword.

"After our kiss, I am such a fool over you that I can hardly contain myself," I tell him with as much sarcasm as I can muster. "All I want to do is nice things that make you happy. Sure, I'll make whatever bargain you want, so long as you kiss me again. Go ahead and run. I definitely won't shoot you in the back."

He blinks a few times. "Hearing you lie outright is a bit disconcerting."

"Then let me tell you the truth. You're not going to run because you've got nowhere to go."

I head to the door, flip the lock, and look out. The Bomb is lying on a cot in the sleeping room. The Roach raises his eyebrows at me. The Ghost is passed out in a chair, but he shakes himself awake when we come in. I feel flushed all over and hope I don't look it.

"You done interrogating the princeling?" the Roach asks.

I nod. "I think I know what I've got to do."

The Ghost takes a long look at him. "So are we selling? Buying? Cleaning his guts off the ceiling?"

"I'm going to take a walk," I say. "To get some air."

The Roach sighs.

"I just need to put my thoughts in order," I say. "And then I will explain everything."

"Will you?" the Ghost wants to know, fixing me with a look. I wonder if he guesses how easily promises are coming to my lips. I am spending them like enchanted gold, doomed to turn back into dried leaves in tills all over town.

"I talked with Madoc, and he offered me whatever I wanted in exchange for Cardan. Gold, magic, glory, *anything*. The first part of this bargain is struck, and I haven't even admitted I know where the lost prince might be."

The Ghost's lip curls at the mention of Madoc, but he's silent.

"So what's the holdup?" asks the Roach. "I like all those things."

"I'm just working out the details," I say. "And you need to tell me what you want. Exactly what you want—how much gold, what else. Write it down."

The Roach grunts but doesn't seem inclined to contradict me. He signals with one clawed hand for Cardan to return to the table. The prince staggers, pushing off the wall to get there. I make sure all the sharp things are where I left them, and then I head for the door. When I look back, I see Cardan's hands are deftly splitting the deck of cards, but his glittering black eyes are on me.

I walk to the Lake of Masks and sit on one of the black rocks over the water. The setting sun has lit the sky on fire, set the tops of the trees ablaze.

For a long time, I just sit there, watching the waves lap at the shoreline. I take deep breaths waiting for my mind to settle, for my head to clear. Overhead, I hear the trilling of birds calling to one another as they roost for the night and see glowing lights kindle in hollow knotholes as sprites come awake.

Balekin cannot become the High King, not if there's anything I can do about it. He loves cruelty and hates mortals. He would be a terrible ruler. For now, there are rules dictating our interactions with the human world—those rules could change. What if bargains were no longer needed to steal mortals away? What if anyone could be taken, at any time? It used to be like that; it still is in some places. The High King could make both worlds far worse than they are, could favor the Unseelie Courts, could sow discord and terror for a thousand years.

So, instead, what if I turn Cardan over to Madoc?

He would put Oak on the throne and then rule as a tyrannical and brutal regent. He would make war on the Courts that resisted swearing to the throne. He would raise Oak in enough bloodshed that he would turn into someone like Madoc, or perhaps someone more secretly cruel, like Dain. But he would be better than Balekin. And he would make a fair bargain with me and with the Court of Shadows, if only for my sake. And I—what would I do?

I could go with Vivi, I suppose.

Or I could bargain to be a knight. I could stay and help protect

Oak, help insulate him from Madoc's influence. Of course, I would have little power to do that.

What would happen if I cut Madoc out of the picture? That would mean no gold for the Court of Shadows, no bargains with anyone. It would mean getting the crown somehow and putting it on Oak's head. And then what? Madoc would still become regent. I couldn't stop him. Oak would still listen to him. Oak would still become his puppet, still be in danger.

Unless—unless somehow Oak could be crowned and spirited away from Faerie. Be the High King in exile. Once Oak was grown and ready, he could return, aided by the power of the Greenbriar crown. Madoc might still be able to assert some authority over Faerie until Oak got back, but he wouldn't be able to make Oak as bloodthirsty, as inclined toward war. He wouldn't have the absolute authority that he'd have as a regent with the High King beside him. And since Oak would have been reared in the human world, when he came back to Faerie, hopefully he'd be at least somewhat sympathetic to the place where he was raised and the people he met there.

Ten years. If we could keep Oak out of Faerie for ten years, he could grow into the person he's going to be.

Of course, by then, he might have to fight to get his throne back. Someone—probably Madoc, possibly Balekin, maybe even one of the other minor kings or queens—could squat there like a spider, consolidating power.

I squint at the black water. If only there were a way to keep the throne unoccupied for long enough that Oak becomes his own person, without Madoc making war, without any regent at all.

I stand up, having made my decision. For good or ill, I know what I am going to do. I have my plan. Madoc would not approve of this strategy. It's not the kind he likes, where there are multiple ways to win. It's the kind where there's only one way, and it's kind of a long shot.

As I stand, I catch my own reflection in the water. I look again and realize that it can't be me. The Lake of Masks never shows you your own face. I creep closer. The full moon is bright in the sky, bright enough to show me my mother looking back at me. She's younger than I remember her. And she's laughing, calling over someone I cannot see.

Through time, she points at me. When she speaks, I can read her lips. *Look! A human girl.* She appears delighted.

Then Madoc's reflection joins hers, his hand going around her waist. He looks no younger then, but there is an openness in his face that I have never seen. He waves to me.

I am a stranger to them.

Run! I want to shout. But, of course, that's the one thing I don't need to tell her to do.

The Bomb looks up when I enter. She's sitting at the wooden table, measuring out a grayish powder. Beside her are several spun glass globes, corked shut. Her magnificent white hair is tied up with what looks like a piece of dirty string. A smear of grime streaks over her nose.

"The rest of them are in the back," she says. "With the princeling, getting some sleep."

I sit down at the table with a sigh. I'd been tensed up to explain myself, and now all that energy has nowhere to go. "Is there anything around to eat?"

She gives me a quick grin as she fills another globe and sets it gingerly in a basket by her feet. "The Ghost picked up some black bread and butter. We ate the sausages, and the wine's gone, but there might still be some cheese."

I rummage through the cupboard, take out the food, and then eat it mechanically. I pour myself a cup of bracing and bitter fennel tea. It makes me feel a little steadier. I watch her make explosives for a while. As she works, she whistles a little, off-key. It's odd to hear; most of the Folk are musically gifted, but I like her tune better for being imperfect. It seems happier, easier, less haunting.

"Where will you go when all this is done?" I ask her.

She glances over at me, puzzled. "What makes you think I'm going anywhere?"

I frown at my nearly empty cup of tea. "Because Dain's gone. I mean, isn't that what the Ghost and the Roach are going to do? Aren't you going with them?"

The Bomb shrugs her narrow shoulders and points a bare toe at the basket of globes. "See all these?"

I nod.

"They don't travel well," she says. "I'm going to stay here, with you. You've got a plan, right?"

I am too flummoxed to know what to say. I open my mouth and begin to stammer. She laughs. "Cardan said that you did. That if you were just making a trade, you would have done it already. And if you were going to betray us, you'd have done that by now, too."

"But, um," I say, and then lose my train of thought. Something about how he wasn't supposed to be paying that much attention. "What do the others think?"

She goes back to filling globes. "They didn't say, but none of us likes Balekin. If you've got a plan, well, good for you. But if you want us on your side, maybe you could be a little less cagey about it."

I take a deep breath and decide that if I am really going to do this, I could use some help. "What do you think about stealing a crown? Right in front of the kings and queens of Faerie?"

Her grin curls up at the corners. "Just tell me what I get to blow up."

Twenty minutes later, I light the stub of a candle and make my way to the room with the cots. As the Bomb said, Cardan is stretched out on one, looking sickeningly handsome. He's washed his face and taken off his jacket, which he has folded up under his head for a pillow. I poke him in the arm, and he comes awake instantly, raising his hand as though to ward me off.

"Shhhh," I whisper. "Don't wake the others. I need to talk to you."

"Go away. You told me you wouldn't kill me if I answered your questions, and I did." He doesn't sound like the boy who kissed me, sick with desire, just hours ago. He sounds sleepy, arrogant, and annoyed.

"I am going to offer you something better than your life," I say. "Now, come on."

He stands, shouldering on his jacket, and then follows me into Dain's office. Once we're there, he leans against the doorjamb. His eyes are heavy-lidded, his hair messy from the bed. Just looking at him makes me feel hot with shame. "You sure you brought me here just to talk?"

It turns out that having kissed someone, the possibility of kissing hangs over everything, no matter how terrible an idea it was the first time. The memory of his mouth on mine shimmers in the air between us. "I brought you here to make a deal with you."

His eyebrow goes up. "Intriguing."

"What if you didn't have to go hide somewhere in the countryside? What if there were an alternative to Balekin's being on the throne?" That's clearly not what he was expecting me to say. For a moment, his insouciant swagger fails him.

"There is," he says slowly. "*Me.* Except I would be a terrible king, and I would hate it. Besides, Balekin is unlikely to put the crown on my head. He and I have never gotten on particularly well."

"I thought you lived in his house." I cross my arms over my chest protectively, trying to push away the image of Balekin punishing Cardan. I can't have any sympathy now.

He tips his head back, looking at me through dark lashes. "Maybe living together is the reason we don't get on."

"I don't like you, either," I remind him.

"So you've said." He gives me a lazy grin. "So if it's not me and it's not Balekin, then who?"

"My brother, Oak," I tell him. "I'm not going to go into how, but he's of the right bloodline. Your bloodline. He can wear the crown."

Cardan frowns. "You're sure?"

I nod. I don't like telling him this before I ask him to do what I need, but there's little he can do with the knowledge. I will never trade him to Balekin. There is no one to tell but Madoc, and he already knows.

"So Madoc will be regent," Cardan says.

I shake my head. "That's why I need your help. I want you to crown Oak the High King, and then I'm going to send him to the mortal world. Let him have a chance to be a kid. Let him have a chance at being a good king someday."

"Oak might make different choices than the ones you want him to," Cardan says. "He might, for instance, prefer Madoc to you."

"I have been a stolen child," I tell him. "I grew up in a foreign land for a far lonelier and worse reason than this. Vivi will care for him. And if you agree to my plan, I'll get you everything you asked for and more. But I need something from you—an oath. I want you to swear yourself into my service."

He barks out the same surprised laugh he made when I threw my knife at the desk. "You want *me* to put *myself* in *your* power? Voluntarily?"

"You don't think I'm serious, but I am. I couldn't be more serious." Inside my crossed arms, I pinch my own skin to prevent any twitches, any tells. I need to seem completely composed, completely confident. My heart is speeding. I feel the way I did when I was a child, playing chess with Madoc—I would see the winning moves ahead of me, forget to be cautious, and then be brought up short by a move of his I hadn't predicted. I remind myself to breathe, to concentrate.

"Our interests align," he says. "What do you need my oath for?"

I take a deep breath. "I need to be sure you won't betray me. You're too dangerous with the crown in your hands. What if you put it on your brother's head after all? What if you want it for yourself?"

He seems to think that over. "I'll tell you exactly what I want—the estates where I live. I want them given to me with everything and everyone in them. Hollow Hall. I want it."

I nod. "Done."

"I want every last bottle in the royal cellars, no matter how old or rare."

"They will be yours," I say.

"I want the Roach to teach me how to steal," he says.

Surprised, I don't answer for a moment. Is he joking? He doesn't seem to be. "Why?" I ask finally.

"It could come in useful," he says. "Besides, I like him."

"Fine," I say incredulously. "I will find a way to work it out."

"You really think you can promise all that?" He gives me a considering look.

"I can. I do. And I promise we will thwart Balekin. We will get the crown of Faerie," I tell him heedlessly. How many promises can I make before I find myself accountable for them? A few more, I hope.

Cardan throws himself into Dain's chair. From behind the desk, he gazes at me coolly from that position of authority. Something in my gut twists, but I ignore it. I can do this. I can do this. I hold my breath.

"You can have my service for a year and a day," he says.

"That's not long enough," I insist. "I can't—"

He snorts. "I am sure that your brother will be crowned and gone by then. Or we will have lost, despite your promises, and it won't matter anyway. You won't get a better offer from me, especially not if you threaten me again."

It buys me time, at least. I let out my breath. "Fine. We're agreed."

Cardan crosses the room toward me, and I have no idea what he's going to do. If he kisses me, I am afraid I will be consumed by the hungry and humiliating urgency that I felt the first time. But when he kneels down in front of me, I am too surprised to formulate any thoughts at all. He takes my hand in his, long fingers cool as they curl around mine. "Very well," he says impatiently, not sounding in the least like a vassal about to swear to his lady. "Jude Duarte, daughter of clay, I swear myself into your service. I will act as your hand. I will act as your shield. I will act in accordance with your will. Let it be so for one year and one day . . . *and not for one minute more.*"

"You've really improved the vow," I say, although my voice comes out strained. Even as he said the words, I felt like somehow he got the upper hand. Somehow he's the one in control.

He stands in one fluid motion, letting go of me. "Now what?"

"Go back to bed," I tell him. "I'll wake you in a little while and explain what we've got to do."

"As you command," Cardan says, mocking smile pulling at his mouth. Then he goes back to the room with the cots, presumably to flop down on one. I think about all the strangeness of his being here, sleeping in homespun sheets, wearing the same clothes for days on end, eating bread and cheese, and not complaining about any of it. It almost seems like he prefers a nest of spies and assassins to the splendor of his own bed.

CHAPTER 27

The monarchs of the Seelie and Unseelie Courts, along with the wild unallied faeries who came for the coronation, had made camp on the easternmost corner of the island. They had pitched tents, some in motley, some in diaphanous silks. When I get close, I can see fires burning. Honey wine and spoiled meat perfume the air.

Cardan stands next to me, dressed in flat black, his dark hair combed away from a face scrubbed clean. He looks pale and tired, although I let him sleep as long as I dared.

I didn't wake up the Ghost or the Roach after Cardan swore his oath. Instead, I talked strategy with the Bomb for the better part of an hour. She is the one who got me the change of clothes for Cardan, the one who agreed he might come in useful. Which is how I came to be here, about to try to find a monarch willing to back a ruler other than Balekin. If my plan is going to succeed, I need someone at that feast who is on the side of a new king, preferably someone with the power to keep a dinner party from devolving into another slaughter if things go sideways.

If nothing else, I'll need lots of disruptions to be sure I can get Oak out of there. The Bomb's glass globes aren't going to be enough. What I'll have to offer in exchange, I am not entirely sure. I've spent all my own promises; now I will begin spending the crown's.

I take a deep breath. Once I stand in front of the lords and ladies of Faerie and declare my intent to go against Balekin, there's no going back, no crawling under the coverlets in my bed, no running away. If I do this, I am bound to Faerie until Oak sits on the throne.

We have tonight and half of tomorrow before the feast, before I must go to Hollow Hall, before my plans either come together or come entirely apart.

There's only one way to keep Faerie ready for Oak—I have to stay. I have to use what I've learned from Madoc and the Court of Shadows to manipulate and murder my way into keeping the throne ready for him. I said ten years, but perhaps seven will be enough. That's not so long. Seven years of drinking poison, of never sleeping, of living on high alert. Seven more years, and then maybe Faerie will be a safer, better land. And I will have earned my place in it.

The great game, Locke had called it when he accused me of playing it. I wasn't then, but I am now. And maybe I learned something from Locke. He made me into a story, and now I am going to make a story out of someone else.

"So I am to sit here and feed you information," Cardan says, leaning against a hickory tree. "And you're to go charm royalty? That seems entirely backward."

I fix him with a look. "I can be charming. I charmed you, didn't I?"

He rolls his eyes. "Do not expect others to share my depraved tastes."

"I am going to command you," I tell him. "Okay?"

A muscle jumps in his jaw. I am sure it is no small thing for a prince of Faerie to accept being controlled, especially by me, but he nods.

I speak the words. "I command you to stay here and wait until I am ready to leave this forest, there is imminent danger, or a full day has passed. While you wait, I command you to make no sound or signal to draw any others to you. If there is imminent danger or a day has passed without my return, I command you to return to the Court of Shadows, concealing yourself as well as you are able until you are there."

"That is not too poorly done," he tells me, managing to retain his haughty, regal air somehow.

It's annoying.

"Okay," I say. "Tell me what you can about Queen Annet."

What I know is this: She left the coronation ceremony before any of the other lords or ladies. That means she hates either the idea of Balekin or the idea of any High Monarch. I just have to figure out which.

"The Court of Moths is sprawling and very traditionally Unseelie. She's practical-minded and direct, and she values raw power over other things. I also heard she eats her lovers when she tires of them." He raises his eyebrows.

Despite myself, I smile. It's bizarre to be in this with Cardan, of all people. And weirder still for him to talk with me this way, as he might to Nicasia or Locke.

"So why did she walk out of the coronation?" I ask. "It sounds like she and Balekin would be perfect for each other."

"She has no heirs," he says. "And despairs of ever bearing one. I think she would not have liked to see the wasteful slaughter of an entire line. Moreover, I don't think she would be impressed that Balekin killed them all and still left the dais without a crown."

"Okay," I say, sucking in a breath.

He grabs hold of my wrist. I am shocked by the sensation of his skin warm against mine. "Take care," he says, and then smiles. "It would be very dull to have to sit here for an entire day just because you went and got yourself killed."

"My last thoughts would be of your boredom," I tell him, and head off toward Queen Annet's Unseelie encampment.

No fires burn, and the tents are of a rough greenish fabric the color of swamp. The sentries out in front are a troll and a goblin. The troll is wearing armor painted over in some dark color that seems too close to dried blood for comfort.

"Um, hello," I say, which I realize I need to work on. "I'm a messenger. I need to see the queen."

The troll peers down at me, obviously surprised to find a human before him.

"And who dares send such a delicious messenger to our Court?" I think he might actually be flattering me, although it's hard to tell.

"The High King Balekin," I lie. I figure using his name is the fastest way to get in.

That makes him smile, although not in a friendly way. "What is a king without a crown? That's a riddle, but one to which we all know the answer: no king at all."

The other sentry laughs. "We will not let you pass, little morsel. Run back to your master and tell him that Queen Annet does not recognize him, though she appreciates his sense of spectacle. She will not dine with him no matter how many times he asks or what delectable bribes he sends along with his messages."

"This isn't what you think," I say.

"Very well, tarry with us awhile. I bet your bones would crunch sweetly." The troll is all sharp teeth and mild threat. I know he doesn't mean it; if he meant it, he would have said something else entirely and just gobbled me up.

Still, I back off. There are guest obligations on everyone who came for the coronation, but guest obligations among the Folk are baroque enough that I am never sure if they protect me or not.

Prince Cardan is waiting for me in the clearing, lying on his back, as though he's been counting stars.

He looks a question at me, and I shake my head before I slump down in the grass.

"I didn't even get to talk to her," I say.

He turns toward me, the moonlight highlighting the planes of his face, the sharpness of his cheekbones, and the points of his ears. "Then you did something wrong."

I want to snap at him, but he's right. I messed up. I need to be more formal, more sure that it is my right to be allowed in front of a monarch, as though I am used to it. I practiced everything I would *say* to her but not how I would *get* to her. That part seemed easy. Now I can see that it won't be.

I lie back beside him and look up at the stars. If I had time, I could make a chart and trace my luck in them. "Fine. If you were me, whom would you apply to?"

"Lord Roiben and the Alderking's son, Severin." His face is close to mine.

I frown at him. "But they're not part of the High Court. They haven't sworn to the crown."

"Exactly," Cardan says, reaching out a finger to trace the shape of my ear. The curve, I realize. I shudder, eyes closing against the hot spike of shame. He keeps talking, but he seems to realize what he's been doing and snatches his hand away. Now we're both ashamed. "They have less to lose and more to gain throwing in with a plan that some might call treason. Severin reportedly favors a mortal knight and has a mortal lover, so he'll speak with you. And his father was in exile, so recognition of his Court itself would be something.

"As for Lord Roiben, the stories make him seem like some figure in a tragedy. A Seelie knight, tortured for decades as a servant in the Unseelie Court he came to rule. I don't know what you offer someone like that, but he has a big enough Court that if you got him to back Oak, even Balekin would be nervous. Other than that, I know he has a consort he favors, though she is of low rank. Try not to annoy her."

I remember Cardan drunkenly talking us past the guards on the way out of the coronation. He knows these people, knows their customs. No matter how high-handed he sounds giving advice or how much he bothers me, I would be a fool not to listen. I push myself to my feet, hoping there aren't hectic spots of red coloring my cheeks. Cardan sits up, too, looking as though he's about to speak.

"I know," I say, starting toward the camp. "Don't bore you by dying."

I decide to try my luck with the Alderking's son, Severin, first. His camp is small, as is his domain—a stretch of woods just outside Roiben's Court of Termites and neither Seelie nor Unseelie in nature.

His tent is made of some heavy cloth, painted in silver and green. A few knights sit nearby around a cheerful fire. None of them are in armor—just heavy leather tunics and boots. One is fussing with a contraption to suspend a kettle over the fire and boil water. The human boy I saw with Severin at the coronation, the redhead who caught me staring, is talking with one of the knights in a low voice. A moment later, they both laugh. No one pays me any notice.

I march up to the fire. "Your pardon," I say, wondering if even that is too polite for a royal messenger. Still, I have no choice but to barrel on. "I have a message for the Alderking's son. The new High King wishes to come to an arrangement with him."

"Oh, really?" The human surprises me by speaking first.

"Yes, mortal," I say, like the hypocrite I am. But come on, that's absolutely how one of Balekin's servants would talk to him.

He rolls his eyes and says something to one of the other knights as he stands. It takes me a moment to realize I am looking at Lord Severin. Hair the color of autumn leaves and moss-green eyes and horns curving from behind his brow to just above his ears. I am surprised at the thought of his sitting with the rest of his retinue before a fire, but I recover quickly enough to remember to bow.

"I must speak with you alone," I say.

"Oh?" he queries. I do not respond, and his brows rise. "Of course," he says. "This way."

"You should fix her," the human boy calls after us. "Seriously, glamoured human servants are *creepy*."

Severin doesn't answer him.

I trail behind him into the tent. None of the others follow, although, when we get inside, there are some women in gowns sitting on cushions and a piper playing a little tune. A female knight sits beside them, her sword across her lap. The blade is beautiful enough to catch my eye.

Severin leads me to a low table surrounded by tufted stools and piled with refreshments—a silver carafe of water with a horn handle, a platter of grapes and apricots, and a dish of little honeyed pastries. He gestures for me to sit, and when I do, he settles himself on another stool.

"Eat whatever you wish," he says, making it seem like an offer rather than a command.

"I want to ask you to witness a coronation ceremony," I say, ignoring the food. "But Balekin's not the one who's going to be crowned."

He doesn't look immensely surprised, just slightly more suspicious. "So you're *not* his messenger?"

"I am the next High King's messenger," I say, taking Cardan's ring from my pocket as proof that I have some connection to the royal family, that I am not just making up this story from whole cloth. "Balekin isn't going to be the next High King."

"I see." His affect is impassive, but his gaze is drawn to the ring.

"And I can promise you that your Court will be recognized as sovereign, if you help us. No threat of conquest from the new High King. Instead, we offer you an alliance." Fear crawls up my throat, and I almost can't say the last words. If he won't help me, there's some chance he'll betray me to Balekin. If that happens, things get a lot more difficult.

I can control a lot, but I cannot control this.

Severin's face is unreadable. "I am not going to insult you by asking whom you represent. There is only one possibility, the young Prince Cardan, of whom I hear many things. But I am not the ideal candidate to help you, for the very reasons your offer is so tempting. My Court is afforded little consequence. And more, I am the son of a traitor, so my honor is unlikely to be given weight."

"You're going to Balekin's banquet already. All I need from you is aid at the critical moment." He's tempted, he admitted as much. Maybe he just needs some more convincing. "Whatever you've heard about Prince Cardan, he will make a better king than his brother."

At least there I am not lying.

Severin glances toward the edge of the tent, as though wondering who can overhear me. "I will help you so long as I am not the only one. I say this as much for your sake as for mine." With that, he stands. "I wish you and the prince well. If you need me, I will do what I can."

I get up off the stool and bow again. "You are most generous."

As I leave his camp, my mind whirls. On one hand, I did it. I managed to speak with one of the rulers of Faerie without making a fool of myself. I even kind of persuaded him to go along with my plan. But I still need another monarch, a more influential one, to agree.

There is one place I have been avoiding. The largest camp belongs to Roiben of the Court of Termites. Notoriously bloodthirsty, he won both of his crowns in battle, so he has no reason to object to Balekin's blood-soaked coup. Still, Roiben seems to feel much the way Annet of the Court of Moths does, that Balekin is of little consequence without a crown.

Maybe he won't want to see one of Balekin's messengers, either. And, given the size of his encampment, I can't even imagine the number of guardians I would have to pass in order to speak with him.

But possibly I could sneak in. After all, with so many of the Folk around, what is one person more or less?

I gather up a bundle of fallen branches, large enough to be a respectable contribution to a fire, and walk toward the Termite Camp with my head down. There are knights posted around the perimeter, but, indeed, they pay me little mind as I walk past.

I feel giddy with the success of my plan. When I was a child, sometimes Madoc would have to stop in the middle of a game of Nine Men's Morris. The board would remain as it was, waiting for us to resume. All through the day and the night, I would imagine my moves and his countermoves until, when we sat down, we were no longer playing the original game. Most often what I failed to do was accurately anticipate his next moves. I had a great strategy for me, but not for the game I was in.

That's how I feel now, walking into the camp. I am playing a game opposite Madoc, and while I can spin out plans and schemes, if I can't accurately guess his, I am sunk.

I drop the kindling beside a fire. A blue-skinned woman with black teeth regards me for a moment and then goes back to her conversation with a goat-footed man. Dusting the bark from my clothes, I walk toward the largest tent. I keep my step light and my stride easy and even. When I find a patch of shadow, I use it to crawl under the edge of the cloth. For a moment, I lie there, half hidden on both sides and completely hidden on neither.

The inside of the main tent is lit with lanterns burning with green alchemical fire, tinting everything a sickly color. In every other way, however, the interior is lush. Carpets are layered, one over another. There are heavy wooden tables, chairs, and a bed piled with furs and brocade coverlets stitched with pomegranates.

But on the table, to my surprise, are paper cartons of food. The green-skinned pixie who was with Roiben at the coronation uses chopsticks to bring noodles to her mouth. He sits beside her, carefully breaking apart a fortune cookie.

"What does it say?" the girl asks. "How about 'the trip you told your girlfriend would be fun ended in bloodshed, as usual.' "

"It says, 'Your shoes will make you happy today,'" he tells her, voice dry, and passes the little slip across the table for her verification.

She glances down at his leather boots. He shrugs, a small smile touching his lips.

Then I'm dragged roughly out from my hiding place. I roll onto my back outside the tent to find a knight standing above me, her sword drawn. There is no one to blame but myself. I should have kept moving, should have found a way to hide myself inside the tent. I should not have stopped to listen to a conversation, no matter how surprising I found it.

"Get up," the knight says. Dulcamara. Her face shows no recognition of me, however.

I stand, and she marches me into the tent, kicking me in the legs once we get there so I topple onto the rugs. I have cause to be thankful for their plushness. For a moment, I let myself lie there. She presses her boot against the small of my back as though I am some felled prey.

"I caught a spy," she announces. "Shall I snap its neck?"

I could roll over and grab her ankle. That would throw her off balance for long enough that I could get up. If I twisted her leg and ran, I might be able to get away. At worst, I'd be on my feet, able to grab a weapon and fight her.

But I came here to have an audience with Lord Roiben, and now I have one. I stay still and let Dulcamara underestimate me.

Lord Roiben has come around from the table and bends over me, white hair falling around his face. Silver eyes regard me pitilessly. "And whose Court are you a part of?"

"The High King's," I say. "The true High King, Eldred, who was felled by his son."

"I am not sure I believe you." He surprises me both with the mildness of the statement and with the assumption that I am lying. "Come, sit with us and eat. I would hear more of your tale. Dulcamara, you may leave us."

"You're going to feed it?" she asks sulkily.

He does not answer her, and after a moment of stony silence, she seems to remember herself. With a bow, she leaves.

I go to the table. The pixie regards me with her inkdrop-black eyes, like Tatterfell's. I notice the extra joint in her fingers as she reaches for an eggroll. "Go ahead," she says. "There's plenty. I used most of the hot mustard packets, though."

Roiben waits, watching me.

"Mortal food," I say, in what I hope is a neutral way.

"We live alongside mortals, do we not?" he asks me.

"I think *she* more than lives *beside* them," the pixie objects, looking at me.

"Your pardon," he says, and waits. I realize they really expect me to eat something. I spear a dumpling with a single chopstick and stuff it into my mouth. "It's good."

The pixie resumes eating noodles.

Roiben gestures to her. "This is Kaye. I imagine you know who I am since you snuck into my camp. What name might you go by?"

I am unused to such scrupulous politeness being afforded to me—he's doing me the courtesy of not asking for my true name. "Jude," I say, because names have no power over mortals. "And I came to see you because I can put someone other than Balekin on the throne, but I need your help to do it."

"Someone better than Balekin or just someone?" he asks.

I frown, not sure how to answer that. "Someone who didn't murder most of his family onstage. Isn't that automatically better?"

The pixie—*Kaye*—snorts.

Lord Roiben looks down at his hand, on the wooden table, then back at me. I cannot read his grim face. "Balekin is no diplomat, but perhaps he can learn. He's obviously ambitious, and he pulled off a brutal coup. Not everyone has the stomach for that."

"I almost didn't have the stomach to watch it," Kaye says.

"He only sort of pulled it off," I remind them. "And I didn't think you liked him very much, given what you said at the coronation."

A corner of Roiben's mouth turns up. It is a gesture in miniature, barely noticeable. "I don't. I think he's a coward to kill his sisters and father in what appeared to be a fit of pique. And he hid behind his military, letting his general finish off the High King's chosen heir. That bespeaks weakness, the kind that will inevitably be exploited."

A cold chill of premonition shivers up my back. "What I need is someone to witness a coronation, someone with enough power that the witnessing will matter. You. It will happen at Balekin's feast, tomorrow eve. If you'll just allow it to happen and give your oath to the new High King—"

"No offense," Kaye says, "but what do you have to do with any of this? Why do you care who gets the throne?"

"Because this is where I live," I say. "This is where I grew up. Even if I hate it half the time, it's mine."

Lord Roiben nods slowly. "And you are not going to tell me who this candidate is nor how you're going to get a crown on his head?"

"I'd rather not," I say.

"I could get Dulcamara to hurt you until you begged to be allowed to tell me your secrets." He says this mildly, just another fact, but it reminds me of just how horrific his reputation is. No amount of takeout Chinese food or politeness ought to make me forget exactly who and what I am dealing with.

"Wouldn't that make you as much of a coward as Balekin?" I ask, trying to project the same confidence I did in the Court of Shadows, the same confidence I did with Cardan. I can't let him see that I'm scared or, at least, not *how* scared I am.

We study each other for a long moment, the pixie watching us both. Finally, Lord Roiben lets out a long breath. "Probably more of a coward. Very well, Jude, kingmaker. We will gamble with you. Put the crown on a head other than Balekin's and I will help you keep it there." He pauses. "But you will do something for me."

I wait, tense.

He steeples his long fingers. "Someday, I will ask your king for a favor."

"You want me to agree to something without even knowing what it is?" I blurt out.

His stoic face gives little away. "Now we understand each other exactly."

I nod. What choice do I have? "Something of equal value," I clarify. "And within our power."

"This has been a most interesting meeting," Lord Roiben says with a small, inscrutable smile.

As I stand to leave, Kaye winks an inkdrop eye at me. "Luck, mortal."

With her words echoing after me, I leave the encampments and head back to Cardan.

CHAPTER 28

The Ghost is up when we return. He had been out and brought back with him a handful of tiny apples, some dried venison, fresh butter, and several dozen more bottles of wine. He's also brought down a few pieces of furniture I recognize from the palace—a silk-embroidered divan, satin cushions, a shimmering spider-silk throw, and a chalcedony set of tea things.

He looks up from the divan where he is sitting, appearing both tense and exhausted. I think he's grieving, but not in a human way. "Well? I believe I was promised gold."

"What if I could promise you revenge?" I ask, conscious once again of the weight of debts already on my shoulders.

He trades a look with the Bomb. "So she really does have a scheme."

The Bomb settles herself on a cushion. "A secret, which is far better than a scheme."

I grab an apple, go to the table, and then hoist myself onto it. "We're going to walk right into Balekin's feast and steal his kingdom out from under him. How's that for vengeance?"

Bold, that's what I need to be. Like I own the place. Like I am the general's daughter. Like I can really pull this off.

The corner of the Ghost's mouth turns up. He takes out four silver cups from the cupboard and sets them before me. "Drink?"

I shake my head, watching him pour. He returns to the divan but rests at the edge as though he's going to have to jump up in a moment. He takes a big swallow of wine.

"You spoke of the murder of Dain's unborn child," I say.

The Ghost nods. "I saw your face when Cardan spoke of Liriope and when you understood my part in it."

"It surprised me," I say honestly. "I wanted to think Dain was different."

Cardan snorts and takes the silver cup that was meant for me as well as his own.

"Murder is a cruel trade," says the Ghost. "I believe Dain would have been as fair a High King as any prince of the Folk, but my father was mortal. He would not have considered Dain to be good. He would not have considered me good, either. You'd do well to decide how much you care for goodness before you go too far down the road of spycraft."

He's probably right, but there's little time for me to consider it now. "You don't understand," I tell him. "Liriope's child lived."

He turns to the Bomb, clearly astonished. "*That's* the secret?"

She nods, a little smug. "That's the scheme."

The Ghost gives her a long look and then turns his gaze to me. "I don't want to find a new position. I want to stay here and serve the next High King. So, yes, let's steal the kingdom."

"We don't need to be good," I tell the Ghost. "But let's try to be fair. As fair as any prince of Faerie."

The Ghost smiles.

"And maybe a little fairer," I say with a look at Cardan.

The Ghost nods. "I'd like that."

Then he goes to wake the Roach. I have to explain all over again. Once I get to the part about the banquet and what I think is going to happen, the Roach interrupts me so many times I can barely get a sentence out. After I'm done speaking, he removes a roll of vellum and a nibbed pen from one of the cabinets and notes down who ought to be where at what point for the plan to work.

"You're replanning my plan," I say.

"Just a little," he says, licking the nib and beginning to write again. "Are you concerned over Madoc? He won't like this."

Of course I am concerned about Madoc. If I wasn't, I wouldn't be doing any of this. I would just hand him the living key to the kingdom.

"I know," I say, gazing at the dregs of wine in the Ghost's glass. The moment I walk into the feast with Cardan on my arm, Madoc will know I am running a game of my own. When he discovers that I am going to cheat him out of being regent, he'll be furious.

And he's at his most bloodthirsty when he's furious.

"Do you have something appropriate to wear?" the Roach asks. At my surprised look, he throws up his hands. "You're playing politics. You and Cardan need to be turned out in splendor for this banquet. Your new king will need everything to look right."

We go over the plans again, and Cardan helps us map out Hollow Hall. I try not to be too conscious of his long fingers tracing over the paper, of the sick thrill I get when he looks at me.

At dawn, I drink three cups of tea and set out alone for the last person I must speak with before the banquet, my sister Vivienne.

I go back to my house—Madoc's house, I remind myself, never really mine, never mine again after tonight—as the sun rises in a blaze of gold. I feel like a shadow as I climb the spiral stairs, as I pass through all the rooms I grew up in. In my bedroom, I pack a bag. Poison, knives, a gown, and jewels that I think the Roach will find to be properly extravagant. With reluctance, I leave behind the stuffed animals from my bed. I leave slippers and books and favorite baubles. I step out of my second life the same way I stepped out of my first, holding too few things and with great uncertainty about what will happen next.

Then I go to Vivi's door. I rap softly. After a few moments, she sleepily lets me inside.

"Oh good," she mumbles, yawning. "You're packed." Then she catches sight of my face and shakes her head. "Please don't tell me you're not coming."

"Something happened," I say, resting my bag on the ground. I keep my voice low. There is no real reason to hide that I am here, but hiding has become habit. "Just hear me out."

"You disappeared," she says. "I've been waiting and waiting for you, trying to act like things were fine in front of Dad. You made me worry."

"I know," I say.

She looks at me like she's considering giving me a swift smack. "I was afraid you were *dead*."

"I'm not even a little bit dead," I say, taking her arm and pulling her close so I can speak in a whisper. "But I have to tell you something I know you're not going to like: I have been working as a spy for Prince Dain. He put me under a geas so I couldn't have said anything before his death."

Her delicately pointed eyebrows rise. "Spying? What does that entail?"

"Sneaking around and getting information. Killing people. And before you say anything else, I was good at it."

"O*kay*," she says. She knew something was up with me, but from her face, I can tell that in a million years she wouldn't have guessed this.

I go on. "And I discovered that Madoc is going to make a political move, one that involves Oak." I explain once more about Liriope and Oriana and Dain. By this point, I have told this story enough that it's easy to hit only the necessary parts, to run through the information quickly and convincingly. "Madoc is going to make Oak king and himself regent. I don't know if that was always his plan, but I am sure it's his plan now."

"And that's why you're not coming to the human world with me?"

"I want you to take Oak instead," I tell her. "Keep him away from all this until he gets a little older, old enough not to need a regent. I'll stay here and make sure he has something to come back to."

Vivi puts her hands on her hips, a gesture that reminds me of our mother. "And how exactly are you going to do that?"

"Leave that part to me," I say, wishing that Vivi didn't know me quite as well as she does. To distract her, I explain about Balekin's banquet, about how the Court of Shadows is going to help me get the crown. I am going to need her to prep Oak for the coronation. "Whoever controls the king, controls the kingdom," I say. "If Madoc is regent, you know that Faerie will always be at war."

"So let me get this straight: You want me to take Oak away from Faerie, away from everyone he knows, and teach him how to be a good king?" She laughs mirthlessly. "Our mother once stole a faerie child away—me. You know what happened. How will this be any different? How will you keep Madoc and Balekin from hunting Oak to the ends of the earth?"

"Someone can be sent to guard him, to guard all of you—but, as for the rest, I have a plan. Madoc won't follow." With Vivi, I feel forever doomed to be the little sister, foolish and about to topple over onto my face.

"Maybe I don't want to play nursemaid," Vivi says. "Maybe I will lose him in a parking garage or forget him at school. Maybe I would teach him awful tricks. Maybe he would blame me for all this."

"Give me another solution. You really think this is what I want?" I know I sound like I am pleading with her, but I can't help it.

For a tense moment, we look at each other. Then she sits down hard in a chair and lets her head fall back against the cushion. "How am I going to explain this to Heather?"

"I think Oak is the least shocking part of what you have to tell her," I say. "And it's just for a few years. You're immortal. Which, by the way, is one of the more shocking things you have to tell her."

She gives me a glare fit to singe hair. "Make me a promise that this is going to save Oak's life."

"I promise," I tell her.

"And make me another promise that it's not going to cost you yours."

I nod. "It won't."

"Liar," she says. "You're a dirty liar and I hate it and I hate this."

"Yeah," I say. "I know."

At least she didn't say she hated me, too.

I am on my way out of the house when Taryn opens her bedroom door. She's dressed in a skirt the color of ivy, with stitching picking out a pattern of falling leaves.

My breath catches. I wasn't planning to see her.

We regard each other for a long moment. She takes in that there's a bag over my shoulder and that I'm in the same clothes I wore when we fought.

Then she closes her door again, leaving me to my fate.

CHAPTER 29

Never have I walked through the front doors of Hollow Hall. Always before I have come skulking through the kitchens, dressed as a servant. Now I stand in front of the polished wood doors, lit by two lamps of trapped sprites who fly in desperate circles. They illuminate a carving of an enormous and sinister face. The knocker, a circle piercing its nose.

Cardan reaches for it, and because I have grown up in Faerie, I am not entirely surprised into a scream when the door's eyes open.

"My prince," it says.

"My door," he says in return, with a smile that conveys both affection and familiarity. It's bizarre to see his obnoxious charm used for something other than evil.

"Hail and welcome," the door says, swinging open to reveal one of Balekin's faerie servants. He stares openmouthed at Cardan, missing prince of Faerie. "The other guests are through there," the servant finally manages.

Cardan tucks my arm firmly through his before striding into the entryway, and I feel a rush of warmth as I match his step. I can't afford to be less than ruthlessly honest with myself. Against my better judgment, despite the fact that he is terrible, Cardan is also fun.

Maybe I should be glad of how little it will matter.

But for now, it's immensely unnerving. Cardan is dressed in a suit of Dain's clothes, stolen from the palace wardrobes and altered by a clever-fingered brownie that owed the Roach a gambling debt. He looks regal in different shades of cream—a coat over a vest and loose shirt, breeches and a neckcloth, with the same silver-tipped boots he wore to the coronation, a single sapphire shining from his left ear. He's *supposed* to look regal. I helped choose the clothes, helped make him this way, and yet the effect is not lost on me.

I am wearing a bottle-green gown with earrings in the shape of berries. In my pocket is Liriope's golden acorn, and at my hip is my father's sword. Against my skin, I have a collection of knives. It doesn't feel like enough.

As we cross the floor, everyone turns to look. The lords and ladies of Faerie. Kings and queens of other Courts. The representative from the Queen of the Undersea. Balekin. My family. Oak, standing with Oriana and Madoc. I look over at Lord Roiben, his white hair making him easy to find in the crowd, but he does not acknowledge that we have ever met. His face remains unreadable, a mask.

I am going to have to trust that he will keep his part of the bargain, but I mislike this kind of calculation. I grew up thinking of strategy as finding weaknesses and exploiting them. That I understand. But making people like you, making people want to take your part and be on your side—that I am far less skilled at.

My gaze goes from a table of refreshments to the elaborate gowns to a goblin king crunching on a bone. Then my eyes settle on the Blood Crown of the High King. It rests on a ledge above us, a pillow beneath it. There, it glows with a sinister light.

At the sight, I imagine all my plans coming apart. The thought of stealing it, in front of everyone, daunts me. And yet, having to search Hollow Hall for it would have been daunting, too.

I see Balekin move from speaking with a woman I don't recognize. She's wearing a gown of woven seaweed and a collar of pearls. Her black hair is tied to a crown festooned with more pearls, appearing like webbing above her head. It takes me a moment to puzzle out who she must be—Queen Orlagh, Nicasia's mother. Balekin leaves her and crosses the room toward us with purpose.

Cardan catches sight of Balekin and steers us in the direction of the wine. Bottles and carafes of it—pale green, yellow as gold, the dark purple-red of my heart's own blood. They are redolent of roses, of dandelions, of crushed herbs and currants. The smell alone nearly makes my head spin.

"Little brother," Balekin says to Cardan. He is dressed head to toe in black and silver, the velvet of his doublet so thickly embroidered with patterns of crowns and birds that it looks as heavy as armor. He wears a silver circlet on his brow, matching his eyes. It's not *the* crown, but it is *a* crown. "I've sought high and low for you."

"Doubtless so." Cardan smiles like the villain I've always believed him to be. "I turned out to be useful after all. What a terrible surprise."

Prince Balekin smiles back as though their smiles could duel without the rest of them even being involved. I am sure he wishes he could rail at Cardan, could beat him into doing what he wants, but since the rest of their family died at swordpoint, Balekin must have learned his lesson about needing a willing participant in a coronation.

For the moment, Cardan's presence is enough to reassure people that Balekin will soon be the High King. If Balekin calls for guards or grabs him, that illusion will dissipate.

"And you," Balekin says, turning his gaze to me, viciousness lighting his eyes. "What have you to do with this? Leave us."

"Jude," Madoc says, striding up to stand beside Prince Balekin, who immediately seems to realize I might have *something* to do with this after all.

Madoc looks displeased but not alarmed. I am sure he is thinking me a fool who expects to get a pat on the head for finding the missing prince and cursing himself for not making it more clear that he wanted Cardan brought to *him* and *not* to Balekin. I give him my best blithe smile, like a girl who thinks she has solved everyone's problems.

How frustrating it must be to come so close to your goal, to have Oak and the crown in one place, to have the lords and ladies of Faerie assembled. And then your first wife's bastard throws a spanner in the works by handing the one person most likely to put the crown on Oak's head to your rival.

I note the evaluating look he's giving Cardan, however. He's replanning.

He rests a heavy hand on my shoulder. "You found him." He turns to Balekin. "I hope you're intending to reward my daughter. I am sure it took no small amount of persuasion to bring him here."

Cardan gives Madoc an odd look. I remember what he said about it bothering him that Madoc treated me so well when Eldred barely acknowledged him. But the way he's looking, I wonder if it's just weird to see us together, redcap general and human girl.

"I will give her anything she asks for and more," Balekin promises extravagantly. I see Madoc frown, and I give him a quick smile, pouring two glasses of wine—one light and the other dark. I am careful with them, sly-fingered. I do not spill a drop.

Instead of handing one to Cardan, I offer them both up for Madoc to choose between. Smiling, he takes the one the color of heart's blood. I take the other.

"To the future of Faerie," I say, tapping the globes together, making the glass ring like bells. We drink. Immediately, I feel the effects—a kind of floatiness, as though I am swimming through air. I don't want to even look at Cardan. He will laugh and laugh if he thinks I can't handle a few sips of wine.

Cardan pours his own glass and throws it back.

"Take the bottle," Balekin says. "I am prepared to be very generous. Let us discuss what you'd like, whatever you'd like."

"There's no hurry, is there?" Cardan asks lazily.

Balekin gives him the hard stare of someone barely holding himself back from violence. "I think everyone would like to see the matter settled."

"Nonetheless," Cardan says, taking the bottle of wine and drinking directly from the neck. "We have all night."

"The power is in your hands," Balekin tells him in a clipped way that leaves the "for now" heavily implied.

I see a muscle twitch in Cardan's jaw. I am sure Balekin is imagining how he will punish Cardan for any delay. It weighs down his every word.

Madoc, by contrast, is taking in the situation, evaluating, no doubt, what he can offer Cardan. When he smiles at me and takes another swig of his wine, it's a real smile. Toothy and relieved. I can see he's thinking that Cardan will be easier to manipulate than Balekin ever would have been.

I am suddenly certain that if we went into the other room, Balekin would find Madoc's sword buried in his chest.

"After dinner, I will tell you my terms," Cardan says. "But until then, I am going to enjoy the party."

"I do not have endless patience," Balekin growls.

"Cultivate it," Cardan says, and with a small bow, he navigates us away from Balekin and Madoc.

I leave my glass of wine near a platter of sparrow hearts, pierced through with long silver pins, and weave through the crowd with him.

Nicasia stops us with a long-fingered hand against Cardan's chest, her cerulean hair bright against her bronze gown.

"Where have you been?" Nicasia asks with a glance at our linked arms. She wrinkles her delicate nose, but panic underlines her words. She is feigning calm, like the rest of us.

I am sure that she thought Cardan had to be dead, or worse. There must be many things she wants to ask him, all of which she cannot do in front of me.

"Jude here made me her prisoner," he says, and I have to fight down the urge to step heavily on his foot. "She ties very tight knots."

Nicasia clearly doesn't know whether to laugh. I almost sympathize. I don't know, either.

"Good thing you finally managed to slip her bonds," Nicasia decides on.

He raises both brows. "Did I?" he asks with a haughty condescension, as though she has shown herself to be less clever than he had hoped.

"Must you be like this, even now?" she asks, clearly deciding to throw caution to the wind. Her hand goes to his arm.

His face softens in a way that I am entirely unused to seeing. "Nicasia," he says, pulling himself free. "Stay away from me tonight. For your own sake."

It stings a little, that he has that kindness in him. I don't want to see it.

She gives me a look, doubtlessly trying to decide why his pronouncement doesn't apply to me. But then Cardan is moving away from her, and I go with him. I see Taryn across the room, Locke beside her. Her eyes widen, taking in whom I am standing with. Something passes over her face, and it looks a lot like resentment.

She has Locke, but I am here with a *prince.*

That's not fair. I cannot know she is thinking that from just one look.

"Part one completed," I say, looking away from her. Speaking to Cardan under my breath. "We got here, got in, and are not yet in chains."

"Yes," he says. "I believe the Roach called that 'the easy bit.'"

The plan, as I've explained it to him, has five basic phases: (1) get in, (2) get everybody else in, (3) get the crown, (4) put the crown on Oak's head, and (5) get out.

I take my arm from his. "Don't go anywhere alone," I remind Cardan.

He gives me the tight-lipped smile of someone who's being abandoned and nods once.

I head toward Oriana and Oak. On the other side of the room, I see Severin break off from a conversation and walk toward Prince Balekin. Sweat beads on my lip, under my arms. My muscles tense.

If Severin says the wrong thing, I am going to have to abandon all phases of the plan except for "get out."

Oriana raises both brows as I approach, her hands going to Oak's thin shoulders. He reaches up his hands. I want to swing him up into my arms. I want to ask him if Vivi explained what's going to happen. I want to tell him everything's going to be fine. But Oriana grabs his fingers, pressing them between hers, settling the question of how many lies I could stomach.

"What is this?" Oriana asks me with a nod toward Cardan.

"What you asked," I tell her, following her gaze. Somehow, Balekin has drawn Cardan into his conversation with Severin. Cardan laughs at something Balekin said, looking as comfortably arrogant as I've ever seen him. I am shocked by recognition—if you live your life always afraid, always with danger on your heels, it is not so difficult to pretend away more danger. I know that, but I didn't think, of all people, Cardan would, too. Balekin has his hand on Cardan's shoulder. I can just imagine his fingers digging into Cardan's neck. "It's not easy. I hope you understand there's going to be a price—"

"I'll pay it," she says quickly.

"None of us knows the cost," I snap, and then hope no one notices the sharpness of my tone. "And we're all going to have to pay our share."

My skin has a fine flush on it from the wine, and there's a metallic taste in my mouth. It's nearly time to put the next part of the plan into effect. I glance around for Vivi, but she's across the room. There's no time to say anything to her now, even if I knew what to say.

I give Oak what I hope is an encouraging smile. I have often wondered if my past is the reason I am the way I am, if it has made me monstrous. If so, will I make a monster out of him?

Vivi won't, I tell myself. Her job is to help him care about things other than power, and my job is to care only about power so I can carve out room for his return. With a deep breath, I head toward the doors out into the hallway. I pass the pair of knights and turn a corner, out of their sight line. I gulp down a few breaths before unlatching the windows.

I wait a few hopeful moments. If the Roach and the Ghost climb through, I can explain the crown's location. But, instead, the doors to the banquet open, and I hear Madoc order the knights off. I move so that he can see me. When he does, he comes toward me with purpose. "Jude. I thought you came this way."

"I needed some fresh air," I tell him, which is indicative of how nerved up I am. I have answered the question he hasn't yet asked.

He waves it off, though. "You should have come to me first when you found Prince Cardan. We could have negotiated from a position of strength."

"I thought you might say something like that," I tell him.

"What matters now is that I need to speak with him alone. I'd like you to go inside and bring him out here, so we can talk. All three of us can talk."

I move away from the window, into the open space of the hall. The Ghost and the Roach will be here in a moment, and I don't want Madoc to spot them. "About Oak?" I ask.

As I had hoped, Madoc follows me away from the window, frowning. "You knew?"

"That you have a plan for ruling Elfhame yourself?" I ask him. "I figured it out."

He stares at me as though I am a stranger, but I have never felt less like one. For the first time, we are both unmasked.

"And yet you brought Prince Cardan here, right to Balekin," he says. "Or to me? Is that it? Are we to bargain now?"

"It must be one or the other, right?" I say.

He's growing angry. "Would you prefer no High King at all? If the crown is destroyed, there will be war, and if there's war, I will win it. One way or another, I will have that crown, Jude. And you stand to benefit when I do. There's no reason to oppose me. You can have your knighthood. You can have all the things you've ever dreamed of." He takes another step toward me. We are in striking distance of each other.

"You said, 'I will have that crown.' *You*," I remind him, my hand going to the hilt of my sword. "You've barely spoken Oak's name. He is just a means to an end, and that end is power. Power for you."

"Jude—" he begins, but I cut him off.

"I'll make a bargain. Swear to me that you'll never raise a hand against Oak, and I'll help. Promise me that when he comes of age, you will immediately step down as regent. You'll give him whatever power you'll have amassed, and you'll do it willingly."

Madoc's mouth twists. His hands fist. I know he loves Oak. He loves me. I'm sure he loved my mother, too, in his own way. But he is who and what he is. I know he cannot promise.

I draw my sword, and he does, too, the scrape of metal loud in the room. I hear distant laughter, but here in the hall, we are alone.

My hands are sweating, but this has the feeling of inevitability, as though this is what I was careening toward the whole time, my whole life.

"You can't beat me," Madoc says, moving into a fighting stance.

"I already have," I say.

"You have no way to win." Madoc flicks his blade, encouraging me to come toward him, as though this is just some practice bout. "What can you hope to do with one missing prince, here in Balekin's stronghold? I will knock you down, and then I will take him from you. You could have had anything you wanted, but now you will be left with nothing."

"Oh, yes, let me tell you my whole plan. You've goaded me right into it." I make a face. "Let's not stall anymore. This is the part where we fight."

"At least you're no coward." He rushes at me with such force that even though I block the blow, I am thrown to the floor. I roll into a standing position, but I am shaken. He has never fought me like this, full out. This will be no genteel exchange of blows.

He's the High King's general. I knew he was better than me, but not how much better.

I cheat a glance toward the window. I can't be stronger than him, but I don't need to be. I just need to keep on my feet a little while longer. I strike out, hoping to catch him by surprise. He knocks me back again. I dodge and turn, but he expects the blow, and I have to stumble inelegantly back, blocking yet another heavy chop of his blade. My arms hurt from the strength behind his blows.

This is all happening too fast.

I come in with a series of techniques he's taught me and then use a bit of swordplay I learned from the Ghost. I feign left and then land a clever slice to his side. It's a shallow hit, but it surprises us both when a line of red wets his coat. He thrusts toward me. I jump to one side, and he elbows me in the face, knocking me back to the ground. Blood gushes over my mouth from my nose.

I push myself dizzily to my feet.

I'm scared, no matter how I try to play it off. I was arrogant. I am trying to buy time, but one of his blows could split me in half.

"Surrender," he tells me, sword pointed toward my throat. "It was well tried. I will forgive you, Jude, and we will go back into the banquet. You will persuade Cardan to do what I need him to. All will be as it should be."

I spit blood on the stone tiles.

His sword arm trembles a little.

"*You* surrender," I say.

He laughs, as though I have told a particularly rich joke. Then he stops, grimacing.

"I imagine you're not feeling quite yourself," I tell him.

His sword sags a little, and he looks at me in sudden comprehension. "What have you done?"

"I poisoned you. Don't worry. It was a small enough dose. You'll live."

"The cups of wine," he says. "But how did you know which one I would choose?"

"I didn't," I tell him, thinking that he'll be at least a little pleased by the answer, despite himself. It is the kind of strategy he likes best. "I poisoned them both."

"You will be very sorry," he says. The tremble is in his legs now. I know. I feel the echo of it in my own. But by now, I am used to drinking poison.

I look deep into his eyes as I sheathe my sword. "Father, I am what you made me. I've become your daughter after all."

Madoc lifts his blade again, as though he's going to rush at me one final time. But then it falls from his hand, and he falls, too, sprawling on the stone floor.

When the Ghost and the Roach come in, a few tense minutes later, they find me sitting beside him, too tired to even think of moving his body.

Wordlessly, the Roach hands me a handkerchief, and I start to wipe the blood from my nose.

"On to phase three," the Ghost says.

CHAPTER 30

When I rejoin the feast, everyone is taking their place at the long table. I walk straight to Balekin and curtsy.

"My lord," I say, pitching my voice low. "Madoc asked me to tell you that he is delayed and to begin without him. He wishes you not to worry, but some of Dain's spies are here. He will send you word when he's caught or killed them."

Balekin regards me with slightly pursed lips and narrowed eyes. He takes in whatever traces of blood I couldn't wash from my nostrils and my teeth, whatever sweat I couldn't wipe away. Madoc slumbers in Cardan's old room, and by my calculations, we have at least an hour before he wakes. It feels as though if Balekin looked carefully, he could see that on my face, too.

"You have been more helpful than I would have guessed," Balekin says, resting a hand lightly on my shoulder. He seems to have forgotten how furious he was when I first came in with Cardan and expects me to forget it, too. "Continue and you will find yourself rewarded. Would you like to live as one of us? Would you like to *be* one of us?"

Could the High King of Faerie really give me that? Could he make me something other than human, something other than mortal?

I think of Valerian's words when he tried to glamour me into jumping out of the tower. *Being born mortal is like being born already dead.*

He sees the look on my face and smiles, sure that he has ferreted out the secret desire of my heart.

And, indeed, as I walk to my seat, I am troubled. I should feel triumphant, but, instead, I feel sick. Outmaneuvering Madoc wasn't nearly as satisfying as I wanted it to be, especially since I was able to do it because he never thought of me as someone who would betray him. Perhaps years from now, my faith in this plan will prove justified, but until then I will have to live with this acid in the pit of my stomach.

The future of Faerie depends on my playing a long game and playing it perfectly.

I spot Vivi, sitting between Nicasia and Lord Severin, and I give her a quick smile. She gives me a grim one in return.

Lord Roiben looks at me askance. Beside him, the green pixie whispers something in his ear, and he shakes his head. At the other end of the table, Locke kisses Taryn's hand. Queen Orlagh looks over at me curiously. There are only three mortals here—Taryn, me, and the redhead with Severin—and from the way she regards us, Orlagh is imagining mice presiding over a convocation of cats.

Above hangs a chandelier made from thin sheets of mica. Tiny glowing faeries are trapped inside for the purpose of adding a warm glow to the room. Occasionally, they fly, making shadows dance.

"Jude," Locke says, touching my arm, startling me. His fox eyes crinkle in amusement. "I admit, I am a little jealous to see Cardan parading you around on his arm."

I take a step back. "I don't have time for this."

"I liked you, you know," he says. "I like you still."

For a moment, I wonder what would happen if I hauled off and punched him.

"Go away, Locke," I tell him.

His smile returns. "The thing I like best is how you never do what I imagine you will. For instance, I didn't think you'd duel over me."

"I didn't." I pull away from him and head to the table, a little unsteady on my feet.

"There you are," Cardan says as I take my place beside him. "How has the night been going for you? Mine has been full of dull conversations about how my head is going to find itself on a spike."

My hands shake as I take my place. I tell myself that it's just the poison. My mouth is dry. I find myself without the wit for verbal sparring. Servants set down dishes—roasted goose shining with currant glaze, oysters and stewed ramps, acorn cakes and whole fish stuffed with rose hips. Wine is poured, dark green with pieces of gold floating in it. I watch them sink to the bottom of the glass, shining sediment.

"Have I told you how hideous you look tonight?" Cardan asks, leaning back in the elaborately carved chair, the warmth of his words turning the question into something like a compliment.

"No," I say, glad to be annoyed back into the present. "Tell me."

"I cannot," he says, then frowns. "Jude?" I may never be used to the sound of my name on his lips. His brows draw together. "There's a bruise coming up on your jaw."

I take a deep drink of water. "I'm fine," I tell him.

It's not long now.

Balekin stands and raises his glass.

I shove back my chair, so that I am on my feet when the explosion happens. For a moment, everything is so loud that it feels like the room is tilting sideways. The Folk scream. Crystal goblets fall and shatter.

The Bomb has struck.

In the confusion, a single black bolt flies from a shadowed alcove and sinks into the wooden table right in front of Cardan.

Balekin leaps to his feet. "There," he shouts. "The assassin!" Knights run toward the Roach, who leaps out of the gloom and shoots again.

Another bolt flies toward Cardan, who pretends to be too stunned to move, just the way we practiced. The Roach explained to Cardan in great detail how it would be much safer to be still, much easier to miss him that way.

What we didn't count on is Balekin. He knocks Cardan out of the chair, throws him to the floor, and covers Cardan's body with his own. As I stare at them, I realize how little I've understood their relationship. Because, yes, Balekin hasn't noticed that the Ghost has climbed onto the ledge with the Blood Crown. Yes, he sent his knights after the Roach, allowing the Bomb to bar the doors of this room.

But he has also reminded Cardan of why not to go forward with this plan.

I have been thinking of Balekin as the brother Cardan hated, as the brother who'd murdered their whole family. I'd forgotten that Balekin is Cardan's family. Balekin is the person who raised him when Dain plotted against him, when his father sent him from the palace. Balekin is all he has left.

And, although I am sure Balekin would make for a terrible king, one who would hurt Cardan along with many others—I am equally sure that he would give Cardan power. Cardan would be allowed to be cruel, so long as it was clear that Balekin was crueler.

Putting the crown on Balekin's head was a safe bet. Much safer than trusting me, than believing in some future Oak. He's pledged himself to me. I just need to take care he doesn't find some way around my commands.

I am a beat behind, and it's harder to push through the crowd than I thought, so I am not where I told the Ghost I would be. When I look up at the ledge, he's there, moving out of shadow. He throws the crown, but not to me. The Ghost tosses the crown to my identical twin. It falls at Taryn's feet.

Vivi has taken Oak's hand. Lord Roiben is pushing through the crowd.

Taryn picks up the crown.

"Give it to Vivi," I call to her. The Ghost, realizing his mistake, draws his crossbow and points it at my sister, but there's no way to shoot his way out of this. She gives me a terrible, betrayed look.

Cardan struggles to his feet. Balekin is up, too, striding across the room.

"Child, if you do not give that to me, I will cut you in half," Balekin tells Taryn. "I will be the High King, and when I am, I will punish any who inconvenienced me."

She holds it out, looking between Balekin and Vivi and me. Then she looks at all the lords and ladies watching her.

"Give me my crown," Balekin says, walking toward her.

Lord Roiben steps into Balekin's path. He presses his hand to

Balekin's chest. "Wait." He hasn't drawn a blade, but I see the shine of knives under his coat.

Balekin tries to push Roiben's hand away, but he does not move. The Ghost has his crossbow trained on Balekin, and every eye in the room is watching him. Queen Orlagh is several steps away.

Violence hangs heavily in the air.

I move toward Taryn to get in front of her.

If Balekin draws a weapon, if he throws away diplomacy and simply charges, the room seems ready to explode into bloodshed. Some will fight on his side, some against. No vows to the crown matter now, and watching him murder his own family hasn't left anyone feeling safe. He has brought the lords and ladies of Faerie here to win them over; even he seems to see that more murder is unlikely to do that.

Besides, the Ghost can shoot him before he gets to Taryn, and he wears no armor under his clothes. No matter how heavy the embroidery, it will not save him from a bolt to the heart.

"She's only a mortal girl," he says.

"This is a lovely banquet, Balekin, son of Eldred," Queen Orlagh says. "But sadly lacking in amusements before now. Let this be our entertainment. After all, the crown is secure in this room, is it not? And you or your younger brother are the only ones who can wear it. Let the girl choose whom she will give it to. What does it matter, if neither of you will crown the other?"

I am surprised. I thought Queen Orlagh was his ally, but then I suppose Nicasia's friendship with Cardan might have made her favor him. Or perhaps she favors neither of them and only wants the sea to have greater power, by diminishing the power of the land.

"This is ridiculous," he says. "What of the explosion? Didn't that entertain you sufficiently?"

"It certainly piqued *my* interest," Lord Roiben says. "You seem to have lost your general somewhere as well. Your rule hasn't even formally begun, but it certainly appears chaotic."

I turn to Taryn and close my fingers over the cool metal of the crown. Up close, it is exquisite. The leaves seem to grow out of the dark gold, to be living things, their stems crossing over one another in a delicate knotwork.

"Please," I say. There is still so much that's bad between us. So much anger and betrayal and jealousy.

"What are you doing?" Taryn hisses at me. Behind her, Locke is looking at me with an odd gleam in his eyes. My story just got more interesting, and I know how much he loves story above all else.

"The best I can," I say.

I tug, and for a long moment, Taryn holds fast. Then she opens her hand, and I stagger back with the crown.

Vivi has brought Oak as close as she dares. Oriana stands with the crowd, clasping and unclasping her hands. She must notice Madoc's absence, must be wondering what I meant when I spoke of a price.

"Prince Cardan," I say. "This is for you."

The crowd parts to let him through, the other key player in this drama. He walks to stand to one side of me and Oak.

"Stop!" Balekin shouts. "Stop them immediately." He draws a blade, clearly no longer interested in playing politics. Around the room, more swords are unsheathed in a terrible echo of his. I can hear the hum of enchanted steel in the air.

I reach for Nightfell at the moment the Ghost lets his bolt fly.

Balekin staggers back. I hear the sound of indrawn breaths all around the room. Shooting the king, even if he's not wearing a crown, is no small thing. Then, as Balekin's sword falls to the ancient rug, I see where he was shot.

His hand is pinioned to the dining table by a crossbow bolt. One that appears to be iron.

"Cardan," Balekin calls. "I know you. I know that you'd prefer I did the difficult work of ruling while you enjoyed the power. I know that you despise mortals and ruffians and fools. Come, I have not always danced to your piping, but you haven't the stomach to truly cross me. Bring me the crown."

I gather Oak close to me and put the crown into his hands, so that he can see it. So that he can get used to holding it. Vivi pats him encouragingly on his back.

"Bring me the crown, Cardan," Balekin says.

Prince Cardan turns on his elder brother the same cool and calculated gaze with which he has regarded so many other creatures before he's torn the wings from their back, before he's cast them into rivers or sent them from the Court entirely. "No, brother. I do not think that I will. I think that if I did not have another reason to cross you, I would do it for spite."

Oak looks up at me, searching for confirmation that he's doing okay in the face of all this shouting. I nod with an encouraging smile.

"Show Oak," I whisper to Cardan. "Show him what he's supposed to do. Kneel down."

"They're going to think—" he starts, but I interrupt him.

"Just do it."

Cardan kneels, and a hush goes through the crowd. Swords are returned to sheaths. Movements slow.

"Oh, this *is* amusing," says Lord Roiben in a low voice. "Who might that child be? Or whose?" He and Queen Annet share a very Unseelie smile.

"See?" Cardan says to Oak, and then makes an impatient gesture. "Now the crown."

I look around at the lords and ladies of Faerie. Not one of their faces is friendly. All of them appear wary, waiting. Balekin's expression is wild with fury, and he pulls against the bolt, as though he might rip his hand in half before he allowed this to happen. Oak takes a hesitant step toward Cardan, then another.

"Phase four," Cardan whispers to me, still believing we're on the same side.

I think of Madoc, dozing away upstairs, all his dreams of murder. I think of Oriana and Oak being forced apart for years. I think of Cardan and how he will hate me. I think of what it means to make myself the villain of the piece. "For the next full minute, I command you not to move," I whisper back.

Cardan goes utterly still.

"Go ahead," Vivi says to Oak. "Just like we practiced."

And with that, Oak puts the crown down on Cardan's head, to rest on his brow. "I crown you." Oak's little-kid voice is uncertain. "King. High King of Faerie." His eyes go to Vivi, to Oriana. He's waiting for one of them to tell him he did well, that he is done.

People gasp. Balekin gives a howl of fury. There is laughter and outrage and delight. Everyone likes a surprise, and the Folk like one more than almost anything else.

Cardan looks at me with helpless rage. Then, the full minute of my command up, he rises slowly to his feet. The fury in his eyes is familiar, the glitter of them like banked fire, like coals burning hotter than flames ever could. This time I deserve it. I promised he was going to be able to walk away from the Court and all its manipulations. I promised he would be free from all this. I lied.

It's not that I don't want Oak to be the High King. I do. He will be. But there's only one way to make sure the throne remains ready for him while he learns everything he needs to know—and that's if someone else occupies it. Seven years and Cardan can step down, abdicate in Oak's favor and do whatever he wants. But until then, he's going to have to keep my brother's throne warm.

Lord Roiben sinks to one knee, as he promised. "My king," he says. I wonder what that promise will cost. I wonder what he will ask us for, now that he has helped give Cardan a crown.

And then the cry goes up around the room, from Queen Annet to Queen Orlagh and Lord Severin. From the other side, Taryn stares at me, clearly shocked. To her, I must seem mad, to put someone I despise on the throne, but there is no way for me to explain myself. I sink to my knees along with everyone else, and so does she.

All my promises have come due.

For a long moment, Cardan just looks around the room, but he has little choice, and he must know it. "Rise," he says, and we do.

I step back, fading into the throng.

Cardan has been a prince of Faerie all his life. No matter what he wants, he knows what's expected of him. He knows how to charm a crowd, how to entertain. He orders the broken glass cleared away. He has new goblets brought out, new wine poured. The toast he gives—to surprises and to the benefits of being too drunk to show up for the first coronation—causes all the lords and ladies to laugh. And if I notice that his hand grips his wineglass tightly enough to turn his knuckles white, then I imagine I am the only one who does.

Yet I am surprised when he turns to me, eyes blazing. It feels as though the room is empty but for us. He lifts his glass anew, mouth curving in a mockery of a smile. "And to Jude, who gave me a gift tonight. One that I plan to repay in kind."

I try not to visibly flinch as glasses lift around me. Crystal rings. More wine flows. More laughter sounds.

The Bomb elbows me in the side. "We came up with your code name," she mouths. I hadn't even seen her come in past the locked doors.

"What?" I feel as tired as I have ever felt, and yet, for seven years, I will not be able to truly rest.

I expect her to say *The Liar.* She gives me a tricksy grin, full of secrets. "What else? The Queen."

It turns out I still don't know how to laugh.

EPILOGUE

I stand in the middle of Target, pushing the cart while Oak and Vivi pick out bedsheets and lunch boxes, skinny jeans and sandals. Oak looks around in mild confusion and pleasure. He keeps picking up things, puzzling over them, and then setting them down again. In the candy aisle, he adds bars of chocolate to the cart, along with jelly beans, lollipops, and chunks of candied ginger. Vivi doesn't stop him, so I don't, either.

It's odd to see Oak with his horns glamoured away, his ears looking as round as mine. It's odd to see him in the toy aisle, trying out a scooter with an owl-shaped backpack over one arm.

I expected that it would be hard to persuade Oriana to let him go with Vivi, but after Cardan's coronation, she agreed that Oak being away from the Court for a few years was for the best. Balekin is imprisoned in a tower. Madoc woke in a rage, only to find that his moment for seizing the crown was past.

"So he's really your brother, right?" Heather asks Vivi as Oak kicks off on the scooter, flying through the greeting card aisle. "You could tell me if he was your son."

Vivi laughs delightedly. "I've got secrets, but that's not one of them."

Heather wasn't thrilled about Vivienne showing up with a child and a half-baked explanation about why he had to live with her, but she didn't kick them out. Heather's sofa pulled out into a bed, and they agreed he could sleep there until Vivi found a job and they were able to afford a larger apartment.

I know Vivi isn't going to get conventional work, but she will be fine. She will be better than fine. In another world, given our parents and our past, I would have kept on encouraging Vivi to trust Heather with the truth. But for now, if she feels like she has to keep the deception going, I am hardly in a position to contradict her.

As we stand in the checkout line and Vivi pays for her haul with leaves glamoured to seem like bills, I think again of the aftermath of the banquet-turned-coronation. Of the blur of the Folk eating and joking. Of everyone marveling over Oak, who appeared both pleased and panicked. Of Oriana, clearly not sure whether to congratulate me or to slap me. Of Taryn, quiet, considering, holding tightly to Locke's hand. Of Nicasia giving Cardan a lingering kiss on his royal cheek.

I have done the thing, and now I must live with what I have done.

I have lied and I have betrayed and I have triumphed. If only there was someone to congratulate me.

Heather sighs and smiles dreamily at Vivi as we load our purchases into the trunk of Heather's Prius. Back at the apartment, Heather takes some premade pizza dough out of her fridge and explains how to make personal pies.

"Mom will visit me, won't she?" Oak asks as he places pieces of chocolate and marshmallows on top of his dough.

I squeeze his arm as Heather sticks the food in the oven. "Of course she will. Think of being here with Vivi as an apprenticeship. You learn what you need to know, and then you come home."

"How will I know when I've learned it, since I don't know it now?" he asks.

The question sounds like a riddle. "Come back when returning feels like a hard choice instead of an easy one," I answer finally. Vivi looks over, as though she's overheard. Her expression is thoughtful.

I eat a slice of Oak's pizza and lick the chocolate off my fingers. It's sweet enough to make me wince, but I don't mind. I just want to sit with them a few more moments before I have to fly back to Faerie alone.

When I dismount from my ragwort steed, I head to the palace. I have rooms there now—a vast sitting area, a bedroom behind latching double doors, and a dressing area with empty closets. All I have to hang in them is what I took out of Madoc's estates and a few things I got at Target.

Here is where I will live, to keep Cardan close, to use my power over him to ensure things go smoothly. The Court of Shadows will grow beneath the castle, fed on being both the High King's spies and his keepers.

They'll have their gold, straight from the king's hand.

What I have not done, not really, is spoken with Cardan. I left him with only a few commands, the familiar hatred in his face enough to make a coward out of me. But I am going to have to talk to him eventually. There is no profit in my putting it off any longer.

Still, it is with a heavy heart and leaden steps that I make my way to the royal rooms. I knock, only to be told by a prim-seeming manservant with flowers braided in his blond beard that the High King has gone to the great hall.

I find him there, lounging on the throne of Faerie, looking out from the dais. The room is empty except for us. My footfalls echo as I move across the floor.

Cardan is dressed in breeches, a waistcoat, and another coat over that, fitted in his shoulders, tapered in sharply at the waist and falling to his midthigh. The cloth is uncut velvet in a deep burgundy, with ivory velvet at the lapels, shoulders, and waistcoat. Stitching in golden thread covers the whole, matched by golden buttons and golden buckles on his tall boots. At his throat is a ruff of pale owl feathers.

His black hair falls in opulent curls around his cheeks. The shadows bring out the sharpness of his bones, the length of his lashes, the merciless beauty of his face.

I am horrified by how much he looks like the King of Faerie.

I am horrified by my own impulse to bend my knee to him, my own desire to let him touch my head with a ringed hand.

What have I done? For so long, there was no one I trusted less. And now I must contend with him, must match my will to his. His oath does not seem enough of an antidote against his cleverness.

What in the world have I done?

I keep walking, though. I keep my expression as cold as I know how. He's the one who smiles, but his smile is colder than any stiff face could be. "A year and a day," he calls out. "Blink and that will be over. And what will you do then?"

I draw closer to him. "I hope I can persuade you to remain king until Oak is ready to return."

"Maybe I will acquire a taste for ruling," he says coolly. "Maybe I won't ever want to give it up."

"I don't think so," I say, although I've always known that was one possibility. I've always known that removing him from the throne might be harder than putting him there.

I have a bargain with him for a year and a day. I have a year and a day to come to a bargain for longer than that. *And not for one minute more.*

His grin widens, shows teeth. "I don't think I will be a good king. I never wanted to be one, certainly not a good one. You made me your puppet. Very well, Jude, daughter of Madoc, I will *be* your puppet. You rule. You contend with Balekin, with Roiben, with Orlagh of the Undersea. You be my seneschal, do the work, and I will drink wine and make my subjects laugh. I may be the useless shield you put in front of your brother, but don't expect me to start being useful."

I expected something else, a direct threat, perhaps. Somehow, this is worse.

He rises from the throne. "Come, have a seat." His voice is replete with danger, lush with menace. The flowering branches have sprouted thorns so thickly that petals are barely visible.

"This is what you wanted, isn't it?" he asks. "What you sacrificed everything for. Go on. It's all yours."

ACKNOWLEDGMENTS

Thank you to my writer friends who saw me through the scheming and imagining and writing and editing of this book. Thank you, Sarah Rees Brennan, Leigh Bardugo, Kelly Link, Cassandra Clare, Maureen Johnson, Robin Wasserman, Steve Berman, Gwenda Bond, Christopher Rowe, Alaya Dawn Johnson, Paolo Bacigalupi, Ellen Kushner, Delia Sherman, Gavin Grant, Joshua Lewis, Carrie Ryan, and Kathleen Jennings (who drew beautiful pictures during a workshop, thereby producing my favorite critique ever).

Thanks, too, to everyone at ICFA who gave me feedback after I read the first three chapters out loud.

Thank you to everyone at Little, Brown Books for Young Readers, who have supported my weird vision. Thanks especially to my amazing editor, Alvina Ling, Kheryn Callender, Lisa Moraleda, and Victoria Stapleton.

And thank you to Barry Goldblatt and Joanna Volpe for shepherding the book through its various trials and tribulations.

Thanks most of all to my husband, Theo, for talking through so much of this book with me over many years, and to our son, Sebastian, for distracting me from the writing and giving me a fuller heart.

Turn the page for a sneak preview of

AVAILABLE JANUARY 2019

PROLOGUE

Jude lifted the heavy practice sword, moving into the first stance—readiness.

Get used to the weight, Madoc had told her. *You must be strong enough to strike and strike and strike again without tiring. The first lesson is to make yourself that strong.*

It will hurt. Pain makes you strong.

She planted her feet in the grass. Wind ruffled her hair as she moved through the stances. One: the sword before her, canted to one side, protecting her body. Two: the pommel high, as though the blade were a horn coming from her head. Three: down to her hip, then in a deceptively casual droop in front of her. Then four: up again, to her shoulder. Each position could move easily into a strike or a defense. Fighting was chess, anticipating the move of one's opponent and countering it before one got hit.

But it was chess played with the whole body. Chess that left her bruised and tired and frustrated with the whole world and with herself, too.

Or maybe it was more like riding a bike. When she'd been learning to do that, back in the real world, she'd fallen lots of times. Her knees had been scabby enough that Mom thought she might have scars. But Jude had taken off her training wheels herself and disdained riding carefully on the sidewalk, as Taryn did. Jude wanted to ride in the street, fast, like Vivi, and if she got gravel embedded in her skin for it, well, then she'd let Dad pick it out with tweezers at night.

Sometimes Jude longed for her bike, but there were none in Faerie. Instead, she had giant toads and thin greenish ponies and wild-eyed horses slim as shadows.

And she had weapons.

And her parents' murderer, now her foster father. The High King's general, Madoc, who wanted to teach her how to ride too fast and how to fight to the death. No matter how hard she swung at him, it just made him laugh. He liked her anger. *Fire,* he called it.

She liked it when she was angry, too. Angry was better than scared. Better than remembering she was a mortal among monsters. No one was offering her the option of training wheels anymore.

On the other side of the field, Madoc was guiding Taryn through a series of stances. Taryn was learning the sword, too, although she had different problems than Jude. Her stances were more perfect, but she hated sparring. She paired the obvious defenses with the obvious attacks, so it was easy to lure her into a series of moves and then score a hit by breaking the pattern. Each time it happened, Taryn got mad, as though Jude were flubbing the steps of a dance rather than winning.

"Come here," Madoc called to Jude across the silvery expanse of grass.

She walked to him, sword slung over her shoulders. The sun was just setting, but faeries are twilight creatures, and their day was not even half done. The sky was streaked with copper and gold. She inhaled a deep breath of pine needles. For a moment, she felt as though she were just a kid learning a new sport.

"Come spar," he said when Jude got closer. "Both of you girls against this old redcap." Taryn leaned against her sword, the tip of it sinking into the ground. She wasn't supposed to hold it that way—it wasn't good for the blade—but Madoc didn't reprimand her.

"Power," he said. "Power is the ability to get what you want. Power is the ability to be the one making the decisions. And how do we get power?"

Jude stepped beside her twin. It was obvious that Madoc expected a response, but also that he expected the wrong one. "We learn how to fight well?" she said to say *something.*

When Madoc smiled at her, she could see the points of his bottom cuspids, longer than the rest of his teeth. He tousled her hair, and she felt the sharp edges of his clawlike nails against her scalp, too light to hurt, but a reminder of what he was nonetheless. "We get power by taking it."

He pointed toward a low hill with a thorn tree growing on it. "Let's make a game of the next lesson. That's my hill. Go ahead and take it."

Taryn dutifully trooped toward it, Jude behind her. Madoc kept pace, his smile all teeth.

"Now what?" Taryn asked, without any particular excitement.

Madoc looked into the distance, as though he was contemplating and discarding various rules. "Now hold it against attack."

"Wait, what?" Jude asked. "From you?"

"Is this a strategy game or a sparring practice?" Taryn asked, frowning.

Madoc brought one finger under her chin, raising her head until she was looking into his golden cat eyes. "What is sparring but a game of strategy, played at speed?" he told her with a great seriousness. "Talk with your sister. When the sun reaches the trunk of that tree, I will come for my hill. Knock me down but once and you both win."

Then he departed for a copse of trees some ways away. Taryn sat down on the grass.

"I don't want to do this," she said.

"It's just a game," Jude reminded her nervously.

Taryn gave her a long look—the one that they gave each other when one of them was pretending things were normal. "Okay, so what do *you* think we should do?"

Jude looked up into the branches of the thorn tree. "What if one of us threw rocks while the other did the sparring?"

"Okay," Taryn said, pushing herself up and beginning to gather stones into the folds of her skirts. "You don't think he'll get mad, do you?"

Jude shook her head, but she understood Taryn's question. What if he killed them by accident?

You've got to choose which hill to die on, Mom used to tell Dad. It had been one of those weird sayings adults expected her to understand, even though they made no sense—like "one in the hand is worth two in the bush" or "every stick has two ends" or the totally mysterious "a cat may look at a king." Now, standing on an actual hill with a sword in her hand, she understood it a lot better.

"Get into position," Jude said, and Taryn wasted no time in climbing the thorn tree. Jude checked the sunmark, wondering what sort of tricks Madoc might use. The longer he waited, the darker it would get, and while he could see in the dark, Jude and Taryn could not.

But, in the end, he didn't use any tricks. He came out of the woods and in their direction, howling as though he were leading an army of a hundred. Jude's knees went weak with terror.

This is just a game, she reminded herself frantically. The closer he got, though, the less her body believed her. Every animal instinct strained to run.

Their strategy seemed silly now in the face of his hugeness and their smallness, in the face of her fear. She thought of her mother bleeding on the ground, recalled the smell of her insides as they leaked out. The memory felt like thunder in her head. She was going to die.

Run, her whole body urged. *RUN!*

No, her mother had run. Jude planted her feet.

She made herself move into the first position, even though her legs felt wobbly. He had the advantage, even coming up that hill, because he had momentum on his side. The stones raining down on him from Taryn barely checked his pace.

Jude spun out of the way, not even bothering to try to block the first blow. Putting the tree between them, she dodged his second and third. When the fourth one came, it knocked her to the grass.

She closed her eyes against the killing strike.

"You can take a thing when no one's looking. But defending it, even with all the advantage on your side, is no easy task," Madoc told her with a laugh. She looked up to find him offering her a hand. "Power is much easier to acquire than it is to hold on to."

Relief broke over her. It was just a game, after all. Just another lesson.

"That wasn't fair," Taryn complained.

Jude didn't say anything. Nothing was fair in Faerie. She had learned to stop expecting it to be.

Madoc hauled Jude to her feet and threw a heavy arm over her shoulders. He drew her and her twin in for an embrace. He smelled like smoke and dried blood, and Jude let herself sag against him. It was good to be hugged. Even by a monster.

Keep reading for a special short story,

A VISIT TO THE IMPOSSIBLE LANDS

Kaye Fierch perched on the fire escape outside her building, espresso in her hand, breathing the iron-tinged summer scents of the city—garbage and smoke, cooking meat, the river, fresh-poured asphalt, and rot. It was well after three in the morning and one of her favorite times to watch over the streets below, to see friends staggering home, arms thrown about one another. To see businesspeople stumble, wondering how it got so late. To see the traffic of excess, people wringing a few more giddy moments from a day, eager to do something memorable—whether they'd *want* to remember it or not—before the sun came up.

Part of her was tempted to take off her shirt and glide around the sky on the delicate moth's wings folded tight against her back. To follow the twinkling lights of the cars below, streaming over bridges and through the grid of roads, to soar over the river. Another part of her wanted a second espresso.

"I didn't see you there at first. I thought you might not be home," came a voice from behind her, a trace of the otherworldly in his accent. Lord Roiben, king of the Court of Termites. Her boyfriend—or maybe something more than that since she'd completed a quest and been made his official *consort,* a relationship stage entirely outside the quizzes in *Cosmo* magazine.

She turned to grin at him. He was wearing a worn black T-shirt, making his white hair and silvery eyes look starker by the contrast. He'd recently cut his hair. It used to fall over his shoulders in a shining pool, but now it was choppy and barely long enough to hang in his eyes.

He reached out his fingers and she took them, letting him help her climb back over the windowsill as though she were a great lady atop a horse instead of on a metal stair.

"You look tired." She slid back into her apartment and went to put the coffee cup in the sink.

"Tired of being too long from your side," he said, which made her snort in sheer incredulity.

He gave her a smile in return. She knew he liked that she didn't take him too seriously, when everyone else in his life treated him with vast deference.

They'd always lived apart. Kaye had started a coffee shop with her friends called Moon in a Cup, which had evolved to sell more and more magical pastries and potions. Now there was a secret menu of gillyflower scones and espressos cut with tears, and all the magical Folk of New York stopped by to have meetings or breakfast or assignations. Meanwhile, Roiben had been ruling over two fractious courts, merged into one highly unstable Court of Termites, named for the sprawling Unseelie palace built beneath a graveyard on a hill.

Roiben insisted that it pleased him that Kaye didn't have to deal with the raw fury of the Unseelie Court and the delicate machinations of the Seelie Court, that he loved having an escape—her apartment, her life, her arms.

But over the years, watching the exhausted way he slept on a simple mattress in a messy apartment, hearing the surprised pleasure of his laughter, feeling the desperate hunger of his kisses, she'd become more and more afraid that he wasn't telling her the whole truth.

He'd been given to the last Unseelie queen to be her knight, forced to do her bidding no matter how terrible, forced to endure whatever cruelties she could devise. Kaye worried that he'd developed low standards for happiness.

"So," she asked, "how long have I got you this time?"

Roiben was skilled at keeping his own counsel, but she read something in the twitch of his lip and the set of his jaw.

She raised a single eyebrow.

"I wish for you to come with me on a journey," he said, spreading his hands in acknowledgment of being caught out. "There is to be a great coronation, the passing of the crown of the High King of Elfhame to his son, and I want you to accompany me. I can promise that we will dance and drink and that there will be time for very little else but merriment. And there is no one I would rather be merry with."

She frowned at him, despite those flattering words. A week before, they'd talked about going to a lake somewhere, with a little tree house, away from everything, with only fireflies to rule over. Instead, they were going to the High Court for what was bound to be bullshit.

"There will be dozens of lords and ladies," he said. "And we, lost among them, wholly unremarkable and entirely forgotten. Elfhame is three islands with the sea all around, where mermaids come to sun themselves on the black rocks. I am told it's beautiful."

"And you're really going to swear fealty to this new guy?" she asked, dubious about Roiben's ability to be unremarkable anywhere.

"I have promised Prince Dain that I would come and consider it. But yes, most like. A High Monarch would give me an excuse to curb the Unseelie Court's appetites without being seen to prefer the Seelie ways." Roiben touched her hair lightly in that odd way he had, as though he half-expected his fingers to pass through her, as though she might be made of glamour and smoke and his own hopeless longings. "And because it is wearying to be always at war."

"Very well," she said. "I'll go to your thing. You promise we're going to have fun?"

"How could it be otherwise?" he asked, which ought to have been her first warning.

That was how she wound up at the High Court in Elfhame, dressed in a silky slip, combat boots, and a lot of eyeliner. Standing near Dulcamara, she couldn't help noticing the nervous looks courtiers kept throwing in Roiben's direction and the wide berth their whole party was getting. Roiben himself was in serious conference with the new Alderking and seemed to be politely pretending not to notice how many of the Folk were terrified of him.

Wholly unremarkable, my ass, she thought.

"What's their problem?" Kaye asked Dulcamara, glaring at a troll until he turned his gaze elsewhere.

Dulcamara shrugged. Her red hair was braided into an elaborate and somehow menacing knot on top of her head, her black armor polished to a shine. Kaye, in deference to the fanciness of the occasion, had put a sparkly green clip in her hair to match the color of her skin, but she was feeling that maybe she should have dressed up a lot more.

"Lord Roiben makes a menacing figure," Dulcamara said finally, when it became clear that Kaye was waiting for some kind of response. "And one with a reputation for popping off the heads of monarchs."

Kaye couldn't actually argue with that. "Which one is Prince Dain?" she asked.

Dulcamara frowned in concentration. "Not here yet. The princesses are—that's Elowyn, Caelia, and Rhyia. And beside them is the eldest prince, Balekin."

"Eldest, but not inheriting?" Kaye asked.

"The High King passed over his two eldest and chose the third. To sire six children is unusual in Faerie," Dulcamara said. "Most Folk are lucky if, in a hundred years, they beget a single child. Two is considered a great blessing. Six is vulgar fortune."

"You named only five," Kaye said.

Dulcamara gestured toward the crowd. "The sixth is there. The youngest prince, Cardan, dancing with that mortal girl."

Kaye's eyebrows went up. She'd met the only other mortal she'd noticed, a nervous-looking redhead who'd come along with the new Alderking. He'd been a little startled by the contrast between Kaye's green skin, inkdrop eyes, and mortal way of speaking, but had quickly decided she might know the answers to some of his questions about the reels that were being played. Despite her own mother being in a band for pretty much ever, Kaye hadn't, and the boy had wandered off to find someone who did.

This mortal was a girl, dressed in gloves and a long gown that appeared like the sky at night. She was of medium height, with hair the red-brown of a willow tree. She had soft features and the solid grace of someone used to living in her body. An acrobat perhaps. Or a soldier.

The tall faerie boy who held her in his arms had a mess of black hair. His cheeks were painted in silver, his eyes edged in black kohl, and he looked drunk, his crown askew. The girl was glaring at him, and Kaye wondered how they wound up dancing together. Then she noticed the way *he* was looking at *her*. But that made things even more puzzling.

"Who's the girl?" Kaye asked.

"The general has two human wards," Dulcamara returned. "That's one of them. They're twins, but I can't tell them apart."

"Like widderkins changelings," Kaye said. She'd been a changeling herself, dropped into the mortal world with a lot of warding, not even discovering she was a pixie until she was a teenager. What would it be like to be a human who didn't understand human stuff, the way she still wasn't sure she understood Faerie?

Maybe if she'd grown up in this world, parties like this coronation would make more sense to her. She looked over at Roiben and he caught her eye, his smile easy. If she walked over to him, he would draw her into the conversation, but trying to talk would only highlight her ignorance. At times like this, she felt the strain of having a foot in two worlds. Roiben belonged here and she wanted to believe she belonged with Roiben, but that turned out to be no simple calculation.

Across the room, the prince walked away from the human girl, leaving her standing alone as figures whirled around her. After a moment, she headed toward the dais. The prince paused his retreat to watch her go with an expression Kaye recognized—the look of someone who wondered if the other person might be made of glamour and smoke, if they might fade away with a touch. Roiben had looked at her that way.

Then the prince went to a table, where he lifted a pitcher of wine to his mouth, not bothering with a glass, tipping the vessel back until the dark liquid streamed over his chin.

Kaye walked toward him on impulse, with some idea that if he was guzzling wine, he wouldn't be that hard to draw into conversation. After all, if Roiben was going to pledge fealty to this guy's brother, she'd better get to know the family.

"You're Prince Cardan," Kaye said with what she hoped was a half-decent curtsy. Raven feathers covered the top of his doublet, gleaming in blues and purples like an oil slick. Up close, she could see that he'd smeared his eye makeup.

Putting down the pitcher and wiping off his chin with the back of his gloved hand, he narrowed his gaze. She wondered if he was going to order her to step back ten paces.

"My name is Kaye," she told him. "From the Court of Termites." She waved vaguely toward where Roiben and Dulcamara and all the others were standing, hoping that would give him pause were he thinking of scolding her for talking to him.

A sneer pulled up a corner of his mouth. "Ah, come to watch your fearsome Lord Roiben bend a knee to my brother. Were I you, I would quit your king's court before you are made part of this one."

"I wouldn't expect a prince to say that," Kaye said.

"But then what do you know of princes?" he asked.

"Fair enough," she said. Right then, she wasn't sure she knew anything about anything.

All around them, bells rang out, signaling that the coronation was to begin soon. The musicians stilled their playing, and only the hum of conversation filled the hall.

An ogre, startled, knocked into the table, sending a pile of pomegranates rolling down the wood. They knocked into plates of sweets and against the pitcher of wine, sending it careening off the table. Prince Cardan caught the handle deftly, although she hadn't seen him so much as look in that direction.

He smirked. "Care for a glass? If so, you'll have to find an actual glass."

"Should I get Roiben to reconsider joining the High Court?" she asked. When Roiben was a young knight, he'd sworn himself into the service of the beautiful queen he loved. That had been a big mistake. If he was about to make another, Kaye would like to prevent it if she could.

"Could you?" Prince Cardan returned, gaze heavy-lidded. She searched his face for some sign of whether to trust his judgment, an impossible task. "I doubt he'd thank you for the advice," he went on. "Kings are notoriously fickle. They ill-reward that which stings their pride."

"Bad kings, maybe," she said.

Cardan snorted, as though she'd said something particularly amusing. He cut a pointed look toward Roiben. The Alderking's son had gone and Roiben was talking to a woman from the Undersea with dripping wet hair and pink gills that ran like three slashes just beneath her jawline. "Is he kind, then, your lord?"

Kaye rolled her eyes at him. Roiben's reputation wasn't for being *kind*, that much was true. But that didn't mean he wasn't. Maybe it was the same with Dain. Maybe Prince Cardan didn't know anything.

"Ruling is like wine," Cardan said, lifting the pitcher. "It brings out the worst in anyone who takes too deep a draught, yet we all want a taste."

"Even you?" Kaye asked.

He looked away, his gaze going toward the dais, and Kaye realized he was looking at the girl. The mortal girl. "What I want," he said, "is for Dain never to get the throne. Failing that, I'd love to see the whole Court of Termites walk out of here without your king's pledging anything. But then it is my nature to only want things I cannot have."

"So tell me something," Kaye said. "If joining this court is so bad, tell me something I can take back to Roiben, something that will give him doubts?"

Cardan shook his head. "What is there to say? First my brother will seem one way, and then another, and then, well, by then there will be no help possible, no help at all. But why would your king listen to either of us in preference to the newly anointed High King of Elfhame?" He handed the pitcher of wine to her. "Drown your cares. Tonight we dance through the leather of our shoes and celebrate my father's abandoning the rest of his children."

Before she was able to come up with a response, he staggered into the crowd.

Kaye stared after him, unnerved.

As she walked back to Roiben, Prince Cardan's last words echoed in her ears. Many times she'd wished that Roiben would just abdicate his throne, but she'd never considered how his people would feel.

Abandoned.

"What if I told you not to swear to Prince Dain?" Kaye asked, hooking her hand in his. His long fingers were cool to the touch as he raised her palm to his lips.

His eyebrows went up. "Then I won't," he said after a moment, simply and a little terrifyingly. She wanted him to trust her, of course, but she wasn't sure she deserved *that* much trust. "Is there a particular reason?" he went on.

"I have a bad feeling," she said, hoping she wasn't making a huge mistake.

"It will make things a touch awkward," he said after a moment. "We would be well served to leave the isles tonight, before the newly anointed High King Dain attempts to force the matter."

Which meant, she guessed, that not swearing fealty was going to be really, really bad. Like, maybe act-of-war bad. But before she could ask, King Eldred began to speak. Kaye realized Cardan wasn't on the stage with the rest of his family. Had he left the court after all? Kaye hoped so, for his sake.

"When this is over, I want to come back to Faerie," she whispered. "With you."

He narrowed his eyes at her. "Whatsoever do you mean?"

Around them, the Folk called out the words to acknowledge High King Eldred's abdicating his throne. But Kaye had realized Roiben was never going to do that—and probably shouldn't. Unless she wanted them to live on the edges of each other's lives, she was going to have to change.

"I could give the coffee shop to Corny and Luis and live in the Palace of Termites," she said. "I want to help you with your job." Now that she'd come to a decision, Kaye felt embarrassed. He might not expect her to be all that helpful. She was occasionally clever, but Kaye often had the sinking feeling that she used her cleverness to get away with being lazy.

Also, she wasn't sure if calling ruling a kingdom a "job" was insulting or not.

Also, she might have just talked him into a war.

She grew even more embarrassed at the way he stared. He seemed utterly thrown. Finally, after an overlong silence, he said, "I love you too well for that."

"So it's good enough for you, but not for me?" She put her hands on her hips. "And I'm supposed to—what? Be happy when I know you're not? Be happy enough for both of us?"

He looked as though he was about to say something, but then swallowed the words.

On the dais, a representative from the Unseelie Courts was drawing swirls over Prince Dain's skin with blood to prepare him for the coronation. Roiben probably wanted Kaye to just shut up and pretend to be interested in what was happening, but she was feeling pettish and rejected and couldn't seem to stop talking. "Happiness isn't something to carefully measure out in spoonfuls as though it's medicine," she said. "I don't need you to suffer to prove your love, and I definitely don't need you to hide your suffering. I want to shoulder half our burden."

"Love shouldn't mean shouldering what has naught to do with you," he said.

"But it does," she said. "That *is* what it means. That's exactly what it means."

"You will tire of it," he spat, real anger in his voice. "You will tire of it and you will tire of me."

She stepped back, dropping his hand, and they stared at each other for a long moment, too shocked to speak.

Many times, Kaye had wondered over his loving her. She hadn't guessed he had doubts about her, too. How could he, when he was the Unseelie king, born into the Gentry, a tortured and famous knight of Faerie? When he came into Moon in a Cup, conversation grew hushed, laughter ceased. And after he left, customers talked a lot about how they wanted to bone him.

"I drink a lot of coffee," she said, trying for lightness. "My motto is 'never tired.'"

"Faerie is a deadly place, as you well know," he returned, grim, and she felt certain her joke had been a misstep. "Replete with horror and cruelty and caprice. But even knowing that, you still cannot know what it is for it to occupy the whole of your days and all your nights."

"I have been in Faerie lots of times," Kaye said. "It's not *all* bad. And the Court of Termites is different now that you're in charge. You've changed it."

Just then, the hall seemed to inhale as one. Someone screamed. Kaye turned back to the dais in time to see one of the princes had his sword out. She couldn't remember his name, but the one who wasn't Cardan and wasn't Dain was threatening the others. A moment later, his blade pierced Princess Elowyn's throat. The princess went to her knees, everything drenched in red. The blood poured from her throat the way wine had poured from Cardan's pitcher.

Dulcamara grimaced. Even Roiben flinched.

"Why did he do that?" Kaye demanded. Maybe she really should have been paying better attention. "That's not part of the ceremony, is it?"

"Perhaps you'd like to expound on your earlier point," Roiben drawled, his hand going to the hilt of his own sword. "About how Faerie is 'not all bad'?"

"You're not seriously going for the 'I told you so' right now, are you?" Kaye demanded.

His eyes were on the violence, and his voice was very dry. "Admit I've won this argument."

But then it became clear that the royal guard was in on the scheme, and Roiben wanted to go up there himself and do something. Dulcamara and several of his other knights had to hold him back as the rest of the royal family was slaughtered, one by one. Screaming filled the hall. Kaye looked around for the youngest prince, but he was nowhere to be seen.

"Let me go," Roiben was saying to Dulcamara. "I order you—"

"You can't cut through the whole guard," she said, interrupting him before he could finish the sentence. "Don't be a fool."

On the dais, Balekin was engaged in a lot of yelling about the crown, which turned out to be cursed.

"Of course," Kaye said to no one in particular, feeling a little nauseated. "Of course it's cursed."

She was starting to think that all crowns were.

It's like one of those shows where people move to another country for love.

That was what Luis had told her a week and a half later, when she was packing up her stuff and giving Corny the keys to Moon in a Cup. He'd started it with her, after all, and Val was going to help him run it, along with Ravus, her troll boyfriend, who concocted a goodly percentage of the potions they sold. Luis, out of medical school and done with his residency, was busy being a doctor.

"There's a yumboe who roasts her own beans out in Brooklyn," Kaye told them. "Delicious, but she's in high demand and fickle about availability. For backup beans, there's a family just outside Newark. Mortal. They've got a whole setup in their garage."

"I know," Corny said for what he clearly felt was the millionth time.

"And for pastries, there's no one better than that bucca up north in Kingston. His garden is full of flowers and he adds charmed glazes according to his whims," Kaye went on. "Mostly they're fun, but occasionally they're a bit alarming."

"Yes," Corny said. "We know what we're doing. Go be the lady of the manor. We're *fine*."

She told them about her resources for faerie fruit pastries. She reminded them about the little iron ball glued to the edge of the wooden counter, to touch money against before putting it in the register to make sure it wasn't glamoured leaves.

"You're not going that far away," Corny said. "We'll see you all the time. You're even going to have your phone with you. I'll text you, I promise."

"Reception is terrible under the hill," she reminded him, but he just gave her a look because, of course, she wasn't trapped there. She could go outside and get his texts. If something went wrong, she could come back.

She had wings. She could *fly* back.

Besides, he didn't really need her.

With no more excuses, Kaye gave them all hugs and said her goodbyes. Then she took her garbage bags of clothes and her cardboard box of novelty mugs, and she started in the direction of the train station.

It's like one of those shows where people move to another country for love, Kaye thought. *Except in this one, he hasn't asked me to come.*

Roiben wasn't in his rooms when she arrived under the hill in the Court of Termites. She barged in anyway, sending servants into fits. She was allowed to be there, of course, to stretch out on his tapestry bedcovers, sit for as long as she liked in his sinister chairs, and order anything she desired from the kitchens. But she did not usually start putting stuff away in the armoire—or redecorating.

A page came in, pale as paper, wearing brown livery and sporting a pair of tiny goat horns. "My lady," the page said. "May I offer you some assistance?"

"Oh, yes," Kaye said. "I have something for you to send to the new High King of Elfhame." Prince Cardan had turned up after all. As one of his vassals, she was pretty sure she owed him a present now and again—besides, she'd found the perfect thing.

"Yes, but..." the page began.

Reaching into the box, Kaye took out a paper-and-twine-wrapped package and handed it over. "And you can tell Roiben I'm staying."

With a nervous bow and a wince at her not using Roiben's title, the goat-horned faerie went out.

Not too long after, the Termite king himself arrived. Clad in flat black with shoulder plates that resembled the carapaces of beetles, he wore a look of someone caught between surprise and suspicion.

"And just what do you suppose you are doing?" he asked, taking in the clothes, the chibi sushi throw pillow Kaye had arranged on one chair, the dumpster-salvaged painting she'd propped against a wall. His voice had a chill in it.

"I told you I was coming to Faerie." She hoped she didn't sound as nervous as she felt.

"I thought I'd made my point at the coronation," he said. "In fact, never has a point been so quickly supported by fate."

"Yes, fine, you made your point," Kaye said. "You won the argument. Faerie is dangerous. But I know you better than you think and I am tougher than you think and I am not going to get tired of you. Maybe of all the rest of Faerie sometimes, but never of you."

"And if I do not want you here?" he said, voice still cold.

She took a deep breath and deployed the only weapon at her disposal. "Then you must tell me so. Tell me that you don't want me. Say you don't want me here and I'll go."

He stared at her intently for a long moment. Finally, he slumped down in the chair with the sushi pillow. A smile pulled at his mouth, and it was one of those rare moments when he seemed very young.

"Since I cannot lie," Roiben said, "I suppose you must stay."

Sometime later, the boy who had once been Prince Cardan lounged on the throne of Elfhame. A page from one of the lower courts came in with a package, setting it before him and bowing deeply. Cardan stared at the brown-paper wrapping, sealed with the waxen stamp of the Court of Termites. He opened it with trepidation.

There, in his long fingers, was a black coffee mug of the sort that mortals used. He spun it in his hands until he saw the writing on one side.

I RULE, it read.

High King Cardan gazed upon the message with great bafflement, and then, after a moment, his mouth lifted with the beginnings of a smile.

"I suppose that I do," he said to himself, holding out the cup to be filled with wine. "But what sort of ruler will I be?"

Sharona Jacobs

HOLLY BLACK

is the award-winning author of internationally bestselling fantasy novels, including *Tithe: A Modern Faerie Tale*, The Spiderwick Chronicles (with Tony DiTerlizzi), the Magisterium series (with Cassandra Clare), *The Coldest Girl in Coldtown*, *The Darkest Part of the Forest*, *The Cruel Prince*, and *The Wicked King*. She lives in western Massachusetts in a house with a secret door.